T. W. (Thomas William) Allies, Charles Passaglia

St. Peter

His Name and His Office

T. W. (Thomas William) Allies, Charles Passaglia

St. Peter
His Name and His Office

ISBN/EAN: 9783744653244

Printed in Europe, USA, Canada, Australia, Japan

Cover: Foto ©Raphael Reischuk / pixelio.de

More available books at **www.hansebooks.com**

ST. PETER
HIS NAME AND HIS OFFICE

BY

T. W. ALLIES, K.C.S.G.

WITH A PREFACE

BY THE

REV. LUKE RIVINGTON, M.A.

LONDON
CATHOLIC TRUTH SOCIETY
21 WESTMINSTER BRIDGE ROAD, S.E.
1895

TO

PETER,

PRINCE OF THE APOSTLES,

THE ROCK OF THE CHURCH,

AGAINST WHICH THE GATES OF HELL SHALL NOT PREVAIL,

THE BEARER OF THE KEYS,

THE BINDER AND LOOSER ON EARTH AND IN HEAVEN,

THE CONFIRMER OF HIS BRETHREN,

THE SHEPHERD OF THE FOLD.

PREFACE.

The Catholic Truth Society owes a real debt of gratitude to Mr. Allies for permission to reprint this valuable work. It is largely drawn, as Mr. Allies himself says in the original preface, from Father Passaglia's learned work on the Prerogatives of St. Peter. That work is now very scarce, and is written in Latin. Mr. Allies has not simply translated it, which would have been of comparatively little use for the general public; but he has freely utilized its arguments and adapted it to the needs of the ordinary English reader. The subject is of the highest importance at the present moment. Nothing is more likely to tend to that re-union for which our present Holy Father has urged us to redouble our prayers, than a clear exposition of the Scriptural grounds on which the supremacy of the Pope rests. Amongst the large number of reviews of a recent work [1] by the writer of this introduction, quite a considerable proportion made the remark that the historical argument must be taken a step further and based on Holy Scripture.

[1] *The Primitive Church and the See of Peter*, by the Rev. Luke Rivington. Longmans, 1894.

But this had been already done by Mr. Allies in the volume now reprinted, and with a vigour and expository power which, for so small a compass, seem to leave nothing to be desired.

The present volume presents, as the writer has said in his original preface, the whole chain of Scriptural evidence for the primacy and prerogatives of St. Peter. On this he remarks : " This chain of evidence is so strong, that, when I first saw it completely drawn out, it struck my own mind, brought up in the prejudices of Protestantism, with the force of a new revelation. I put to myself the question—Is it possible that they who specially profess to draw their faith from the written Word of God, would refuse to acknowledge a doctrine set forth in Holy Scripture with at least as strong evidence as the Godhead of our Lord itself, if they could see it not broken up into morsels, like bits of glass reflecting a distorted and imperfect image, according to the fashion of citing separate texts without regard to the proportion of the faith, but presented in a complete picture on the mirror of God's Word ? " He presently adds : " The importance of the argument, as it affects the Papal Supremacy, which is but a summary of the whole cause at issue between Protestantism in every shape, and the Church of Christ, cannot be over-rated. If St. Peter be already set forth in Scripture as the head and bond of the Apostolic

College, if he be delineated as the Supreme Ruler who succeeds our Lord Himself in the visible government of His Church on earth, there becomes at once the strongest ground for expecting that such a Ruler will be continued as long as the Church herself lasts. Thus a guiding clue is given to us among all the following records of antiquity."

This is most true : and the present writer is able to say that the Anglican theory of Church government never seemed to him secure after the day when he finished a careful perusal of the following pages. It seemed that the Papal theory *ought* to be found at work in the Church, since it stands out so plainly in Holy Scripture. But those who, like myself, have been brought up with Anglican interpretations of Early Church History, are naturally disposed to think that there must be something wrong in this estimate of the Scriptural argument, because its *natural sequel* is not, according to their reading of history, found in the early Church.

I venture, therefore, to put before such the following line of argument. Take the life of the Church when her records are ample. Do not take refuge in the silence of scanty records. Take the life of the Church at Chalcedon, and work backwards. See her at Ephesus. Carry on your investigation through the earlier centuries, and

interpret glimpses seen in these centuries by
what you have seen in its full-blown acceptance
at Ephesus and Chalcedon. See how the life is
really one through all these centuries. Explain
the obscure by that which is plain, and not *vice
versâ.* And then return to Holy Scripture, and
consider how that form of unity, which obtained
in the fifth century, had been clearly delineated by
our Lord, and is seen in actual working, in its
great fundamental principle, immediately after
Pentecost. The outline sketched by His Divine
Hand finds its fulfilment in the exercise of Papal
government at Ephesus and Chalcedon; and the
teaching of St. Leo on the prerogatives of his See
is but the echo of the teaching of our Lord on the
position of Peter.

One more remark. Mr. Allies has rightly called
attention to the cumulative nature of the Scriptural evidence for the prerogatives of St. Peter. It
is a study of the evidence as a whole that will
enable a man to see the hollowness of the usual
objections against those prerogatives. Take a
single instance. An objection is based on the
fact that, on one occasion, the Apostles " sent
Peter and John " to Samaria (Acts viii. 14). Mr.
Allies rightly points out that St. Peter was amongst
the senders. Passaglia also shows from the nature
of the work to be done, and the peculiar relationship between the Jews and the Samaritans, that

there was a certain congruity in the Head of the Apostles engaging in it. But an Anglican writer has recently said : " The fact that the Apostles sent St. Peter and St. John to confirm the Samaritans, is proof positive that St. Peter was not the supreme ruler of the others. That two equal Apostles should be sent by the College of Apostles—that is natural. That the subject Apostles should send their supreme pontiff and also one of their fellow-subjects on a joint mission—that is incredible." (Puller's *Primitive Saints*, p. 117.) This writer would have been preserved from the mistake which he here makes, had he remembered what Josephus relates about a contemporary " joint mission " to Rome. The Jews sent to Nero ten legates from amongst their princes, also their High Priest, Ishmael, and, with him, another high ecclesiastical functionary. There is, therefore, nothing "incredible" in two persons of un-equal rank being sent on a "joint mission " in those times.

But any one who reads in the following pages the relationship between St. Peter and St. John on other occasions, will see at once that St. John is sent, not as the equal (except in the possession of the Apostolate) of St. Peter, but simply as his companion. And the context is so decisive against Mr. Puller's misconception, that Mr. Allies is able to say, and is justified in saying : " Nothing but an inequality of rank between Peter and John will account for Luke's narration here ".

This is only one instance of how a superficial objection is met by a study of the Scriptural evidence as a whole.

I will only add that this little work is one which will admit of real study. The argument is sustained throughout; and the threads are carefully and brilliantly gathered up in a summary. But to a careful reader these pages will be found to suggest even more than they state. " Open Thou mine eyes; and I will consider the wondrous things of Thy law."

LUKE RIVINGTON.

August, 1895.

CONTENTS.

CHAPTER IX.—THE NATURE, MULTIPLICITY, AND FORCE OF PROOF FOR ST. PETER'S PRIMACY.

ST. PETER, HIS NAME AND HIS OFFICE.

CHAPTER I.

THE NAME OF PETER PROMISED, CONFERRED, AND EXPLAINED.

OUR Lord tells us that He came upon earth to " finish a work "; and He likewise tells us what that work was, the setting up a living society of men, who should dwell in Him and He in them; on whom His Spirit should rest, with whom His presence should abide, until the consummation of all things. For, the evening before His Passion, " lifting up His eyes to heaven, He said, Father, the hour is come. . . . I have glorified Thee on the earth : I have finished the work which Thou gavest Me to do. . . . I have manifested Thy name to the men whom Thou hast given Me out of the world. Thine they were, and to Me Thou gavest them; and they have kept Thy word. . . . Holy Father, keep them in Thy name, whom Thou hast given Me; that they may be one, as We also are. While I was with them, I kept them in Thy name. . . . And now I come to Thee. . . . I pray not that Thou shouldst take them out of the world, but that Thou shouldst keep them from evil. . . . As Thou hast sent Me into the world, I also have sent them into the world. And for them do I sanctify Myself, that they also may be sanctified in truth. And not for them only do I pray, but for those also who through their word shall believe in Me; that they all may be one, as Thou, Father, in Me, and I in Thee; that they also may be one in Us; that the world may believe that Thou hast sent Me. And the glory which Thou hast given to Me, I have given to them, that they may be one, as We also are one. I in them, and Thou in Me; that they may be made perfect in one; and the world may know that Thou hast sent Me, and hast loved them as Thou hast loved Me. . . . And I have made known Thy name to them, and will make it known; that the love wherewith Thou hast loved Me may be in them, and I in them." [1]

In these terms the Eternal Word condescends to declare to us that the fruit of His Incarnation, the "finished work" which His Father had given Him to do, was the establishment of a society whose unity in "truth" and "love" should be so perfect, that He exemplifies it by the indwelling in each other of the Divine Persons; which should be perpetual and visible for ever, so that the world by it and in it should recognise His own mission, and believe in the Sender; and that the dowry of this society, thus perpetually visible, should be the equally perpetual possession of truth—the revelation of God's will—and of love, which is conformity to it. And He based these unexampled promises on no less a guarantee than the almighty power

---

[1] John xvii.

and ineffable goodness of His Father, witnessed by His own dwelling amongst us in our flesh.

Elsewhere He termed this society His Church, declared that He would " build it on a rock, and that the gates of hell should not prevail against it ".[1]

He told those whom He had set over it to go forth in His name, and " to teach all nations what-soever He had commanded them," adding the solemn engagement on His own part, " Behold, I am with you all days, even to the consummation of the world ".[2]

His whole teaching is full of reference to it, setting forth its nature with every variety of illustration, enfolding it, as it were, with an ex-uberance of divine charity.

But two conceptions run through every illustra-tion, and are involved in its primary idea, nay, as this was the finished work of His Incarnation, so are they found in His adorable Person from which His work springs. These conceptions are Unity and Visibility.

As the mystery of the Incarnation consists in the union of the divine and human natures, in one Person, and in the assumption of a body, that is, matter, by the one uncreated, incomprehensible, and invisible Being, whereby He becomes visible, so Unity and Visibility are the unfailing marks of His Church, and enter into every image of it, in such a manner that without them the image loses its point and significancy.

[1] Matt. xvi. 18.　　　　　　[2] Matt. xxviii. 19, 20.

Accordingly He proclaims the Church which He was founding to be " the Kingdom of God," and "the Kingdom of Heaven," thus bringing before us the conceptions of order, government, power, headship on the one hand, dependence on the other, and a host of mutual relations between the Sovereign and the people, significantly remarking that " a kingdom which is divided against itself must fall ". Now, a kingdom without unity is a contradiction in terms, and a kingdom of God on earth, which cannot be seen, would be for spirits and not for men.

So He calls it a " city seated on a mountain," which "cannot be hid"; answering to His prophet's words, " the city of the great King," " His rest, and His habitation for ever".[1]   Here again are embodied the notions of order, government, conspicuous majesty, impregnable strength.

Thus He inspires His Apostle to call it "the house of God, the pillar and ground of the truth ".[2]   The house must have its head, the family their father; the knowledge of that father's will is the truth which rests upon the family as its support and pillar. Outside of the family that knowledge may be lost, together with the will to obey the father and to love him ; but within it is a living tradition, " familiar to the ear as household words ". As long as the Master and the Father is there, a perpetual light from His face is there too upon His children and His servants. Divide the house, or corrupt its

<hr/>

[1] Matt. v. 14 ; Ps. xlvii. 2 ; cxxxi. 13, 14.
[2] 1 Tim. iii. 15.

internal life, and the idea of the house is destroyed; while an invisible house is an absurdity.

Again, the Lord, calling Himself "the Good Shepherd, who giveth His life for the sheep,"[1] terms His Church the sheep-fold, and declares that as there is one Shepherd, so there must be one fold.

But, rising yet in nearness to the Divine Person of the Word Incarnate, from whose side sleeping on the cross she is moulded, the Church is called His Spouse, as united to Him in eternal wedlock, "a great Sacrament," or mystery; and even yet more, His Body, as supported by the continual influx of her Head ; and all her members are called "flesh of His flesh, and bone of His bones ".[2]

It is evident, then, that in these promises and illustrations are set forth, as belonging to their object, a visible unity, a perpetual possession and maintenance of the truth, and the closest union with God, founded upon a most supernatural indwelling of the Godhead in a society of men on earth, the founding of which was the "finished work" of God the Word Incarnate. *Were these promises to fail in any respect*—which is utterly impossible, for while heaven and earth shall pass away, no word of their Maker can pass away—*it is plain that our ground for trusting in any promises of Holy Writ whatsoever would be demolished.* The whole Christian revelation rests on the imperishable life of the Church ; because the corruption or division of the Church would falsify the written records of

---

[1] John x. 11-16.   [2] Eph. v. 32, 30.

our faith, in which, after the doctrine of the Blessed
Trinity, and the Godhead of our Lord, no truth is
so deeply imbedded as the perpetual existence and
office of the Church.

We have seen the idea of King, Lord, Master,
Father, Shepherd, Husband, and Head, running
through the delineation of the Church. And no
society is complete without its ruler. Such was
our Lord, while on earth—the *visible* ruler of a
visible Church. " While I was with them, I kept
them in Thy name." He went forth from His
baptism to win souls. The water became wine in
His presence. He bade men follow Him, and they
followed. Power went forth from Him, and healed
diseases. Grace flowed from His lips and conquered hearts. An innumerable multitude sur-
rounded Him, of all ages and conditions. "And
going up into a mountain, He called unto Him
whom He would Himself; and they came to Him.
And He made that twelve should be with Him, and
that He might send them to preach." [1]

Here, then, the true Israel chooses the future
princes of His house, who should sit with Him on
thrones, judging the twelve tribes. Already, while
yet with His Church, He is preparing for her future
government, when His visible presence shall be
taken from her. In three years all shall be accomplished, but when " the covenant should have been
confirmed with many in one week, and in the half
of the week the victim and the sacrifice should
fail "; [2] when His Apostles should see Him no

[1] Mark iii. 13. [2] Dan. iv. 26.

longer; was any one ordained to take that all-important place of supreme ruler which He had filled? For upon earth He had been in two relations to His Church: her Founder, and her Ruler. The former office belonged to His single Person; in its nature it could not pass to another; the work was finished once and for ever. But the latter office was, in its nature, likewise perpetual. How, then, should the charge of visible ruler, as man among men, be executed, when His Person was withdrawn, when He ascended up on high, when all power in heaven and earth was indeed given into His hands, and so the headship of spiritual influence and providential care; but when, nevertheless, that sacred Body was withdrawn into the tabernacle of God, and the Bridegroom was taken away for a time, and the voice and visible presence "what they had seen, and heard, and handled, of the word of life"[1] "was with them and kept them" no longer? Should His Church, which had been under one visible ruler from the beginning, now have her government changed? Or had He marked out any one among the Twelve to succeed to His own office of visible headship, and to be "the greater," and "the ruler"[2] among His brethren, His own special representative and vicar?

To answer this question, we must carefully observe and distinguish what is said and what is given to the Apostles *in common*, and what to any one of their number *in particular;* the former will

---

[1] 1 John i. 1.   [2] Luke xxii. 26.

instruct us as to their equality, the latter as to the pre-eminence which any one enjoyed over the rest, and in what it consisted.

Just, then, as at a certain period of His ministry, our Lord, out of the multitude who followed Him, selected twelve, to be His special attendants upon earth, and, when He should be taken up, to be the heralds of His Gospel among all nations : so out of the twelve He from the beginning distinguished one, marked him out for a peculiar and singular office, connected him with Himself in a special manner, and after having through the whole of His ministry given him tokens and intimations of his future destination, at last expressly nominated him to take His own place, and preside among his brethren. His dealing with this Apostle forms one connected whole, in which there is nothing abrupt or inharmonious, out of keeping, or opposed to what He said to others. What is at first obscurely intimated is afterwards expressly promised, again in fresh terms corroborated, and at last, in yet other language, but of the like force, most significantly conveyed,[1] while it is attested by a number of incidental notices scattered through the whole Gospel history. Thus[2] it becomes necessary to consider each particular, as well as the whole sum of things said, *proper* and *peculiar* to this Apostle ; to weigh first their *separate* and then their *joint* force, and only at last to form a united judgment upon all.

---

[1] See John i. 42 ; Mark iii. 16 ; Matt. xvi. 18 ; Luke xxii. 32 ; John xxi. 15.   [2] Passaglia, pp. 35-37.

We are searching into the will of the Divine Founder of our faith, which He has not only communicated to His Church in a living tradition, but in this case likewise ordered to be set forth in authentic written documents. These alone we are here considering, and the point in question is whether He decreed that all the Twelve should share equally in that divine mission and authority which He had received from the Father, or whether, while bestowing on them all very high and distinctive powers, He yet appointed one, namely Simon, the son of Jonas, to preside over the rest in His own place. We have, then, to consider all in these documents which is said peculiar to such Apostle, pointing out singular gifts and prerogatives, and carrying with it special authority of government. And we must remember that where proofs are numerous and complex, some which in themselves are only probable and accessory, yet have their force on the ultimate result. But this result must be drawn from a general view of the whole, and will collect in one the sum of proof both probable and certain.

Again, where many various causes concur, some more and some less, to produce a certain effect, the force of such effect is the force of all these causes put together, not of each by itself alone. Or where many witnesses are examined, whose evidence differs in value, although the testimony of some be in itself decisive, yet the verdict must be given after a consideration and review of all.

Now, the first mention which we have of the

Apostle Simon is full of signification. Our Lord
had only just begun His ministry; He had been
lately baptized, and as yet had called no disciples.
But two of John the Baptist's disciples, hearing
their master name Jesus "the Lamb of God,"
follow Him, are kindly received by Him, and one
of them, being Andrew, Simon's brother, finds
Simon, and says to him, "We have found the
Messias. And he brought him to Jesus. And
Jesus looking on him said, Thou art Simon the
son of Jonas; thou shalt be called Cephas, which
is interpreted Peter:"[1] as if He would say, By
birth thou art Simon, son of John; but another
and a higher lot is in store for thee. I will give
thee another name which thou shalt bear, a name
in itself signifying the place which thou shalt hold
in My Church. Thou shalt be called, and thou
shalt be, the Rock.

For why, when a vast multitude of our Lord's
words and actions have been omitted, was this
recorded for us, save that a deep meaning lay in
it? Or what could that meaning be when our
Lord, for the first time looking on Peter, promised
to him and to him alone, a new name, and that a
name given in prophecy to himself, a name declaring by its very sound that he should be laid by the
builder, as a foundation of the structure about to
be raised? So in the fourth century St. Chrysostom
comments on the text, calling him " the foundation
of the Church, he that was really Peter" (the
Rock) " both in name and in deed"; and a little

---

[1] John i. 35-42.

after St. Cyril of Alexandria, "with allusion to the rock He transferred His name to Peter, for upon him He was about to found His Church".[1] The Creator of the world does not give a name for nothing. His word is with power, and does what it expresses. Of old, "He spake and they were made; He commanded and they were created". Now, too, He speaks, at the first dawn of His great spiritual restoration. When as yet nothing has been done, and not a stone of the divine building reared, He who determines the end from the beginning looks upon one who seemed a simple fisherman, and at first beholding him, He takes Simon, the son of Jonas, out of the roll of common men; He marks him for a future design; He wraps him in a prophetic title; He associates him with His own immovable power. Of Himself it has been said,[2] "Behold I will lay a stone in the foundation of Sion, a tried stone, a corner-stone, a precious stone, founded on the foundation. He that believeth, let him not hasten." And again, "The stone which the builders rejected, the same is become the head of the corner: this is the Lord's doing, and it is wonderful in our eyes". And again, "A stone was cut out of a mountain without hands; and it struck the statue upon the feet thereof that were of iron and clay, and broke them in pieces. But the stone that struck the statue became a great mountain, and filled the whole

[1] St. Chrysostom on the text. St. Cyril on John i. 42.
[2] Isa. xxviii. 16; Ps. cxvii. 22; Dan. ii. 35; Zach. iii. 9; Eph. ii. 20.

cxiii. 22

earth." And again, " Behold the stone that I
have laid before Jesus : upon one stone there are
seven eyes ; behold, I will grave the graving
thereof, saith the Lord of Hosts ; and I will take
away the iniquity of that land in one day ". In
reference to which St. Paul said of Christians,
that they are " built upon the foundation of the
apostles and prophets, Jesus Christ Himself being
the chief corner-stone ; in whom all the building,
being framed together, groweth up into a holy
temple in the Lord ". It is plain, then, that our
Lord, " both by the Old and New Testament, is
called a stone ". [1]

But this which He had of Himself, and by virtue
of His own divine power, as the Word of God, He
would communicate in a degree, and by dependence
on Himself, to another. This is no modern interpretation, but the very words of St. Ambrose :
"Great is the grace of Christ, who bestowed
almost all His own names on His disciples. I,
said He, am the light of the world, and yet He
granted to His disciples the very name in which
He exulted, by the words, Ye are the light of the
world. Christ is the Rock, but yet He did not
deny the grace of this name to His disciple, that
he should be Peter, because he has from the Rock
firm constancy, immovable faith." [2]

In the third century, Origen, on this very text,
observes : " He said he should be called Peter, by
allusion to the Rock, which is Christ, that as a

---

[1] Theodoret on Dan. ii. 34.
[2] Ambrose on Luke, lib. 6, n. 97.

man from wisdom is termed wise, and from holiness holy, so too Peter from the Rock ". And in the fifth, St. Leo paraphrases the name thus: " While I am the inviolable Rock, the Cornerstone, who make both one, the foundation beside which no one can lay another; yet thou also art the rock, because by My virtue thou art established so as to enjoy by participation the properties which are peculiar to Me ".[1]

Here, then, we have three facts: 1. That our Lord having twelve Apostles whom He chose, loved, and honoured, above all His other disciples, yet promised to one only a new name;[2] and, 2. This a name in the highest degree significative, and most deeply prophetical of a particular office ; and, 3. A name peculiar to Himself, as the immovable foundation of the Church. This happened in the first year of His ministry, before, as it would appear, either Peter or any other Apostle was called.

The promise thus emphatically made to Simon, "Thou shalt be called the Rock," our Lord fulfilled in the second year of His ministry, when He distinguished the twelve Apostles from the rest of

[1] Serm. iv. 2.

[2] For the name Boanerges, which in one place is given to the two sons of Zebedy, is in the first place a joint name ; secondly, it is nowhere else referred to, and does not take the place of their birth-names; thirdly, it indicates not an official dignity, but an inward disposition. We cannot doubt that such a name bestowed on the two brothers was a mark of great distinction, but, for the above reasons, it cannot come into competition with the name of Peter. See Passaglia, p. 44, n. 38.

His disciples, giving them authority to teach, and
power to heal sicknesses and to cast out devils.
Then, says St. Mark, "to Simon He gave the
name of Peter "; and St. Matthew, " The names
of the Twelve Apostles are these: the first, Simon,
who is called Peter;" and St. Luke, " Simon,
whom also He named Peter ".[1]   And by this
name He marked him out from amongst all his
brethren, and united him to Himself.   " He
changes, too," says Tertullian, " Peter's name
from Simon, because also as Creator He altered
the names of Abraham, Sara, and Oshua, calling
the last Jesus, and adding syllables to the others,
but why did He call him Peter?.   If for the
strength of his faith, many solid substances
would lend him a name from themselves.
Or was it because Christ is both the Rock and
the Stone, since we read that He is set for a
stone of stumbling and a rock of offence?   I omit
the rest.   And so it was His pleasure to communicate to the dearest of His disciples, in a
peculiar manner, a name drawn from the figures
of Himself, I imagine, as being nearer than one
drawn from figures not of Himself."[2]

It is, then, setting a seal on His former acts,
drawing out and corroborating their meaning, that
He once more, and in the most emphatic way of
all, recurs to this name, attaching to it the most
signal promises, and establishing its prophetic
power.   In the third year of His ministry our

[1] Mark iii. 14; Matt. x. 1; Luke vi. 14.
[2] Cont. Marcion. l. 4, c. 13.

Lord "came into the quarters of Cesarea Philippi; and He asked His disciples, saying, Whom do men say that the Son of Man is ? But they said, Some John the Baptist, and others Elias, and others Jeremias, or one of the prophets. Jesus saith to them, But whom say ye that I am ? Simon Peter answered and said, Thou art Christ, the Son of the living God. And Jesus answering, said to him, Blessed art thou, Simon Bar Jona, because flesh and blood hath not revealed it to thee, but My Father who is in heaven. And I say to thee, that thou art Peter ; and upon this rock will I build My Church, and the gates of hell shall not prevail against it. And I will give to thee the keys of the kingdom of heaven. And whatsoever thou shalt bind on earth, shall be bound also in heaven ; and whatsoever thou shalt loose on earth, it shall be loosed also in heaven."

When we reflect that the first act of our Lord to Peter was to look upon him, and to promise him this name, a token of His omnipotence to Simon yet knowing him not, as that seeing him under the fig-tree was to Nathanael of His omniscience ; and that when He chose His twelve Apostles, it is said markedly, " to Simon He gave the name of Peter," the force of His reply cannot well be exceeded. The promise of our Lord answers part by part to the confession of His Apostle. The one says, " Thou art the Christ," that is, the anointed one ; the other, " Thou art Peter," that is, the Rock, the name which I gave thee Myself: My own title with which I invested thee. The one adds, " The

Son of the living God"; the other, "And upon this
rock I will build My Church," that is, as it is true
what thou confessest, that I am "the Son of the
living God," so My power as such shall be shown
in building My Church upon thee whom I have
named the Rock, "and the gates of hell shall not
prevail against it". Not only this, but I will
unfold to thee the full meaning of thy name, and
declare the gifts which accompany it. "And I
will give to thee the keys of the kingdom of
heaven." [1] That is, "The root and the offspring
of David," "The holy one and the true one, He
that hath the key of David; He that openeth and
no man shutteth; shutteth and no man openeth;"
as He gave to thee to share His name of the Rock,
so He shall give to thee to bear in His name His
own symbol of supreme dominion, the key which
opens or shuts the true city of David; all ages
shall own thee, all nations acknowledge thee, as
The Bearer of the Keys; as long as My Church
shall last, against which the gates of hell shall not
prevail, thy office shall last too; as long as there
are souls to be saved, they shall pass by thy
ministry into the gate of the Church. And further,
as long as there need in My spiritual kingdom laws
to be promulgated, precepts issued, sins forgiven,
"whatsoever thou shalt bind upon earth, it shall
be bound also in heaven; and whatsoever thou
shalt loose on earth, it shall be loosed also in
heaven".

Who, indeed, can adequately express the gifts

[1] Apoc. xxii. 16; iii. 7.

which the world's Creator and Redeemer here promises to His favoured servant? Thus in the fourth century St. Chrysostom labours to set them forth. "See how He raises Peter to a higher opinion of Himself; and reveals and shows Himself to be the Son of God by these two promises. For what belongs to God alone, to loose sins, and to render the Church immovable in such an assault of waves, and to make a fisherman more solid than any rock, when the whole world was at war with him, these are what He promises to give him; as the Father addressing Jeremias, said, 'I have made thee an iron pillar and a wall,' but him to one nation, whereas the other to the whole world. Willingly would I ask those who wish to diminish the dignity of the Son, which are the greatest gifts, those which the Father gave to Peter, or those which the Son. For the Father bestowed on Peter the revelation of the Son; but the Son disseminated that of the Father and of Himself through the whole world; and *put into the hands of a mortal man power over all things in heaven, when He gave the keys to him* who extended the Church through the whole world, and showed it to be firmer than the heaven." [1] And not many years later St. Leo says, "That which the Truth ordered remains; and blessed Peter persisting in that strength of the rock which he received, has not deserted the guidance, once undertaken, of the Church. For thus was he set before the rest, that while he is called the Rock, while he is declared

[1] St. Chrys. on Matt. 16, Hom. 54.

to be the foundation, while he is appointed the door-keeper of the kingdom of heaven, while he is advanced to be the judge of what shall be bound and what loosed, with the condition that his sentence shall be ratified even in heaven, *we might learn through the very mysteries of the names given to him, how he was associated with Christ.*[1] This association passed, indeed, into the very mind of the Church, for among all the titles given by fathers and councils and liturgies to Peter, and expressing his prerogatives, the one contained in this name is the most frequent. Thus he is termed, "the rock of the Church,"[2] "the rock of the Church that was to be built,"[3] "underlying the building of the Church,"[4] "receiving on himself the building of the Church,"[5] "the immovable rock,"[6] "the rock which the proud gates of hell prevail not against,"[7] "the most solid rock,"[8] "he to whom the Lord granted the participation of His own title, the rock,"[9] "the foundation second

---

[1] St. Leo, Serm. 3 on his anniversary.

[2] Hilary of Poitiers on Matt. xv. n. 6; on Ps. cxxxi. n. 4; on the Trinity, 1. 6, n. 20. Gregory Naz. Orat. 26, p. 453. Ambrose in his first hymn, referred to also by Augustine, Retract. lib. 1, c. 21, and Epiph. in ancor. n. 9.

[3] Tertullian de Monogam. c. 8. Origen on Ps. i. quoted by Eusebius, Hist. 1. 6, c. 25. Cyprian, Ep. 71, and Firmilian, among Cyprian's letters, 74.

[4] Basil cont. Eunom. lib. 2, n. 4. Zeno, lib. 2, tract. 13, n. 2.

[5] By the same.   [6] Epiphan. Hær. 59, n. 7.

[7] August. in. Ps. cont. par. Donati. Leo, serm. 98.

[8] Theodoret, ep. 77.

[9] Maximus of Turin, Serm. pro natali Petri et Pauli.

from Christ,"[1] "the great foundation of the Church,"[2] "the foundation and basis,"[3] "founding the Church by his firmness,"[4] "the support of the Church,"[5] "the Apostle in whom is the Church's support,"[6] "the support of the faith,"[7] "the pillar of the Church,"[8] and by an authority sufficient alone to terminate all controversy, the great Council of Chalcedon,[9] "the rock and foundation of the Catholic Church, and the basis of the orthodox faith".[10]

Thus, then, we have the name of Peter first promised, next conferred, then explained. And further light will be shed on this by the consideration of the purpose for which names in Holy Writ were bestowed by divine command on individuals, or their former names changed.

Now, of names opposed in Scripture there would seem to be three classes.[11] The first and most common are *commemorative*, and are for the purpose of recording and handing down to posterity re-

---

[1] Greg. Nazian. in Hom. archieratico inserta.

[2] Origen on Exod. hom. 5, n. 4.

[3] Gallican Sacramentary, edited by Mabillon, t. i., Mus. Ital. p. 343. Synod of Ephesus, act 3.

[4] Peter Chrysologus, serm. 154.

[5] Ambrose on Virginity, c. 16.

[6] Ambrose on Luke, lib. iv. n. 70.

[7] Chrysostom, Hom. on debtor of ten thousand talents, tom. iii. p. 4.

[8] Philip, legate of the Apostolic See, in Act 3 of Council of Ephesus.

[9] Council of Chalcedon, act 3, in deposing Dioscorus.

[10] For the above references see Passaglia, p. 400.

[11] Vid. Passaglia, p. 54, note 47.

markable facts. Such are Peleg, "because in his
days the earth was *divided*"; Isaac, from the
laughter of his father and mother; Issachar, a
reward; Manasseh, "God hath made me to *forget*
my labours"; Ephraim, "God hath made me to
grow";[1] and a multitude of others.

The second class may be termed *significative*,
being imposed to distinguish their bearers from
others by some quality. Such are Jacob, the
supplanter; Esau; Edom, the red; Moses, the
taken or saved; Maccabæus; Boanerges.[2]

The third and highest class are *prophetic*, and
as such evidently can be imposed by God alone,
who foresees the future. They are twofold: 1.
Those which fore-signify events concerning not
so much their bearers as others; such are Shear-
jashub, "the remnant shall return"; Jezrael, "I
will visit"; Lo-ruhamah, "not pitied"; Lo-ammi,
"not my people".   2. Those which point out the
office and destiny of their bearers; such as Noah,
rest ; Israel, a prince before God ; Joshua, Saviour;
Sarah, princess; John, in whom there is grace;
and, after the divine name of Jesus, "who saves
His people from their sins,"[3] Abraham, and Cephas,
or Peter, which two neither commemorate a past
event, nor signify a quality or ornament already
possessed, but are wholly prophetic, inasmuch as

---

[1] Gen. x. 25; xvii. 19; xxx. 18; xli. 51, 52.

[2] Gen. xxv. 26; xxvii. 36: xxv. 25; xxv. 30; Exod. ii. 10;
1 Macc. ii. 4; Mark iii. 17.

[3] Isa. vii. 3.; Os. i. 4, 6, 9; Gen. v. 29; xxxii. 28; Numb. xiii.
17; Gen. xvii. 15; Matt. iii. 1.

they shadow out the dignity to which the leaders of the two covenants are divinely marked out by the very imposition of their name.

For it will perhaps bring out the pre-eminence and superior authority of Peter, if we consider the very close resemblance and almost identity of the dispensation into which God entered with Abraham, and that which Christ gave to Peter. But first we must observe how the more remarkable things occurring in the New Testament were foretold by types, images, parallelisms, and distinct prophecies in the Old. How[1] both our Lord, the Evangelists, and the Apostles, take pains to point out the close agreement between the two covenants; how the ancient ecclesiastical writers do the like in their contests with early heretics, or in recommending the truth of the Christian faith either to Jew or Gentile. They considered scarcely any proof of the Gospel superior to that which might be drawn by grave and solid inference from the anticipation of Christian truths in the old covenant. Now, among such truths, what concerns Peter is surely of signal importance, as it affects the whole judgment on the form of government which our Lord instituted for His Church.

Again, it may be taken as an axiom that, as a similitude of causes is inferred from a similitude of effects, so a resemblance of the divine counsels may be inferred from a resemblance of exterior manifestations. As effects are so many steps by which we rise to the knowledge and discernment

[1] Passaglia, p. 51,

of causes, so divine manifestations are tokens which unfold God's eternal decrees. Thus if the series of dealings which constitute God's dispensation to Abraham be very much like that other series in which the Scriptures of the New Testament set forth the dispensation given to Peter, we may conclude, first, that the two dispensations may be compared; and, secondly, that from their resemblance, a resemblance in the divine purpose may be deduced.

First,[1] then, " God at sundry times, and in divers manners, speaking to the fathers " of that covenant of grace, into which He had already entered with our first parents, said to Abram, " Go forth out of thy country,' and from thy kindred, and out of thy father's house, and I will make of thee a great nation ". But when in the last days He began to fulfil that covenant, and to declare His will by His Son, Jesus said to Simon and Andrew, " Follow Me, and I will make you to become fishers of men," and to Simon specially, " Fear not, for henceforth thou shalt catch men ".[2]

Abram hearkened to God calling him: "So Abram went out as the Lord had commanded him;" and Simon as readily obeyed Christ's vocation: "And immediately leaving their nets they followed Him ".[3]

God rewarded Abraham's obedience by the

---

[1] Passaglia, p. 52.
[2] Gen. xii. 1 ; Mark i. 16, 17 ; Luke v. 10,
[3] Gen. xii. 4 ; Mark i. 18,

promise of a new name: " Neither shall thy name be called any more Abram, but thou shalt be called Abraham ". So Christ honoured Simon, saying, " Thou art Simon, the son of Jonas ; thou shalt be called Cephas ".[1]

No sooner had God unfolded the dignity shadowed forth in the promised name, and bestowed that dignity on Abraham, than He required of him a signal instance of faith and love: " God tempted Abraham, and said to him, Take thy son, thine only begotten, whom thou lovest, and offer him for a holocaust ". So Christ required of Simon a proof of faith and of superior love before He either unfolded the excellence of the promised name, or adorned him with that excellency: " He saith to them, Whom say ye that I am ? " " Simon, son of Jonas, lovest thou Me more than these ? "[2]

And both were no less ready to show the fortitude of their faith and love than they had been ready to follow the divine calling. For, " Abraham stretched forth his hand, and took the sword to sacrifice his son "; and " Simon Peter answering, said, Thou art the Christ, the Son of the living God "; and again, " Yea, Lord, Thou knowest that I love Thee ".[3]

Then, as the bestowal of the new name was the reward of the obedience with which each had followed his vocation, so God, moved by their

---

[1] Gen. xvii. 5 ; John i. 42.
[2] Gen. xxii. 1 ; Matt. xvi. 15 ; John xxi. 15.
[3] Gen. xxii. 10; Matt. xvi. 16; John xxi. 15.

remarkable ensuing faith and charity, explained
the dignity contained in that name, and bestowed
it when so explained. The following refers to
the explanation : " By Myself have I sworn,
because thou hast done this thing," and " Because flesh and blood hath not revealed it to
thee, but My Father who is in heaven. And I
say unto thee."

But as to the dignity bestowed, it should be
remarked that it is divine, and communicated to
each with this resemblance : *First*, that Abraham
thereby becomes the source and parent of all the
faithful, and Peter their base and foundation ; the
one, the author of a seed which should equal in
number the stars of the heaven and the sand of
the sea ; the other, the Rock of the Church, which
should embrace all nations, tribes, and languages.
God says to Abraham, " And multiplying I will
multiply thy seed as the stars of heaven and as
the sand which is on the sea-shore ". But Christ
to Peter, " And upon this rock I will build My
Church ". *Secondly*, the blessing thus bestowed
from above upon each was not one which should
rest in their single persons, but from them and
through them should be extended to the universal
posterity and society of the faithful ; so that all
who should believe, to the consummation of time,
should gain through them blessing, stability, and
victory over the assault of enemies and the gates
of hell. The promise to Abraham is clear : " Thy
seed shall possess the gate of their enemies, and
in thy seed shall all the nations of the earth be

blessed;" nor less so to Peter, "And the gates
of hell shall not prevail against it".

But the high excellence of this dignity, embracing, as it does, the whole company of the faithful,
was presignified in the very meaning of the name
imposed. For of Abraham's name we read, "And
thy name shall be Abraham, for a father of many
nations have I made thee". Exactly resembling
is what is said of Peter's appellation, "Thou art
Peter, the Rock, and upon this rock I will build
My Church".

Nay, we may put in parallel columns the two
promises, thus—

| 1. Thy name shall be Abraham, | 1. Thou art Peter, |
| 2. For a father of many nations have I made thee: | 2. And upon this rock I will build My Church: |

and just as in the former the second clause contains
the reason of the first, so in the latter likewise the
two clauses cohere, as the name and its explanation.
Again, the dignity of the one is expressed as that
of the Father; of the other as that of the Rock.
Further, those alone can share the blessing of
Abraham, who are born of his spirit; and those
alone the stability divinely granted to Peter,
who refuse by any violence, or at any cost, to be
separated from him.

But Abraham was thus raised to be the friend
of God, associated in the divine Fathership, and
made the teacher of posterity; and therefore, as
being such, God would show him His counsels,
that through him they might descend to his
children. "And the Lord said, Can I hide from

Abraham what I am about to do? for I know
that he will command his children and his household after him to keep the way of the Lord." In
a precisely similar way, when God would call the
Gentiles to the light of the Gospel, He showed it
by a special revelation to Peter alone: "There
came upon him an ecstasy of mind; and he saw
the heaven opened; and this was done thrice".
And the reason of so preferring Peter was God's
decree, that through him other Christians, even
the Apostles themselves, might be informed, and
convinced. "You know that in former days God
made choice among us that by my mouth the
Gentiles should hear the word of the Gospel and
believe." "And thou, when thou art converted,
confirm thy brethren." [1]

Finally, as God pronounces Abraham blest,
so Christ pronounces Peter; and as He made
Abraham the source and fountain-head of blessing
and strength to all others, so no less did Christ
make Peter. Of the first we read, "I will bless
thee, and will make thy name great, and thou
shalt be a blessing"; of the second, "Blessed art
thou, Simon Bar Jona;—and upon this rock I
will build My Church".

In one word, the parallel is as follows between
Abraham and Peter. Both receive a remarkable
call, and follow it; both are promised and receive
a new, and that a prophetical name; of both signal
instances of faith and love are required; both
furnish these, and therefore do not lose the increase

[1] Gen. xviii. 17; Acts x. 10; xv. 7; Luke xxii. 32.

of their reward; to Abraham his prophetical name is explained, and to Peter likewise; Abraham understands his destination to be the Father of all nations, and Peter that he is made the Rock of the universal Church; Abraham is called blest, and so Peter; to Abraham it is revealed that no one, save from him, and through him, shall share the heavenly blessing; to Peter that all, from him, and through him, shall gain strength and stability; it is only through Abraham that his posterity can promise itself victory over the enemy, and only through being built on Peter, the Rock, that the Church will triumph over the gates of hell; in fine, if Abraham, as the teacher of the faithful, is instructed in the divine counsels with singular care, not less is shown to Peter, whom Christ has made the doctor and teacher of all believers.

The gifts thus bestowed on Abraham and Peter are *peculiar*, for they are read of no one else in the Holy Scriptures; they are not only *gifts*, but a *reward* for singular merit; and in their own nature they cannot be *general*. As by them Abraham is put into a relation of *Fathership*, so that all the faithful become his children, so Peter being called and made the rock and *Foundation* of the Church, all its members have a dependence on him.

And if these gifts are *peculiar*, no less do they convey a singular *dignity* and *pre-eminence*. For it follows that, as St. Paul says, all the faithful are children of Abraham,[1] being heirs not of his

---

[1] Gal. iii. 7.

flesh, but of his spirit and faith; so no one is, or can be, a part of the Church's building, who rests not on Peter as the foundation. For the same God who said to Abraham, "Thy name shall no longer be called Abram, but Abraham shall be thy name," said also to Simon, "Thou shalt not be called Simon, but Cephas"; the same God who said to the former, "In thee shall all families of the earth be blessed," said to the latter, "Upon this Rock I will build My Church".

What is the source of this pre-eminence in both? To both the same objection may be made, and for both the same defence.

How should blessing and adoption be propagated from Abraham, as a sort of head, into the whole body of the faithful? Because Abraham is considered as joined with that mighty Seed his offspring, whence *in chief* and *primarily* the salvation of all depends; because Abraham is made by *participation* partner of that dignity which *naturally* and *substantially* belongs to the Seed that was to spring from him. God Himself has told us this, and His Apostle St. Paul explained it. For as we read that it was said to Abraham, "In thee shall all nations of the earth be blessed," so God Himself has told us that *in thee, by thee,* means *in, by thy seed.* Hence St. Paul: "To Abraham were the promises made, and to his seed. He saith not, seeds, as of many, but as of one, And to thy seed, which is Christ."[1] So that the divine words, "In thee shall all nations of the earth be

---

[1] Gal. iii. 16,

blessed," give this meaning: "As thou shalt give flesh to My only begotten Son whom I cherish in My bosom, whence He shall be called at once ' the Son of God and the Son of Abraham,'[1] so He makes thee a partner of His dignity and excellence, whence, if not the source and origin, yet thou shalt be a broad stream of blessing to be poured out on all nations ".

Now, just in the same manner is Peter the Rock of the Church, and the cause next to Christ of that firmness with which the Church shall remain impregnable to the end. For therefore is he the Rock and Foundation of the Church, because he has been called into a sort of unity with Him of whom it is said, " Behold, I lay in Sion a chief corner-stone, elect, precious, and he that believeth on it shall not be ashamed ": and in whom, as Paul explains, "the whole building fitly framed together increaseth unto a holy temple in the Lord ".[2] Therefore is he the Church's Rock, because as he, by his own confession, declared the Godhead of the Foundation in chief, " Thou art the Christ, the Son of the living God," so from Him, who is the chief and substantial Foundation, he received the gift of being made partner in one and the same property: " And I too say unto thee, that thou art Peter, and upon this rock I will build My Church ; " one with Me by communication of My office and charge, My dignity and excellency. Hence the stability of Peter is that of Christ, as the splendour of the ray is that of

[1] Matt. i. 1.   [2] Isa. xxviii. 16; Eph. ii. 21.

the sun; Peter's dignity that of Christ, as the river's abundance is the abundance of the fountain. Those who diminish Peter's dignity may well be charged with violating the majesty of Christ; those who are hostile to Peter, and divorced from him, stand in the like opposition to Christ.

Now, this parallel is an answer[1] to those who object to Peter's supereminence as the Foundation, that this dignity is entirely divine, surpassing by an almost infinite degree the capacity of man. For is not that a divine dignity which consists in the paternity of all the faithful? Is not that prerogative beyond man's capacity by which one becomes the author of a blessing diffused through all nations? Yet no one denies that such a dignity and such a prerogative were granted to Abraham. In divine endowments, therefore, their *full* and *natural possession* must be carefully distinguished from their *limited* and *analogous participation*. The one, as inherent, cannot fall to the creature's lot; the other, as transferable, may be granted as God pleases. For what further removed from man than the Godhead? Yet it is written, "I have said, Ye are Gods".[2]

Not weightier is the other objection, that the office of being the Foundation is too important to be entrusted to human care. Was there less difficulty in blessing being diffused from one man among all nations? Rather we must look on man not as he is by, and of, himself, apart from God, and left to his own weakness, but as upborne by

---

[1] Passaglia, p. 58.   [2] Ps. lxxxii. 6, with John x. 34.

divine power, according to the promise, " Behold,
I am with you all days, until the consummation
of the world ". Who can doubt that man, in
union with God, may serve for a foundation, and
discharge those offices in which the unity of a
structure consists ? It is confidently and constantly objected, that " other foundation no man
can lay besides that which is laid, which is Jesus
Christ ".[1] As if what has been laid by Christ
Himself, and consists in the virtue of Christ alone,
can be thought other than Christ ; or as if it were
unusual, or unscriptural, for things proper to
Christ to be participated by men. Therefore the
chief difficulties against Peter's pre-eminence, and
character as the Foundation, seem to spring from
the mind failing to realize the supernatural order
instituted by God, and the perpetual presence of
Christ watching over His Church.

Thus it is no derogation to Abraham's being
the Father of the faithful, or to the hierarchy of
the Church instituted by Christ Himself, that our
Lord says, " Call none your father upon earth, for
one is your Father who is in heaven ";[2] inasmuch
as Scripture abundantly proves that divine gifts
are richly conferred upon men. What more divine
than the Holy Spirit ? Yet it is written, " And
I will ask the Father, and He shall give you
another Paraclete, that He may abide with you
for ever ".[3] What a higher privilege than filial
adoption ? Yet it is said, " Ye have received the
spirit of filial adoption, by which we cry, Abba,

[1] Cor. iii. 11.   [2] Matt. xxiii. 9.   [3] John xiv. 16.

Father".[1]   What a greater treasure than co-
inheritance with Christ?   Yet we read, "But if
children, also heirs : heirs of God, but joint heirs
with Christ".[2]   What higher than the vision of
God?   Yet St. Paul bears witness, "We see
now through a glass darkly, but then face to
face".[3]   What more wonderful than the power of
remitting sins?   Yet this very power is granted
to the Apostles : "Whose sins you shall forgive,
they are forgiven them".[4]   What further from
human weakness than the power of working
miracles?   Yet Christ establishes this, "Amen,
amen, I say unto you, he that believeth on Me,
the works which I do shall he do also, and greater
works than these shall he do".[5]   Indeed, the
participation and communion of heavenly gifts
have the closest coherence with that supernatural
order, which God in creating man chose, and to
which He called fallen man back through His
only begotten Son ; with that dispensation of
Christ by which He loved the Apostles as He
Himself was loved by the Father, by which He
called them, "not servants, but friends,"[6] and
gave them that glory which He had Himself
received from the Father.   And the tone of mind
which denies Peter's prerogative as the Foundation
of the Church, under pretence that it is a usurpa-
tion of divine power, tends to deny some one or
all of the privileges just cited, and, as a fact, does
deny some of them.   It is wonderful to see how

---

[1] Rom. viii. 15.   [2] Rom. viii. 17.   [3] 1 Cor. xiii. 12.
[4] John xx. 23.   [5] John xiv. 12.   [6] John xv. 9, 15.

only common and vulgar things are discerned by modern eyes, where the Fathers saw celestial and divine gifts.[1] Those without the Church have fallen away as well from the several parts and privileges, from what may be called the standing order of the Incarnation, as from its final purpose and scope; and it is much if they would not charge with blasphemy that glorious saying put forth by the greatest of the Eastern, as by the greatest of the Western Fathers, "that God became man, in order that man might become God".[2]

Was, then, St. Chrysostom wrong when he said that our Lord, in that passage of Matthew, showed a power equal to God the Father by the gifts which He bestowed on a poor fisherman? "He who gave to him the keys of the heavens, and made him Lord of such power, and needed not prayer for this, for He did not then say, I prayed, but, with authority, I will build My Church, and I will give to thee the keys of heaven."[3] Was he wrong when he called him "the chosen of the Apostles, the mouth-piece of the disciples, the head of the band, the ruler over the brethren"?[4] or where he saw these prerogatives in the very name of Peter, observing, "When I say Peter, I mean the impregnable rock, the immovable foun-

---

[1] Passaglia, p. 442, n. 28.

[2] 'Ο τοῦ Θεοῦ Λόγος ἐνηνθρώπησεν ἵνα ἡμεῖς θεοποιηθῶμεν. St. Athan. de Incarn. Factus est Deus homo, ut homo fieret deus. St. Aug. Serm. 13, de Temp.

[3] St. Chrys. tom. vii. 786. Hom. 82, in Matt.

[4] Tom. viii. 525. Hom. 88 in Joan.

dation, the great Apostle, the first of the disciples " ? [1]

To sum up, then, what has been hitherto said, we have advanced so far as this ; first the promise, and then the bestowal of a new name, expressing a singular pre-eminence, and in its *proper* sense befitting Christ alone, have distinguished Simon from the rest of the Apostles. But much more the power signified by that name, and explained by the Lord Himself, carries far higher Peter's privilege, and indicates him to be the possessor of authority over the Apostles. For if Simon is the Rock of the Church, and if the property of Foundation, on which the structure of the Church rests, belongs to him immediately after Christ, and analogously with Christ, there arises this relation between Christ and Simon, that as He is first, and chiefly, and by inherent power, so Simon is secondarily, by participation and analogy, that which underlies, holds together, and supports the Apostles and the whole fabric of the Church.

Now, such a relation carries with it not merely precedency of honour, but superior authority. The strength of the Apostles lay in their union with Christ, and subordination to Him. The like necessity of adhering to Peter is expressed in his new name. Take away that subordination, and you destroy the very image by which the Lord chose to express Peter's dignity ; and you remove, likewise, Peter's participation in that property which the Lord communicated to him in the name

[1] Hom. 3, de Pœnitentia.   Tom. ii. 300.

of the Rock. For if the Apostles needed not to be joined with him, he had no title to be called the Foundation ; and if he had no co-active power over the Apostles, he did not share the property by which Christ is the Rock and Foundation. Thus the name, and the dignity expressed by the name, show Peter to have been singly invested by the Lord with both honour and power superior to the Apostles.[1]

[1] Passaglia, pp. 48, 49.

CHAPTER II.

EDUCATION AND FINAL DESIGNATION OF PETER TO BE THE RULER WHO SHOULD CONFIRM HIS BRETHREN.

HAVING promised[1] and bestowed on Simon a new name, prophetic of the peculiar position which he was to occupy in the Church, and having set forth the meaning contained in that name in terms so large and magnificent, that, as we have seen, the greatest Saints and Fathers have felt it impossible to exhaust their force, our Lord proceeded to *educate* Peter, so to say, for his especial charge of supreme ruler. He bestowed upon him, in the course of His ministry, tokens of preference which agree with the title thus solemnly conferred; and He instructed him with all the care which we should expect to be given to one who was to become the chief doctor of Christians. Such instruction may be said to consist in two things : a more complete knowledge of the Christian revelation, and a singular apprehension of its divine proofs.

Now, innumerable as are the particulars in which the Christian revelation consists, they may yet be gathered up mainly in two points, which

---

[1] Passaglia, p. 68.

meet in the person of our Lord, and are termed
by the ancient Fathers who have followed this
division, the *Theology*, and the *Economy*. There
is the Divine Nature, that *"form of God,"* which
our Lord had from the beginning in the bosom of
the Father; and there is the human nature, that
"form of a servant," which "in the economy or
dispensation of the fulness of times" He assumed,
in order that He might purchase the Church with
His blood, and "re-establish all things in heaven
and on earth".[1] All, therefore, in the Christian
faith which concerns "the form of God" is termed
the Theology; all which contemplates *"the form
of a servant,"* the Economy.

But the heavenly origin and certain truth of
both these parts of Christian faith are proved
partly by the fulfilment of prophecy, and partly by
the working of miracles. To both our Lord perpetually appealed, and His Apostles after Him,
and those who have followed them. One, then,
who was to be the chief ruler and doctor of
Christians, needed especial instruction in the
Theology, and Economy, especial assurance of
the fulfilment of prophecy, and the working of
miraculous power. Now, Peter was specially
selected for this instruction and that assurance.

The whole teaching of our Lord, indeed, and
the innumerable acts of power and words of grace
with which it was fraught, were calculated to
convey these to all the Apostles. But while they
were witnesses in common of that teaching in

[1] Eph. i. 10.

general, some parts of it were disclosed only to
Peter and the two sons of Zebedy. Perhaps
there is no incident in the Gospel history, which
set forth in so lively a manner, and so convincingly
proved, the mysteries concerning the union of
"the form of God" and "the form of a servant,"
as the Transfiguration. The retreat to the "high
mountain apart," and in the midst of that solitary
prayer, "the face shining as the sun," and "the
robes white as light," the presence of Moses
and Elias, conversing with Him on the great
sacrifice for sin, "the bright cloud which encompassed them," and the voice from out of it,
proclaiming "This is My beloved Son, in whom
I am well pleased : hear Him "; so impressed
themselves on the great Apostle, that after long
years he appealed to them in proof that he and
his brethren had not taught " cunningly devised
fables, when they made known the power and
presence of the Lord Jesus Christ, but had been
eye-witnesses of His majesty, when He received
from God the Father honour and glory, this voice
coming down to Him from the excellent glory,
' This is My beloved Son, in whom I have pleased
Myself : hear ye Him '. And this voice we heard
brought from heaven, when we were with Him
in the holy mount." Among all the Apostle's
experience of the three years' ministry, by the
shore and on the waves of the lake of Galilee, in
the cornfields or on the mountain side, in the
noonday heat or midnight storm, even in the
throng which cried "Hosannah !" and " Crucify

Him ! " this stood out, until "the laying aside of his fleshly tabernacle," as " the Lord had signified to him ".[1] For [2] what indeed was not there?— the plurality of Persons in the Godhead, the Father and the Son, the true, and not adopted, Sonship of the latter, His divine mission unto men ; the new order of things resulting from it, and the summing up under one head of all things in heaven and in earth; the sealing up and accomplishing of the law and the prophets, by the presence of their representatives, Moses and Elias, a most wonderful and transporting miracle ; and the command implicitly to obey Him in whom the Father was well pleased. Thus the Transfiguration may be termed the summing up of the whole Christian revelation.

But now of this we read that "after six days Jesus taketh unto Him *Peter*, and James, and John his brother, and bringeth them up into a high mountain apart ". These three alone of the twelve. Yet does he not associate the sons of Zebedy with Peter in this privilege ? Needful no doubt it was that so splendid an act should have a suitable number of witnesses, and that as His future glory should have three witnesses from heaven, and as many from earth,[3] so this, its rudimental beginning, should be attested by three as from heaven, God the Father, Moses, and Elias, and by three from earth, Peter, James and John. Dear to Him, likewise, next to Peter, and most privileged after Peter, were the sons of Zebedy; yet a distinction

2 Pet. i. 14.   [2] Passaglia, p. 69.   [3] 1 John v. 6, 7.

is seen in the mode in which they are treated even
when joined together in so great a privilege.   For
in all the three accounts Peter is named first :
" He taketh to Him Peter, and James, and John ".
They likewise are called by their birth-name, he
by his prophetic appellation of the Rock ; they are
silent, but he speaks : "Peter answering, said;"
nor only speaks, but in the name of all : "It is
good *for us* to be here," as if their leader.   And,
fifthly, he is named specially, they as his companions : " but Peter, *and they that were with him,*
were heavy with sleep ".[1]   Thus even when three
are associated in a special privilege above the
twelve, Peter is distinguished among the three.

But if there was one other occasion on which
above all "the form of the servant" was to be set
forth in the most awful, and the most endearing
light, it was on that evening, " the hour" of evil
men and "the power of darkness," when " the
righteous Servant who should justify many" was
about to perform the great, central, crowning act
of His mediation.   Then we read that " He said
to His disciples, Sit you here, till I go yonder and
pray ".[2]   And then immediately "taking with Him
Peter, and the two sons of Zebedy, He began to
grow sorrowful and to be sad ".   Yet here again,
even in the association with the sons of Zebedy,
Simon is distinguished, for he is named first ; and
by the illustrious name of Peter, the Rock ; and
as the leader of the others, for, says Matthew,
Christ after His first prayer, " comes to His

[1] Luke ix. 32.   [2] Matt. xxviii. 36.

disciples, and finds them sleeping, and *says to
Peter*, What, could *ye* not watch with Me one
hour ?" Why the change of number, Peter in the
singular, *ye* in the plural ? Why the blame of
Peter, involving the blame of the rest ? Because
the members are censured in the head.

In these two signal instances our Lord, while
preferring Peter and the two sons of Zebedy to the
rest of the Twelve, yet marks a gradation likewise
between them and Peter. And these two set forth
the Theology and Economy, in the most emphatic
manner.

And as the supreme preceptor must not only be
acquainted with the truth which he has to deliver,
but with the evidence on which it rests, so is Peter
specially made a witness of his Lord's "power
and presence" and "the works which no other
man did". In that remarkable miracle of raising
to life the ruler of the synagogue's daughter we
read : " He admitted not any man to follow Him,
but Peter and James, and John the brother of
James ;" [1] where, as before, and always, Peter is
mentioned first, and by the prophetic name of his
Primacy.

From [2] all which we gather four points : 1.
Several things are mentioned in the Gospels which
Christ gave to Peter, and not to the rest of the
Apostles; 2. But nothing which He gave to them
together, and not to Peter with them. 3. What
He seemed to give to them in common, yet accrue
to Peter in a special manner, who appears among

---

[1] Mark v. 35.   [2] Passaglia, p. 72.

the Apostles not as one out of the number, but
their destined head, by the name, that is, of Peter,
so markedly promised, bestowed, and so wonderfully explained by our Lord, of which, as we have
seen, St. Chrysostom, an Eastern Patriarch, as
well as a great Saint and Father, observed, "When
I say Peter, I mean the impregnable Rock, the
immovable foundation, the great Apostle, the first
of the disciples". 4. Either we are not to take
Christ's dealing as the standard of Peter's dignity
and destination, or we must admit that he was
preferred to the rest, and made the supreme teacher
of the faithful.

St. Matthew records the incidents of the officers
asking for the payment of the didrachma which
all the children of Israel were bound to contribute
to the Temple; and his words show us a fresh
instance of honour done to Peter, and a fresh note
of his superiority. "When they were come to
Capharnaum, they that received the didrachma
came to Peter, and said to him, Doth not your
Master pay the didrachma?"[1] But why should
they come to *him*, and ask, not if *his* Master, but
"your" Master, the Master of all the Apostles,
paid the census, save that it was apparent, even to
strangers, that Peter was the first, and most pro-
minent of the company? Why use him rather
than any of the others, for the purpose of approaching Christ? "As Peter seemed to be the first of
the disciples." says St. Chrysostom, on the text,
"they go to him." The context naturally suggests

[1] Matt. xvii. 23.

this reason, and the ancient commentators remarked it.   But what follows is much more
striking. Peter answered, Yes, that is, that his
Master observed all the laws of Moses, and this
among the number. As he went home he purposed, no doubt, to ask our Lord about this
payment, but "when he was come into the house
Jesus prevented him," having in His omniscience
seen and heard all that had passed, and He proceeded to speak words involving His own high
dignity, followed by a singular trial of Peter's faith,
and as marked a reward of it when tried. "What
thinkest thou, Simon?   The kings of the earth, of
whom do they receive tribute or custom? of their
own children or of strangers?   And he said, Of
strangers. Jesus said to him, Then the children
are free."   Slight words in seeming, yet declaring
in fact that most wonderful truth which had
formed so shortly before Peter's confession, and
drawn down upon him the yet unexhausted promise; for they expressed, I am as truly the natural
Son of that God, the Sovereign of the temple, for
whom this tribute is paid, as the children of earthly
sovereigns, who take tribute, are their sons by
nature. Therefore by right I am free. "But that
we may not scandalize them, go to the sea and
cast in a hook; and that fish which shall first
come up, take: and when thou hast opened its
mouth, thou shalt find a stater; take that, and
give it to them for Me and thee." Declaring to
His favoured disciple afresh that He is the true,
and not the adopted, Son of God, answering his

thoughts by anticipation, and expressing His knowledge of absent things by the power of the Son of
God, He tries his faith by the promise of a fresh
miracle, which involved a like exercise of divine
power. Peter, in proceeding to execute His command, must make that confession afresh by deed,
which he had made before by word, and which his
Lord had just repeated with His own mouth.
How else could he go to the lake expecting to
draw at the first cast a fish in whose mouth he
should find a coin containing the exact amount
due to the Temple for two persons? But what
followed? What but a most remarkable reward
for the faith which he should show.? "Take that,
and give it to them for Me and thee." There are
looks, there are tones of the voice, which convey
to us more than language. So, too, there are acts
so exceedingly suggestive, that without in any
formal way proving, they carry with them the force
of the strongest proof. And so, perhaps, never did
our Lord in a more marked manner *associate* Peter
with Himself than here. It was a singular distinction which could not fail to strike every one
who heard it. Thus St. Chrysostom exclaims,
" You see the exceeding greatness of the honour" ;[1]
and he adds, "wherefore, too, in reward for his
faith He connected him with Himself in the payment of the tribute " ; and he remarks on Peter's
modesty, "for Mark, the disciple of Peter, seems
not to have recorded this incident, because it
pointed out the great honour bestowed on him ;

[1] On Matt. Hom. 58, n. 2.

but he did record his denial, while he was silent as
to the points which made him conspicuous, his
Master perhaps begging him not to say great
things about him". Indeed, *how* could one of the
disciples be more signally pointed out than by this
incident, as " the faithful and wise steward, whom
the Lord would set over His household, to give
them their portion of food in due time "?

Other Fathers, as well as St. Chrysostom, did not
fail to see such a meaning in this passage ; but let
us take the words of Origen as pointing out the
connection of this incident with the important
question following. His words are : " It seems to
me that (the disciples) considering this a very
great honour which had been done to Peter by
Jesus, in having put him higher than the rest of
His disciples, they wished to make sure of what
they suspected by asking Jesus, and hearing His
answer, whether, as they conceived, He judged
Peter to be greater than them ; and they also
hoped to learn the cause for which Peter was
preferred to the rest of the disciples. Matthew,
then, wishing to signify this by these words, ' take
that, and give it to them for Me and thee,' added,
' on that day the disciples came to Jesus, saying,
Who, thinkest Thou, is the greater in the kingdom
of heaven ?' " [1]

For, indeed, why should they immediately ask
this question ? The preceding incident furnishes
a natural and sufficient cause. The Apostles, it
seems, were urged by the plainness of Christ's

[1] Origen on the text, in Matt., tom. xiii. 14.

words and acts to inquire who among them should
have the chief authority. Who will not agree
with St. Chrysostom : " The Apostles were touched
with a human infirmity, which the Evangelist too
signifies in the words, ' in that hour,' when He had
honoured him (Peter) before them all. For though
of James and John one of the two was the first-
born" (alluding to an opinion that the tax was paid
by the first-born), " He did nothing like it for
them. Hence, being ashamed, they confessed their
excitement of mind, and do not say plainly, Why
hast thou preferred Peter to us ? Is he greater
than we are ? For this they do not dare ; but they
ask indefinitely, Who is the greater ? For when
they saw three preferred to the rest, they felt
nothing like this ; but when one received so great
an honour they were pained. Nor were they
kindled by this alone, but by putting together
many other things. For He had said to him, ' I
will give to thee the keys,' and ' Blessed art thou,
Simon Bar Jona,' and here, ' Give it to them for
Me and for thee '; and also they were pricked at
seeing his confidence and freedom of speech." [1]

Thus their question, if it did not express, at least
suggested this meaning, " Speak more plainly and
distinctly whether Peter is to be the greater and
the chief in the Church, and accordingly among
us," and so they seem to have drawn from our
Lord's act a conclusion which they did not see in
the promising or bestowing the prophetic name
of Peter, nor even in the promises conveyed in

---

[1] St. Chrysostom on the text, Hom. 58, tom. vii. p. 587.

explaining that name, and were vexed at the preference shown to him.

And if[1] any be inclined to conclude from hence
that our Lord's words and acts to Peter had not
been of any marked significancy, they should be
reminded that the very clearest and plainest things
were sometimes not understood by the Apostles,
before the descent of the Holy Spirit on them.
This was specially the case with the things which
they were disinclined to believe. Thus our Lord
again and again foretold to them His passion in
express terms, but we are told, " they understood
none of these things ".[2] He foretold, too, His
resurrection, yet they did not in the least expect
it, and they became at length fully assured of
the fact before they remembered the prediction.
Strange as these things seem, yet probably every
one's private experience will furnish him with
similar instances of a veil being cast upon his
eyes, which prevented his discerning the most
evident things, towards which there was generally
some secret disinclination.

But[3] how did our Lord answer their question ?
Did He remove at once the ground of their jealousy
by declaring that in the kingdom of heaven no
one should have pre-eminence of dignity, but the
condition of all be equal ? On the contrary, He
condemns ambition and enjoins humility, but likewise gives such a turn to His discourse as to
insinuate that there would be one pre-eminent

---

[1] Passaglia, p. 77, note 38.

[2] Luke xviii. 34.   [3] Passaglia, p. 78.

over the rest. "Jesus calling unto Him a little
child, set him in the midst of them, and said,
Amen I say unto you, unless you be converted
and become as little children, you shall not enter
into the kingdom of heaven."[1] Then He adds,
"Whosoever therefore shall humble himself as
this little child, he is the greater in the kingdom
of heaven". Thus He did not exclude the pre-
eminence of that "greater one," about which they
asked, but pointed out what his character ought
to be. But this will be much clearer from a like
inquiry, and the answer to it, recorded by St.
Luke.

For even at the Last Supper, our Lord having
told them that He should be betrayed, and was
going to leave them in the way determined for
Him, there was not only an inquiry among them
which of them should do that thing, but also, so
keenly were their minds as yet, before the coming
down of the Holy Spirit, alive to the desire of
pre-eminence, and so strongly were they persuaded
that such a superior had not been excluded by
Christ, but rather marked out and ordained, "there
was a strife among them which of them should
seem to be greater". Now our Lord meets their
contention thus: "The kings of the Gentiles lord
it over them, and they that have power over them
are called beneficent. But you not so; but he
that is the greater among you, let him become as
the younger; and he that is the leader, as he that
serveth. For which is greater, he that sitteth at

[1] Matt. xviii. 2.

table, or he that serveth? Is not he that sitteth at table? But I am in the midst of you as he that serveth. And you are they who have continued with Me in My temptations; and I dispose to you, as My Father hath disposed to Me, a kingdom; that you may eat and drink at My table in My kingdom; and may sit upon thrones judging the twelve tribes of Israel." [1]

Now [2] in this speech of our Lord we may remark four points:—

1. What is omitted, though it would seem most apposite to be said;

2. What is affirmed, if not expressly, yet by plain consequence;

3. What comparison is used in illustration;

4. What meets with censure and rejection.

1. First, then, though the Apostles had twice before contended about pre-eminence, yet our Lord neither there, nor here, said openly that He would not prefer any one over the rest, nor appoint any one to be their leader. Yet the importance of the subject, His own wisdom, and His love towards His disciples, as well as His usual mode of acting, seemed to demand that, had it been His will for no one of them to be set over the rest, He should plainly declare it, and thus extinguish all strife. No less a matter was at issue than the harmony of the Apostles with each other, the peace of the Church, and the success of the divine counsel for its government. Moreover, the Gospels represent Him to us as continually removing doubts, clearing

[1] Luke xxii. 25.　　　　[2] Passaglia, p. 77.

up perplexities, and correcting wrong judgments among His disciples. Let us recall to mind a very similar occasion, when the mother of the sons of Zebedy with her children came before Him, asking " that these my two sons may sit the one on Thy right hand and the other on Thy left, in Thy kingdom ". He rejected their prayer at once, saying, " To sit on My right or My left hand is not Mine to give to you, but to them for whom it is prepared by My Father ".[1]   The silence, therefore, of Christ here, under such circumstances, is a proof that it was not the divine will that all the Apostles should be in such a sense equal that no one of them should hold a superior authority over the rest.

2. But eloquent as this silence is, we are not left to trust to it alone, for our Lord's words point out, besides, the institution of one superior. " The kings of the Gentiles," He says, " lord it over them ; and they that have power over them are called benefactors. But you not so : but he that is the greater among you, let him become as the younger ; and he that is the leader, as he that serveth." *A greater* and *a leader*, then, *there was to be*. Our Lord's words contain two parallel propositions repeated.   1. There is among you one who is the greater, let him, then, be as the younger.   2. There is among you one who is the leader, let him be as he that serveth. Thus our Lord's meaning is most distinct that they should have a superior.

[1] Matt. xx. 20.

But in the very similar passage about the sons of Zebedy, lest any should conclude that no one of the Apostles was to be superior to the rest, He called them to Him, and said, " You know that the princes of the Gentiles lord it over them, and they that are the greater exercise power upon them. It shall not be so among you, but whosoever will be the greater among you, let him be your minister; and he that will be the first among you shall be your servant. Even as the Son of Man is not come to be ministered unto, but to minister, and to give His life a redemption for many." Where He tells them His will, not that no one of the Apostles should be "great" and "first," but what the type and model should be which that "great" and "first" one should imitate, even the Son of Man who came to minister.

3. For to make this quite certain, there, and here too, He directs us to a particular comparison, by which He explains and concludes His discourse, "For who is greater, he that sitteth at table, or he that serveth? Is not he that sitteth at table? But I am among you as he that serveth. . . . And I dispose unto you, as My Father disposed unto Me, a kingdom." Here our Lord sets Himself before His Apostles as the exemplar both of the rule which the superior was to exercise, and of the temper and character which he was to show. As He had been speaking of the kingdoms of the Gentiles, so He now points out to them in contrast the true kingdom which He was disposing unto

them.   The Church as it had been from the
beginning, was to be the model of what it should
be to the end.   Now all confess that in that
Church, Christ had held the place of "the First,"
"the Great One," "the Ruler".   And now He
explains that one of His Apostles should occupy
that place of His, and occupying it should be of a
like temper with Himself, who had been the
minister and servant of all.   And it may be remarked that the same word is here applied to him
who should *rule* among the disciples, which expresses the dignity of Christ Himself in the
prophecy of Micah, quoted in Matt. ii. 6, "Out
of thee shall go forth[1] *the ruler*, who shall be
shepherd over my people Israel".   For Christ
says, "He that is the greater among you, let him
be as the younger; and *he that ruleth*, as he that
serveth.   *For* who is greater, he that sitteth at
meat, or he who serveth?   But *I* am among you
as he that serveth."   "I dispose to you a kingdom,
as My Father disposed to Me:" let him who
follows Me in place, follow Me in character.

But, 4, what does our Lord censure and
reject from His Church?   It is plain that He
compares kingdom with kingdom, and the kingdom of heaven, which is the Church, with
human kingdoms, and, moreover, that the negative quality as to which, in the clause "But
you not so," the two are compared, is, *not* the
fact that there is pre-eminence and rule in both,
but a certain *mode* of exercising them.   This is

[1] ἡγούμενος.

the pomp and ambition expressed in the words,
"lording it," "exercising authority," "are called
beneficent". As again is shown in the repeated
declaration that what had been most alien from
the spirit of His own ministry, should not appear
in the ministry that He would establish after Him.
Now, He had shown no pomp and pride of
dominion, but yet He had shown the dominion
itself in the fullest sense, the power of passing
laws, enjoining precepts, defining rites, threatening
punishments, governing, in fine, His Church, so
that He had been pre-eminently "the Lord".
Lastly, this is shown in the words recorded by St.
John, as said shortly after on this same occasion.
"You call Me Master and Lord, and you say well,
for so I am. If I, then, your Lord and Master,
have washed your feet, you also ought to wash
one another's feet: *for I have given you an example,*
that as I have done unto you, so you also may do."[1]

Now, nothing can show more strongly than
this discourse the pre-eminence and authority
which our Lord was going to establish in one of
His Apostles over the rest. For here we have
His intention disclosed that in His kingdom,
which is the Church, some one there should be
"the Great," "the First," and "the Ruler," who
should discharge, in due proportion and analogy,
the office which He Himself, before He returned
to the Father, had held. But before we consider
further who this one was, let us look at the subject
from a somewhat different point of view.

[1] John xiii. 15.

And[1] here we must lay down three points, the
first of which is, that our Lord, during His life
on earth, had acted in two capacities, the one as
the Author and Founder, the other as the Head
and Supreme Ruler of His Church. His functions
in the former capacity are too plain to need en-
larging upon. He disclosed the objects of our
faith; He instituted rites and sacraments; He
provided by the establishment of a ministry for
the perpetual growth and duration of the Church.
It was in this sense that He spoke of Himself to
His Apostles, as "the Master," who could share
His prerogatives with no one: "But be not you
called Rabbi, for one is your Master, and all you
are brethren".[2] Thus is He "the Teacher," "the
Master," throughout the Gospel.

But He likewise acted as the Head of His
Church, with the dignity and authority of the
chief visible Ruler. He was the living bond of
His disciples; the person around whom they
grouped; whose presence wrought harmony;
whose voice terminated contention among them;
who was ever at hand to solve emergent difficulties.
Thus it is that prophecy distinguished Him as
"the Lord," "the King," "the Shepherd"; "on
whose shoulders is the government," "who should
rule His people Israel". And His Church answers
to Him in this capacity, as the family, the house,
the city, the fold, and the kingdom.

Thus His relation to the Church was twofold:
as Founder, and as Supreme Pastor.

[1] Passaglia, p. 82.   [2] Matt, xxiii. 8.

Secondly, the Church shares her Lord's pre-rogative of unchangeableness, and as He is " Jesus Christ the same yesterday, to-day, and for ever," so she, His mystical Body, in her proportion remains like herself from the beginning to the end. The Church and Christianity are bound to each other in a mutual relation ; the Church is Christianity embodied ; Christianity is the Church in conception ; the consistency and identity which belong to Christianity belong likewise to her ; neither can change their nature, nor put on another form.

But, *thirdly*, the Church would be unlike herself, if, having been from her very cradle visibly ad-ministered by the rule of One, she fell subsequently, either under no rule at all, according to the doctrine of the Independents, or under the rule of the multitude, according to the Calvinists, or under the rule of an aristocracy, as Episcopalians imagine. A change of government superinduces a change of that substantial form which constitutes a society. But this holds in her case especially, above all other societies, as she came forth from the creative hand of her Lord, her whole organiza-tion instinct with inward life, her government *directly* instituted by God Himself, in which lies her point of distinction from all temporal polities.

For imagine that, upon our Lord's departure, no one had been deputed to take the visible head-ship and rule over the Church. How, without ever fresh revelations, and an abiding miraculous power, could that complex unity of faith, of worship, and of polity, have been maintained, which the Lord has set forth as the very sign and token of His Church?[1] A multitude scattered throughout the most distant regions, and naturally differing in race, in habits, in temperament, how could it possibly be joined in one, and remain one, without a powerful bond of unity? Hence, in the fourth century, St. Jerome observed, "The safety of the Church depends on the dignity of the supreme Priest, in whom, if all do not recognize a peculiar and supereminent power, there will arise as many schisms in the Church as there are Priests".[2] And the repentant confessors out of Novatian's schism, in the middle of the third century, " We know that Cornelius (the Pope) has been elected Bishop of the most holy Catholic Church, by Almighty God, and Christ our Lord.— We are not ignorant that there is one God, one Christ the Lord, whom we confessed, one Holy Spirit, and that there ought to be one Bishop in the Catholic Church."[3] And these words, both of St. Jerome, and of the confessors, if they primarily apply to the diocesan Bishop among his Priests and people, so do they with far greater force apply to the chief Bishop among his brethren in the whole Church. Now, as our Lord willed that His Church should do without fresh revelations, and new miracles, such as at first accredited it, and that it should preserve unity; and as, when it was a little flock, which could be

---

[1] John, chaps. x., xiii., xvii.
[2] Dialog, cont. Lucif, n. 9,   [3] St, Cyprian, Ep. 46.

assembled in a single room, it had yet one visible Ruler, how can we doubt that He willed this form of government to remain, and that there should be one perpetually to rule it in His name, and preserve it in unity, since it was to become co-extensive with the earth?

Again, we may ask, was the condition of fold, house, family, city, and kingdom, so repeatedly set forth in Holy Scripture, to belong to the Church only while Christ was yet on earth, or to be the visible evidence of its truth for ever? Do these terms exhibit a temporary, or a perpetual state? Each one of these symbols by itself, and all together, involve one visible Ruler; therefore, so long as the Church can be called with truth the one house, the one family, the one city, the one fold, the one kingdom, so long must it have one visible and supreme Ruler.

But once grant that such a one there was after our Lord's departure, and no one can doubt that one to have been Peter. It is easier to deny the supreme Ruler altogether, than to make him any one but Peter. The whole course of the Gospels shows none other marked out by so many distinctions. Thus, even those who wish to refuse a real power to his Primacy, are compelled by the force of evidence to allow him a Primacy of order and honour.

But nothing did our Lord more pointedly reject than the vain pomp of titles and honours. In nothing is His own example more marked than in that He exercised real power and supreme

authority without pomp or show. Nothing did
He enjoin more emphatically on the disciple who
should be the "Great One," and "the Ruler,"
among his brethren, than that he must follow his
Master in being the servant of all. A Primacy,
then, consisting in titles and mere precedency, is
of all things most opposed to the spirit and the
precepts of our Lord. And so the Primacy which
He designated must be one of real power and pre-
eminent authority.

And this brings us back to the passage of St.
Luke which we were considering, where four
things prove that Christ had such a headship in
view. First, the occasion, for the Apostles were
contending for a place of real authority. The
sons of Zebedy expressed it by sitting on His right
hand and on His left, that is, holding the second
and the third place of dignity in the kingdom.

Secondly, the double comparison which our
Lord used, the one negative, the other affirmative :
in the former, contrasting the Church's ruler with
the kings of the Gentiles, He excluded pomp and
splendour, lordship and ambition; in the latter,
referring him to His own example, who had the
most real and true power and superiority, He
taught him to unite these with a meekness and an
attention to the wants of his brethren, of which
His own life had been the model.

Thirdly, the words "the First," "the Greater,"
and "the Ruler," indicate the pre-eminence of the
future head, for as they appear in the context, and
according to their Scriptural force, they indicate

not a vain and honorary, but a real authority, one of them being even the very title given to our Lord.

And, fourthly, this is proved by the object in view, which is, maintaining the identity of the Church, and the form which it had from the beginning, and preserving its manifold unity. As to its identity, and original form, it is needless to observe that Christ exercised in it not an honorary but a real supremacy, so that under Him its government was really in the hands of one, the Ruler. As to the preservation of its unity—and especially a unity so complex—the very analogy of human society will sufficiently teach us that it is impossible to be preserved without a strong central authority. Contentions can neither be checked as they arise, nor terminated when they come to a head, without the interference of a power to which all yield obedience. And the living example of those religious societies which have not this power is an argument whose force none can resist. Where Peter is not, there is neither unity of faith, nor of charity, nor of external regimen.

No sooner[1] then had our Lord in this manner pointed out that there should be one hereafter to take His place on earth and to be the Ruler of his brethren, expressing at the same time the toilsome nature of the trust, and the duty of exercising it with the spirit which He, the great model, had shown, than, turning His discourse from the

Passaglia, p. 89.

Apostles, whom hitherto He had addressed in common, to Peter singly, He proceeded to designate
Peter as that one, to assure him of a singular privilege, and to enforce upon him a proportionate duty.

And first, a break in the hitherto continuous discourse is ushered in by the words, " And the Lord
said," and what follows is fixed to Peter specially,
by the reiteration of his name, " Simon, Simon,
behold Satan hath desired to have you, that he
may sift you as wheat " : to have *you*, that is, not
Peter alone, but all the Apostles, the same you,
whom in the preceding verses He had so often
repeated, " you not so," " but I am in the midst
of you," " but you are they that have continued
with Me," " and I dispose to you a kingdom,"
" that you may eat and drink with Me " ; and what
follows ?   What was the resource provided by the
Lord against this attack of the great enemy on all
His fold ?   " But I have prayed for *thee*, that *thy*
faith fail not : and thou being once converted confirm thy brethren."   Not " I have prayed for *you*,"
where all were assaulted, " that *your* faith fail not,"
but I have prayed for *thee*, Peter, that *thy* faith fail
not ! Nothing can be more emphatic than this
change of number, when our Lord throughout all
His previous discourse had used the plural, and
now continuing the plural to designate the persons
attacked, uses the singular to specify the person
for whom He has prayed, and to whom He assures
a singular privilege, the fruit of that prayer.
Nothing could more strongly prove that this
address was special to Peter.

Nor less evident is the singular dignity of what is here promised to him. First of all, it is the fruit of the prayer of Christ. Of what importance must that be which was solicited by our Lord of His Father, and at a moment when the redemption of the world was being accomplished, and when His passion may be said to have begun ? Of what importance that which was to be the defence of not Peter only, but all the disciples, against the most formidable assault of the great enemy, who had demanded [1] them as it were to deliver them over to punishment ? And this was " that thy faith fail not ". How is it possible to draw any other conclusion here than what St. Leo in the fifth century expressed so clearly before all the Bishops of Italy ? " The danger from the temptation of fear was common to all the Apostles, and all equally needed the help of the divine protection, since the devil desired to dismay all, to crush all ; and yet a special care of Peter is undertaken by our Lord, and He prays peculiarly for the faith of Peter, as if the state of the rest would be more sure, if the mind of their chief were not conquered. In Peter, therefore, the fortitude of all is protected, and the help of divine grace is so ordered, that the firmness which through Christ is given to Peter, through Peter is conferred on the Apostles." [2] And if such is the importance of the help secured, no less is the charge following : " And thou, being once converted, confirm thy brethren ". To confirm

---

[1] ἐξητήσατο. The word in classic Greek has this force.

[2] Serm. 4, c. 3.

others, is to be put in an office of dignity and
authority over them. And his brethren were
those whom our Lord till now had been addressing
in common with him ; to whom He had just disclosed "a Greater" and "a Ruler" "among"
them ; that is, the Apostles themselves. Among
these, then, when our Lord's visible presence was
withdrawn, Peter was to be the principle of
stability, binding and moulding them into one
building. For one cannot fail to see how this
great promise and prophecy answers to those in
Matthew. There our Lord, as Architect, promised
to lay Peter as the foundation of the Church,
against which the gates of hell should not prevail :
here, being about to leave the world, when His
own work was finished, to ascend unto His Father,
and to assume His great power and reign, He
makes Peter as it were the Architect to carry on
the work which was to be completed by *His* grace
and authority, but by human co-operation. So
exact is the resemblance that we may put the two
promises in parallel columns to illustrate each
other :—

Thou art Peter, and upon this Rock I will build My Church ; and the gates of hell shall not prevail against it.	But I have prayed for thee, that thy faith fail not ; and thou, being once converted, confirm thy brethren.

But light is thrown on the greatness of this pre-
eminence thus bestowed on Peter of confirming his
brethren, if we consider that the term is applied
to the Father, the Son, and the Holy Spirit, as
bestowing by inherent power what is here granted

by participation. Of the Father it is said, " To Him that is able to *establish* you according to my Gospel—the only wise God, through Jesus Christ, be honour and glory ". And again, " Now He that *confirmeth us* with you in Christ, and that hath anointed us, is God " ; and again, " The God of all grace, who hath called us unto His eternal glory in Christ Jesus, after you have suffered a little, will Himself perfect you, *confirm*, establish you ".[1] Of Christ likewise : " As therefore you have received Jesus Christ the Lord, walk ye in Him, rooted and built up in Him, and *confirmed* in the faith ". And " waiting for the manifestation of our Lord Jesus Christ, who also will *confirm* you unto the end without crime ". And again: " Now our Lord Jesus Christ Himself exhort your hearts, and *confirm* you in every good word and work ".[2] And the Holy Spirit is continually mentioned as the author of this gift, when, for instance, to Him is ascribed " the teaching all truth," " the leading into all truth," " the bringing to mind " all things which Christ had said. And St. Paul prays " that He would grant you, according to the riches of His glory, to be *strengthened* by His Spirit with might unto the inward man ".[3]

What, therefore, is proper to the most Holy Trinity, and given in the highest sense by the Father, the Son, and the Holy Ghost, it was the will of Christ should be shared by Peter, according

[1] Rom. xvi. 25 ; 2 Cor. i. 21 ; 1 Pet. v. 10.
[2] Col. ii. 6; 1 Cor. i. 7 ; 2 Thess. ii. 16.
[3] John xvi. 13 ; xiv. 16, 26 ; Eph. iii. 16.

as man is capable of it. That is, it was His pleasure that the same man, whom He had intimately associated with Himself by communicating to him His prerogative to be the Rock, should be closely joined with the Blessed Trinity, by participating in that privilege, whereby, together with the Father and the Holy Spirit, He is the confirmation and stability of the faithful. But if any rule there can be whereby to measure pre-eminence and dignity, it is surely that which is derived from participation of divine properties and offices. And the closer that by these Peter is shown to have approached to God, the higher his exaltation above the rest of his brethren, who, as it has been observed, are the Apostles. To them he is the Rock, and them he is to confirm. Thus Theophylact, in the eleventh century, commenting on this text, says, " The plain meaning of this is, that, since I hold thee as the ruler of My disciples, after thou shalt have wept over thy denial and repented, confirm the rest. For this belongs to thee as being after Me the rock and support" (literally, confirmation) " of the Church. Now, one may see that this is said not only of the Apostles, that they are confirmed by Peter, but also concerning all the faithful until the consummation of the world."

But looking more closely into the nature of this dignity, since Christ, by the bestowal of heavenly gifts, caused Peter to be conspicuous through the firmness of his own faith, and through the charge of confirming the faith of his brethren, we can call it by no fitter name than a Primacy of faith. For it has these two qualities: it cannot fail itself; and it confirms others. And for the authority which it carries, such a Primacy of faith cannot even be imagined without at the same time imagining the office by which Peter was bound to watch over the firmness and integrity of the common faith. In this office two things are involved : first, the right to, and therefore the possession of, all things necessary for its fulfilment; and secondly, the duty by which all were bound to agree in the profession of one faith with Peter. So that Peter's dignity, rightly termed the Primacy of faith, mainly consists in the supreme right of demanding from all an agreement in faith with him.

It [1] remains to explain the proper force of the word *confirm*. Now, this is a term of architecture, and as such is joined with other terms relating to that art, as by St. Peter, "the God of all grace . . . Himself fit you together" (as living spiritual stones), "confirm, strengthen, ground you ".[2] It means, to make anything fit so firmly that it cannot be shaken. Thus in Holy Writ it frequently bears metaphorically a moral significa- tion, such as encouraging, supporting, as we say, confirming the resolution, as in the passage just quoted; and again, " Be watchful, and *confirm* the things that remain, which are ready to die ".[3] Now, it cannot be doubted that the phrase " confirm thy brethren," carries a moral sense very like that in which the word *confirm*, when applied to the spiritual building of the Church, is

<hr>

[1] Passaglia, p. 563.   [2] 1 Pet. v. 10.   [3] Apoc. iii. 2.

used of God and of Christ,[1] from whom the Church has both its being and its perseverance to the end, and again of the Apostles, who strengthen the flock entrusted to them by the imparting spiritual gifts, as St. Paul says, " I long to see you, that I may impart unto you some spiritual grace to strengthen you";[2] or, again, of Bishops, who, as sent by the Apostles, and charged by the Holy Spirit with the government of the Church, are bid to be watchful and see that those who stand do not fall, and those who are in danger do not perish.[3] Accordingly, when it is said to Peter, " And thou, in thy turn, one day confirm thy brethren," *the charge and office are laid upon him, as an architect divinely chosen, of holding together, strengthening, and keeping in their place, the several parts of the ecclesiastical structure.*

But what are these *parts* to be confirmed, and what is the *nature* of the confirmation ?

As to the first question there can be no controversy, it being determined by the words " confirm *thy brethren* ": and it is plain, from what is said above, that by brethren are meant the Apostles. He had, therefore, the Apostles committed to his charge *immediately;* but likewise, the rest of all the faithful *mediately.* When a person has been named by Christ to confirm the Apostles expressly, the nature of the case does not allow that the whole congregation of believers be not in their persons committed to him. The care of the

---

[1] Rom. xvi. 25 ; 1 Thess. iii. 13 ; 2 Thess. ii. 17 ; 1 Pet. v. 10.
[2] Rom. i. 11.   [3] Apoc. iii. 2.

flock is manifestly involved in the care of the shepherds; and no one in his senses can doubt that the man who is charged to support the pillars, is charged to keep in their place the inferior stones.

And as to the *nature* of the confirmation, it is for protection against the fraud of the great enemy. And the danger lay in losing the faith. Peter, then, is charged to confirm, in such sense that neither the pillars of the Church, nor its inferior parts, may, by the loss of faith, be moved from their place, and so severed from the Church's structure. No charge can be higher than such an office of confirmation; nor for anything need we to be more thankful to our Saviour; but, particularly, nothing can more distinctly show the divinely appointed relation between Peter on the one hand, and on the other, the rest of the Apostles, and the whole company of the faithful; nothing define more clearly the special authority of Peter; that is, to protect and strengthen the unity of the faith, and to possess all powers needed for such protection.

This charge was given after that by the prayer of Christ the privilege had been gained for Peter's faith, *that it should never fail.* Hence, that faith is become, in virtue of such prayer, the infallible standard of evangelical truth: as St. Cyprian expressed it of old, "that faith of the Romans, which perfidy *cannot* approach".[1] It follows that all the faithful owe to it obedience. And Peter's

[1] St. Cyprian, Ep. 55.

authority rests on a double title, *external* of
mission, *internal* of spiritual gift : the former contained in the words of Christ the legislator, " And
thou,[1] in thy turn, one day confirm thy brethren ";
the latter, in the words of Christ the bestower of
all gifts, " But I have prayed for thee, that thy
faith fail not ".

More than a thousand years ago two Easterns
seem to have expressed all this, one the Bishop
Stephen, suppliantly approaching Pope Martin I.,

---

[1] As far as the *words* by themselves go, it is the opinion of the
best commentators that they may be equally well rendered,
"And thou, when thou art converted," or "And thou, in thy turn,
one day," etc. But as it is impossible to bring a discussion
turning on a Hebrew idiom conveyed in a Greek word before the
English reader, we must here restrict ourselves to the proof
arising from the *sense* and *context*. And here one thing alone,
among several which may be urged, is sufficient to prove that the
sense preferred in the text, " And thou, in thy turn, one day confirm thy brethren," is the true one. For the other rendering
supposes that the time of Peter's conversion would also be the
time of his confirming his brethren ; whereas this was far otherwise. He was converted by our Lord looking on him that same
night shortly after his denial, and "immediately went out and
wept bitterly". But he did not succeed to the charge of confirming his brethren till after our Lord's ascension. It must be added
that the collocation of the original words καὶ σὺ ποτὲ ἐπιστρέψας
στήριξον is such as absolutely to require that the joint action
indicated by them should belong to the same time, and that an
indefinite time expressed by ποτέ. Now this would be false
according to the rendering, " And thou, when thou art converted,
confirm thy brethren," for the conversion was immediate and
definite, the confirmation distant and indefinite ; whereas it
exactly agrees with the rendering, " And thou, in thy turn, one
day confirm thy brethren ".

Those who wish to see the whole controversy admirably drawn
out, may find it in Passaglia, b. ii. ch. 13.

in the Lateran Synod of A.D. 649, and speaking of
" the blessed Peter, in a manner special and
peculiar to himself, having above all a firm and
immutable faith in our Lord God, to consider
with compassion, and confirm his spiritual
partners and brethren when tossed by doubt:
inasmuch as he has received power and sacerdotal
authority, according to the dispensation, over all,
from the very God for our sakes incarnate ".[1] And
Theodore, Abbot of the Studium, at Constantinople, addressing Pope Paschal I., A.D. 817, in the
midst of persecution from the state, as if he were
Peter himself: " Hear, O Apostolic Head, O
shepherd of the sheep of Christ, set over them by
God, O doorkeeper of the kingdom of heaven, O
rock of the faith upon which the Catholic Church
is built. For Peter art thou, who adornest and
governest the See of Peter. To thee, said Christ
our God, ' And thou, in thy turn, one day confirm
thy brethren '. Behold the time, behold the place,
help us, thou who art ordained by God for this.
Stretch forth thy hand as far as may be: power
thou hast from God, because thou art the chief of
all."[2]

Now let us[3] view in its connection the whole
scope of our Lord's discourse. We shall see how
naturally the contest of the Apostles arose out of
what He had told them, and how well the former
and the latter part of His answer harmonize
together, and terminate that contest. We learn

[1] Mansi, Concilia, x. 894.
[2] Baronius, Annal., A.D. 817, xxi.   [3] Passaglia, p. 545.

from St. John's record of this divine conversation, that our Lord besought His Father, saying, "While I was with them in the world, I kept them in Thy name . . . but now I come to Thee": that is, so long as I was with them visibly in the world (for invisibly I will always be with them, and nurture them with the spiritual influx of the Vine), I kept them united in Thy name; "but now I come to Thee," I leave the world, I relinquish the office of visible head. It remains, that by the appointment of another visible head, Thou shouldst entrust him with My office, provide for the conspicuous unity of all, and preserve them joined to each other and to Us. So St. Luke tells us, that no sooner had our Lord declared to the Apostles, "the Son of Man indeed goeth according to that which is determined," than they began to have a strife among them, "which of them should seem to be the greater". For they had heard that Christ would withdraw His visible presence, and they had heard Him also earnestly entreating of the Father to provide for their visible unity. Accordingly, the time seemed at hand when another was to take this office of visible head; hence their questioning, who should be the greater among them. Now, our Lord does not reprove this inference of theirs, but He does reprove the temper in which they were coveting pre-eminence. For, engaged as they were in the strife, He warned them that the person who should be "the Greater and the Ruler" among them must follow in the discharge of his office the rule and the standard which *He* had set up in His own conduct, and not that which the kings of the Gentiles follow. Thus, setting these in sharp contrast, He proceeds: " The kings, indeed, of the nations lord it over their subjects, and love high titles, and to be called benefactors; but I, though Lord and Master amongst you, have dealt otherwise, as you know. For I have exercised, not a lordship, but a servitude; I have not sat at table, but waited ; I have not cared for titles, but called you friends and brethren. Let this example then be before you all, but especially before him who is to be the greater and the ruler among you. For I appoint unto you, and dispose of you, as My Father hath disposed of Me ; of Me He hath disposed that through humiliation, emptying of Myself, ignominy, and manifold temptations, I should gain the kingdom, reach the joys of heaven, and obtain all power in heaven and on earth. So likewise dispose I of you, that through humility, sufferings, reproaches, hunger, thirst, and all manner of temptations, you may reach whither I have, come, being worthy, after your hunger and your thirst, to eat and drink at My table in My kingdom ; after being despised and dishonoured, to sit on thrones, judging the twelve tribes of Israel. Now, hitherto you have trodden with Me this royal way full of sorrows, and have continued with Me in My temptations. But little will it profit to begin, if you persevere not to the end. None shall be crowned, save he who has contended lawfully ; none be saved, but he who perseveres to the end. Will you remain with me still in your temptations to come, and when I am no longer present with you visibly, to protect and exhort, will you preserve your steadfastness ? Simon, Simon, behold ! I see Satan exerting all his force to overcome your purpose, and to destroy the fidelity which you have hitherto shown Me. I see the danger to your faith and your salvation approaching. But I, who, when visibly present with you, left nothing undone to guard, protect, and strengthen you visibly, so, too, when separated from your bodily sight, will yet not leave you without a visible support. Wherefore, Peter, I have prayed for thee, that thou fail not, and thou, in thy turn, one day confirm thy brethren. Remember that thou hast to discharge that part visibly towards thy brethren, which I, while yet mortal, and visible, discharged ; remember that I therefore had special care of thee, because it was My will that thou, confirmed by My prayers, shouldst confirm thy brethren, My disciples, and My friends." [1]

Now, from [2] what has been said, it appears that Peter in Holy Scripture is set forth as the source and principle of ecclesiastical unity under a double but cognate image, as Foundation, and as Confirmer. Of the former we will here say nothing further, but a few consequences of the latter it is desirable here to group together.

[1] Passaglia, p. 547.   [2] Ibid. p. 571.

I. The unity, then, which consists in the profession of one and the same faith, is conspicuous
among those [1] modes of unity by which Christ has
willed that His Church should be distinguished.
Now, first, St. Paul declares that the whole
ministerial hierarchy, from the Apostolate downwards, was instituted by our Lord, for the sake of
obtaining and preserving this unity. " He gave
some Apostles, and some Prophets, and other
some Evangelists, and other some pastors and
doctors, for the perfecting " (literally, the fitting
in together, the same word in which St. Peter had
used in his prayer, ch. v. 10), " of the saints, for
the work of the ministry, for the edifying of the
body of Christ; until we all meet into the unity of
faith, and of the knowledge of the Son of God,
unto a perfect man, unto the measure of the age
of the fulness of Christ." [2] To this living hierarchy
he expressly attributes preservation from doctrinal
error, proceeding thus : " That henceforth we be
no more children tossed to and fro, and carried
about with every wind of doctrine by the wickedness of men, by cunning craftiness by which they
lie in wait to deceive". And, secondly, this
hierarchy itself was knitted and gathered up into
a monarchy, and its whole force and solidity made
to depend on association with Peter, to whom
alone was said, " But I have prayed for thee, that
thy faith fail not "; to whom alone was enjoined,
" And thou, in thy turn, one day confirm thy
brethren ".

[1] For which see hereafter, ch. 7.   [2] Eph. iv. 11.

II. Accordingly the pre-eminence of Peter is well expressed by the words,[1] " Primacy of faith," " chiefship of faith," " chiefship in the episcopate of faith," meaning thereby a peculiar authority to prescribe the faith, and determine its profession, and so protect its unity and purity. This is conveyed in the words of Christ, Confirm thy brethren. Thus St. Bernard [2] addressed Innocent II., "All emergent dangers and scandals in the kingdom of God, specially those which concern the faith, are to be referred to your Apostolate. For I conceive that we should look especially for reparation of the faith to the spot where faith cannot[3] fail. That indeed is the prerogative of his see. For to whom else was it once said, ' I have prayed for thee, Peter, that thy faith fail not ' ? Therefore what follows is required of Peter's successor : ' And thou, in thy turn, one day confirm thy brethren '. And this is now necessary. It is time for you, most loving father, to recognize your chiefship, to approve your zeal, and so make your ministry honoured. In that you clearly fulfil the part of Peter, whose seat you occupy, if by your admonition you confirm hearts fluctuating in faith, if by your authority you crush those who corrupt it."

---

[1] Petrus uti audivit, vos autem quid me dicitis ? *Statim loci non immemor sui primatum egit :* primatum confessionis utique, non honoris ; primatum fidei, non ordinis.—Ambros. de Incarn. c. 4, n. 32, tom. 2, p. 710.

[2] Ep. 190, vol. 1, p. 649.

[3] Observe the exact identity with St. Cyprian's expression nine hundred years earlier, Ep. 55, quoted p. 60.

III. All who have received the ministry of the word, and the charge of defending the faith and preserving unity, and are "ambassadors in Christ's name," have a claim to be listened to, but he above all who holds the chiefship of faith, and who received the charge, " Confirm thy brethren ". He therefore must be the supreme standard of faith, which is just what St. Peter Chrysologus, in the fifth century, wrote to Eutyches : " We exhort you in all things, honourable brother, to pay obedience to what is written by the most blessed Pope of the Roman city ; for St. Peter, who both lives and rules in his own see, grants to those who ask for it the truth of faith ".[1]

IV. And in this prerogative of Peter, to be heard above all others, we find the meaning of certain ancient expressions. Thus Prudentius calls him, " the first disciple of God " ;[2] St. Augustine, " the figure of the Church ";[3] St. Chrysostom, " the mouthpiece of the disciples, and teacher of the world ";[4] St. Ephrem Syrus, " the candle, the tongue of the disciples, and the voice of preachers";[5] St. Cyril of Jerusalem, " the prince of the Apostles, and the highest preacher of the Church ".[6] In these and such-like continually recurring expressions we recognize his chiefship in the epis-

---

[1] Twenty-fifth letter among those of St. Leo.
[2] Con. Symmachum, lib. 2, v. 1.
[3] Sermon 76.   [4] Hom. 88, on John.
[5] Encom. in Petrum et cæteros Apostolos.
[6] Cat. xi. n. 3 : Ὁ πρωτοστάτης τῶν Ἀποστόλων καὶ τῆς ἐκκλησίας κορυφαῖος κήρυξ.

copate of faith, his being the standard of faith, and his representing the Catholic faith, as the branches are gathered up in the root, and the streamlets in the fountain.

V. Our Lord [1] has most solemnly declared, and St. Paul repeated, that no one shall be saved without maintaining the true and uncorrupt faith. Of this Peter's faith is the standard and exemplar. Accordingly, by the law of Christ, unity with the faith of Peter is necessary to salvation. This law our Lord set forth in the words, "Confirm thy brethren". And to this the Fathers in their expressions above quoted allude.

VI. The true faith and the true Church are so indivisibly united, that they cannot even be conceived apart from each other, faith being to the Church as light to the sun. But the true faith neither is, nor can be, other than that which Peter, "the first disciple of God," "the teacher of the world," "the mouthpiece of the disciples," and "the confirmer of his brethren," holds and proposes to others. No communion, therefore, called after Christ, which yet differs from that faith, can claim either the name or dignity of the true Church.

VII. If any knowledge have a special value, it is surely that by which we have a safe and ready test of the true faith and the true Church. It is of the utmost necessity to know and embrace both, and the means of reaching them are proportionably valuable. Now that test abides in Peter, by keeping

[1] Mark xvi. 16; John iii. 18; Rom. iii. 3, etc.

which before us we can neither miss the true faith nor the true Church. For no other true faith can there be than that which he delivers, who received the charge of confirming his brethren, nor other true Church than what Christ built, and is building still. Hence the expression of St. Ambrose, "Where Peter is, there is the Church " : [1] and of Stephen of Larissa, to Pope Boniface II. (A.D. 530), " that all the Churches of the world rest in the confession of Peter ".[2]

VIII. With all these agrees that famous and most early testimony of St. Cyprian, that men " fall away from the Church into heresy and schism so long as there is no regard *to the source of truth, no looking to the head*, nor keeping to the doctrine of our heavenly Master. If any one consider and weigh this, he will not need length of comment or argument. It is easy to offer proofs to a faithful mind, because in that case the truth may be quickly stated." [3] And then he quotes our Lord's words to Peter, Matt. xvi. 16, and John xxi. 17, adding, " upon him being one He builds His Church ". Therefore that Church can neither be torn from the one on whom she is built, nor profess any other faith, save what that one, who is Peter, proposes.

[1] Ambros. in Ps. l. n. 30.
Mansi, tom. viii. 746.   [3] De Unitate Ecclesiæ, 3.

CHAPTER III.

THE INVESTITURE OF PETER.

OUR Lord has hitherto, while on earth,[1] ruled as its visible head that body of disciples which He had chosen out of the world, and which His Father had given Him. And this body He for the first time called the Church in that famous prophecy[2] wherein He named the person, who, by virtue of an intimate association with Himself, the Rock, should be its foundation, and the duration of which until the consummation of the world, He pronounced at the same time, in spite of all the rage of " spiritual wickedness in high places " against it, because it should be founded upon the rock which He should lay.

Secondly, He had, at that period of His ministry when He thought it meet, the second year, selected out of the rest of His disciples, after ascending into a mountain and continuing the night long in prayer, twelve whom He named Apostles—as before and above all sent by Him— for " He called whom He would Himself, and they came to Him," to whom " He gave authority over unclean spirits, to cast them out, and to heal every disease and every weakness," whom He

---

[1] Passaglia, p. 93. [2] Matt. xvi. 16.

chose also "to be with Him," His personal attendants, "and to send them to preach"; to whom, moreover, He subsequently made a promise that whatever they should bind on earth should be bound in heaven, and whatever they should loose on earth should be loosed in heaven.[1]

Thirdly, as at a certain time in His ministry, that is the second year, He had selected twelve to be nearer His person than the rest of His disciples, so at a yet later time, the third year of His ministry, He had set apart one out of the twelve, to whom from the very first, and before either he, or any one, had been called to be an Apostle, or even, as it would seem, a disciple, He had given a prophetic name; whom by word and deed, in correspondence with that name, He designated to be the future rock of His Church, to be the Bearer of the keys, which opened or shut the entrance to His mystical Holy City, to be endued with power *singly* to bind and to loose; and whom at last, on the very eve of His being taken away from His disciples, He pointed out as the future "First one," "Greater one," or "Ruler," among them, having, as such, had given to him a *special* and *singular* charge, after the departure of the Head, to "confirm his brethren".

It is manifest that this was all which, before His offering Himself up for the sin of the world, and the withdrawal of His visible presence thereupon ensuing, He could do for the government of His Church. For as long as He was there, the Son

[1] Matt. x. 1; Mark iii. 13-15; Luke vi. 12, 13; Matt. xviii. 18.

of Man among men, seen, felt, touched, and handled, the sacred voice in their ears, and the divine eyes gazing bodily upon them, He was not only the fountain of all headship and rule, but He exercised in His own person the highest functions of that headship and visible rule. He daily encouraged, warned, corrected, taught, united them ; in short, to use His own words, " while He was with them, He kept them in His Father's name". [1]

But now another time, and other dangers were approaching. The sword was drawn which should " strike the shepherd," there was a fear that " the sheep would be scattered," not only for a moment, but for ever. To meet this the care of the Divine Guardian was necessary in a further disposition of those powers which He received at His resurrection from the dead. For henceforth His visits, as of a risen King, were to be few and sudden, when He pleased, and at times they expected not, " for forty days appearing to them and speaking of the kingdom of God," and as soon as His final injunctions had been thus royally given, " the heavens were to receive Him till the time of the restoration of all things ". The Apostles could no longer " be with Him," as before, nor He " keep them," as in the days of His flesh.

How, then, does He complete the ministerial hierarchy which sprung from His own Divine Person on earth, and which is to rule His Church and represent that person from His first to His second coming ?

[1] John xvii. 12,

Now, first, we must remark, that while great care is taken to make known to all the Apostles the resurrection of the Lord, yet a special solicitude is shown with regard to that one who was to be " the Ruler ". Thus the angels, announcing the fact to the holy women at the sepulchre, " He is risen, He is not here, behold the place where they laid Him," add, " but go, tell His disciples *and Peter*, that He goeth before you into Galilee ".[1] The expression indicates his superior place, as when Peter, himself delivered from prison, re-counted to the disciples at the house of Mark his escape, and added, " Tell these things to James and to the brethren," where no one fails to see the pre-eminence given to James by such a mention of him, that Apostle being the Bishop of Jerusalem and so put over the brethren, and, with himself, one of those who " seemed to be pillars ". Again, to Peter our Lord appeared first among the Apostles. St. Paul, exhibiting a sort of sum of Christian doctrine, as he says " the Gospel which I preached unto you," begins, " I delivered unto you first of all that which I also received, how that Christ died for our sins according to the Scriptures ; and that He was buried, and that He rose again the third day, according to the Scriptures ; and that He was seen by Cephas, and after that by the eleven ". By him alone, first, then by them in conjunction with him. And further, St. Paul's words seem to express a sort of descending ratio, " Then was He seen by more than five hun-

[1] Mark xvi. 6.

dred brethren at once, of whom many remain until this present, and some are fallen asleep. After that He was seen by James, then by all the Apostles. And last of all He was seen also by me, as by one born out of due time. For I am the least of the Apostles."[1] And while they were yet in doubt, and for joy could not receive the marvellous tidings when brought by the women, as soon as our Lord appeared to Peter their hesitation was removed, and the two disciples returning from Emmaus—themselves full of His wonderful conversation with them—" found the eleven gathered together and those that were with them, saying, The Lord is risen indeed, and hath appeared to Simon," as the Church in her exultation repeats, where philologists tell us that the Greek *and* bears what is often the Hebrew meaning, and signifies " for," as if no doubt could remain any longer of their happiness, when Peter had become a witness of it.

These are indications of superiority, slight perhaps in themselves if they stood alone, but not slight as bearing tacit witness to a fact otherwise resting on its own explicit evidence. If one of the Apostles was destined to be the head of the rest, this is what we should have expected to happen to that one, and this did happen to Peter, who is elsewhere made the head of the Apostles.

But now we come to those most important injunctions which our Lord gave to His Apostles after His resurrection, concerning the government

[1] 1 Cor. xv. 1-9.

of His Church. And here it becomes necessary to mark with the utmost accuracy what He said and what He gave to all the Apostles in common, and what to Peter in particular.

First of all, then, we may remark our Lord's care to redeem the promises which He had made to the Twelve, and to convey to them their legislative, judicial, and executive powers. These are mentioned by each of the four Evangelists, in somewhat different terms, but alike involving the distinctive Apostolic powers of immediate institution by Christ, and universal mission; as Apostles they are *sent*, and they are sent *by Christ*. The form recorded in St. Matthew is, "All power is given unto Me in heaven and in earth. Go ye, therefore, and make disciples all nations, baptizing them in the name of the Father, and of the Son, and of the Holy Ghost, teaching them to observe all things whatsoever I have commanded you; and behold I am with you all days, even to the consummation of the world."

The form of St. Mark is, "Go ye into the whole world, and preach the Gospel to every creature".

St. Luke refers specially in two passages to the descent of the Holy Ghost, as being Himself as well the Divine "Gift," and the immediate worker of all graces in man, as the principle of the ecclesiastical hierarchy. "And I send the promise of My Father upon you, but stay you in the city till you be endued with power from on high." And again, "Eating together with them, He commanded them that they should not depart from Jerusalem, but should wait for the promise of the Father, which you have heard," saith He, " by My mouth; for John, indeed, baptized with water, but you shall be baptized with the Holy Ghost not many days hence ". " You shall receive the power of the Holy Ghost coming upon you, and you shall be witnesses unto Me in Jerusalem, and in all Judea, and Samaria, and even to the uttermost part of the earth."

The form recorded by St. John is, "As the Father hath sent Me, I also send you. When He had said this, He breathed on them; and He said to them, Receive ye the Holy Ghost; whose sins you shall forgive, they are forgiven them; and whose sins you shall retain, they are retained."[1]

Now, it may be remarked that these passages of the several Evangelists are *identical* in their force; that is, they each convey all those powers which constitute the Apostolate. These are received by all the Apostles in common, and together; and in the joint possession of them consists that *equality* which is often attributed by the ancient writers to the Apostles, as notably by St. Cyprian, " He gives to all the Apostles an equal power, and says, ' As the Father sent Me, I also send you '". And again, " Certainly the other Apostles also were what Peter was, endued with an equal fellowship, both of honour and power ".[2]

And these Apostolic powers, legislative, judicial,

---

[1] Matt. xxviii. 18; Mark xvi. 15; Luke xxiv. 49; Acts i. 4-8; John xx. 21.   [2] De Unitate Ecclesiæ, 3.

and executive, are afterwards referred to as exercised ; as in Acts xv., where the first council passes
decrees which bind the Church ; nay, which go
forth in the joint name of the Holy Ghost, and the
Rulers of the Church, " It hath seemed good to
the Holy Ghost and to us " ;—which are delivered
by St. Paul to the cities to be kept : Acts xvi. 4—
as in Acts xx. 28, where Bishops are charged to
rule the Church, each over his flock, wherein the
Holy Ghost has placed him—as in 1 Cor. v. 1-5,
where St. Paul, " in the name of our Lord Jesus
Christ," excommunicates—as in 2 Cor. x. 6, where
he sets forth his Apostolic power—as in the
Epistles to Titus and Timothy, where he sets
them in authority, enjoins them to ordain Priests
in every city, and commands them to " reprove,"
or " rebuke ".

And all these powers St. Peter, of course, as one
of the Twelve, had received in common with the
rest. The limit to them would seem to lie in their
being shared in common by twelve ; as, for instance,
universal mission dwelling in such a body must
practically be determined and limited somehow to
the different members of that body, or one would
interfere with the other. But there is nothing in
these powers which answers to the images of " the
rock," on which the Church is built, the single
" bearer of the keys," and " confirmer " of his
brethren, which Christ had appropriated to one
Apostle.

In like manner, then, as our Lord fulfilled His
promises to the Twelve, so did He those to St,

Peter, and we find written the committal of an authority to him exactly answering to these images ; an authority, which expresses the full legislative, judicial, and executive power of the head, which can be executed by one alone at a time, and is of its own nature supreme, and responsible to none save God. It remained for our Lord to find an image setting forth all this as decisively as that of the Rock, the Bearer of the keys, and the Confirmer of his brethren.

Once, as He passed along the shores of the lake of Galilee, He had seen two fishermen casting their net into the sea, and had "said to them, Come after Me, and I will make you fishers of men, and immediately leaving their nets, they followed Him". Once again, too, He had gone into the ship of that same fisherman, and sitting, taught the multitudes out of it. And then He bade that fisherman, "who had laboured all the night and taken nothing, to launch out into the deep," and in faith "let down his nets for a draught," whereupon "he enclosed so great a multitude of fishes that the net brake ".[1] And again, in after times, when the fisherman had become an Apostle, that same ship waited on His convenience, and carried Him across the lake. It was there He was asleep when the storm raged, and His disciples in little faith awoke Him, saying, " Master, save us, we perish," not yet knowing that the ship which carried the Lord might be tost, but could not sink.[2] From it they beheld Him walking

[1] Mark i, 16 ; Luke v. 3.   [2] Mark iv. 38 ; Luke viii. 24.

on the sea, in the fourth watch of the night, when Peter, in his fervour, desired to join Him, and going to meet his Lord on the waves, his faith failed him, and he begun to sink, till the Almighty hand supported him, and drew him with it to the ship, which " presently was at the land to which they were going".[1] And now, Peter, and Thomas, and Nathaniel, and the sons of Zebedy, and two others, were once more on that same ship and sea, but no longer with Him who had commanded the winds, and walked on the waves. Once more, too, they[2] toiled all the night, but " caught nothing " ; when, lo, in the morning light, Jesus stood on the shore, but yet unknown to them, and bade them cast the net on the right side of the ship, " and now they were not able to draw it for the multitude of fishes". Thus He revealed Himself to them, and invited them to eat with Him of the fishes which they had caught. " Then Simon Peter went up, and drew the net to land, full of great fishes, one hundred and fifty-three. And although there were so many, the net was not broken : " for, indeed, that draught of great fishes, gathered by Peter at Christ's command, betokened God's elect, whom the Church is to gather out of the sea of this world, who cannot break from the net, which net, therefore, Peter drew to land, even the ever-lasting shore whereon Christ welcomes His own. And after that marvellous banquet of the disciples with their Lord, betokening the never-ending marriage-feast, wherein " the roasted fish

---

[1] John vi. 21.   [2] John xxi. 1-14.

is Christ in His passion," [1] our Lord proceeds to
crown all that series of distinctions, wherewith,
since imposing the prophetic name, He had
marked out Simon, the son of Jonas, to be the
Leader of His disciples : and thus He fulfils
by the side of the lake of Galilee what He
foreshadowed when He first looked upon Peter,
what He promised in the quarters of Cesarea
Philippi, and what He repeated on the eve of
His passion.

It was His will to appoint one to take His
place on earth. Now He had assumed to Himself specially a particular title, under which of old
time His prophets had foretold His advent among
men, and which above all other's expressed His
tender love for fallen man. It had been said of
Him, " I will set up one shepherd over them, and
He shall feed them, even My servant David : He
shall feed them, and He shall be their shepherd ".
And again : " Say to the cities of Judah, behold
your God. . . . He shall feed His flock like a
shepherd : He shall gather together the lambs
with His arm, and shall take them up in His
bosom, and He Himself shall carry them that are
with young."   And, once more, in the very
prophecy by which the chief priests and scribes
declared to Herod that He must be born at
Bethlehem, " For from thee shall go forth the
Ruler, who shall feed (or shepherd) My people
Israel ". Appropriating these predictions to Him-

[1] St. Augustine's 122nd discourse on St. John, who has thus set
forth this chapter ; " Piscis assus Christus est passus ",

self, the Lord had said, " I am the good shepherd.
The good shepherd giveth His life for His sheep.
And other sheep I have which are not of this fold ;
them also I must bring; and there shall be one
fold and one shepherd."[1] And now it was His
pleasure to give this particular title, so specially
His own, to Peter, and to Peter alone, and to
Peter in most marked contrast even with the best-
beloved of His other disciples, and to Peter, thrice
repeating the charge, and varying the expression
of it so as to include the term in its utmost force.
" When, therefore, they had dined, Jesus said to
Simon Peter, Simon, son of John, lovest thou Me
more than these ?   He saith to Him, Yea, Lord,
Thou knowest that I love Thee.   He saith to him,
Feed My lambs.   He saith to him again, Simon,
son of John, lovest thou Me ?   He saith to Him,
Yea, Lord, Thou knowest that I love Thee.   He
saith to him, Feed My lambs.   He saith to him
the third time, Simon, son of John, lovest thou
Me ?   Peter was grieved because He had said to
him the third time, Lovest thou Me ?   And he
said to Him, Lord, Thou knowest all things: Thou
knowest that I love Thee.   He said to him, Feed
My sheep."

Our Lord had before addressed the seven
disciples present in common, " Children, have you
any meat ? "   " Cast the net, and you shall find."
" Bring hither of the fishes which you have caught."
" Come and dine."   But now, turning to one in

---

[1] Ezech. xxiv. 33; Isa. xl. 9-11 ; Mich. v. 2 ; Matt. ii. 6 ; John
x. 11, 14, 16.

particular, He singles him out in the most special
manner, by his name, by asking of him a love
greater than that of any other towards Himself,
by conferring on him a charge, which, as we shall
see, from its extension excludes its being held in
joint possession by any other, and by a prophecy
concerning the manner of his death, which is
wholly particular to Peter. If it is possible by
any words to convey a power and a charge to a
particular person, and to exclude the rest of the
company from that special power and charge, it
is done here.

But, secondly, it is a charge of a very high and
distinguishing nature indeed, for our Lord before
conferring it demands of Peter, as a condition,
greater love towards His own person than that
felt for Him by any of the Twelve—even by the
sons of Zebedy, whom from their zeal He surnamed Boanerges, sons of thunder—even by the
disciple whom He loved, and who lay on His
breast at the last supper. What must that charge
be, the preliminary condition for which is a greater
love for Jesus than that of the beloved disciple?
What shall be a fitting sequel to "Simon, son of
John, lovest thou Me *more* than these?" What,
again, the importance of that office, in bestowing
which our Lord thrice repeats the condition, and
thrice inculcates the charge? The words of God
are not spoken at random, nor His repetitions
without effect. What, again, are the *subjects* of
the charge? They are "My lambs," and "My
sheep"; that is, the fold itself of the Great Shep-

herd. As He said, " If I wash thee not, thou shalt have no part with Me," so those who are not either His lambs or His sheep, form no part of His fold. Others, too, in Holy Writ, are addressed as shepherds, but with a limitation, as, " Take heed to the whole flock *wherein* the Holy Ghost hath placed you bishops," or " Feed the flock of God *which is among you*". And, more largely far it was said, " Go ye, therefore, and make disciples all nations "; and " Go ye into the whole world, and preach the Gospel to every creature ".[1] But they to whom this was said were yet themselves sheep of the Great Shepherd, and in committing the world to them, He did not commit *them* to each other. Whereas here, they too, as His sheep, are committed to one, even Peter; and very expressly, in the persons of James and John, and the rest present, " Lovest thou Me more than these ? " A particular flock is never termed absolutely and simply " the flock," or " the flock of God," but " the flock *which is among you*," " *in which the Holy Ghost hath made you bishops* ". And again, the Apostles are sent in common to the whole world, to preach to all nations, and to form one flock ; but they are twelve, and " power given to several carries its restriction in its division, whilst power given to one alone and over all, and without exception, carries with it plenitude, and, not having to be divided with any other, it has no bounds save those which its terms convey ".[2]

---

[1] Acts xx. 28; 1 Pet. v. 10; Matt. xxviii. 19; Mark xvi. 15.
[2] Bossuet, Sermon on Unity.

What are the terms here? "Feed," and "be
shepherd over" or "rule" "My lambs and My
sheep". The terms have no limit, save that of
salvation itself. Such, then, are the *persons* indicated as subjects of this charge. But what is
the nature of the charge? Two different words
of unequal extent and force in the original, but
both rendered "feed" in the translation, convey
this. One means "to give food" simply, the
other, of far higher and nobler reach, embraces
every act of care and providence in the government of others, under an image the farthest
removed from the spirit of pride and ambition.
Such is even its heathen meaning, and the first
of poets termed Agamemnon by this word, "Shepherd of the people". By this word, St. Paul, and
St. Peter[1] himself, express the power of the Bishop
over his own flock. And so our Lord, here instituting the Bishop of Bishops, the one Shepherd
of the one fold, gives to Peter over all his flock,
the very word given to *Him* in the famous prophecy,
"Thou, Bethlehem, the land of Juda, art not the
least among the princes of Juda : for out of thee
shall come forth the captain that shall *rule* My
people Israel :" the very word which, used of Himself in Psalm ii. to express all His power and
dominion, in His revelation to St. John is spoken
of His own triumphant career, as the Word of
God going forth to battle, "He shall *rule* them
with a rod of iron"; and again, in the same book
is applied by Himself to set forth the honour

---

[1] Acts xx. 28; 1 Pet. v, 10; Ps. ii. 9; Apoc. xix, 15; ii. 27.

which He will give "to him that shall overcome and keep My works unto the end ".[1] Thus, just as in the *persons* pointed out, the *subject* of this charge is *universal*, so in the *terms* by which it is expressed, the *nature* of the power is *supreme*. What the Bishop is to his own flock, Peter is made to "the flock of God ": and this at once, in the most simple, as well as in the most absolute and emphatic manner, by institution from the Chief Shepherd Himself, at the close of His ministry, and by associating Peter singly with Himself in His most distinctive title. If the fold of Christ is equivalent to "the Church of Christ," and "the kingdom of heaven," so to feed and to rule the lambs and the sheep of that fold is equivalent to being "the Rock" of that Church, and "the Bearer of the keys," as well as *the First, the Greater one, and the Ruler* in that kingdom of heaven.

Again, looking at the circumstances under which this charge is received by Peter, it either conveys that special and singular honour and power which we have here set forth, or *none at all*. For Peter had *already* received the full Apostolic authority : he had heard together with the rest of the Apostles those words of power, "As My Father sent Me, I also send you," and the charge following, to bind and to loose. It could not therefore be this power which was here given him, for he had it already. All which James and John, the sons of thunder, ever had given them, he also

---

[1] Ποιμαίνειν used in the text of John, and in all these.

had before these words were uttered. Besides, a power which was to be shared by James and John, and the rest of the Apostles, could not be given in terms which distinguished him from them, "Lovest thou Me *more than these ?*" It could not be the mere forgiveness of his denial, for not only did the Apostolate, since conferred, carry that, but when our Lord appeared to him first of all the Apostles after His resurrection, it was a token of such forgiveness. There remained nothing else to give him, but a presidency over the Apostles themselves, the reward of superior love, as was prophesied and promised to him in reward for superior faith. For these two oracles of our Lord exactly correspond to each other as promise and performance. Their conditions and their terms shed a reciprocal light on each other. In the one there is the great confession, "Thou art the Christ, the Son of the living God"; in the other as singular a declaration, "Lovest thou Me more than these? Yea, Lord." In the one there follows the reward, "And I say to thee, that thou art Peter," etc.: and in the other a like reward, "Feed My lambs, be shepherd over My sheep". The one is future, "I will build, I will give, thou shalt bind, thou shalt loose": the other present, "Feed, and be shepherd". What concerns "the Church and the kingdom of heaven" in the one, concerns "the fold" in the other. And the promise and performance are singularly restricted to Peter —"I say unto thee, thou art Peter"—"Simon, son of John, lovest thou Me more than these ?"

And then Peter received the promise of the supreme episcopate *before all* and *by himself*, under the terms that he should be the Rock, by being built on which the Church should never fall, that he should be the Bearer of the keys in the kingdom of heaven, and that *singly* he should bind and loose in heaven and on earth; so *after* his own Apostolate and that of the rest had been completed, *by himself*, and as the crown of the divine work, he received the fulfilment of that supreme episcopate, under the terms, " Feed My lambs, be shepherd over My sheep ". And as a part out of that magnificent promise made to him *singly*, was afterwards taken and made to the Apostles *jointly* with him, for so " it was the design of Jesus Christ to put first in one alone what afterwards He meant to put in several; but the sequel does not reverse the beginning, nor the first lose his place. That first word, ' whatsoever thou shalt bind,' said to one alone, has already ranged under his power each one of those to whom shall be said, ' Whatsoever ye shall remit '; for the promises of Jesus Christ, as well as His gifts, are without repentance; and what is once given indefinitely and universally is irrevocable:"[1] so when Peter and the rest already possessed the whole Apostolate, the commission to go and preach to the whole world, and to make disciples of all nations, a power was added to Peter to make up what was promised to him originally; the Apostles themselves, with the whole fold, were

---

[1] Bossuet, Sermon on Unity.

put under his charge; he represented the person of the Great Shepherd: and the divine work was complete.

Thus the powers of the Apostolate and the Primacy are not antagonistic, but fit into and harmonize with each other. In the college of the Twelve, as before inaugurated, and sent forth into the whole world, something had been wanting, save that " by the appointment of a head, the occasion of schism was taken away ":[1] and Satan would have shaken the whole fabric, but that there was one divinely set to "confirm the brethren ". He who " kept them " once, when " with them," by His personal presence, now kept them for evermore by the word of His power, issued on the shore of the lake of Galilee, but resounding through every age, clear and decisive, amid the fall of empires, and the change of races, and heard by all His flock to the utmost of the isles of the sea, till the day of the Son of Man comes,—" Simon, son of John, lovest thou Me more than these? Feed My lambs : Feed My sheep."

And that the universal and supreme authority over the Church of Christ was in these words committed to Peter by the Lord, is the belief of antiquity. Thus, St. Ambrose, in the West : " It is not doubtful that Peter believed, and believed because he loved, and loved because he believed. Whence, too, he is grieved at being asked a third time, Lovest thou Me ? For we ask those of whom we doubt. But the Lord does not doubt, but asks

[1] St. Jerome.

not to learn, but to teach him whom, on the point
of ascending into Heaven, He was leaving, *as it
were, the successor and representative of His love.* [1]
It is because he alone out of all makes a profession,
that *he is preferred to all.* Lastly, for the third
time, the Lord asks him, no longer *hast* thou *a
regard* (diligis me) for Me, but *lovest* (amas) thou
Me : and now he is ordered to feed, not the lambs,
as at first, who need a milk diet, nor the little
sheep, as secondly, but the more perfect sheep,
*in order that he who was the more perfect might have
the government.*" [2] In the East, St. Chrysostom :
" Why then, passing by the rest, does He converse
with him on these things ? *He was the chosen of
the Apostles, and the mouthpiece of the disciples, and
the head of the band.* Therefore, also Paul once
went up to see him rather than the rest. It
was, besides, to show him, that for the future he
must be bold, as his denial was done away with,
that *He puts into his hands the presidency over the
brethren.* And He does not mention the denial,
nor reproach him with what had past ; but He
says, If thou lovest Me, *rule the brethren,* and show
now that warm affection which on all occasions
thou didst exhibit, and in which thou didst exult,
and the life which thou didst offer to lay down for
Me, now spend for My sheep." Again, " Thrice
He asks the question, and thrice lays on him the
same command, showing at how high a price He
sets *the charge of His own sheep*". Again, " He was
put in charge with the direction of his brethren ".

---

[1] Amoris sui veluti vicarium.　　[2] In Lucum, lib. 10, n. 175.

" He made him great promises, *and put the world into his hands.*" Thus John and James, and the rest of the Apostles, were committed to Peter, but never Peter to them : and he adds, " But if any one asks, How then did James receive the throne of Jerusalem ? I would reply that He elected Peter *not to be the teacher of this throne, but of the whole world.*" And in another place, " Why did He shed His blood to purchase those sheep *which He committed to Peter and his successors?* With reason then said Christ, ' Who is the faithful and prudent servant whom his Lord had set over His own[1] house ? ' " Theophylact repeated, seven hundred years later, the perpetual tradition of the East : " He puts into Peter's hands the headship over the sheep of the whole world, and to no other but to him gives He this; first, because he was distinguished above all, and the mouthpiece of the whole band ; and secondly, showing to him that he must be confident, as his denial was put out of account ". And if St. Leo, a Pope, declares that "though there be among the people of God many priests and many shepherds, yet Peter rules all by immediate commission, whom Christ also rules by sovereign power,"[2] the great Eastern, St. Basil, assigned an adequate reason for this near a century before, when he viewed all pastoral authority in the Church as included in this grant to Peter, declaring that the spiritual "ruler is none else but one who represents the person of

[1] St. Chrys. in Joan. Hom. 88, pp. 525-527 ; and De Sacerdot. lib. 2, tom. i. p. 372.   [2] St. Leo, Serm. 4.

the Saviour, and offers up to God the salvation of those who obey him, and this we learn from Christ Himself *in that He appointed Peter to be the shepherd of His Church after Himself*".[1]

But especially must we quote St. Cyprian, because to that equality of the Apostles as such, before referred to by us, by considering which without regard to the proportion of faith some have been led astray, he adds the full recognition of the Primacy, and urges its extreme importance. Thus quoting the promise and the fulfilment, " Thou art Peter," etc., and " Feed My sheep," he goes on, " Upon him being one He builds His Church ; and *though* He gives to all the Apostles an equal power, and says, 'As the Father sent Me, I also send you,' etc., yet in order to manifest unity He has, by His own authority, so placed the source of the same unity as to begin from one. Certainly the other Apostles also were what Peter was, endued with an equal fellowship both of honour and power, but a commencement is made from unity, that the Church may be set before us as one."[2] That is, the Apostles were equal as to the powers bestowed in John xx. 23-25, but as to those given in Matt. xvi. 18, 19, Luke xxii. 31-33, and John xxi. 15-18, "the Church was built upon Peter alone," and he was made the source and ever-living spring of ecclesiastical unity.

Yet clearly as our Lord in this charge associates

[1] St. Basil, Constit. Monas. xxii. tom. ii. p. 573.
[2] St. Cyprian, de Unit. 3.

Peter with Himself, puts him over his brethren, the other Apostles, and fulfils to him all that He ever promised, as to making him "the First," "the Greater one," and "the Ruler or Leader," by that one title of "the Shepherd," in which is summed up all authority over His Church, and the very purpose of His own divine mission, "to seek and to save that which was lost," still a touch of tenderness is added by the Master's hand, which brings out all this more forcibly, and must have told personally on Peter's feelings and those of his fellow-disciples, as the highest and most solemn consecration to his singular office. For when the Lord spoke that parable, "I am the good shepherd," He added, as the token of the character, "The good shepherd giveth his life for his sheep". And so now, appointing Peter to take His place over the flock, He adds to him this token also: "Amen, amen, I say to thee, When thou wast younger thou didst gird thyself, and didst walk where thou wouldst, but when thou shalt be old, thou shalt stretch forth thy hands, and another shall gird thee, and lead thee whither thou wouldst not". "When thou wast younger, thou didst gird thyself," alluding, perhaps, to that impulse of affection with which, just before, as soon as Peter heard from John that it was the Lord standing on the shore, "He girt his coat about him and cast himself into the sea," for his love waited not for the slowness of the boat. Thus He taught Peter that the chiefship to which He was appointing him, that "care of all the

Churches," as it required a different spirit to fulfil
it from that which prevailed among "the kings of
the nations," so it led to a different end, the last
crowning act of a life-long self-sacrifice, which
began by being the servant of all, ran through a
thousand acts of humiliation and anxiety, and
was to be completed in the martyrdom of cruci-
fixion. And so in his death, as well as in his
charge of visible head of the Church, he was to be
made like his Lord, and after the manner of the
Good Shepherd, whom he succeeded, should lay
down his life for his sheep. For "this He said
signifying by what death he should glorify God.
And when He had said this, He saith to him,
Follow Me;" with far deeper meaning now than
when those words of power were first uttered to
him beside that lake. Then it was "Follow Me,
and I will make you fishers of men". Now it is,
"Follow Me, and I will associate thee with My
life and with My death, with My charge and with
its reward. This shall be the proof of thy great
love, to be obedient even to death, and that the
death of the cross." Such was the anointing
which the first Primate of the Church received to
the triple crown. "Follow thou Me." Like his
divine Master, he was during the whole of his
ministry to have the cross set before his eyes, and
laid upon his heart as the certain end of his
course. And thus Peter "received power and
sacerdotal authority over all, from the very God
for our sakes incarnate":[1] thus he followed in the

[1] Stephen of Dora, in the Lateran Synod, A.D. 649. Mansi, x. 893.

steps of the Good Shepherd, as he succeeded to His office. And therefore, having accomplished his mission and triumphed on the Roman hill, from Rome he speaks through the undying line of his spiritual heirs, and feeds the flock of Christ.

CHAPTER IV.

THE CORRESPONDENCE AND EQUIVALENCE OF THE GREAT TEXTS CONCERNING PETER.

BEFORE we compare together more exactly what was said to the Apostles in common, and what to Peter in particular, it is desirable to consider briefly two other points, which will complete the evidence furnished by the Gospels.

1. If, then, the question[1] to be decided by documents is, whether several persons are to be accounted equal in rank, honour, and authority, or whether one of them is superior to the rest, it will be an unexceptionable rule to observe whether they are spoken of in the same manner. For words are signs of ideas, and set forth as in a mirror the mind's conceptions. A similarity of language, therefore, will indicate a similarity of rank ; a distinction of language, especially if it be repeated and constant, will show a like distinction of rank. Let us apply this rule to the mode in which the Evangelists speak of Peter and of the other Apostles.

Now, to express one of rank and his attendants, the Evangelists often use the phrase, a person *and those with him.* Thus Luke vi. 4, " David and

---

[1] Passaglia, p. 106.

those that were with him"; and Matt. xii. 3 with
Mark ii. 25, " Have ye not read what David did
when himself was a hungered and *those that were
with him?"* Of our Lord and the Apostles it is
said, Mark iii. 11, " And He made twelve, *that they
should be with Him"*: and xvi. 10, " She went and
told *them that had been with Him"*. And Acts iv.
13, the chief priests " knew them," Peter and John,
" that *they had been with Jesus"*. And Matthew
xxvi. 69, Peter is reproached, " Thou also *wast
with Jesus"*. Now, just so the Evangelists speak
of Peter. Our Lord having on one occasion left
the Apostles for solitary prayer, St. Mark writes,
i. 36, " And Simon *and they that were with him"*
followed after Him". Again, the woman with the
issue of blood having touched the Lord, when He
asked, " Who is it that touched Me?" St. Luke
says, viii. 45, "all denying, Peter *and they that were
with him* said," etc. And on the occasion of the
Transfiguration, " Peter and *they that were with
him,"* being James and John. Just as after the
resurrection Luke writes, Acts ii. 14, " Peter
standing up with the eleven"; verse 37, " They
said to Peter and to the rest of the Apostles";
v. 29, " Peter and the Apostles answering said ".
And the angels to the holy women, Mark xvi. 7,
" Go tell His disciples and Peter ".

It is then to be remarked that Peter is the *only*
Apostle who is put in this relation to the rest.
Never is it said " James," or " John and the rest
of the Apostles," or, "and those with him ".
Peter is named, and the rest are added in a mass,

and this happens in his case continually, never in the case of any other Apostle.

No adequate cause can be alleged for this but the Primacy and superior rank of Peter, which was ever in the mind of the Evangelist, and is sometimes indicated by the prophetic name, for as often as Simon is called Peter, he is marked as the foundation of the Church, according to the Lord's prophecy. And long before contentions about the prerogatives of Peter arose, the ancient Fathers attributed it to his Primacy that he was thus named expressly and first, the others in a mass, or in the second place.

According, then, to the rule above-mentioned, Peter, by the mode in which the Evangelists speak of him, is distinguished from the other Apostles, and his position with regard to the rest is described in the very same phrase which is used to express the superiority of David over his men, and even of our Lord over the Twelve. And for this there seems no adequate cause, but that special association of Peter with Himself indicated in the name, and the promises accompanying it in Matt. xvi.

2. Again, four[1] catalogues of the Apostles exist,[2] and in each of these Peter is placed first. And in the three which occur in the Gospels (that of Luke in the Acts being a more brief repetition of his former one), the prophetic name Peter is indicated as the reason for his being thus placed first. So

---

[1] Passaglia, p. 109.
[2] Matt. x. 2-5 ; Mark iii. 16-19 ; Luke vi. 14-17 ; Acts i. 13.

Mark: "And to Simon He gave the name Peter. And James the son of Zebedy, and John the brother of James; and He named them Boanerges, which is the sons of thunder:" for which reason, that the Lord had given them a name, though it was held in common, and not, like that of Peter, expressive of official rank, but personal qualities, Mark seems to set these two before Andrew, whom both in Matthew and in Luke they follow. Again, Luke says, "He chose twelve of them, whom also He named Apostles, Simon whom He surnamed Peter, and Andrew his brother," etc. "The *first* of all, and the chief of them, he that was illiterate and uneducated," says St. Chrysostom;[1] and Origen long before him, observing that Peter was always named first in the number of the twelve, asks, What should be thought the cause of this order? He replies, it was constantly observed because Peter was "more honoured than the rest," thus intimating that he no less excelled the rest on account of the gifts which he had received from heaven, than "Judas through his wretched disposition was truly the last of all, and worthy to be put at the end".[2] But much more marked is Matthew in signifying the superior dignity of Peter, not only naming him at the head in his catalogue, but calling him simply and absolutely "the first". "And the names of the twelve Apostles are these, The first, Simon, who is called Peter, and Andrew his brother, James," etc.

[1] St. Chrysostom on Matt. Hom. 32.
[2] Origen on John, tom. 32, n. 5, t. 4, p. 413.

Now, that *second* and *third* do not follow, shows that "first" is not a numeral here, but designates rank and pre-eminence. Thus in heathen authors this word "first" by itself indicates the most excellent in its kind : thus in the Septuagint occur, "first friend of the king," "first of the singers," "the first priest,"[1] *i.e.*, the chief priest. So our Lord, "whichever among you will be first;" "Bring forth the first robe;" and St. Paul, "sinners, of whom I am first,"[2] *i.e.*, chief. Thus "the first of the island," Acts xxviii. 7, means the chief magistrate; and "first" generally in Latin phraseology, the superior, or prince.

Such, then, is the rank which Matthew gives to Peter, when he writes, "the first Simon, who is called Peter".

It should also be remarked that, whenever the Evangelists have occasion to mention *some* of the Apostles, Peter being one, he is ever put first. Thus Matthew, "He taketh unto Him Peter, and James, and John his brother"; and Mark, "He admitted not any man to follow Him, but Peter, and James, and John the brother of James"; and "Peter, and James, and John, and Andrew asked Him apart"; and "He taketh Peter, and James, and John with Him"; and Luke, "He suffered not any man to go in with Him, but Peter, and James, and John, and the father and mother of the maiden"; and "He sent Peter and John"; and John, "There were together Simon Peter, and Thomas, who is called

---

[1] 1 Paral. xxvii. 33 ; Neh. xii. 45 ; 2 Paral. xxvi. 20.
[2] Matt. xx. 27 ; Luke xv. 22 ; 1 Tim. i. 15.

Didymus, and Nathaniel who was of Cana in
Galilee, and the two sons of Zebedy, and two
others of His disciples ".[1] This rule would seem
to be invariable, though James and John are not
always mentioned next after him.

An attempt has been made to evade the force of
these testimonies, by giving as a reason for Peter
being always thus named first, that he was the
most aged of all the Apostles, and the first called.
Even were it so, such reasons would seem most
inadequate, but unfortunately they are neither of
them facts.   For as to age, antiquity bears witness
that Andrew was Peter's elder brother.   And as
to their calling, St. Augustine has observed, " In
what order all the twelve Apostles were called,
does not appear in the narrations of the Evangelists, since not only not the order of the calling,
but not even the calling itself of all is mentioned,
but only of Philip, and Peter, and Andrew, and of
the sons of Zebedy, and of Matthew the publican,
termed also Levi.   But Peter was both the first
and the only one who separately received a name
from Him." [2]   As it may be conjectured from the
Gospels that Christ said to Philip first of all
" Follow Me," John i. 44, he has the best right to
be considered the first called.

Now the two classes of facts just mentioned, as
to the mode in which the Evangelists speak of
Peter in combination with the other Apostles,

---

[1] Matt. xvii. 1 ; Mark v. 37 ; xiii. 3 ; xiv. 33 ; Luke viii. 51 ;
xxii. 8 ; John xxi. 2.

[2] De Consensu Evang. lib. ii. c. xvii. n. 39.

prove directly and plainly his *Primacy*, while they do not *directly* prove, save Matthew's title of *First*, nor are they here quoted to prove, the *nature* of that Primacy, which rests, as we have seen, on other and more decisive texts.

At length, then, we have before us the whole evidence of the Gospels, and having considered it, piece by piece, may now take a general view. It is time to gather up the several parts of this evidence, and, claiming for each its due force, to present the sum of all before the mind. For distinct and decisive as certain texts appear, and are, even by themselves, yet when they are seen to fit into a whole system, and perfectly to harmonize together, they have much greater power to convince the mind which really seeks for truth. But moral evidence generally, and especially that which results from a study of the Holy Scripture, is not intended to move a mind in a lower condition than this; a mind, that is, which loves something else better than the truth.

Thus out of the body of His disciples we see our Lord choosing Twelve, and again, out of those Twelve, distinguishing One by the most singular favours. This distinction even begins *before* the selection of the Twelve, and has its root in the very commencement of our Lord's ministry: for, as we have seen, it was when Andrew first led his brother Simon before Christ, that He " looked upon him," and promised him the prophetic name which revealed his Primacy, and his perpetual relation to the Church of God. The name thus promised is

in due time bestowed, and solemnly recorded by
the three Evangelists, at the appointment of the
Apostles, as the reason why he is invariably set at
their head; Matthew, still more distinctly expressing it in his Primacy, "*the first*, Simon, who
is called Peter". And their whole mode of mentioning him, and exhibiting his relation to the
other Apostles, shows that this Primacy was, when
they wrote, ever in their minds. It comes out in
the most incidental way, as when Mark writes
"Simon, and they that were with him, followed
after" Christ: or Luke, "Peter, and they that
were with him, said"; as naturally as they write,
"David, and those that were with him"; or of
our Lord Himself, and the Apostles, "those that
had been with Him".[1] Again this preference of
Peter is shown by our Lord, both at the Transfiguration and the Agony: where, even when the two
next favoured of the Apostles are associated with
Him as witnesses, yet there is evidence of Peter's
superiority in the mode with which the Evangelists
mention him. Great as the dignity was of the two
sons of thunder, they are yet ranged under Peter
by Luke, with that same phrase which we have
just been considering. "Peter, and they that
were with him, were heavy with sleep." And our
Lord, at the Agony, says to Peter, "could not *you*,"
that is, all the three, "watch with Me one hour?"[2]
Again, how incidentally, yet markedly, does
Matthew show that this superiority of Peter over

---

[1] Mark i. 36; Luke viii. 45; Matt. xii. 3; Mark ii. 25; xvi. 10.
[2] Luke ix. 32; Matt. xxvi. 40.

others was apparent even to strangers, when he writes, that the officers who collected the tribute for the temple, came to *him*, and said, " Does not *your* Master" (the Master of all the Apostles) "pay the didrachma ? "[1] Much more significant is the incident immediately following, when our Lord orders him to go to the sea, to cast a hook, and to bring up a fish, which shall have a stater in his mouth, adding, " Take that, and give it to them for Me, and for thee " : a token of preference so strong, and of association so singular, that it set the Apostles on the immediate inquiry, who should be the greater among them : the answer to which we will revert to presently.

And this designation of Peter to his high and singular office becomes even more striking, if we contrast what our Lord did and said to him with what He did and said to another Apostle, who *in another way* is even in some respects preferred to Peter himself. For, " the disciple whom Jesus loved," who lay on His breast at supper, to whom was committed at the most sorrowful of all moments the domestic care of the Virgin Mother, has in the affection of our Lord his own unapproachable sphere. But as Peter does not come into competition with him here, so neither in another view he with Peter. His distinction is private, and in the nature of personal affection : Peter's is public, and in the nature of Church government. To one is committed the Mother of the Lord, the living symbol of the Church, the most blessed of all creatures,

[1] Matt. xvii. 24.

and that, when her full dignity and blessedness stood at length revealed in the full Godhead of her Son, yet whose throne was intercessory, apart from rule on earth : to the other is committed the Church herself, her championship in the time of conflict, the rudder of the vessel on the lake, till with Christ it should reach the shore. Each of these, so eminent and unapproachable in his way, has that way apart ; and when Peter, on receiving his final commission, turned about and saw his best-loved friend following, and ventured to ask, "Lord, and what shall this man do?" our Lord replied with something like a reproof, "What is that to thee? Follow thou Me.". These distinct preferences of the two Apostles were indicated by Tertullian, when he wrote, "Was anything concealed from Peter, who was named the rock on which the Church should be built, who received the keys of the kingdom of heaven, and the power to bind and loose in heaven and on earth? Was anything, too, concealed from John, the most beloved of the Lord, who lay upon His breast, to whom alone the Lord foresignified the traitor Judas, whom He committed in His own place as Son to Mary?"[1]

But to return. Our Lord, after encompassing Peter during His whole ministry with such tokens of preference, and a preference specially belonging to his office, and designating it, appears to him first of all the Apostles after His resurrection. And yet all the proofs which we have been here

[1] De Præsc. c. 22.

summing up of Peter's pre-eminence, are but collateral and subordinate: though by themselves tenfold more than any other can claim, yet Peter's authority does not rest *mainly* on them. And this likewise is true of another class of facts concerning Peter, which yet carries with it much force, and when once remarked, never leaves the thoughtful mind. It is his great predominance in the sacred history over the rest of the Twelve. A single incident or expression distinguishing him is perhaps all that falls to the lot of another Apostle, as when " Philip saith unto Him, Lord, show us the Father and it sufficeth us "; and the Lord replies, " Have I been so long time with you, and yet hast thou not known Me, Philip ? " Or as Thomas, at a moment of danger, " said to his fellow-disciples, Let us also go that we may die with Him ".[1] But Peter's name is wrought into the whole tissue of the Gospel history; he is perpetually approaching the Lord with questions : " Lord, how oft shall my brother sin against me, and I forgive him ? until seven times ? " The rest suffer the Lord in silence to wash their feet, but Peter is overcome at the sight. " Lord, dost Thou wash my feet ? Thou shalt never wash my feet;" "Lord, not my feet only, but also my hands and my head ".[2] Thus in the whole New Testament, John, who is yet mentioned oftener than the rest, occurs only thirty-eight times; but in the Gospels alone, omitting the Acts and the Epistles, Peter is mentioned twenty-three times by Matthew, eighteen by Mark,

---

[1] John xiv. 8 ; xi. 16.   [2] Matt. xviii. 21 ; John xiii. 6.

twenty by Luke, and thirty by John.[1] More especially it is the custom of the Evangelists, when they
record anything which touches all the Apostles, almost invariably to exhibit Peter as singly speaking
for all, and representing all. Thus when Christ
asked them all equally, " But whom say ye that I
am? Simon Peter answered and said". He told them
all equally " That a rich man shall hardly enter
into the kingdom of heaven,"[2] whereupon " Peter
answering said to Him, Behold, we have left all
things, and followed Thee : what therefore shall
we have ? " And when " Jesus said to the twelve,
Will you also go away ? "[3] at once we hear "Simon
Peter answered and said, Lord, to whom shall we
go ? Thou hast the words of eternal life." And a
very remarkable occasion occurs where our Lord
had been telling to His disciples the parable of the
watchful servant, upon which Peter said to Him,
" Lord, dost Thou speak this parable to us, or
likewise to all ? "[4] And the reply seems by anticipation to express the very office which Peter was
to hold. " Who, then, is the faithful and wise
steward, whom his lord setteth over his family, to
give them their measure of wheat in due season?"
Now it looks not like an equal, but a superior, to
anticipate the rest, to represent them, to speak
and act for them. St. Chrysostom drew the conclusion long ago. " What then says Peter, the
mouthpiece of the Apostles ? Everywhere im-
petuous as he is, the leader of the band of the

---

[1] Passaglia, p. 134.   [2] Matt. xix. 23.
[3] John vi. 67.   [4] Luke xii. 41.

Apostles, when a question is asked of all, he replies."[1] No other cause can be assigned for the care of the Evangelists in setting before us so continually his words and acts, in bringing him out, as the second object, after Christ. But though his future place in the Church is a reason for this, and this, again, a token of that singular preeminence, its decisive proof rests on declarations from our Lord's own mouth, expressly circumscribed to him, of singular lucidity, and of force which nothing can evade ; declarations which set forth, under different but coincident images, a power supreme and without equal, and of its own nature belonging to but one at a time. The proofs which we have hitherto mentioned take away all abruptness from these declarations, and show that they embody a great design which runs all through the Gospel ; but the office itself rests upon these, and by these is most clearly and absolutely defined.

Thus, when our Lord, in answer to a great confession of His Apostle, " Thou art the Christ, the Son of the living God," replies, " And I too say unto thee, Thou art Peter, and upon this rock I will build My Church " : every one must feel how it adds to the cogency of the reply, that the name, which He is explaining, was not the person's natural name, but first promised, and then given, by that same Lord, who now attaches other promises and prophecies to it. This fact serves, among others, to fix the whole which follows to

[1] In Matt. Hom. 54.

Peter individually, and to introduce what follows as part of a design which before had been intimated : for what follows no more belongs to the other Apostles, than the name Peter belongs to them : and a name, on the other hand, so promised, and so given, naturally looks, as it were, to such a result. To say solemnly of a man, when first seen, " Thou art called Simon, but thou shalt be called The Rock," and to make nothing of him when so called, would be, if ascribed to any one, a dull and pointless thing ; but what shall we say, when the speaker is God ? It is a new thing for God the Word to speak with little meaning, or to speak and not to do : and so now He does what He had long designed. And what is it that He does ? He sets up a governor who is never to be put down. He inaugurates a Church against which Hell shall rage, but in vain : He establishes a government at which the nations shall rage, the kings of the earth set themselves, and the rulers take counsel together, for ever, but to their own confusion. He does what He alone could do, and so the answer is worthy of the confession, " Thou art the Christ, the Son of the living God ".

" Blessed[1] art thou, Simon Bar-Jona, for flesh and blood hath not revealed it unto thee, but My Father who is in heaven. *And I too say unto thee,* in return for what thou hast said to Me, and to show, like My Father, My good will towards thee, and what I say, as the Almighty Word of the Father, by My power I fulfil, *that thou art Peter,*

[1] Passaglia, p. 510.

the Rock, and so partaker with Me of that honour whereby I am the chief Rock and Foundation ; *and upon this Rock,* which I have called thee, *I will build My Church,* which, therefore, with Me for its architect, shall rest on thee, to thee adhere, and from thee derive its conspicuous unity : *and the gates of hell,* even all the powers of the enemy, *shall not prevail against it,* nor take that which, by My Godhead, is established upon thee, but rather yield to it the victory. *And to thee,* whom, as Supreme Architect, I have marked out for the Rock and Foundation of My Church, as King and Lord *I will give the keys of the kingdom of heaven* and the supreme authority over My Church, and will make thee sharer with Me in that dignity, by which I hold the keys of heaven and of earth, *and whatsoever,* in virtue of that authority and as associated in My dignity, *thou shalt bind upon earth, shall be bound in heaven,* and there shall be no matter relating to My Church, and the kingdom of heaven, but shall be subject to thy legislative and judicial power, which shall reach the heaven itself: for it is a power at once human and divine; human, as entrusted to a man, and administered by a man ; divine, as a participation of that right by which I am, in heaven and on earth, Supreme Lawgiver and Judge ; *and whatsoever thou shalt loose upon earth shall be loosed in heaven.''*

Thus it is that the most famous Fathers and Bishops, the most distinguished Councils, the most various nations, have understood our Lord's words, and this is their meaning, according to the fixed laws of grammar, of rhetoric, of philosophy, and of logic, as well as by the testimony of history, and in accordance with the principles of theology. Let us mention certain consequences which follow from them.

These words [1] of Christ are, in the most marked manner, addressed to Peter *only* among the Apostles, and are, therefore, with their meaning, *peculiar* to him. And they designate pre-eminence in the government of the Church. They have, therefore, the two qualities which render them a suitable testimony to establish his Primacy among the Apostles.

Now, if persons differ in rank and pre-eminence, they must be considered not equals, but absolutely unequal. And such pre-eminence Peter had, deriving from Christ, the Founder, a superior rank in the Church's ministry. Therefore, the college of the Apostles must be termed absolutely unequal, and all the Apostles, compared with Peter, absolutely unequal.

But as inequality may be manifold, as of age, calling, honour, order, jurisdiction, and power, its nature and its degree must be sought in that property which belongs to one over the rest. So that we must determine, by the authority of the Scriptures, from those gifts which were promised to Peter alone, the nature and the degree of that inequality which subsisted between him and the other Apostles.

The gifts promised to Peter alone, are contained

[1] Passaglia, p. 518.

in these words of Christ, recorded by Matthew: and therefore, from their nature and inherent qualities, we must judge of the sort and the extent of inequality put by Christ between Peter and the rest.

These are summed up in the four following: I. That Peter is the Rock, on which the Church was to be built by Christ, the Chief Architect. II. That the impregnable strength which the Church was to have against the gates of hell, depended on its union with Peter, as the divinely laid foundation. III. That by Christ, the King of kings, and Lord of lords, Peter is marked out as next to Him, and after Him, the Bearer of the keys in the Church's heavenly kingdom. IV. And that, accordingly, universal power of binding and loosing is promised to him, leaving him responsible to Christ alone, the supreme Lawgiver and Judge. Therefore the nature of the prerogatives expressed in these four terms must be our standard both of the character and degree of inequality between the Apostles and Peter, and of the power of the Primacy promised to Peter.

But these terms mark authority, and plainly express jurisdiction and power; the inequality, therefore, is one relating to jurisdiction and power; and Peter's pre-eminence likewise such.

That these terms, which contain Peter's prerogatives, really do express jurisdiction and authority, may be thus very briefly shown. The first, "Thou art Peter, and upon this rock I will build My Church," is drawn from architecture, exhibiting

between Peter and the Church, which includes
also the Apostles, the relation which exists between the foundation and the superstructure.
This is one of dependence, by which accordingly
the Apostles must maintain an indivisible union
with Peter : which relation of dependence, again,
cannot be understood without the notion of
superior jurisdiction in Peter, for these are cor-
relative. The second term corroborates this ; for
it is a plain duty, and undoubted moral obligation, to be united to him, if severed from whom,
the words of Christ do not entitle you to expect
stability or victory over the gates of hell. Now,
"the gates of hell shall not prevail against it,"
most plainly express that perseverance and victory
are promised to no one by Christ, who does not
remain joined with Peter. So much for the *duty*
which binds all Christians, and the Apostles
among them, to avoid separation from Peter as
their destruction. But such duty involves the
faculty and authority on Peter's part of enjoining
on all without exception the maintenance of unity,
and of keeping from the whole body the sin of
schism, which, again, expresses his superior
jurisdiction. Yet plainer and more striking is
the *third ;* for in the words, "And I will give to
thee the keys of the kingdom of heaven," it is
foretold that Peter, in regard to the kingdom
of heaven, and therefore to all Christians, whether
teachers or taught, subjects or prelates, shall discharge the office of the bearer of the keys; with
which jurisdiction and authority are indivisibly

united. But in the *fourth*, there is no matter relating to the heavenly kingdom, which is not subjected by this promise to Peter's authority. " Whatsoever thou shalt bind," "whatsoever thou shalt loose " ; but this is in its own kind without limit, a full legislative and judicial power. Thus these four terms exactly agree with each other, and express, severally and collectively, prerogatives by which Peter is admitted to a singular and close association with Christ ; and therefore is pre-eminent among the Apostles by his Primacy, and his superior authority over the whole Church.

They also show, with no less clearness, that Christ in bestowing these prerogatives and Primacy on Peter, designed to produce the visible unity of His kingdom and Church ; and this in two ways, the first *typically prefiguring* the Church's own unity in Peter, the single Foundation, Bearer of the keys, and supreme Legislator and Judge; the second *efficiently*, as by a principle and cause, *forming, holding together*, and *protecting*, visible unity in that same Peter, as he discharged these functions. For just as the building is based on the foundation, and by virtue of it all the parts are held together, so a kingdom's unity and harmonious administration are first *moulded out* and then *preserved*, in the unity of its supreme authority.

And this Primacy may be regarded from three different points of view ; as it *is in itself*, and as it regards its *efficient* and its *final* cause. As to the first, it consists in superior jurisdiction and

authority; as to the second, it springs from Christ
Himself, who said to Peter alone, "And I too say
unto thee," etc.; as to the third, it *prefigures*,
forms, and *protects* the Church's visible unity.

But to prefigure, to form, and to protect the
Church's unity, being distinct functions, care
must be taken not to confuse them, the former
concerning the Primacy as a type, the two latter
as the origin and efficient cause; and also not
to concede the former while the latter are denied,
which latter make up the Primacy as jurisdictional,
and the instrument effecting unity. Now, Peter
is both the type of unity, its origin, and its
efficient cause.

A long line [1] of Fathers, from the most ancient
downwards, regards Peter as at once the type,
and the origin, and efficient cause of unity; setting it forth as a prerogative of his headship that
no one, whether Apostle, or Prophet, or Evangelist, or Doctor, or Teacher, might separate from
him without the crime of schism. In this consists his Primacy, and in this the famous phrase
of St. Cyprian find its solution, that "the Episcopate is one, of which a part is held by each
without division of the whole".

And, what is like to the preceding, they hold
that Peter is the *continuous* source of all power in
the Church, and that while its plenitude dwells in
his person, a portion of it is derived to the various

---

[1] These testimonies have been set forth at length in another
work, *The See of St. Peter, the Rock of the Church*, etc., pp.
97-118.

prelates under him. No one has set this forth more fully than St. Leo, in the middle of the fifth century, as where he says, that " if Christ willed that other rulers should enjoy aught together with him (that is, Peter), yet never did He give, *save through him*, what He denied not to others ".[1]

There is no one of these consequences but seems to result from the words of our Lord, here solemnly addressed to Peter.

But, recurring to our general view, we find our Lord three several[2] times appealed to by the Apostles to declare who should be the greatest in the kingdom of heaven ; and while on neither of these occasions does He declare to them that there should be no " greater one " among them, though such a declaration would have terminated their rivalry, on the last and most urgent, at the very eve of His departure from them, He sets forth in vivid words what ought to be the character and deportment of the one so to be placed over them ; and then turning His conversation from them in a body to Peter in particular, He charges him, at a future time, when He shall obtain for him the gift of a faith that could not fail, to " confirm his brethren ". Having before dwelt on the full meaning of these words, we need only remark how marvellously they coincide in force with the prophecy which we have just been considering, while they differ from it in expression. They convey as absolutely a supreme authority as the former ; and an authority independent of others,

---

[1] Serm. 4.   [2] Matt. xviii. 1 ; xx. 20 ; Luke xxii. 24-27.

and exclusive of participation; and one which is given for the maintenance of the faith, and of visible unity in that faith. Nor can we imagine a more fitting termination to the whole of our Lord's dealing with His disciples before His passion, than that, when about to be taken from them, He should designate, in words so full of affection and provident care, one who was presently to take His own place among them. "Simon, Simon, I have prayed for thee, that thy faith fail not, and thou in thy turn one day confirm thy brethren."

But if our Lord's preference of Peter, as to rank and dignity in the Church, was during His lifetime consistent and uniform; if, moreover, He made to him, twice, promises so large as to include and go far beyond all that He said to the Apostles in common; and if He took out, as it were, of what He had first promised to Peter a portion which He afterwards promised as their common inheritance to the rest; His dealing with Peter and the Apostles after His resurrection is the exact counterpart to this. The fulfilment is equivalent to the promise. In the fourfold prophecy to Peter, in Matt. xvi., the last member is, "And whatsoever thou shalt bind on earth, it shall be bound also in heaven; and whatsoever thou shalt loose on earth, it shall be loosed also in heaven". That this is a grant of full legislative and judicial power, given to one, we have seen. Now on a later occasion it is repeated to the twelve together, Matt. xviii. 18. *But the other three members of the prophecy made to Peter are never repeated to the twelve.* In the fulfilment the same distinction takes place. To the twelve in common our Lord communicates the power contained in the fourth member of His original promise, saying, John xx. 21, "As the Father hath sent Me, I also send you. Receive ye the Holy Ghost: whose sins ye shall forgive, they are forgiven them: and whose sins ye shall retain, they are retained:" to which the other forms contained in Matt. xxviii. 18, Mark xvi. 15, Luke xxiv. 49, Acts i. 4, 8, of preaching the Gospel to every creature, of waiting for the power of the Holy Ghost wherewith they should be endued, of teaching men to observe all things which He had commanded, are equivalent, though less definite. *But nowhere are the powers contained in the first three members of the prophecy to Peter communicated to the twelve.* As the promises were made to Peter alone originally, so to Peter alone are they, as we shall see, fulfilled. Indeed, it could not be otherwise, for the promises to be the rock of the Church, by coherence with which the Church should be impregnable, and the bearer of the keys, are in their own nature confined to one, and exclusive of participants; and once made by the very Truth Himself to one man, they ranged under his power all his brethren: "For the promises of Jesus Christ, as well as His gifts, are without repentance; and what is once given indefinitely and universally is irrevocable".[1] Besides that, another indisputable principle must be taken into account, viz. "that power given to several carries its restriction

[1] Bossuet, Sermon on Unity.

in its division " : just as if a king before his death
bequeaths the whole administration of his sove-
reignty to a board of twelve councillors, though
the sum of authority so conveyed be sovereign,
yet the share of each individual in the college will
be restricted by the equal right of his colleagues.
Whereas "power given to one alone, and over all,
and without exception, carries with it plenitude, and,
not having to be divided with any other, it has no
bounds save those which its terms convey". Such
was the power originally promised to Peter; and
such, no less, that which was ultimately conveyed.
He stands apart and alone no less in the fulfilment
than in the promise. And under another image,
but one equally expressive with the first, the Lord
conveys an authority as absolute and as exclusive.
The "bounds which its terms convey" are the
whole fold of Christ : "the sheep" no less than
"the lambs " : "to govern" no less than "to
feed ".[1] As the great Architect of the heavenly
city said to Peter, "Thou art the Rock"; as "the
King of kings," who "hath the key of David,"
and "on whose shoulder is the government," said
to Peter, "To thee will I give the keys of the

---

[1] Ποιμαίνειν, gubernare, to govern, the particular word which
our Lord employs to convey His powers to Peter, is also the
particular word which gives such offence to temporal governments,
when acted on by Peter: βόσκειν, pascere, to feed, they find
more endurable, and probably they would all be content, from
the heathen Roman emperors to the present day, to allow *the
Church* to *feed*, so long as *they* are allowed to *govern* the faithful.
The objection on the part of the Church is, that our Lord gave
both to Peter.

kingdom of heaven"; as He "who upholdeth all
things by the word of His power," and "in whom
all things consist," said to Peter, "Confirm thy
brethren" : so to the same Peter, the same
"Great Shepherd of the sheep," said, "Feed My
lambs, be shepherd over My sheep," thus committing to him the chief Apostles themselves who
heard this charge, and causing there to be for
ever "one fold and one shepherd," on earth as
in heaven.

It remains briefly to consider these three
palmary texts in their reciprocal relations to
each other, by which the fullest light is thrown
upon the Scriptural prerogatives of St. Peter.

1. First, then, all these texts are in the most
marked manner circumscribed to Peter *alone*.   In
all he is addressed by name ; in all he is
distinguished by other circumstances from his
brethren at the time present with him ; in all
a special condition is attached belonging to him ;
in the first, superior faith—in the second, faith,
which, by a particular gift, the fruit of Christ's
own prayer, should never fail—in the third,
superior love.   So that, without an utter disregard
of the meaning of words, and the force of the
context, and every law of grammar and philology,
no one of these texts can be extended from its
application to Peter alone, and made common
to the other Apostles.

2. Secondly, the note of *priority in time* is secured
to Peter by the first text, to which the other two
correspond.   Even if the promise in Matt. xviii.

18, made to all the Apostles, were of equal latitude
with that previously made to Peter, which it is
so very far from being that it contains one point
only out of four, yet, the fact that they had been
already ranged by the former under him, and that
he had been promised *singly* what they afterwards
were promised *in common*, would make a vast
difference between them; indeed, the difference
of the Primacy. But, as it is, the very first
mention of the Church is connected with a promise
made to Peter of the highest authority in that
Church, and a perpetual relationship, entering
into its inmost constitutions between it and his
person. Before the Church is formed, it is foretold that Peter shall rule her; before she is set
up against the gates of hell, that, by virtue of her
coherence with him, she should prevail over them.
And the germ of her Episcopate, on which she
is to grow, is sown in his person; just as, in the
last act of our Lord, that Episcopate is delivered
over to him, universal and complete.

3. Thirdly, these three texts are exactly *equivalent* to each other; they each involve and express
the other. They could not have been said of
different persons without contradiction and confusion. He who has one of them must have the
rest. There is variation of image, but identity
of meaning. Thus, the relation between Peter
and the Church is in the first, that of Foundation
and Superstructure; of the heaven-built city,
and of him who holds its keys: in the second,
it is that of the Architect, who, by skill and

authority, won for him, and given to him, by the
Supreme Builder, the Word and Wisdom of God,
maintains every living stone of the structure in
its due place; in the third, it is that of the
supreme and universal Pastor and his whole flock.
In all of these there is the habit of dependence
between the superior and that over which he is
set : in all the need of close coherence with him.
Observe in particular the identity of the second
and third. The special office of the Shepherd
of souls [1] is to lead his flock into suitable pastures;
that is, duly to instruct them in the Divine Word
and Will: the pastoral office is identical with
that of teaching : " He gave some Apostles, some
Prophets, some Evangelists, some Pastors and
Teachers ; " the former are distinguished, the last
united together : where the Apostle observes, that
the whole ministry, from the highest to the
lowest, is organized " to edify the body of Christ
into the unity of faith," and to preserve men
from being " carried about by every wind of
doctrine ". But if this was the design of Christ
as to the whole ministry, and as to each individual teacher, most of all was it in instituting
one supreme and universal Pastor: in him most
of all would be seen the perfect *fitting in together* [2]
of each individual member : he was set up especially for the compacting of each spiritual joint,
the harmony and cohesion of the whole. Here,
then, the office of the universal Pastor or Teacher

---

[1] Passaglia, p. 591.
[2] Ὁ καταρτισμὸς τῶν ἁγίων, Eph. iv. 12.

is precisely equivalent to him who, by another
image, confirms, strengthens, consolidates his
brethren. Thus, in the second text, Christ foretold the third. But the more we contemplate
all the three in their mutual relations, the more
a certain thought suggests itself to the mind.
There is a special doctrine concerning the most
Holy Trinity, the most distinctive of that great
mystery, which expresses the reciprocal indwelling
of the Three Persons. Now, something analogous
may be said of the way in which these three
texts impermeate and include each other, of their
exact equivalence, and distinct, but inseparable
force : of whom one is said, of the same must
all.

4. Fourthly, they all indicate a *sovereign*
authority, *independent* itself, but on which all
others depend; symbolizing power from above,
but claiming obedience from below; immutable
in itself, but by which all the rest are made
proof against change; for it is not to the sheep
that the shepherd is responsible, but to their
owner. It has been said throughout that the one
special mark of Peter's distinction was a peculiar
association with Christ. It is not therefore by
any infringement of equal rights that this authority is set up, but as the representative, the vice-
gerent, of Him in whom all power dwells : who
bore this authority in His own body, and who
committed to another, what was first His own,
both by creation and by purchase—" Feed *My*
sheep ". In all these texts the immediate trans-

ference of authority from the Person of the God-
man is most striking: in Peter He inaugurates
His great theandric dispensation, and forms the
Body which He was to leave on earth. Thus
these texts most clearly express that important
doctrine of antiquity, the keystone of the Church's
liberty from the world, which is the reason why
the world so hates it: " The first See is judged
by no man". So entirely have political ideas
and jealousies infected our mode of judging of
spiritual things—to such a degree is our peculiar
civil liberty made the standard of Church government—that it is necessary to insist again and
again on what to Christians ought to be a first
principle, *viz.*, that " all power and jurisdiction
in the Church, like the Church herself, ought to
rest not upon natural and human authority, but
on the divine authority of Christ. This is the
reason why we may pronounce no otherwise
concerning such jurisdiction, than we know has
been handed down from Christ, its proper Author
and Founder. Now, it is certain that at the same
moment at which Christ instituted the community
called the Church, such a power was introduced,
and entrusted as well to Peter singly as the
head, as to the Apostles under him. Nay, that
power was fixed and constituted, and its Ministers
and Bishops marked out, *before* the Church, that
is, the whole body and commonwealth, had grown
into coherence. And so ecclesiastical jurisdiction
did not first dwell in the community itself, and was
then translated by a sort of popular suffrage and

consent to its magistrates; but from the very first
origin Peter was destined to be single chief of the
future body, and next to him the other Apostles."[1]

5. Fifthly, it must be observed that there is a
definiteness about these texts which belongs in a
far less degree to those forms in which the co-
ordinate and co-equal authority of the Apostles,
as such, is expressed.   This last is left to be
harmonized and brought into operation by the
superior power of the chief.   They are indeed sent
into all the world, they are immediately instituted
by our Lord, they have the promise that His
power shall be with them, and that their sentence
shall stand good in heaven and on earth; but this
promise, which is the most distinct made to them,
has been already gathered up into the hands of
one, and in its practical issue is limited by the
necessity of co-operating with that one; that is,
the authority of Peter includes and embraces
theirs, but theirs is ranged under his.   Theirs is
modified not only by being shared, but by having
his set over them.   Now observe how distinct and
clear, how definite in their meaning, while universal in their range, are the things said of him
alone; 1. That he should be the rock on which
Christ would build His Church; 2. That perman-
ence and victory should belong to that Church for
ever through him; 3. That he should bear the
keys in the kingdom of heaven; 4. That whatever
singly he should bind and loose, should be bound
and loosed in heaven as well as on earth; 5. That

---

[1] Petavius, de Ecc. Hier. lib. iii. c. 14.

he should confirm his brethren, the Apostles themselves being the very first so called; 6. That he
should be the shepherd of the fold. What can
constitute inequality between two parties, if such
a series of promises given to one, and not to the
other, does not ?

6. Sixthly, these promises cannot be contemplated without seeing that the ordinary and regular
government of the Church springs from the person
whom they designate, and in whom they are con-
centrated. To take the last, all spiritual care is
summed up in the word Pastorship, the office of
Priest, Bishop, Metropolitan, Patriarch, and Pope,
rising in degree, and extending in range, but in its
nature the same. On the contrary, Apostles (with
this one exception, in virtue of the Primacy), Prophets, and Evangelists, are extraordinary officers,
attending the opening of the dispensation, but
afterwards dropping off. But the Church, as it
was to endure for ever, and the orderly arrangement of the divine ministry, were summed up in
the Primacy, and flowed forth from it as the full
receptacle of the virtue of God the Word Incarnate. And so it is the head of the ministerial body.
All which is set forth as in a picture to the mind,
in that scene upon the shore of the lake of Galilee,
when the Lord said to Peter, " Feed My sheep ".

7. And, again, Peter was thus made the beginning and principle of spiritual power, as it left the
Person of God the Word, not for once, but for
ever. Long as the structure should endure, its
principle of cohesion must bind it. As the law

of gravitation binds all worlds together in the natural kingdom, and is a *continuous* source of strength and harmony, so should be in the spiritual kingdom that force which the same Wisdom of God established; it goes on with power undiminished; it is the full fountain-head from which all streams emanate; it is the highest image of God's power as the centre and source of all things. This idea is dwelt upon by St. Cyprian and St. Augustine, as well as by Pope St. Innocent,[1] the contemporary of the latter, and was afresh expressed in a synodical letter of the three provinces of Africa to Pope Theodore, in A.D. 646, " No one can doubt there is in the Apostolic See a great unfailing fountain, pouring forth waters for all Christians, whence rich streams proceed, bountifully irrigating the whole Christian world ".[2]

8. And, lastly, in these great promises Peter is specially set forth as the type and the efficient cause of visible unity in the Church. Such was the very purpose of Christ, that His disciples might be one, as He and the Father are one. For this end, in the words of St. Augustine, " He entrusted His sheep to Peter, as to another self, He willed to make him one with Himself "; and in the words of St. Leo, " He assumed him into the participation of His indivisible unity ".[3] But this is seen no less plainly in the words of Christ

---

[1] St. Cyprian, de Unitate, c. 3. St. Aug. to Pope Innocent, Ep. 177, n. 19. Pope Innocent to the Councils of Carthage and Numidia.   [2] Mansi, x. 919.

[3] St. Aug. Serm. 46. St. Leo, Epistle 10.

than in the Fathers; for He made *one* Rock, *one* Bearer of the keys, *one* Confirmer of the brethren, and *one* Shepherd. The union of millions of naturally conflicting wills in the profession and belief of one doctrine is almost the very highest work of divine power; and as grace, that is, the Holy Spirit diffused in the heart, is the inward efficient of this, so the outward, both symbol and instrument, is the Primacy, that "other self" which the Lord left in the world. And as the Church of God through every succeeding age grows and expands, the need of this power becomes greater and not less, and reverence to that "single chair in which unity was to be observed by all,"[1] a more imperative virtue, or rather an ever-deepening instinct, of the Christian mind.

But antiquity itself drew no other conclusions from the concentration of these great privileges in the person of Peter. We have but to go back to a time before the present nationalities of Europe, those jealous foes of Peter's authority, had come into existence, and we find the chief men of France, and Spain, and Italy, interpreting the above texts as we have done. Take one whose testimony from the circumstances of his life ought to be above suspicion. John Cassian was by birth a Scythian, was educated in a monastery at Bethlehem, travelled through Egypt, and made himself acquainted with its most distinguished religious men, went to Constantinople, and was ordained deacon by St. Chrysostom, and afterwards at

[1] St. Optatus, cont. Parm. lib. ii. c. 6.

Rome priest by Pope Innocent I.   On the capture
of Rome by Alaric, he settled at Marseilles, about
the year 410, and there founded two monasteries.
In his work on the Incarnation he says,[1] " Let us
ask him who is supreme, both as disciple among
disciples and as a teacher among teachers, who,
steering the course of the Roman Church, held
the supremacy as well of the faith as of the priesthood. Tell us, therefore, tell us, we pray, O
Peter, Prince of the Apostles, tell us how the
Churches ought to believe.   For just it is that thou
who wast taught of the Lord, shouldst teach us,
and open to us the door whose key thou hast
received.   Shut out all who undermine the
heavenly house, and turn away those who attempt
to make an entry through treacherous caverns
and illicit approaches; because it is certain that
no one shall be able to enter the door of the
kingdom, save he to whom the key placed by thee
in the Church shall open it.   Tell us, therefore,
how we ought to believe that Jesus is the Christ,
and to confess our common Lord."   Again,
fourteen hundred years ago, Maximus, Bishop
of Turin in that day, confessed by his words,
what his successor of the present day bears
witness to by his sufferings; for he writes of
Peter, " As[2] the Good Shepherd he received the
defence of the flock, so that he, who before had
been weak in his own case, might become the
confirmation to all : and he who had been shaken
by the temptation of the question asked him,

[1] Lib. iii. c. 12.   [2] De Petro Apostolo, Hom. 4.

might be a foundation to the rest by the stability of his faith. In fine, for the firmness of his devotion he is called the Rock of the Churches, as the Lord says, ' Thou art Peter, and upon this Rock I will build My Church '. For he is called the Rock, because he was the first to lay the foundations of the faith among the nations, *and because, as an immovable stone, he holds together the framework and the mass of the whole Christian structure.* Peter, therefore, for his devotion is called the Rock, and the Lord is named the Rock by His inherent power, as the Apostle says, ' And they drank of the spiritual rock that followed them, and the rock was Christ '. *Rightly does he merit to share the name, who, likewise, merits to share the work.*" Again, far and wide has the lying story been spread by false-hearted men, who above all things hate the spiritual kingdom which God has set up in the world, that Peter's power has been the growth of gradual encroachment on the secular authority. Now, long before Pelayo renewed the Spanish monarchy in the mountains of the Asturias, and while Augustine, sent by Pope Gregory, was laying the foundation of the English Church, St. Isidore, Bishop of Seville, from 598 to 636, the very highest of the ancient Spanish doctors, wrote thus explicitly to his colleague at Toledo:[1] " But as to the question of the equality of the Apostles, Peter is pre-eminent over the rest, who merited to hear from the Lord, ' Thou shalt be called Cephas. . . .Thou art Peter,

[1] Ad Eugenium Toletanum.

and upon this rock I will build My Church.'
And not from any one else, but from the very
Son of God and the Virgin, he was the first to
receive the honour of the pontificate in the Church
of Christ, to whom also, after the resurrection of
the Son of God, was said by the same, ' Feed My
lambs,' noting by the name of lambs the prelates
of the Churches. And although the dignity of
this power is derived to all Catholic Bishops,
yet in a more special manner it remains for ever
in the Roman Bishop, who is by a certain singular
privilege set as the head over the other limbs.
Whoso, therefore, renders not reverently to him
due obedience, involves himself, as being severed
from the head, in the schism of the Acephali."

It would be easy to multiply such authorities of
a period prior to the formation of all the existing
European states. It was the will of God, providing for His Church, that before the old Roman
society was utterly upheaved from its foundations
by the deluge of the Northern tribes, reverence for
St. Peter's throne should be fixed as an immovable
rock, on which a new Christian civilization might
be founded. Thus Pope Gregory II., writing to
the Emperor Leo the Isaurian, about the year 717,
only sums up the force and effect of all preceding
tradition, when he says, " The whole West turns
its eyes upon us, and, unworthy though we be,
puts complete trust in us, and in that blessed
Peter, whose image you threaten to overturn, but
whom all the kingdoms of the West count for a
God upon earth ".[1]

[1] Mansi, Concil. tom. xii. 972.

CHAPTER V.

ST. PETER'S PRIMACY AS EXHIBITED IN THE ACTS.

THE purpose[1] of St. Luke in writing the Acts
seems to have been to set before us the labours
and sufferings of the Apostles in planting and
propagating the Church. But he has divided the
book very distinctly into two portions; the latter,
from the thirteenth chapter to the end, with one
short exception, is wholly occupied with the
labours of St. Paul, "the vessel of election," in
spreading the faith among the Gentiles, and so
contains the particular history of that Apostle,
and the Churches founded by him. The former,
from the beginning to the end of the twelfth
chapter, embraces the history of the Apostles in
common, and of the whole Church, as it rose at
Jerusalem, and was spread first in Judea, then in
Samaria, and finally extended to the Gentiles.
The former history, then, is universal; the latter,
particular.

Moreover, to use the words of St. Chrysostom,[2]
"We may here see the promises which Christ
made in the Gospels carried into execution, and
the bright light of truth shining in the very actions,

---

[1] Passaglia, p. 138.
[2] Ibid. p. 140.   St. Chrys. in Acta, Hom. 1.

and a great change in the disciples, arising from
the Spirit that had entered into them. . . . You
will see here Apostles speeding on the wing over
land and sea, and men once timid and unskilled,
suddenly changed into despisers of wealth, and
conquerors of glory and all other passions; you
will see them united in the utmost harmony,
without jealousy, which once they had, without
contention for the higher place."

We may say, then, in a word, that the Gospels
are a history of the Head, and the Acts of the
mystical Body. Hence both issue forth from one
and the same fountain and source. The history
of the Head begins with that descent of the Holy
Ghost, whereby Christ was conceived, and "the
race[1] of God and of man became one. For just
as the union of man with woman joins two
families, so, upon Christ assuming flesh, by that
flesh the whole Church became of kin with
Christ, Paul became Christ's kinsman, and Peter,
each one of the faithful, all we, every holy person.
Therefore, says Paul,[2] 'being the offspring of
God,' and again 'we are the body of Christ and
members in particular,' that is, through the flesh,
which He has assumed, we are His kinsmen."
Now, the history of the Body, proceeding from
the same fountain-head, sets before us the Holy
Spirit, who, by descending first on the teachers,
and afterwards on the disciples, exalts and ad-
vances all, and by imparting Himself, imparts

[1] St. Chrys. Hom. in Ascens., and on Acts, tom. iii. p. 773.
[2] Acts xvii. 28, 29, and compare 1 Cor. xii. 12-17 with Eph. iv. 16.

"the proportional deification of man," that is, "the utmost possible assimilation and union with God ".[1] For "the Spirit works in us by His proper power, truly sanctifying and uniting us to Himself into one frame, and making us partakers of the divine nature ":[2] "becoming, as it were, a quality of the Godhead in us, and dwelling in the saints, and abiding for ever ".

Now it is[3] manifest that if the first twelve chapters of the Acts contain the history of the Church from its beginning, and what the Apostles did for its first formation, its growth, and its form of government, all this has the closest connection with the question as to Peter's prerogatives. For the historical accounts in the Acts, which exhibit the *execution* of Christ's promises and intentions, naturally tend to set in the fullest light, and to reveal distinctly, whatever as to the administration of the Church may be less clearly *foretold* in the Gospels. For in itself the *execution* is declaratory of the *enactment*, and supplies a safe rule for understanding and determining the words of institution. Now, if we apply this rule to the present question, it will be apparent that those expressions of the Gospel, which we assigned to the divine institution of the Primacy, cannot be otherwise received without making the *execution* in the Acts at variance with what the Gospels record.

---

[1] Dions. de Cœl. Hier. cap. 1, § 3.
[2] St. Cyril. Thes. lib. xxxiv. p. 352, and lib. ix. on John, p. 810.
[3] Passaglia, p. 143.

For, take it as a still doubtful hypothesis
whether there exist evangelical testimonies of
Peter's *institution* to be head and chief of the
Apostles. What needs it to turn this hypothesis
into certainty? What should we expect of Peter,
if he really had received from Christ the charge
of leading the other Apostles? What but that
he should never follow, but always be at the
head; should close dissensions, weigh and terminate controversies, punish emergent offences,
maintain the general discipline, give the support
of his counsel and authority in need, and leave
undone none of those functions which accompany
the office of head and supreme ruler? Hence
it is plain that there are two ways, the one
absolute, the other hypothetical, by which a
decisive judgment may be drawn from the history
of the Acts, as to whether Peter's Primacy was
instituted in the Gospels. Critics and philoso-
phers are perpetually using both these tests.
Thus, the former, "if a certain work—say the
epistles of the martyr Ignatius—be genuine, it
ought to contain certain characteristics. But it
does contain these and so is genuine." Or absolutely, "a certain work, the epistles of Ignatius,
contains all which we should expect in a genuine
work, therefore it is genuine". The latter infer,
"If bodies be moved by the law of gravitation,
they would pass through a certain space under
such and such a condition. But this they do,
and accordingly are moved by gravitation."
Or absolutely, "Bodies left to themselves pass

through space under such conditions as they would follow, if impelled by gravitation. Accordingly they are so impelled." Now, in the parallel case, " If Christ in the Gospels preordained a form of Church government, which gathered up the supreme power and visible headship into Peter's hands, the *exercise* of such *institution* ought to be found in the Acts. But it is so found. Therefore," etc. Or again, " No one would expect certain acts from Peter, unless he were the head of all the Apostles ; and all would fairly expect those acts of Peter, if they recognized him as so set over all by Christ. Now, in the general history of the Apostles we find such acts recorded of Peter, and that not partially, here and there, but in a complete series. Accordingly the history of the rising Church, exhibited in the first part of the Acts, demands Peter's Primacy for its explanation ; and if we deny that Primacy, and take in another sense the words recording its institution in the Gospel, the history becomes unintelligible."

Now, this reasoning is conclusive in either way, provided only that what we have asserted be really found in the Acts. The proof of this may be either general, or piecemeal and particular. We will take both in order, beginning with the former.

1. First, [1] then, we must repeat, as concerns that whole portion of the Acts containing the history of the universal Church, and all the Apostles, *viz.*, the first twelve chapters, a remark

---

[1] Passaglia, p. 144.

before made as to the Gospels, which is, that Peter singly is more often mentioned than all the rest put together. For Peter's name occurs more than fifty times, the others very seldom, and those who are found the oftenest, John and James, are recorded, the former seven or eight, the latter three or four times. Yet this is a history of them all: Luke is recording the common exertions of all the Apostles in building up the Church. This is the very distinction between the former and the latter portion of his book, which is confined to the labours of St. Paul, leaving aside the rest of the Church. What then is the reason that Peter, in a general history, is so often brought forward, and the rest, either singly or in conjunction, so seldom? Because after our Lord's glorious ascension Peter stood to the eleven in an analogous position to that held by our Lord, so long as He was visible, towards the whole college: because Peter was become the head, and the rest, as members, were ranged under him.

2. Such subordination on their part, such pre-eminence on his, Luke[1] shows yet more clearly, whenever he groups Peter with the rest, by assigning to him the leading place. It frequently happens to him to speak of Peter and the rest together, but on no one occasion does he give Peter any but the first place, and the leading part. Just as the evangelists do with regard to Christ, and the Apostles and disciples, so Luke prefers Peter to the rest, to mark a difference

[1] Acts i. 13 ; ii. 14 ; iii. 1-3; iv. 19; viii. 14.

between the rank and office of Peter, and that of the others.

3. Luke seems to confirm his readers in such a conclusion by the form which he follows of mentioning Peter *directly*, and the rest *obliquely* or *in a mass*. These are instances : " In those days Peter, *rising up in the midst of the brethren*, said " —" Peter, *standing up with the eleven*, lifted up his voice "—" They said *to Peter and to the rest of the Apostles* "—" Peter, *with John*, fastening his eyes upon him, said, Look upon us "—" Peter *and the Apostles* answering, said ".[1] Now, what form of writing could Luke choose, to refute an opinion about the *universal* equality of the Apostles ? Or to show Peter as set over the rest, and to satisfy in this even the most unreasonable ? Either the form which he did choose is calculated to do this, or none such can be found.

4. Add to this that Peter is represented as speaking and answering, when the occasion would suggest that all the Apostles, equally, should disclose their mind. The reproaches of the unbelieving Jews affected not Peter singly, but all alike ; but he alone stands forth, he alone lifts up his voice, and in a long speech brings them to sound reflection. The multitude, struck with compunction, asked not Peter only, but the rest likewise, " What shall we do, men and brethren ? " Yet it is forthwith added, " But *Peter* said to them ". Upon the miracle by which one who had been lame from his mother's womb was healed,

---

[1] Acts i. 15; ii. 14, 37 ; iii. 4 ; v. 29.

"all the people ran together to them," both Peter
and John, but Peter alone speaks, and takes on
himself the defence of the common cause : " Peter
seeing, made answer to the people ".[1] Fresh
instances may be found in chaps. iv. 6, 7, and v. 2,
3. The result of the whole is that Peter is continually " the mouthpiece of the Apostles,"[2]
always takes the lead, and gives his own mind, as
conveying that of the rest.

On what ground does he do this? Was it
from natural fervour of disposition? But it was
the same after he was filled with the Holy Spirit
as before. Was it the result of superior age, or
first calling? but the facts refute this. What
other cause can be suggested save that Primacy
which the Gospels record, and the Acts confirm ?

5. To this we must likewise refer it that Luke,
while he amply describes actions which belong to
Peter, rather hints at than narrates what concerns
the other Apostles. Thus he leaves it to be
understood that the others spoke, while he gives
Peter's discourses entire, and seems to have chosen
them as the principal material of his history. He
simply suggests that miracles were wrought by the
rest, but records particularly what Peter did for
the establishment of the faith. He relates but
very little of those who became Christians by
the exertion of others, but notes at large the
abundant fruit of Peter's teaching. Take an
ancient author's summary of the Acts, " this whole
volume is about the ascension of Christ after the

---

[1] Acts ii. 13, 37, 38 ; iii. 11, 12.   [2] St. Chrysostom.

resurrection, and about the descent of the Holy Spirit on the holy Apostles, and how and where the disciples announced Christ's religion, and all the wondrous deeds which they did by prayer and faith in Him, and about Paul's divine calling from heaven, his apostleship, and fruitful preaching, and in a word about those many great dangers which the Apostles underwent for Christ " : [1] follow, out of this, all which concerns the universal Church in the first twelve chapters, and Peter will be found not only the principal, but well-nigh the only, figure in the foreground.

6. Hence, as the Gospels may be called the history of Christ, so this first part of the Acts may be called the history of Peter; for as Christ occupies each page of the Gospels, so Peter here. Nothing can be more emphatic or more just than St. Chrysostom's words: " Behold him making his rounds on every side, and the first to be found ; when an Apostle was to be chosen, he was the first ; when the Jews were to be told that they were not drunken ; when the lame man was to be healed ; when the multitude was to be addressed, he is before the rest ; when they had to do with the rulers, it is he ; when with Ananias, when healings took place from the shadow, still it is he. Where there was danger, it is he, and where there was dispensation ; but when all is tranquil, they act in common. He sought not the greater honour. But again, when miracles are to be worked, he comes forth before the rest." [2]   What

---

[1] Euthalius, apud Zaccagnium, p. 410.   [2] On Acts, Hom. 21, n. 2.

can prove Peter's pre-eminence if this does not?
But his words on another occasion deserve mention.
Alluding to the title "Acts of the Apostles," which
seems to promise their common history, he
observes, "Yet if you search accurately, the first
part of the book exhibits Peter's miracles and
teaching, but little on the part of the other
Apostles; and after this the whole account is
spent on Paul". But he adds, "How are they
the Acts of all the Apostles? Because, according
to Paul, when one member is glorified, all the
members are glorified with it; the historian did not
entitle them, the Acts of Peter and of Paul, but
the Acts of the Apostles; the promise of the
writer includes them all." [1]   Now, every one
must feel the very high distinction given to Paul
in the latter part of the book, when the historian
turns away from the general history of the Church
to record his particular labours, in which, no doubt,
the object was to show the progress of the Church
among the Gentiles; but with regard to the part
which is common to the whole Church, another
thought is suggested. The history of what Peter
taught and did, to build up and extend the Church,
is considered the common history of the Apostles,
and so inscribed as their Acts. But can this be
called an *accurate* expression, unless Peter had
been the head of the Apostles? It is very plain
that the acts of a head are imputed to the whole
body; to a college of brethren, what its chief
executes; to a city or kingdom, the deeds of its

[1] Hom. on beginning of Acts, n. 8, tom. iii. 764.

prince. But it is not plain how this can be, if the actor be one of a number, and do not exceed his brethren in honour or dignity. Therefore the Acts of Peter could be called, generally, the Acts of the Apostles, only because they were considered the Acts of their head.

Now let us pass from the general view to that in detail.

I. After[1] the Lord's ascension a most important point immediately arose, whether, that is, the number of the Twelve was to be filled up by the election of a new Apostle to take the place of Judas. The will of Christ on this matter was to be learnt ; a witness was to be chosen who should participate in the mission of Christ Himself, according to the words, "As the Father hath sent Me, I also send you," and carry the light of the Gospel to the ends of the world ; and one was to be elected to the dignity of the Apostolate, the highest rank in the Church. It was, therefore, so important a matter, that no one could undertake it save he who had received the vicarious headship of our Lord Himself. Now, the history in the Acts tells us that Peter alone spoke on the subject of substituting a fresh Apostle for Judas ; Peter alone proved from Scripture the necessity of the election, defined the conditions of eligibility, and appointed the mode of election, and presided over and directed the whole transaction.

For Luke begins thus: " In those days," the interval between the Ascension and Pentecost,

---

[1] Passaglia, p. 148,

" Peter rising up in the midst of the brethren,
said ". Here the important prerogative *of initiation*
is shown to belong to Peter, and by the phrase, " in
the midst of the brethren," or " disciples,"—which
is often used of Christ in respect of the Apostles
—his pre-eminence over the disciples is shown.
" Brethren, it behoved that the Scripture should
be fulfilled which the Holy Ghost spoke before by
the mouth of David, concerning Judas, who was
the leader of them that apprehended Jesus, who
was numbered with us, and had obtained part of
this ministry," that is, of the Apostolate.   Then
having mentioned the miserable end of the traitor,
he applies to him the prophecy : " For it is written
in the Book of Psalms, ' Let his habitation become
desolate, and let there be none to dwell therein ' :
and," adding another prophecy from another
Psalm, " ' his bishopric let another take'". [1]
Whence he concludes, " Wherefore of these men
who have companied with us all the time that
the Lord Jesus came in and went out among us,
beginning from the baptism of John, until the day
wherein He was taken up from us, one of these
must be made a witness with us of His resurrection".
In these words Peter plainly points out the *necessity*
of the matter in question, confirms it by the Holy
Scriptures, speaking in the character of their
highest interpreter, and as the appointed teacher
of all ; and, while proposing it to their deliberation,
yet requires their consent ; for the phrase, " wherefore, one *must*," means, " I am not proposing what

[1] Ps. lxix. 26 ; cviii. 8,

may be done or left undone, but declaring and pre-
scribing what is to be done ". So he determines
the conditions of eligibility, and the form of
election. Whereupon his hearers—" the number
of persons together about an hundred and twenty"
—instantly agree unanimously to Peter's proposition, follow its conditions, and complete the
election.

No one can reflect on the above without con-
cluding, that if Peter presided over the rest by the
authority of a divinely chosen headship, no course
could be more becoming, both for Peter and for the
disciples, than this ; and if, on the contrary, Peter
was only one out of many, not having yet even
received the Pentecostal gifts of the Holy Spirit,
and had been entrusted by Christ with no pre-
eminent office in the ministry, nothing could be
more unfitting for both. We have therefore to
infer that Peter " stood in the midst of his
disciples," as a superior among inferiors, not as
an equal among equals, and conceived that the
charge of supplying an Apostle, and filling up the
Apostolic college, belonged in chief to himself,
because he and they alike were conscious that he
was the steward set in chief over the Lord's
family.

But, clear as this is on the face of the narration
itself, fresh light is shed on it by the fact that St.
Chrysostom observed and recorded this very conclusion. For why did Peter alone arise? Why was
he the first and the only one to speak ? " Both [1]

---

[1] Hom. 3, in Act. n. 1-2.

as fervent, and *as one entrusted by Christ with the
flock*, and *as the first of the choir*, he ever first begins
to speak." Why does he allege prophecy? First,
that he might not seem with human counsel "to
attempt a great matter, and one fitted for Christ":
next to imitate his Master, "he always reasons
from the Scriptures". "Why did he not singly
ask of Christ to give him some one in the place of
Judas?" Because "Peter had now improved,"
and overcome his natural disposition. But "*might
not Peter by himself have elected?* Certainly: but
he does not so, that he may not seem partial."
"Why does he communicate this to them," the
whole number of the names? That the matter
may not be contested, nor they fall into strife:
"for" (he alludes to the contention of the Apostles
for the primacy) "if this had happened to themselves, much more would it to the others," that is,
the candidates to succeed Judas. Then he points
out to our admiration " Peter doing this with
common consent, nothing with authority,[1] nothing
with lordship," where we must note that the *abuse*
of a power is only to be feared from one who really
has that power. For again he says, " he first acts
on authority[2] in the matter, *as having himself all
put into his hands*, for to him Christ said, ' And
thou, in thy turn, one day confirm thy brethren ' ".

The college of the Apostles completed, it
followed that the head, if such there were, would,
on every occasion of danger, be the first to protect
it, and to defend its reputation. Now there ensues

---

[1] Αὐθεντικῶς.   [2] Αὐθεντεῖ.

the miracle of the Holy Spirit's descent, and the
gift of tongues, whereupon Luke describes the
various opinions of the astonished multitude, some
of whom "mocking,[1] said, These men are full of
new wine ". That is, they blasphemed the working
of the Spirit, and by the most monstrous calumny
were destroying the good name of the Apostles.
Whereupon, " Peter, standing up with the Eleven,
lifted up his voice and spoke to them : Ye men of
Judea, and all you that dwell in Jerusalem, be this
known to you, and with your ears receive my
words. For these are not drunk as you suppose,
seeing it is but the third hour of the day : but this
is that which was spoken of by the prophet Joel."
Now here, both the *form of the words*, and the
matter, establish Peter's primacy. For the phrase,
" Peter standing up with the Eleven, lifted up his
voice and spoke to them," portrays Peter as the
leader of the band, the master of the family. So
St. Chrysostom,[2] " What means *with the Eleven ?*
They uttered a common voice, and he was the
mouthpiece of all. And the Eleven stand beside
him, bearing witness to his words." And as to
the *matter*, Peter alone fulfils the part of teacher,
by interpreting Scripture, and declaring the agreement of both covenants : Peter alone maintains
the common cause ; Peter alone, representing all,
addresses the multitude in the name of all.
" Observe, too, the harmony of the Apostles :
they gave up to him the office of speaking : "[3] that

[1] Acts ii.   [2] On the Acts, Hom. 4, n. 3.
[3] St. Chrysostom, as before.

is, they yielded to him who was the head, and who, as he says, showed here " the courage," as before " the providential care " of the Head.

After refuting the calumny, Peter goes on in a noble discourse to explain prophecies, and then coming to the dispensation of Jesus, gives the strongest proofs of His resurrection and exaltation to the right hand of the Father, and finally sums up with great force and authority. " Therefore, let all the house of Israel know most certainly, that God hath made both Lord and Christ this same Jesus whom you have crucified."

Now, what [1] is here to our purpose? It is this, that Luke seems only to dwell on what concerns Peter: that Peter, first of all, and in the name of all, performs the office of a witness, laid both on himself and the rest ("ye shall be witnesses to me"; "and you shall give witness "[2]), saying, " This Jesus hath God raised up, of which we all are witnesses ": that first of all, he publicly and solemnly discharges the duty of instruction with authority: that, first of all, he fulfils the charge set by Christ on all the Apostles, " make disciples —teach": that, first of all, he promulgates the necessity of believing in Jesus as the divinely appointed Lord and Christ. Now these are things which, so far from allowing an equality between Peter and the rest of the Apostles, point out in him a headship over them.

Thereupon, the hearers, struck with compunction for having crucified, not merely a just man,

[1] Passaglia, p. 153.   [2] Acts i. 8; John xv. 27.

but the Anointed of the Lord, " said to Peter and
the rest of the Apostles "—here again he alone is
singly named—but of all alike they asked, " Men
and brethren, what shall we do?"   Whereupon,
St. Chrysostom notes,[1] "Here again, where all are
asked, he alone replies ".   For, as Luke goes on,
" Peter said to them": as the leader, he performs
what belongs to all : he alone sets forth the law of
Christ.   " Do penance, and be baptized every one
of you, in the name of Jesus Christ, for the
remission of sins:"   he alone encourages them
with the promised gifts of the Holy Spirit, " and
you shall receive the gift of the Holy Ghost": he
alone continues at length the instruction of the
hearers, "and with very many other words did he
testify and exhort them": he alone declares the
fruit of Christian profession, "save yourselves
from this perverse generation," and he alone it is,
of whose ministry Luke adds, " They, therefore,
that gladly received his word were baptized, and
there were added, in that day, about three
thousand souls ".

And here we see how fitting it was that Peter,
whom Christ had set as the foundation and rock
of the Church, should labour with all his might, as
the chief architect after Him, to build up the
structure.   But what, in the meantime, of the
other Apostles ?   Were not they also architects ?
Yes, but *with* and *under* Peter, whom accordingly
they   attend   and   support.   The   subsequent
additions   to   the   Church's   structure,   and   the

___
[1] On Acts, Hom. 7, n. 1,

course consistently pursued by Peter, will bring
this out yet more clearly.   For of fresh accre-
tions, Luke writes, "Many of them who had heard
the word, believed, and the number of the men
was made five thousand".[1]   Now, whose word was
this ?   Still the word of Peter, who speaks for the
third[2] and fourth time, as he had for the first and
second.

For, as to the third[3] occasion, Luke, after
mentioning Peter and John together, introduces
Peter alone as urging the children of Abraham to
embrace the faith of Christ, and persuading them
that Jesus is the Prophet, promised by God
through Moses in Deuteronomy.   And as to the
fourth,[4] he writes, "Then Peter, filled with the
Holy Ghost, said to them——"   But was he
alone present ? not so, for the council "setting
them," not him, but John as well as Peter, "in
the midst, they asked," on which Chrysostom[5]
observes, "See how John is on every occasion
silent, while Peter defends him likewise".   That
is, John was silent, as knowing that the lead
belonged to Peter, and Peter spoke, because the
Head defends not himself only, but the members
committed to him.

Now, reviewing these first four chapters of the
Acts, let us ask these questions.   Had Peter held
the authority of head among the Apostles, what
would he have done ?   He would have filled up
the Apostolic college, carefully watched over it,

---

[1] Acts iv. 4.   [2] Acts iii. 12-26 ; iv. 8-19.   [3] Acts iii. 11, 12-26.
[4] Acts iv. 7, 8.   [5] On Acts, Hom. 8, n. 2.

protected its several members. But this is just what he did. Again, had Christ made him the supreme teacher and doctor, what would he have done? He would have disclosed, first to the Apostles themselves, and to the disciples, and then to the multitude, who were to be converted, the secrets of the divine will laid up in the Scriptures; he would have shown the agreement between the dispensation of Christ, and the oracles of the Old Testament, and so have proved that Jesus was the Messiah. But this he repeatedly did. Once more, had Christ made him the chief among the builders of the Church, what would have been his office? He would have been the very first to set his hand to the work, and to construct the building with living stones; he would have held the other workmen under his control, so that the edifice might rise worthy of Christ, and exactly answering to His promises. But does not the history give precisely this picture of him, and does not the Church which Peter raised answer exactly to the archetype prescribed by the Lord? "All they that believed were together, and had all things common:" "the multitude of believers had but one heart and one soul:" what is this but the counterpart of that divine prayer, "that they all may be one, as Thou, Father, art in Me, and I in Thee, that they also may be one in Us, that the world may believe that Thou hast sent Me"?[1]

II. To take another point. The office[2] of

---

[1] Acts ii. 44; iv. 32; John xvii. 21.   [2] Passaglia, p. 157.

authoritative teaching is in the New Testament
closely connected with the power of working
miracles, so that Christ not only said of Himself,
" If I had not come and spoken to them, they
would not have sin ; but now they have no excuse
for their sin": but likewise added, " If I had not
done among them the works that no other man
hath done, they would not have sin : but now
they have both seen and hated both Me and My
Father": [1] to show that, while faith depended on
preaching and authoritative instruction, these also
needed the power of *works* to conciliate conviction.
In accordance with which, when He first sent out
His Twelve to preach, He not only charged them
what to say, " The kingdom of· heaven is at
hand," [2] but added the fullest miraculous power,
" heal the sick, raise the dead, cleanse the lepers,
cast out devils ". And when more solemnly
sending them, not to one people, but to all
nations, " Go ye into the whole world, and preach
the Gospel to every creature," He adds their
warrant, " these signs shall follow them that
believe. In My name they shall cast out devils,
they shall speak with new tongues, they shall take
up serpents:" and the Evangelist subjoins, "They
going forth preached everywhere, the Lord working withal, and confirming the word with signs
that followed ". [3]

Remembering, then, this very close connection
between the authority of Apostolic teaching and
the power of working miracles, we may fix a

[1] John xv. 22-24.   [2] Matt. x. 7.   [3] Mark xvi. 15-17.

criterion for recognizing the exercise of the supreme office in teaching. Suppose any one of the Apostles to have been invested at the commencement of the Church with this office, how may he be ascertained? If any one is found invariably the first to announce the word of truth, and likewise to confirm it with miracles, you may suppose him to be that one. Suppose, again, that Luke intended to represent one of the Apostles as the supreme teacher. How may it be safely inferred? If, in the course of his narration, he continually exhibits one as eminent above all the rest in preaching the Gospel and guaranteeing it by signs. These are not tests arbitrarily chosen, but naturally suggested. And both exactly fit to Peter, and to Peter alone. For he, in this history of the universal Church, is the first, nay, well-nigh the only one, both to preach and to support his preaching by miracles. And Luke takes pains to relate no less his miracles than his discourses, and scarcely describes with any detail either the one or the other, of any but Peter.

Nay, his mode of writing suggests a parallel between himself and St. John in his Gospel, as if it were no less Luke's intention to show Peter invested with the supreme office, than John's to set forth Christ as the head and teacher of the Apostolic college; and no less Luke's purpose to accredit the Church by Peter's miracles, than John's[1] by the miracles of Christ to establish faith in Him as the true Son of God. For the circum-

[1] John xx. 21.

stances of each narration point to this similarity of design. As St. John subordinates the group of Apostles entirely to the figure of Christ, so Luke, very slightly sketching the rest, is profuse in detail of what concerns Peter, and marks him as set over all. As John in recording the miracles of Christ dwells on the points which prove His divine mission and origin from the Father, so Luke directs his narration to exhibit the beginning, the growth, and the authority of the Church, as due to Peter's miracles. We will mark two further resemblances. *First*, the miracles which Luke records of Peter seem cast in the same type as those of Christ. Compare the first one with that told by John, ch. v.

John v. 5-9. " There was a certain man there that had been eight and thirty years under his infirmity. Him when Jesus had seen lying, and knew that he had been now a long time, He saith to him, Wilt thou be made whole? The infirm man answered Him, Sir, I have no man, when the water is troubled, to put me into the pond. For whilst I am coming another goeth down before me. Jesus said to him, Arise, take up thy bed, and walk. And immediately the man was made whole, and he took up his bed and walked."

Acts iii. 2-8. " And a certain man, who was lame from his mother's womb, was carried, whom they laid every day at the gate of the temple, which is called Beautiful. He, when he had seen Peter and John about to go into the temple, asked to receive an alms. But Peter, with John, fastening his eyes upon him, said, Look upon us. But he looked earnestly upon them, hoping that he should receive something of them. Peter said, Silver and gold I have none, but what I have, I give thee. In the name of Jesus Christ of Nazareth, arise and walk. And taking him by the right hand, he lifted him up, and forthwith his feet and soles received strength, and he, leaping up, stood, and walked."

How often had the hand of the Lord—as here

that of Peter—healed the sick, given the blind sight, cured the leper, and raised the dead ! But if Peter's miracle in healing Æneas of the palsy carries[1] one back immediately to the poor man let down through the roof before our Lord, there is a yet more exact identity between the great miracle of Christ raising Jairus' daughter, and Peter raising Dorcas. In the one case, the Lord " having put them all out, taketh the father and the mother of the damsel, and them that were with Him, and entereth in where the damsel was lying, and taking the damsel by the hand, He said to her, Talitha cumi, which is, Damsel, arise, and immediately the damsel rose up and walked ". In the other case, Peter came into the upper chamber, " and all the widows stood about him weeping— and they being all put forth, Peter, kneeling down, prayed, and turning to the body, he said, Tabitha, arise. And she opened her eyes, and seeing Peter, she sat up,[2] and giving her his hand he lifted her up." But how perfect the resemblance of the following.

Luke iv. 40. "And when the sun was down, all they that had any sick with divers diseases brought them to Him. But He, laying His hands on every one of them, healed them. And devils went out from many."

Acts v. 15. "Insomuch that they brought forth the sick into the streets, and laid them on beds and couches, that, when Peter came, his shadow, at the least, might overshadow any of them, and they might be delivered from their infirmities. And there came also together to Jerusalem a multitude out of the neighbouring cities, bringing sick persons, and such as were troubled with unclean spirits, who were all healed."

[1] Compare Acts ix. 33, with Mark ii. 3-11.
[2] Mark v. 40 ; Acts ix. 39.

The second point of resemblance is, that the
multitude regarded Peter among the Apostles as
before they had regarded Christ: for, putting the
rest of the Apostles in the second place, they
flocked to him, and besought his aid. So that
Luke, briefly saying of them, that "by the hands
of the Apostles were many signs and wonders
wrought among the people,"[1] goes on to Peter,
and of him relates the unheard-of wonders just
described, assigning to the miracles wrought by
him, "that the multitude of men and women
who believed in the Lord was more increased".
It is just as when "there came to Jesus great
multitudes, having with them the dumb, the blind,
the lame, the maimed, and many others ; and they
cast them down at His feet, and He healed them".[2]
And the fuller the resemblance these incidents
show between Peter and Christ, the more evident
their proof that Peter's ministry must be considered
a continuation of that which Christ began.

III. We proceed[3] to the order predetermined
by our Lord in the propagation of His Church.

Of Himself He had said, though the Redeemer
of all, that He was not sent, that is, as an Apostle,
actually to preach, "save to the lost sheep of the
house of Israel" : and on first sending His Apostles,
He gave them this commission, "Go ye not into
the way of the Gentiles, and into the city of the
Samaritans enter ye not, but go ye rather to the
lost sheep of the house of Israel". But when
about to ascend to the Father, He tells them

[1] Acts v. 12-14.   [2] Matt. xv. 30.   [3] Passaglia, p. 163.

"You shall receive the power of the Holy Ghost coming upon you, and you shall be witnesses unto Me in Jerusalem, and in all Judea, and Samaria, and even to the uttermost part of the earth ":[1] that is, that they should set up His kingdom through all the world, proceeding by gradual steps, from Jerusalem to Judea, thence to Samaria, and at length "to every creature" in the whole world.

Now, the history of the Acts shows the exact accomplishment of this order, and it likewise shows that Simon Peter was the one elected chief instrument for carrying out these successive propagations of the Church. What we have said already shows this as to the mother Church of Jerusalem, and, before proceeding to the Gentile Churches, we will trace the same instrumentality as used to bring the Samaritans into the universal kingdom.

The persecution ensuing on the proto-martyr Stephen's death caused, by our Lord's providence, the dissemination of many believers through Judea and Samaria, while the Apostles alone remained at Jerusalem. Amongst those who thus "went about preaching the word of God," Philip the deacon came to Samaria, and many of the people, hearing his words and seeing his miracles, were converted and baptized. But the Church thus commenced by the preaching of the deacon would have dried up without hope of progress, had it not received the assistance of those whom Christ had set in the place of fathers, and who could bestow the gifts of the Holy Ghost. For "the Church is

[1] Matt. xv. 24; x. 5; Acts i. 8.

in the bishop,"[1] and, as St. Jerome said of a faction which had a deacon for its author, "With the man the sect also perished, because a deacon could ordain no clerk after him. But it is not a Church which has no priest." Accordingly when "the Apostles, who were in Jerusalem, had heard that Samaria had received the word of God, they sent unto them Peter and John,"[2] who "laid their hands upon them, and they received the Holy Ghost". The providence of Christ, then, so ordered the propagation of His kingdom as to choose Peter and John to complete and perfect the Samaritan Church. But was this on equal terms, or is no superior dignity and authority apparent in Peter over John? A regard to the words of Luke, and the series of acts recorded, will prevent such a misconception. For he mentions Peter and John, but he sets Peter first; and in his record of what happened to Simon, John acts the second part, and it is Peter alone who teaches, commands, judges, and condemns, with authority, as the head and supreme ruler. Simon Magus, tempted by beholding the gifts of the Holy Spirit visibly bestowed on imposition of the Apostles' hands, "offered them money," to both Peter and John. But Peter alone replies, and not only so, but condemns his profaneness, enlarges on his guilt, and solemnly declares that the gifts of God are not purchasable with money. "Keep thy money to thyself to perish with thee, because thou hast

[1] St. Cyprian, Ep. 69. St. Jerome, Dialogue con. Luciferianos.
[2] Acts viii. 14.

thought that the gift of God may be purchased
with money:" he discloses Simon's secret thoughts,
"for thy heart is not right in the sight of God";
he inflicts on him excommunication, "thou hast
no part nor lot in this matter"; he exhorts him
to repent, "do penance therefore from this thy
wickedness, and pray to God, if perhaps this
thought of thy heart may be forgiven thee". Now
here John, the next of the Apostles in rank, is with
Peter, yet he does not speak, teach, or enjoin:
Peter does all this singly. He answers Simon's
question, lances and probes the most secret wound
of his conscience, declares how divine gifts are
given, proscribes the plague of simony, orders
penance, and inflicts excommunication on a
scandalous public offender. Thus the twenty-
second of the Apostolic Canons runs, "If any
bishop, priest or deacon, hath obtained this dignity
by money, let him and his ordainer be deposed,
and altogether be deprived of communion, as
Simon Magus was by Peter". Nothing but an
inequality of rank between Peter and John will
account for Luke's narration here. But if John
was inferior to Peter, much more the rest.

But there is another proof of his superiority here,
in that God caused Simon Peter to engage Simon
Magus. Thus, by His providence, "reaching from
end to end mightily, and ordering all things
sweetly," the first-born of Christ is brought to
conflict with the "first-born of the devil," the
chief of teachers with the earliest of heretics, and
prime of that long brood of the evil one, who are

to persecute " the seed of the woman ". Thus ancient writers record that Peter afterwards went to Rome on purpose to expose the acts of this same Simon. Thus they mention his engaging with the famous Alexandrine Apion, the enemy of the Jewish and the Christian faith alike. And hence, too, probably the very ancient writer (whoever he was) of the Epistle of Clement to St. James, begins it by recording how " Simon, for his true faith and his firm grounding in doctrine, was appointed to be the foundation of the Church, and for this very reason by Jesus Himself with most true augury had his name changed to Peter, the first-fruits of our Lord, the first of the Apostles, to whom first the Father revealed the Son, whom Christ with reason blessed, the called and the elect His guest and comrade, the good and the proved disciple, *he who, as the most able of all, was commanded to illuminate the West, the darker quarter of the world*, and who was enabled to succeed ".

But as to what is said, that " the Apostles who were in Jerusalem *sent* to the Samaritans Peter and John," it must be remembered, that at the head of those thus *sending* was Peter himself, and that next to him John was the most distinguished of the Apostolic college. And since it is evident from all that we have hitherto seen, that in whatever concerned the Apostles equally, Peter took the leading part, and in their common deliberations exercised the initiative, it must be concluded that he was likewise the first author of this resolution, to send himself and John to the Samaritans. And

this is confirmed by our seeing that in the fulfilment of this mission he discharges the offices, and
acts with the authority, of head. To none else
could the execution of a fresh advance in the propagation of the Church be committed ; and so
great, besides, were the jealousies between the
Jews and Samaritans, that it needed no less than
Peter's authority to induce the Jewish converts to
receive them into the bond of the same society.

IV. But now we [1] draw nigh to the revelation of
that great " mystery which in other generations
was not known to the sons of men—that the
Gentiles should be fellow-heirs, and of the same
body, and co-partners of His promise in Christ
Jesus by the Gospel," whereby was brought to
pass the prophecy, " from the rising of the sun
even to the going down My Name is great among
the Gentiles, and in every place there is sacrifice,
and there is offered to My Name a clean oblation ".[2]
The hour was come " when the true adorers were
to adore the Father in spirit and in truth " throughout every region of the world purchased with the
blood of the Son of God, and of this event, expected
during four thousand years, God, by an unexampled
honour, disclosed to Peter, and through Peter, the
time and the manner. This greatest of purposes,
after His own ascension, Christ left to be revealed
through him to whom He had committed the
feeding of His sheep.

While Peter [3] was " passing through all," that
is, exercising his general supervision as primate of

---

[1] Passaglia, p. 174.   [2] Eph. iii. 5 ; Mal. i. 11.   [3] Acts ix. 32.

X. i-48

the Church, God sent His angel " in a vision
manifestly " to " a certain man in Cesarea named
Cornelius, a centurion of that which is called the
Italian band, a religious man, and fearing God
with all his house, giving much alms to the people,
and always praying to God ".   And the angel says
to him : " Thy prayers and thine alms are ascended
for a memorial in the sight of God, and now send
men to Joppa, and call hither one Simon, who is
surnamed Peter ; he will tell thee what thou must
do ".   Though God then sends an angel, it is left
to *Simon, who is surnamed Peter*, to declare His
counsel, in what affected the salvation of innumerable souls.   Other Apostles there were to whom
had been said equally, " Go ye into the whole
world and preach the Gospel to every creature,"
and "Ye shall be witnesses to Me both in Jerusalem
and in all Judea, and Samaria, and to the uttermost parts of the earth " ; and " as the Father
hath sent Me, I also send you".   Yet putting aside
all these, as on so many other occasions, Peter is
preferred, and that because to him alone was said,
" on this rock I will build My Church," and again,
" Feed My lambs, be shepherd over My sheep ".
Fitting it was that, when the wall between the
Jews and Gentiles should be taken away, by him
specially all should be collected into one, on whom,
as the divinely laid foundation, all were to rest.
Fitting, again, that the Lord's prophecy, " Other
sheep I have which are not of this fold ; those also
I must bring ; and they shall hear My voice ; and
there shall be one fold and one shepherd," should

be fulfilled chiefly by his ministry to whom the Lord had committed His own office of universal visible pastor. For the Church, in her very birth, and in the whole process of her growth, bore this upon her forehead, that *universality* as well as *unity* belonged substantially to Peter, and that it was no less his function to gather up all nations into the mould of unity by his ministration as the one chief shepherd, than to embrace them all in the wide circuit of his love. Therefore it is a marvellous agreement in which the *institution* of the Primacy has a corresponding *execution ;* and as the latter confirms the former, so from the former you might anticipate the latter before it was recorded in the sacred history.

But in the meantime, while the messengers of Cornelius were approaching the house in which Peter was a guest, "there came upon him an ecstasy of mind, and he saw the heaven opened, and a certain vessel descending, as it were a great linen sheet let down by the four corners from heaven to the earth, wherein were all manner of four-footed beasts, and creeping things of the earth, and fowls of the air " ; and while Peter is fixed in contemplation, " there came a voice to him, Arise, Peter, kill and eat," that he might understand how " by his preaching he was to make a sacrifice to the Lord of those who were represented by these animals, bringing them into the divine service through the mysteries of the Lord's passion," [1] which he not yet understanding, replies, " Far be

[1] Bede on this text.

it from me, for I never did eat anything that is
common or unclean ". Then the heavenly "voice
spoke to him again the second time, That which
God hath cleansed, do not thou call common.
And this having been done thrice, presently the
vessel was taken up into heaven."

Here three things are set forth : first, that as
the ark of Noah contained all sorts of animals,
clean and unclean, so the fold of Christ was to
gather from Jews and Greeks and barbarians "a
great multitude, which no man could number, of
all nations and tribes and peoples and tongues " ;[1]
secondly, that the blessings of Christ concerned all
who did not reject the proffered grace ; thirdly,
that the elaborate system of Mosaic ordinances
concerning meats, rites, and ceremonies, had fallen
to the ground. But to whom is disclosed, first and
immediately, this whole dispensation of the first
principles on which the Church was to be propagated ? To none other but Peter, " To me hath
God shown to call no man common or unclean ".
Now, the undoubted knowledge of this dispensation
must appear of the greatest moment, whether in
itself, or as concerns the Jews, of whom the earliest
Church consisted, or the Apostles, by whose
ministry it was to be extended. And yet, by that
providence which is ever over His Church, the
wisdom of God so ruled it that through Peter
alone the Apostles should be taught when they
were first to approach the Gentiles, and discharge
their office of witnesses before all nations without

[1] Apoc. vii. 9.

distinction. And that because He had made Peter
" the Greater one " and " the Leader " of all, and
put him in His own place, and constituted him
supreme teacher in these words, " Confirm thy
brethren ". Thus Epiphanius,[1] in the fourth
century, says that the charge of bringing the
Gentiles into the Church was laid upon all the
Apostles, " but most of all on holy Peter ".
Why this *most of all* ? Because, while he had
heard with the rest, " Make disciples of all
nations," he had singly and peculiarly received
the charge of the whole fold, and of the Apostles
as part of it.

But Peter, still pondering on the vision, hears a
fresh voice from the Spirit, " Behold, three men
seek thee. Arise, therefore, get thee down, and
go with them, doubting nothing, for I have sent
them." He accompanies the messengers and
finds Cornelius, " his kinsmen and his special
friends "; he asks why they have sent for him,
whereupon Cornelius informs him of what had
passed, and concludes, " Now therefore all we are
present in thy sight, to hear all things whatsoever
are commanded thee by the Lord ". Peter in
reply sets forth to them the heads of Christian
doctrine, and as he comes to the words " to Him
all the prophets gave testimony, that by His
name all receive remission of sins, who believe in
Him," " the Holy Ghost fell upon all them that
heard the word " of life and truth from his lips.
And the Jewish Christians who were with him,

[1] Hær. 28, s. 3.

being astonished at this reception of Gentiles into the Church by the Holy Spirit's visible descent, Peter cries, "Can any man forbid water, that these should not be baptized, who have received the Holy Ghost as well as we?" "Words," says St. Chrysostom,[1] "of one almost assaulting any that would forbid, and say that should not be," and so "he commanded them to be baptized in the name of the Lord Jesus"; for Peter also, like his Lord,[2] preached in person, but baptized by the hands of others.

Are not then the prerogatives of Peter written legibly on this whole narration? First, among all the Apostles he alone is chosen to consecrate to God the first-fruits of the Gentiles. Again, through him, as the teacher of all, God makes known to the Apostles themselves when the door was to be opened to the Gentiles. Thirdly, without advising with the rest, he enlarges the fold of Christ, which in Christ's place he ruled, with the accession of the Gentiles. Fourthly, the building of the Church is thus referred to him alone. Further, he gathers up to himself the Church which is made out of Jews, Samaritans, and Gentiles; as the foundation he sustains the whole; and when constructed, he binds it together. Lastly, Luke, without having recorded a single speech of any other Apostle, has given five of Peter, thus showing that Peter's words, as well as his actions, had a higher importance than theirs in the history of the Church's birth and growth;

---

[1] Hom. 24 on the Acts, n. 1.   [2] John iv. 2.

for, indeed, in the history of the head that of the body is included.

On Peter's[1] return to Jerusalem, "the Apostles and brethren who were in Judea, having heard that the Gentiles also had received the word of God,"[2] "they that were of the circumcision contended with him," because he had "gone in to men uncircumcised, and ate with them". Hereupon Peter set forth to them the whole series of events, upon which "they held their peace and glorified God, saying, God then has also to the Gentiles given repentance unto life". Now, some in late times have attempted to derogate from Peter's authority on the strength of this incident. On the other hand, St. Chrysostom, not satisfied with setting forth Peter's rank, and assigning his whole apology to a most gracious condescension, continues, "See how he defends himself, and *will not use his dignity as the Teacher*, for he knew that the more gently he spoke with them, the surer he was to win them".[3] And what expression can signify Peter's rank more markedly than *the Teacher*? And Gregory the Great sets forth Peter's distinctions, how he alone had received the keys, walked on the waters, healed with his shadow, killed with his word, and raised the dead by his prayer; then he goes on, "and because, warned by the Spirit, he had gone in to Cornelius, a Gentile, a question was raised against him by the faithful, as to wherefore he had gone in to the Gentiles, and eaten with them, and received them

---

[1] Passaglia, p. 181. [2] Acts xi. 1-4. [3] On Acts, Hom. 24, n. 2.

in baptism. And yet the same first of the Apostles, filled with so great a grace of gifts, supported by so great a power of miracles, answers the complaint of the faithful by an appeal not to authority but to reason. . . . For if, when blamed by the faithful, he had considered the authority which he held in holy Church, he might have answered, that the sheep entrusted to the shepherd should not venture to censure him. But if, in the complaint of the faithful, he had said anything of his own power, he would not have been the teacher of meekness. Therefore he quieted them with humble reason, and in the matter where he was blamed even cited witnesses. If, therefore, *the Pastor of the Church, the Prince of the Apostles*, having a *singular* power to do signs and miracles, did not disdain, when he was censured, humbly to render account, how much more ought we sinners, when blamed for anything, to disarm our censurers by a humble defence." [1]

Here it occurs to observe with what different eyes Holy Scripture may be read, for just where persons determined to deny Peter's authority find an excuse for their foregone conclusion, the Fathers draw arguments to praise the moderation with which he exercised that same superior authority.

V. But [2] founded as we have seen the Church to have hitherto been, and at each step of its course advanced, mainly by the authority of Peter, it could not hope to remain in a vigorous and

---

[1] Lib. 9, Ep. 39.   [2] Passaglia, p. 188.

united state without the continual exercise of *judicial* and *legislative* power, and diligent *inspection*. Nor is there, in fact, one of these which Peter did not exercise, and that in a manner to indicate the ruler set over all. For as to the judicial power, do we not hear him saying, "Tell[1] me whether you sold the land for so much"; and "Ananias, why hath Satan tempted thy heart, that thou shouldst lie to the Holy Ghost, and by fraud keep part of the price of the land? Whilst it remained did it not remain to thee? And after it was sold, was it not in thy power? Why hast thou conceived this thing in thy heart? Thou hast not lied to men but to God." And presently the sentence comes forth from him who binds in heaven as well as on earth. "Behold the feet of them who have buried thy husband are at the door, and they shall carry thee out." Here, then, we have Peter, in the midst of the Apostles, yet acting singly as the supreme judge, and defender of ecclesiastical discipline, on which St. Chrysostom says, "For Peter was terrible, punishing and convicting the thoughts, to whom they adhered the more both for the sign, and his first speech, and his second, and his third. For he it was who did the first sign, and the second, and the present, which seems to me double, one to convict the thoughts, and another to kill with his command." Then, asking why nobody had announced her husband's death to Sapphira, "This was fear of the Teacher; this

[1] Acts v. 8, 3.

respect of the disciples; this obedience ":[1] where he is mentioned not as *a* teacher, but the supreme and chief one.

Yet though the other Apostles were judges, with power to bind and to loose, though they were present, and concerned, for " Ananias bringing a certain part, laid it at the feet of the Apostles," not of Peter only, it was not they, but Peter, who entered on the cause of Ananias and Sapphira, passed sentence, and inflicted punishment. Why did he judge singly a cause which was brought before the common tribunal of the Apostles? Because Peter was to have the Primacy in all things; because from him the model of ecclesiastical judgments was to be taken; because the charge of maintaining ecclesiastical discipline belonged in chief to him as the head.

VI. But no less [2] markedly does Luke represent Peter as everywhere visiting the Churches, providing for them as universal pastor, and exercising herein the administrative Primacy. " The Churches," he says, " throughout all Judea, and Galilee, and Samaria, had peace, being edified and walking in the fear of the Lord, and were multiplied by the consolation of the Holy Ghost. And it came to pass *that Peter, as he passed through, visiting all*, came to the saints who dwelt at Lydda." [3] In illustration of this we may remember Paul's charge to Titus : [4] " For this cause I left thee in Crete, that thou shouldst set in order the things that are

---

[1] On Acts, Hom. 12.
[2] Passaglia, p. 190.
[3] Acts ix. 31.- 32
[4] Titus i. 5.

wanting, and shouldst ordain priests in every city, as I also appointed thee ". And again, what Luke writes of Paul himself: " After some days Paul said to Barnabas, Let us return and visit our brethren in all the cities wherein we have preached the word of the Lord, to see how they do ".[1] And what Eusebius,[2] from St. Clement, relates of St. John, that he visited with authority the Churches of Asia, which he had either founded, or specially attended to. By these passages we see the nature of Peter's visitation, that it was pastoral, and likewise the difference between his and these others, for they were *local*, but his *universal*. Titus acted in Crete, the special sphere of his labour, to which St. Paul the founder of that Church had appointed him. Paul and Barnabas propose to visit " our brethren *in every city in which we have preached the word of the Lord* " ; St. John exerts visitatorial power over the Churches of that province wherein he dwelt, and that too, apparently, when he was the sole survivor of the Apostolic college, yet did not go into other parts. But Peter's charge is œcumenical, and therefore his visitation universal. He inspects the labours of others, as well as his own. For he was not the only Apostle at Jerusalem, nor had he singly built up all the Churches of Judea, Galilee, and Samaria, yet he alone makes a progress from Jerusalem to all these Churches. Though not the Bishop of Jerusalem, over which the Apostle James presides, he goes everywhere, as

---

[1] Acts xv. 36.　　　　[2] Hist. Ecc. Lib. 3, ch. 2

"the Bishop of Bishops".[1] No other reason coherent with Scripture can we find for this universal inspection of Peter; for all the Apostles were indeed pastors, but he alone set over the whole fold; he alone not limited, like Paul, "to the brethren in every city wherein he had preached". He differs from all others as the universal from the particular, and so St. Chrysostom says of him in this very passage, "Like a general he went round surveying the ranks, seeing what portion was well massed together, what in order, what needed his presence. Behold him making his rounds in every direction." [2]

VII. Further,[3] we may see the deference paid to this supreme authority of Peter by the Apostles and Ancients at Jerusalem, on occasion of that severest dissension which threatened the unity of the Church, and kindled the greatest agitation, the question whether Gentile converts should be bound to obey the Mosaic ritual law. For "the [4] Apostles and Ancients having assembled to consider of this matter," after "there had been much disputing, Peter, rising up, said to them". But why does Peter first rise and decide the cause? Because he was first of the Apostles, and as such supreme arbiter in controversy. But consider what he says: "Men and brethren, you know that in former days God made choice among us, that by my mouth the Gentiles should hear the word of the Gospel, and believe". *By my mouth*, he appeals to

---

[1] So called by Arnobius, on Psalm cxxxviii.
[2] On Acts, Hom. 21, n. 2.   [3] Passaglia, p. 192.   [4] Acts xv. 6.

their knowledge of his election by God to the
singular privilege of receiving the Gentiles : in
virtue of that election he claims and exercises
authority. "And God, who knoweth the hearts,
gave testimony, giving unto them the Holy Ghost,
as well as unto us, and put no difference between
us and them, purifying their hearts by faith."
God, therefore, has already decided this controversy, by my ministry, whom He specially called
thereunto, and by the effects which He caused to
accompany it. Then, using words full of force,
being, indeed, very like those in which he had
answered to Ananias and Sapphira, he continues,
"Now, therefore, why tempt you God, to put a yoke
upon the neck of the disciples, which neither our
fathers, nor we, have been able to bear ? But by
the grace of our Lord Jesus Christ, we believe that
we shall be saved, in like manner as they also."
" How full of power are these words," is the comment of Chrysostom ; [1] " he says here what Paul
has said at great length in the Epistle to the
Romans." And then, speaking of the heads of
Paul's doctrine, he adds, " The seeds of all this lie
in Peter's discourse ". This, then, is a *decision*, and
given in no hesitating manner, but with severe
censure of those who maintained the opposite, as
" tempting God," words suitable for him only to
use who had authority over all. But how did the
Council receive them ? Though " there had been
much disputing before," though the keenest feelings had been excited, and the point involved the

[1] Hom. 32, n. 1.

strongest prepossessions of the Jewish converts, "all the multitude held their peace". They acquiesced in Peter's judgment, and now readily "heard Barnabas and Paul telling what great signs and wonders God had wrought among the Gentiles by them". It follows, then, that on a capital point, and in the first Council of the Church, Peter occupied a position which befits only the supreme judge of controversies, so that had we no other evidence but this place whereby to decide upon his rank and office, his pre-eminence would be evident. "See," says St. Chrysostom, "he first permits a discussion to arise in the Church, and then he speaks." [1]

But is this affected by other persons likewise speaking and voting, as Paul and Barnabas ? or by St. James likewise giving his sentence, as an Apostle ? or by the whole matter being settled by common consent ? As little as to be *head* involves being *all ;* as to preside over the rest takes from them the power of deliberation and resolution. Rather it is the office of the Head and the President to take the initiative, and point out the course which others are to follow.

For those here present were teachers, and had the prerogative of hearing and judging, as well as Peter ; they were bound to weigh the matter in controversy to the best of their power, and to decide on it according to the proportion of faith. They stood to Peter in a relation, not of simple obedience, as the ordinary members of the flock,

---

[1] Hom. 32, tom. ix. p. 250.

but of judges, who, though responsible to his
superintendence, yet are really judges, pass sentence, and decree by inherent authority. It is no
part of the idea of a judge, that he should be
supreme and irresponsible : this is the *special*
privilege of the one supreme judge. Objections
such as these, therefore, do not take from Peter
his Primacy, and quality of Head, but claim for
Paul, Barnabas, James, and other Apostles, the
judicial authority and office, which they undoubtedly possessed.

Nor again, that not Peter only, but all, passed
the decree in common, as it is written : " It
seemed good to the Holy Ghost, and to us " ; and
as Paul and Timothy " delivered to the cities the
decrees to keep that were decreed by the Apostles
and Ancients ". [1] For a decree made in common
by many shows not an equality of power in each,
but a competent authority to join in that decree.
Such acts proceed, not only from equal, but from
unequal assemblies. A question, therefore, terminated by common decision, and laws established
by common consent, do indeed prove a power to
deliberate and decree common to all participating,
but do not prove that all and every of the judges
were equal in their privileges, for who gives to the
Ancients the same authority as to the Apostles ?

This inequality is elsewhere established, and
rests on its own proof, but bearing it in mind, we
shall see that Peter is the first and chief author
of this common decree, and that laws passed by

[1] Acts xv. 28 ; xvi. 4.

common consent depend on him primarily as
Head. Most unsuspicious witnesses of this are
the ancient writers, and this is the very conclusion
which they drew from the account of this Council.
Thus, Tertullian, in the second century, speaking
of Peter's singular prerogatives, says, "On him
the Church was built, that is, through him: it was
he who hanselled the key. This is it. ' Ye men
of Israel, hear these words. Jesus of Nazareth, a
man approved of God among you,' etc. He, too,
first by Christian baptism opened the approach of
the heavenly kingdom, by which offences, hereto-
fore bound, are loosed, and those not loosed are
bound, according to true salvation. And Ananias
he bound with the chain of death : and him that
was weak in his feet he delivered from his disease.
But likewise, in that discussion as to maintaining
the law, Peter, first of all, instinct with the Spirit,
and preluding with the vocation of the Gentiles,
says, ' And now why tempt ye the Lord, by imposing a yoke on the brethren, which neither we
nor our fathers have been able to bear ? But by
the grace of Christ we believe that we shall be
saved, as also they.' *This* SENTENCE *both loosed what
was given up of the law and kept binding what was
reserved*."[1] As clearly, St. Jerome, in the fourth
century, writes, that Peter "used his wonted
freedom, and that the Apostle James *followed his
sentence,* and all the ancients at once *acceded to it,
and that the decree was drawn upon his wording* ".[2]

[1] De Pudicitia, c. 21.
[2] St. Jerome, Ep. 75, inter Augustinianas, tom. ii. p. 171.

A little later Theodoret wrote to St. Leo, thus:
" If Paul, the preacher of the truth, the trumpet
of the Holy Spirit, hastened to the great Peter,
to carry from him the solution to those at Antioch,
at issue about living under the law; much more
do we, poor and humble, run to your Apostolic
throne, to receive from you healing for the wounds
of the Churches ".[1] Why does he here call Peter
the *great*, or say that Paul hastened to him for solution of a grave contention ? Did not Paul go to
all the Apostles ? But Peter was the head among
them, and had a power in chief—a power above
the rest, a " more special " power—of binding and
loosing.

VIII. One other[2] instance there is of Peter's
superior dignity, and therefore importance, in the
Apostolic college, which if, perhaps, less direct
than some of the foregoing, is even more persuasive. For there was an Apostle associated,
as we have seen, by our Lord with Peter and John
in several favours not granted to the rest; one
who with John received from Him the name of
Boanerges; the elder brother of John, who with
him had once asked to sit on the Lord's right
hand and on His left in His kingdom. Now,
Luke is led in the course of his narrative to
mention the martyrdom of this great and favoured
Apostle; the first likewise of the Apostolic choir
who drank, as he had promised, of his Lord's
chalice, and sealed his labours and trials with his

---

[1] Theodoret, Ep. 113, tom. iii. p. 984.
[2] Passaglia, p. 197.

blood. The occasion was a great and striking
one. It is thus recorded by Luke: "And at the
same time Herod the King stretched forth his
hands to afflict some of the Church. And he
killed James, the brother of John, with the sword."
This is the first and the last time that he is
mentioned by himself in Luke's inspired history
of the universal Church. Great as he was, so
eminently favoured by his Lord, the elder brother
of John, nothing is said of the Church's anxiety
for his danger, her prayers for his release, her
sorrow at his loss, or her exultation at his triumph
by witnessing unto blood. He passed to his
throne in heaven with this short record. The
more emphatic is the contrast following. "And
seeing that it pleased the Jews, he proceeded to
take up Peter also. Now it was in the days of the
azymes. And when he had apprehended him, he
cast him into prison, delivering him to four files
of soldiers to be kept, intending after the pasch to
bring him forth to the people. Peter therefore
was kept in prison. *But prayer was made without
ceasing by the Church unto God for him.*" That is,
by the instinct of self-preservation she prayed for
her head. A few years later another Apostle, after
glorious labours by land and sea, and missions of
unrivalled success, was seized and imprisoned in
this same city of Jerusalem, and in danger of his
life. But we do not hear of prayers being offered
up without ceasing even for Paul, the doctor of
the nations. The Church's safety was not bound
up with his, any more than with that of James,

and therefore not even of the great preacher " in
labours more abundant than all," are we told that
in the hour of danger "prayer was made without
ceasing by the Church unto God for him ". James
and Paul were most distinguished *members*, but
Peter was more. This was an honour reserved
for the Head alone, as the life of the Head was
peculiarly precious to the whole body. Thus St.
Chrysostom explains it : " The prayer is a proof
of affection : they all sought for a Father, a kind
Father ".[1] And then Luke proceeds to give at
length Peter's delivery out of prison by the angel,
and his departure in safety to another place. But
there is no other solution of such a difference in
recording what happened alike to James, to Peter,
and to Paul, but that Peter held the place of father
in the Lord's family, of commander in His army,
of steward in His household, delivering to each of
His servants their measure of wheat in due season.

The result,[2] then, of our particular inquiry in
the Acts is to demonstrate two things, that Peter
discharged the office of Father and Head in the
Lord's family, and that the Church received and
admitted him when so acting, with a consciousness
that such was the will of Christ.

Now, this office did not consist in "lording it "
over his brethren, in assuming high titles, and
interfering with the ministry of others when exercised in its due course, in rejecting their assistance,
or impeding the unanimous exercise of their counsel.
On the contrary, the Lord had before prescribed

[1] On Acts, Hom. 26, n. 2.   [2] Passaglia, p. 198.

that "the greater" among them should be as the younger, and "the leader" as he that ministers, proposing to them Himself as the great model, who had exercised the highest power with the utmost gentleness, and, being, "the Lord," had become "the servant of all". What, then, did this office of Primate consist in? We must say that Peter was undoubtedly such, if he constantly exercised the power of a head in building up the Church, in maintaining discipline, in reconciling dissensions, and in general administration. Now, it would be doing Peter wrong to suppose that he usurped as peculiar to himself what equally belonged to all the Apostles; or that, having received the special power of the Holy Ghost, he did not fulfil his own advice to others, "not to lord it over the clergy, but to be made a pattern of the flock".[1] And the four points just mentioned may be reduced to a triple authority, a Primacy *magisterial, judicial*, and *legislative*. Let us take in at one glance what has been said of Peter in regard to each of these.

As to the *magisterial*, or power of authoritative teaching, and general administration, Peter is constantly taking the lead, he is the mouthpiece of the Apostles: he alone, or he first, by teaching plants the Churches; he alone, or he in chief, completes them when planted; he it is who by divine revelation given to himself, discloses to the rest the dispensation of God; and he in words full of power sets forth to these assembled in council the course which they are to pursue.

[1] 1 Pet. v. 3.

As to the *judicial*, none other judgments are found in that portion of the Acts which contains the history of the whole Church, save those of which he was either the *sole* or the *chief* author. Alone he took cognizance of Ananias and Sapphira, and alone he punished them. And Simon he censured in chief, and excommunicated.

As to the *legislative*, Peter alone promulgated the law as to receiving the Gentiles; alone he pre-scribed that for abrogating the Mosaic ceremonial ordinances; and he was the chief author of the decree which expressed in terms his own previous act, and was put forth in common by the Apostles and Ancients.[1]

Again, compare the *institution* of the Primacy with its *exercise*. Its institution consisted in three things: 1. That Peter was named by Christ the foundation of the Church, with whom its whole fabric was most intimately to cohere, and from whom it should derive visible unity and impregnable strength; 2. That the authority of universal pastor, and the care of the whole fold, was committed to him; 3. That to him belonged the confirmation of his brethren, and a power of the keys to which all were subject. Now consider the execution.

As foundation of the Church, he gathers up to himself congregations from the Jews, the Samaritans, and the Gentiles.

As universal pastor, he collects from these

---

[1] " Princeps hujus fuit decreti," says St. Jerome to St. Augus-tine, Ep. 75, n. 8, inter Augustinianas.

three the flock, nourishes, defends, inspects it,
and fills up one place of highest rank in the
ministry forfeited by the traitor.

As confirmer of the brethren, he disclosed to
them the heavenly vision signifying the universal
calling of the Gentiles, and the abrogation of the
Mosaic law. He acts in the Lord's household as
the bearer of the keys, going to all parts, defending
and inspecting all. By himself he binds and looses,
calling Ananias and Sapphira to his tribunal, and
excommunicating the first heretic.

So exactly, then, do the institution of the
Primacy and the acts of Peter fit into each other,
that from the former you may predict the latter,
and from the latter prove the former. They are
like cause and effect, or an *a priori* and an *a
posteriori* argument. They are a reciprocal confirmation to each other ; just as if by time you
calculate the sun's rising, and see the diffusion
of his light, from his having risen you infer his
light, and from his light conclude that he has
risen.

Nor in the Apostolic Church does any one
appear to resist or question this office of Peter.
Rather upon him all eyes are fixed, for him all
are anxious ; no Abiram rises up against him with
the words of rebellion : " Thou takest too much
upon thee, seeing all the congregation are holy,
every one of them, and the Lord is among them :
wherefore then liftest thou up thyself above the
congregation of the Lord ? " [1]   No Aaron in a

---

[1] Num. xvi. 3 ; xii. 2,

moment of delusion cries, " Did the Lord speak by
Moses only ? hath He not spoken also by us ? "

Yet Peter acts not like one out of a number, and
occasions of contention are not wanting, strong
prepossessions and keen feelings.[1]   He is everywhere; his pre-eminence and his control are
universal : he can act with severity, and there are
some impatient even of a just control.   When
Ananias and Sapphira fell dead at his feet, none
murmured.   When he exclaimed, in full council,
" Now, therefore, why tempt you God ?" the
whole multitude was silent.   When he explained
the reception of the Gentiles, those who had murmured " held their peace, and glorified God ".[2]

But had Peter not possessed, by divine commission, the authority which he exercised, it is
clear, from the conduct of Paul, that he would
have met with opposition from each in proportion
to his advance in Christian perfection.   Paul's
censure of his indulgence to the prejudices of the
circumcision, proceeding as it did from charity,
shows this.   But what would Paul, and what
would the other Apostles have done, had they seen
Peter perpetually taking the lead, and exercising
the power of a head, without any special title
thereto ?   Would they not have resisted him to
the face, and before all, and declared that there was
no difference of authority between them ?   Yet, not
a trace of such resistance appears, while on number-
less occasions the Apostles, and the whole assembly
of the faithful, yield to him the Primacy, a sign truly

---

[1] Acts vi. 1; xv. 2; xi. 2.   [2] Acts xi. 18.

that they recognized in him one who had received
the place of Christ as visible Head among them.

The place of Christ *as visible Head*, for infinite
indeed is the distance between Christ and Peter,
as to the headship of mystical influx and the
source of grace. Neither he nor any creature has
part with Christ as to this latter, of which Paul
writes, "that God had set all things under His
feet, and given Him to be Head over all to the
Church, which is His body, the fulness of Him
who filleth all in all"; of which again, "from
whom the whole body, being compacted and fitly
joined together, by what every joint supplieth,
according to the operation in the measure of every
part maketh increase of the body, unto the edifying
of itself in charity"; and "the husband is the head
of the wife, as Christ is the head of the Church,
and He is the Saviour of His body": and all this
"to present it to Himself a glorious Church, not
having spot or wrinkle or any such thing".[1]   In
this sense Headship belongs to Christ, not only
first and chiefly, but absolutely and solely. But
as to the Headship of external government and
visible unity, though here also the same Apostle
calls Him, "the head of the body the Church, who
is the beginning, the first-born from the dead;
that in all things He may hold the primacy,"[2] to
this Christ Himself has in a measure associated
Peter by saying to him specially, "Feed My sheep
—follow thou Me".

And observe how that divine injunction was ful-

---

[1] Eph. i. 22; iv. 15; v. 23, 27.   [2] Col. i. 18.

filled. For as, following our Lord with loving gaze through the Gospels, we see every object grouped about that heavenly figure of His; as our eyes rest ever upon Him in the synagogue, in the market-place, among the crowd, before the Pharisees, the elders, the chief priests, healing the sick, raising the dead, supporting and animating His disciples —so turning to the Acts we see a human copy indeed of that divine portrait, but still one wrought by the Holy Spirit out of our redeemed flesh and blood. We see the fervent Apostle treading in his Master's steps, the centre and the support of his brethren, the first before the Council and before the people, ready with his words and his deeds, uttering to the dead, as the echo of his Lord, "Arise," and healing the sick with his shadow. With reason, then, do the inspired writers use of Peter and of Christ similar forms of speech, and as they write, "Jesus and His disciples," "there went with Him His disciples," "there He abode with His disciples," so they write, "Peter standing up with the Eleven," "they said to Peter and to the rest of the Apostles," "Peter and the Apostles answering". What above all is remarkable is to observe the same *proportion* between the figure of Peter and the Apostles in the first twelve chapters of the Acts, as between the figure of our Lord and the Apostles in the Gospel. Such was the power and the will of the Divine Master when He said, "Feed My sheep; follow thou Me". Such the truth of the disciple, answering, "Lord, Thou knowest all things, Thou knowest that I love Thee".

CHAPTER VI.

TESTIMONY OF ST. PAUL TO ST. PETER'S PRIMACY.

IN leaving the Gospels and the Acts we quit those writings in which we should expect, beforehand, that divine government to be set forth, which it pleased our Lord to establish for His Church. In exact accordance with such expectation we have seen the institution of the Apostolic College, and of St. Peter's Primacy over it, described in the Gospels, and the history in the Acts of its execution and practical working. Both institution and execution have been complete in their parts, and wonderfully harmonious with each other. But in the other inspired writings of the New Testament, comprising the letters of various Apostles, and specially St. Paul, we had no reason to anticipate any detailed mention of Church government. The fourteen Epistles of St. Paul were written incidentally on different subjects, no one of them leading him to set forth, with any exact specification, that divine hierarchy under which it was the pleasure of the Lord that His Church should grow up. Moreover, it so happened that[1] the circumstances of St. Paul's calling to be an Apostle, and the opposition which he some-

[1] Passaglia, p. 206.

times met with from those attached to Jewish usages, caused him to be a great defender of the Apostolic dignity, as bestowed upon himself, and continually to assert that he received it not of men, but of God.   Had there, then, been no recognition at all of St. Peter's superior rank in the Apostolic College to be found in his writings, it would not have caused surprise to those who consider the above reasons.   And proportionably strong and effective is the recognition of that rank, which, though incidental, does occur, and that several times.   If, then, St. Paul, being so circumstanced, selected expressions which seem to indicate a distinction of dignity between the Apostles and St. Peter, they claim a special attention, and carry a double force.   Now, on putting these together, we shall find that they show not merely a distinction of dignity, but a superior authority in Peter.

The first are four several passages in the first Epistle to the Corinthians, in all of which St. Peter holds the higher place, and in two is moreover mentioned singly, whilst the rest are mentioned only in mass.   These are the following: "Now this I say, that every one of you saith, I indeed am of Paul; and I of Apollo; and I of Cephas; and I of Christ".   Again: "All things are yours, whether it be Paul, or Apollo, or Cephas, or the world, or life, or death, or things present, or things to come, for all are yours, and you are Christ's, and Christ is God's".   Again: "Have we not power to carry about a woman, a sister, as well as the rest of the Apostles, and the brethren of the Lord, and Cephas?" And once more: "That He was seen by Cephas, and after that by the eleven".[1] First, we may remark that the place of dignity in a sentence varies[2] according to its nature : if it *descends*, such place is the first ; but if it *ascends*, it is the farthest point from the first. Now in the first instance the discourse ascends, for what can be plainer than that it terminates in Christ, as in the supreme point? "Every one of you saith, I indeed am of Paul, and I of Apollo, and I of Cephas, and I of Christ;" so St. Chrysostom observes, " It was not to prefer himself before Peter that he set him last, but to prefer Peter even greatly before himself. For he speaks in the ascending scale:" and Theodoret, "They called themselves from different teachers : now he mentioned his own name and that of Apollo ; but he adds also the name of the chief of the Apostles ".[3] As plain is this in the second instance, where St. Paul, developing his thought, " all things are yours," adds, " whether Paul, or Apollo, or Cephas," or if that be not sufficient, "the world" itself, which, carried away in a sort of transport, he seems to divide into its parts, "or life, or death, or things present, or things to come, all," I repeat, "are yours": but only, you are not your own, "you are Christ's, and Christ is God's". In all which, from human

---

[1] 1 Cor. i. 12 ; iii. 22 ; ix. 5 ; xv. 5.

[2] Passaglia, pp. 124-126.

[3] St. Chrys. in 1 Cor. Hom. 3, n. 2. Theodoret on text.

instruments, who plant and water, he rises up to God, the ultimate source, the beginning and the end. Stronger yet is the third passage, for being in the very act of setting forth the dignity of his own Apostolate, " Have we not power," he says, "to lead about a sister, a woman, as well as the rest of the Apostles, and the brethren of the Lord, and Cephas?" Now, whether "the rest of the Apostles" here means those who in the looser signification are so called, as " the Apostles of the Churches," and "Andronicus and Junias—who are of note among the Apostles," [1] or the original Twelve, the ascending scale is equally apparent. For why is Peter distinguished by name from all the rest? Why alone termed by his prophetical name? St. Chrysostom, again, tells us why. " Look at Paul's wisdom. *He puts the chief the last. For there he puts that which was strongest among the principal. For it was not so remarkable to show the rest doing this, as him that was chief, and had been entrusted with the keys of heaven.* But he puts not him alone, but all, as if he would say, whether you look for inferiors, or superiors, you have examples of all. For the brethren of the Lord, being delivered from their first unbelief,[2] were among the principal, though they had not reached the height of Apostles, and, therefore, he put them in the middle, with the highest on the two sides :"[3] words in which he seems to indicate that Peter was as excellent among the Apostles,

---

[1] 2 Cor. viii. 23 ; Rom. xvi. 7.   [2] John vii. 5.
[3] In 1 Cor. Hom. 21, n. 2.

as they among the rest of the disciples, and the Lord's brethren.

Of the superiority contained in the fourth passage, we have spoken above, under another head, and therefore proceed to much more remarkable testimonies of St. Paul.

In the Epistle to the Galatians, St. Paul has occasion[1] to defend his Apostolic authority, and the agreement of the Gospel which he had preached with that of the original Apostles. After referring to his marvellous conversion, he continues, "immediately I condescended not to flesh and blood; neither went I to Jerusalem to the Apostles, who were before me, but I went into Arabia, and again I returned to Damascus. Then, after three years, I went to Jerusalem, to visit Peter, and I tarried with him fifteen days. But other of the Apostles I saw none, saving James, the brother of the Lord." At length, then, St. Paul goes to Jerusalem, and that with a fixed purpose, "to visit Peter". But why Peter only, and not the rest of the Apostles, and the brethren of the Lord?[2] Why speaks he of these, and of James himself besides, as if he would intimate that he had little care of seeing them? No other answer can be given to such queries than is shadowed out in the prophetic name of Peter, and contained in the explanation of it given by Christ Himself, "Upon this Rock I will build My Church".

For, to prove this, let us go back once more to

---

[1] Passaglia, p. 208.   [2] Gal. i. 16-19.

witnesses beyond suspicion, who wrote a thousand
years before the denial of Peter's Primacy began.
The Greek and Latin Fathers see here a recognition of his chief authority. Thus Theodoret,
" Not needing doctrines from man, as having received it from the God of all, he gives the fitting
honour to the chief ". Theodoret follows St.
Chrysostom, who had said, " After so many great
deeds, needing nothing of Peter, nor of his instruction, but being his equal in rank, for I will say no
more here, still he goes up to him as to the greater
and elder " ; his equal in the Apostolic dignity,
and the immediate reception of his authority from
Christ, but yet his inferior in the range of his
jurisdiction, Peter being " greater and elder ".
And he goes on, " He went but for this alone, to
see him and honour him by his presence. He
says, I went up to visit Peter. He said not to *see*
Peter, but to *visit* Peter, as they say in becoming
acquainted with great and illustrious cities. So
much pains he thought it worth only to see the
man." And he concludes, " This I repeat, and
would have you remember, lest you should suspect
the Apostle, on hearing anything which seems said
against Peter. For it was for this that he so
speaks, correcting by anticipation, that when he
shall say, I resisted Peter, no one may think these
words of enmity and contention. For he honours
the man, and loves him more than all. For he
says that he came up for none of the Apostles,
save him." Elsewhere, St. Chrysostom, commenting on the charge, Feed My sheep, asks, " Why,

then, passing by the rest, does He converse with him (Peter) on these things?" And he replies, Peter " was the one preferred among the Apostles, and the mouthpiece of the disciples, and the head of the band : *therefore*, too, Paul then went up to visit him *rather than the rest*".[1] Tertullian, the most ancient of the Latins, says, " Then, as he relates himself, he went up to Jerusalem for the purpose of becoming acquainted with Peter, that is, according to duty, and the claim of their identical faith and preaching ":[2] the *duty* which Paul had to Peter; the *claim* which Peter had on Paul. In the fourth century, Marius Victorinus observes : " After three years, says he, I came to Jerusalem ; then he adds the cause, to see Peter. For if the foundation of the Church was laid in Peter, as is said in the Gospel, Paul, to whom all things had been revealed, knew that he was *bound* to see Peter, as one to whom so great an authority had been given by Christ, not to learn anything from him."[3] The writer called Ambrosiaster, as his works are attached to those of St. Ambrose, and contemporary with Pope Damasus (A.D. 366-384), remarks, " It was proper that he should desire to see Peter, because he was first among the Apostles, to whom the Saviour had committed the care of the Churches ". St. Jerome, more largely, says, " Not to behold his eyes, his cheeks, or his countenance, whether he were thin or stout, with

---

[1] Theodoret and Chrysostom on the text, and on John, Hom. 88.   [2] De Præsc. c. 23.

[3] Comm. in Gal. i. 18.   Mai nova collectio, tom. 3.

nose straight or twisted, covered with hair, or as Clement, in the Periods, will have it, bald.   It was not, I conceive, in the gravity of an Apostle, that after so long as three years' preparation, he could wish to see anything human in Peter.   But he gazed on him with those eyes with which now he is seen in his own letters.   Paul saw Cephas with eyes such as those with which all wise men now look on Paul.   If any one thinks otherwise, let him join all this with the sense before indicated, that the Apostles contributed nothing to each other. For even in that he seemed to go to Jerusalem, in order that he might see the Apostle, it was not to learn, as having himself too the same author of his preaching, but *to show honour to the first Apostle.*" [1]   Our own St. Thomas sums up all these in saying, " The doctor of the Gentiles, who boasts that he had learnt the Gospel, not of man, nor through man, but instructed by Christ, went up to Jerusalem, conferred concerning the faith *with the head of the Churches*, lest perchance he might run, or had run, in vain ". [2]

These last words lead us attentively to consider the passage which follows in St. Paul.   At a subsequent period the zealots of the law had raised against him a report that the Gospel which he preached differed from that of the Twelve.   At once to meet and silence such a calumny, he tells us that " after fourteen years, I went up again to Jerusalem, with Barnabas, taking Titus also with

[1] Ambrosiaster and St. Jerome on the text.
[2] St. Thomas Cant. Epist. lib. i. 97.

me. And I went up according to revelation, and," assigning the particular purpose, " conferred with them the Gospel which I preach among the Gentiles, but apart with them who seemed to be something ; lest, perhaps, I should run, or had run, in vain ". Then, having proved the identity of his doctrine with that of those who "seemed to be something," that is, Peter, James, and John, though to him they "added nothing," he specifies Peter among these, and proceeds to draw a singular parallel between, on the one hand, Peter, as accompanied by James and John, and himself, as working with Barnabas and Titus. If we set the clauses over against each other,.this will be more apparent.

When they had seen that to me was committed the Gospel of the uncircumcision,	as to Peter was that of the circumcision ;
For He who wrought in Peter, to the Apostleship of the circumcision,	wrought in me also among the Gentiles ;
James, [1] and Cephas, and John, who seemed to be pillars,	gave to me and Barnabas the right hands of fellowship ;

[1] An argument has been drawn by some against St. Peter's Primacy from St. Paul here placing St. James first. Now as to this we must remark that some most ancient manuscripts, and the original Latin version, read " Peter, and James, and John," and that this is'followed by Tertullian, Chrysostom, Ambrose, Ambrosiaster, Augustine, Theodoret, Jerome, Irenæus, Gregory of Nyssa, and Cassiodorus, of whom Jerome is the more important, in that he had studied so many ancient commentaries before writing his own. But supposing that the vulgar reading is the true one, Peter's being once placed by St. Paul between St. James and St. John will not counterbalance the vast positive evidence for his Primacy. Those who wish to see the probable reasons why

where it would appear that James and John stand in the like relation to Cephas, as Barnabas and Titus, just before mentioned, to Paul. And St. Chrysostom, who, it must be remarked, reads Cephas, and not James, first, as do some manuscripts and many Fathers, observes, " Where it was requisite to compare himself, he mentions Peter only, but where to call a testimony, he names three together, and with praise, saying, ' Cephas, and James, and John, who seemed to be pillars ' ". And further, Paul " shows himself to be of the same rank with them, and matches himself not with the rest, but with the leader, showing that each of them enjoyed the same dignity," [1] that is, of the Apostolic commission, and the divine co-operation. And Ambrosiaster explains the parallel : " Paul names Peter only, and compares him to himself, as having received the Primacy *for the founding of the Church*, he being in like manner elected to hold a Primacy *in founding the Churches of the Gentiles*, yet so that Peter, if occasion might be, should preach to the Gentiles, and Paul to the Jews. For both are found to have done both." And presently, " By the Apostles who were the more illustrious among the rest, whom for their stability he names pillars, and who were ever in

St. James was here placed first, may consult Passaglia, b. 1, c. 14, who treats of the question at length. Perhaps St. Paul, narrating historically a past incident, recalled them to his recollection *in the order of time* in which they received him : and St. James, residing constantly at Jerusalem, might very probably have seen him first.

[1] St. Chrys. in Gal. c. 2.

the Lord's secret council, being worthy to behold His glory on the mount " (here Ambrosiaster confuses James the brother of the Lord, with James the brother of John), " by these he declares to have been approved the gift which he received from God, that he should be worthy to hold the Primacy in the preaching of the Gentiles, as Peter held it in the preaching of the circumcision. *And as he assigns to Peter for companions distinguished men among the Apostles, so he joins Barnabas to himself: yet he claims to himself alone the grace of the Primacy as granted by God, like as to Peter alone it was granted among the Apostles.*" [1]

Now, Baronius proves that the above words cannot be taken of a division of jurisdiction, and that the singular dignity of Peter is marked in them. " For as a mark of his excellence Christ Himself, who came to save all men, with whom there is no distinction of Jew and Greek, was yet called ' minister of the circumcision,' by Paul (Rom. xv. 8), a title of dignity, according to Paul's own words, for theirs was ' the adoption of children, and the glory, and the testament, and the giving of the law, and the service of God, and the promises,' while ' the Gentiles praise God for His mercy '. But just as Christ our Lord was so called minister of the circumcision, as yet to be the Pastor and Saviour of all, so Peter too was called the minister of the circumcision, in such sense as yet to be by the Lord constituted (Acts ix. 32) pastor and ruler of the whole flock. Whence St. Leo, ' Out of the

---

[1] Comm. on Gal. ii. 7, 8.

whole world Peter alone is chosen to preside over
the calling of all the Gentiles, and over all the
Apostles and the collected Fathers of the Church,
so that though there be among the people of God
many priests and many shepherds, yet Peter rules
all by immediate commission, whom Christ also
rules by sovereign power '." [1]

The parallel, then, drawn by Paul between himself and Peter, distinctly conveys that as he was
superior to Barnabas and Titus, and used their co-
operation, so was Peter among the Apostles, and
specially the chief ones, James and John, as their
leader and head.   For what is the meaning of the
words, " He who wrought in Peter to the Apostleship of the circumcision " ?   Was the Apostleship
of the circumcision entrusted to Peter only ?   It
needs no proof that it was also entrusted to James
and John, nay, Paul himself immediately says so :
" They gave to me and Barnabas the right hands
of fellowship, that *we* should go unto the Gentiles,
and *they* unto the circumcision ".   Why, then, does
Paul so express himself as to intimate that the
Gospel of the circumcision was given to Peter
only ?   For the same reason that he said that to
himself " was committed the Gospel of the uncircumcision," and that God " wrought in me also
among the Gentiles ".   Now Barnabas likewise had
been separated [2] by the Holy Ghost Himself for
the Gentile mission ; Barnabas, too, and Titus
were discharging the office of ambassadors for

[1] Baron. Ann. A.D. 51, § 29.   St. Leo, Serm. 4.
[2] Acts xiii. 2.

Christ among the Gentiles: "that *we*," Paul says, not I, "should go to the Gentiles". The terms, therefore, used by Paul both of himself and Peter, do not *exclude* the rest, but express the *superiority* of the one named singly before the rest, as if he alone held the charge. Their fittest interpretation, then, will be, "The Apostles saw that the Gospel of the uncircumcision was no less given to me *above* the rest, than the Gospel of the circumcision to Peter *above* the rest; for He who wrought in Peter *above* the rest in the Gospel of the circumcision, wrought also in me *above* the rest in the Gospel of the uncircumcision". But what can set forth St. Peter's dignity more remarkably, than to exhibit him in the same light of superiority among the original Apostles, as St. Paul was among St. Barnabas and his other fellow-workers?

Further confirmation of this is given by the argument with which he refutes the calumny urged against him of disagreement with the Apostles. For while he appeals to them *in general*, and to his union with them, he likewise *specifies* the point which favoured that union. It was the parallel between himself and Peter, as we have seen; it was the exact resemblance between his mission and that of Peter, which was the cause of their joining hands: they approve Paul's Apostleship because they see that it follows the type of Peter's.

And other words of Paul which follow, prove not only the point of his own cause, but the source of Peter's singular privileges. "But when Cephas was come to Antioch, I withstood him to the face,

Gal. 2: 11-21

because he was to be blamed : for before that some came from James, he did eat with the Gentiles ; but when they were come he withdrew, and separated himself, fearing them who were of the circumcision. And to his dissimulation the rest of the Jews consented, so that Barnabas also was led by them into that dissimulation. But when I saw that they walked not uprightly unto the truth of the Gospel, I said to Cephas before them all, If thou, being a Jew, livest after the manner of the Gentiles, and not as the Jews do, how dost thou compel the Gentiles to live as the Jews ? " For why did Paul here censure Peter *only ?* By his own account not only Peter, but the rest, and Barnabas himself amongst them, set apart as he was by the Holy Ghost to preach to the Gentiles, did not defend Christian liberty, as they ought to have done. Why, then, does he single out Peter among all these, resist him to the face, and so firmly censure all, in his person ? No answer can be given but one : that by this dissembling of Peter the zealots of the law gathered double courage to press against Paul their calumny of dissension from Peter, and to infer that he had run in vain, from the indulgence which Peter showed ; that Peter's authority with all was so great that his example drew the pastors and their flocks alike to his side, and that it was requisite to correct the members in the head. From this St. Chrysostom proves that it was really the Apostle Peter, which some, as we shall soon see, denied : " For to say, that I resisted him to the

face, and to put this as a great thing, was to show
that he had not reverenced the dignity of his
person. But had he said it of another, that I
resisted him to the face, he would not have put it
as a great thing. Again, if it had been another
Peter, his change would have not had such force
as to draw the rest of the Jews with him. For he
used no exhortation, nor advice, but merely dis-
sembled, and separated himself, and that dissembling and separation had power to draw after
him all the disciples, *on account of the dignity of his
person.*" [1]   Again, another writer of the fourth
century tells us this : " Therefore he inveighs
against Peter alone, in order that the rest might
learn in the person of him who is the first ".[2]   It
was, then, Peter's Primacy, and the necessity of
agreeing with him thence arising, which led Paul
to resist him publicly, and disregarding the conduct of the rest, to direct an admonition to him
alone.   " So great," St. Jerome tells us, on these
two passages, " was Peter's authority, that Paul
in his epistle wrote, ' Then after three years I
went to Jerusalem to see Peter, and I tarried with
him fifteen days '.   And again in what follows,
' After fourteen years I went up again to Jerusalem
with Barnabas, taking Titus also with me.   And
I went up according to revelation, and conferred
with them the Gospel which I preach among the
Gentiles,' *showing that he had no security in preaching*

---

[1] Hom. on " I resisted him to the face," n. 15.
[2] Ambrosiaster on Gal. ii. 14.

the Gospel, unless it were confirmed by the sentence of Peter, and those who were with him." [1]

But this passage,[2] concerning the reprehension of St. Peter by St. Paul, has afforded so signal an instance "of the unlearned and unstable wresting Scripture to their own proper destruction,"[3] that we must dwell a little longer upon it. First, the Gnostics and the Marcionites quoted it to accuse the Apostles of ignorance, and to favour their own claim to a progressive light. In Peter, they would have it, there was still a taint of Judaism. Next Porphyry, who "raged against Christ like a mad dog,"[4] tried by this passage to weaken the authority of the Apostles, and to convict Paul of ambition and rashness, who censured the first of the Apostles and the leader of the band, not privately, but openly before all, as St. Chrysostom and St. Jerome tell us. Julian the Apostate succeeded these, and tried, by means of Paul's contention with Peter, to bring discredit on the religion itself. For who, he asked, could value a religion whose chief teachers were guilty of hypocrisy, ignorance, and ambition? And in complete accordance with the spirit of these, all, who, since the sixteenth century, have attempted to impugn St. Peter's prerogatives, have rested their chief effort on the exaggeration and distortion of this reprehension. "This," says Baronius, "is the stone of stumbling and rock of offence, on which a great number have dashed

---

[1] Epist. inter Augustin. 75, n. 8.
[2] Passaglia, p. 217.   [3] 2 Pet. iii. 16.   [4] St. Jerome.

themselves. For those, who without any diligent consideration have superficially interpreted a difficult statement, have gone so far in their folly as either to accuse Paul of rashness for having inveighed against Peter not merely with freedom, but wantonness, or to calumniate Peter as a hypocrite, for acting with dissimulation; or to condemn both, for not agreeing in the same rule of faith."[1]

In most remarkable contrast with these stand out three several interpretations, which prevailed in early times, all differing from each other in points, but all equally careful to maintain the dignity of Peter, and to clear up the conduct of Paul. First, from St. Clement of Alexandria in the second century up to St. Chrysostom in the fourth, we find a number of Greek writers asserting that it was not the Apostle Peter, who was here meant, but another; St. Jerome gives their reasons thus: "There are those who think that Cephas, whom Paul here writes that he resisted to the face, was not the Apostle Peter, but another of the seventy disciples so called, and they allege that Peter could not have withdrawn himself from eating with the Gentiles, for he had baptized Cornelius the centurion, and on his ascending to Jerusalem, being opposed by those of the circumcision who said, 'Why hast thou entered in to men uncircumcised, and eaten with them?' after narrating the vision, he terminates his answer thus: 'If, then, God hath given to them the same

[1] Ad. Ann. 51, § 32.

grace as to us who believe on the Lord Jesus
Christ, who was I that I should withstand God ? '
On hearing which they were silent, and glorified
God, saying : ' Therefore to the Gentiles, also,
God hath given repentance unto life '. Especially
as Luke, the writer of the history, makes no
mention of this discussion, nor even says that
Peter was at Antioch with Paul ; and occasion
would be given to Porphyry's blasphemies, *if we
could believe either that Peter had erred, or that Paul
had impertinently censured the prince of the Apostles.*"[1]

But this interpretation, contrary both to internal
evidence and to early tradition, and suggested
only by the anxiety to defend St. Peter's dignity,
did not prevail. Another succeeded, supported by
St. Chrysostom, St. Cyril, and the greatest Greek
commentators, and for a long time by St. Jerome,
even more remarkably opposed to the apparent
sense of the passage, and only, as it would seem,
dictated by the same desire to defend the dignity
of St. Peter, and the conduct of St. Paul.
Admitting that it was really Peter who was here
mentioned, they maintained that it was not a real
dissension between the two Apostles, but apparent
only, and arranged both by the one and the other,
to terminate the question more decidedly. St.
Chrysostom[2] sets forth at great length this
opinion : " Do you see," says he, " how St. Paul
accounts himself the least of all saints, not of

---

[1] St. Jerome on Gal., ch. ii.

[2] Homily on the text " I resisted him to the face," n. 8, tom.
iii. p. 368.

Apostles only? Now, he who was so disposed with respect to all, both knew how great a prerogative Peter ought to enjoy, and reverenced him most of all men, and was disposed towards him as he deserved. And this is a proof. The whole earth was looking to Paul; there rested on his spirit the solicitude for the Churches of all the world. A thousand matters engaged him every day; he was besieged with appointments, commands, corrections, counsels, exhortations, teachings, the administration of endless business; yet giving up all these, he went to Jerusalem. And there was no other occasion for this journey save to see Peter, as he says himself: 'I went up to Jesusalem to visit Peter'. Thus he honoured him, and preferred him to all men." Suspecting, too, that an accusation against Peter's unwavering faith might be brought from the words, "fearing those of the circumcision," he breaks out, "What say you? Peter fearful and unmanly? Was he not for this called Peter, that his faith was immovable? What are you doing, friend? Reverence the name given by the Lord to the disciple. Peter fearful and unmanly! Who will endure you saying such things?"

Now compare[1] together these two interpretations of the Greek Fathers with that of the reformers and their adherents since the sixteenth century. A more complete antagonism of feelings and principles cannot be conceived. I. There is not a Greek Father who does not infer the

[1] Passaglia, p. 232.

singular authority of Peter from the first and
second chapter of the Epistle to the Galatians.
There is not an adherent of the reformers who
does not trust that he can draw from those same
chapters matter to impugn St. Peter's Primacy.
II. The Greek Fathers anxiously search out every
point which may conduce to Peter's praise.   The
adherent of the reformers suppresses all such, and
seems not to see them.   III. If anything in Paul's
account seems at first sight to tell against Peter's
special dignity, the Greek Fathers are studious
carefully to remove it ; the adherents of the
reformers to exaggerate it.   IV. The Greek
Fathers prefer slightly to force the obvious meaning of the words, and to desert the original
interpretation rather than set Apostles at variance
with each other, or admit that Peter, the chief of
the Apostles, was not treated with due deference.
The adherents of the reformers intensify everything, take it in the worse sense, and are the more
at home the more bitterly they inveigh against
Peter.

Now turn to the third interpretation, that of the
Latin Fathers.   They admit both that it was
Peter and that it was a real dissension, but they
are as anxious as the Greek to defend Peter's
dignity.   Thus Tertullian:[1] "If Peter was blamed
—certainly it was a fault of *conduct*, not of
preaching".   And Cyprian:[2] "Not even Peter,
whom first the Lord chose, and upon whom He
built His Church, when afterwards Paul disagreed

---

[1] De Præsc. c. 24.   [2] Cyprian, Ep. 71.

with him respecting circumcision, claimed aught proudly, or assumed aught arrogantly to himself, saying that he held the Primacy, and that obedience rather was due to him by those younger and later ". And Augustine: " Peter himself received with the piety of a holy and benighted humility what was with advantage done by Paul in the freedom of charity. And so he gave to posterity a rarer and a holier example, that they should not disdain, if perchance they left the right track, *to be corrected even by their youngers*, than Paul, that even *inferiors* might confidently venture to resist *superiors*, maintaining brotherly charity, in the defence of evangelical truth. For better as it is on no occasion to quit the proper path, yet much more wonderful and praiseworthy is it, willingly to accept correction, than boldly to correct deviation. Paul then has the praise of just liberty, and *Peter of holy humility ;* which, so far as seems to me according to my small measure, had been a better defence against the calumnies of Porphyry, than the giving him greater occasion of finding fault : for it would be a much more stinging accusation that Christians should with deceit either write their epistles, or bear the mysteries of their God."[1]

Now, to see[2] the fundamental opposition between the Greek and Latin Fathers and the reformers, let us observe that, though there are three ancient interpretations of this passage, differing from each other, the first denying that

[1] Ep. 82, n. 22.   [2] Passaglia, p. 240.

Cephas, so reprehended by Paul, was the chief of the Apostles, the second affirming this, but reducing the whole contention to an arrangement of prudence between the two Apostles, and the third maintaining the reality of the reprehension, yet all three have in common the reconciling Peter's chief dignity with the reprehension of him, and the two latter, besides, are much more careful to admire his modesty, than Paul's liberty, and make the most of every point in the narration setting forth Peter's Primacy. On the other hand the reformers use this reprehension as their sharpest weapon against his authority, praise Paul's liberty to the utmost in order to depress that authority, hunt out everything against Peter, and pass over everything for him. It is equally evident that their motive in this runs counter to the faith universal in the Church during the first four centuries; and that their inference cannot be accepted without rejecting all Christian antiquity, and the very sentiments expressed by Paul himself, as we have seen, towards Peter.

But as to the reprehension itself, it would seem to have been not on a point of *doctrine* at all, but of *conduct.* St. Peter had long ago both admitted the Gentiles into the Church, and declared that they were not bound to the Jewish law. But out of regard to the feelings of the circumcised converts, he pursued a line of conduct at Antioch which they mistook to mean an approval of their error, and which needed, therefore, to be publicly cleared up. Accordingly, Peter's fault, if any there

were, amounted to this, that having, with the best
intention, done what was not forbidden, he had
not sufficiently foreseen what others would thence
infer contrary to his own intention. Can this be
esteemed either a dogmatic error, or a proof of his
not holding supreme authority ? But the *event*
being injurious and contrary to the truth of the
Gospel, why should not Paul admonish Peter
concerning it ? But very remarkable it is, that he
quotes St. Peter's own example and authority,
opposes the antecedent to the subsequent fact, and
maintains Gospel liberty by Peter's own conduct.
St. Chrysostom remarked this. " Observe his
prudence. He said not to him,. Thou dost wrong
in living as a Jew, but he alleges his former mode
of living, that the admonition and the counsel may
seem to come not from Paul's mind, but from the
judgment of Peter already expressed. For had he
said, Thou dost wrong to keep the law, Peter's
disciples would have blamed him, but now, hearing that this admonition and correction came not
from Paul's judgment, but that Peter himself so
lived, and held in his mind this belief whether
they would or would not, they were obliged to be
quiet.'' [1]

----

[1] Hom. on text, n. 17.

CHAPTER VII

ST. PETER'S PRIMACY INVOLVED IN THE FOURFOLD UNITY OF CHRIST'S KINGDOM.

THE doctrine[1] of St. Paul has brought us to a most interesting point of the subject, what, namely, is the principle of unity in the Church. A short consideration of this will show us how the office of St. Peter enters into and forms part of the radical idea of the Church, so that the moment we profess our belief in one holy Catholic Church, the belief is likewise involved in that Primacy of teaching and authority which makes and keeps it one.

The principle of unity, then, is no other than " the Word made flesh " : that divine Person who has for ever joined together the Godhead and the Manhood. Thus, St. Paul speaks to us of God " having made known to us the mystery of His will, according to His good pleasure, which He purposed in Himself, in the dispensation of the fulness of times, *to gather together under one head all things in Christ, both which are in heaven and which are on earth* " : at whose resurrection, " He set all things under His feet, and gave Him to be Head over all to the Church, which is His body, the ful-

---

[1] In this chapter I have availed myself of Passaglia, b. 1, c, 25, and b. 2, c. 11.

ness of Him who filleth all in all ". And again,
" the head of every man is Christ ; . . . and the
head of Christ is God ". " And we being many
are one body in Christ, and every one members
one of another : " [1] as again he sets forth at length
in the twelfth chapter of the first Epistle to the
Corinthians, calling that one body by the very
name of Christ.

With one voice the ancient Fathers [2] exult in
this as the great purpose of His Incarnation.
"The work," says St. Hippolytus, [3] "of His taking
a body, is the gathering up into one head of all
things unto Him." " The Word Man," says St.
Irenæus, [4] " gathering all things up into Himself,
that as in super-celestial, and spiritual, and
invisible things, the Word of God is the chief, so
also in visible and corporeal things He may hold
the chiefship, assuming the Primacy to Himself,
and joining Himself as Head to the Church, may
draw all things to Himself, at the fitting time."
And again, " The Son of God was made Man
among men, to join the end to the beginning, that
is, man to God " ; or, as Tertullian says, [5] " that
God might show that in Himself was the evolution
of the beginning to the end, and the return of
the end to the beginning ". And Œcumenius,

---

[1] Eph. i. 9, 22 ; 1 Cor. xi. 2 ; Rom. xii. 5.

[2] See Petavius, de Incarn. lib. 2, c. 7 and 8, for the following quotations.

[3] Hippolytus, quoted by Anastasius, p. 216.

[4] Irenæus, lib. iii. 18, and iv. 37.

[5] De Monogamia, c. 5.

" Angels and men were rent asunder : God then joined them, and made them one through Christ ". St. Gregory Thaumaturgus breaks out, " Thou art He that didst bridge over heaven and earth by Thy sacred body ". And Augustine, [1] " Far off He was from us, and very far. What, so far off as the creature and the Creator ? What, so far off as God and man ? What, so far off as justice and iniquity ? What, so far off as eternity and mortality ? See how far off was ' the Word in the beginning, God with God, by whom all things were made '. How, then, was He made nigh, that He might be as we, and we in Him ? ' The Word was made flesh.' " " Man, being assumed, was taken into the nature of the Godhead," says St. Hilary : [2] and St. Chrysostom, [3] " He puts on flesh, that He who cannot be held may be holden " : " dwelling with us," says Gregory [4] of Nazianzum, " by interposing His flesh as a veil, that the incomprehensible may be comprehended ". " For since," adds St. Cyril, [5] " man's nature was not capable of approaching the pure and unmixed glory of the Godhead, because of its inherent weakness, for our use the only-begotten one put on our likeness." " In the assumption of our nature," says St. Leo, [6]

---

[1] Augustine, 21 Tract. in Joannem.

[2] Hilary on Psalm 68.

[3] St. Chrys. tom. 5 (Savile), Hom. 106.

[4] Greg. Naz. Orat. 36.

[5] St. Cyril, Dialog. 1, de Trin. p. 399.

[6] St. Leo, 5th Serm. on Nativity, c. 4 and 5, 12th Serm. on Passion, c. 3.

" He became to us the step, by which through Him
we may be able to mount unto Him : " " the
descent of the Creator to the creature is the
advance of believers to things eternal : " and, " it
is not doubtful that man's nature has been taken
into such connection by the Son of God, that, not
only in that man who is the first-born of all creation, but even in all His saints, there is one and the
same Christ : and as the Head cannot be divided
from the limbs, so neither the limbs from the
Head. For though it belong not to this life, but
to that of eternity, that God be all in all, yet even
now He is the undivided inhabitant of His temple,
which is the Church." For all the above is contained in our Lord's own words, "that they all
may be one, as Thou, Father, in Me, and I in
Thee," on which St. Athanasius [1] says, " that all,
being carried by Me, may be all one body and one
spirit, and reach the perfect man " :—" for, as the
Lord having clothed Himself in a body, became
man, so we men are deified by the Word, being
assumed through His flesh ". St. Gregory [2] of
Nyssa has unfolded this idea thus : " Since from
no other source but from our lump was the flesh
which received God, which, by the resurrection,
was together with the Godhead exalted ; just as in
our own body the action of one organ of sense
communicates sympathy to all that which is united
with the part, so, just as if the whole nature (of

---

[1] St. Athanasius, Orat. 3, contr. Arian. tom. 1, p. 572. Oxf.
Trans. p. 403.

[2] Greg. Nyss. tom. 2, p. 524. Catechet, Oratio, c. 32,

man) were one living creature, the resurrection of
a part passes throughout the whole, being communicated from the part to the whole, according to
the nature's continuity and union ". And another,[1]
interpreting the words, "that they all may be one,"
" thus I will, that they being drawn into unity, may
be blended with each other, and becoming as one
body, may all be in Me, who carry all in that one
temple which I have assumed ; the temple,
namely, of His Body". And lastly, St. Hilary[2]
deduces this not only from the Incarnation, but
from the Blessed Eucharist. " For, if the Word
be really made flesh, and we really receive the
Word as flesh in the food of the Lord, how is He
not to be thought to remain in us naturally, since,
both in being born a man, He assumed the nature
of our flesh, never to be severed from Him, and has
joined the nature of His flesh to the eternal nature
under the sacrament of the flesh to be communicated to us ? "

So deep in the junction of the divine and human
natures in our Lord's adorable Person lies the root
of unity for that humanity which He purchased
with His blood. It is in virtue of this headship
that the whole mystical body is one, and "we all
members one of another ". By this Headship our
Lord nourishes and cherishes the Church, and
communicates to her incessantly that stream of
grace by which she lives. And as this Headship
flows from the union of the Godhead and Manhood,

[1] Ephrem, Patriarch of Antioch, quoted by Photius, cod. 229.
[2] St. Hilary, de Trin. lib. 8, n. 13.

so it is inseparable from His Person, and incommunicable. But He has Himself, in His parting
discourse, recorded by St. John, dwelt upon the
great Sacrament of unity, the result of this Headship, and set it forth as the sign and seal of His
own divine mission, and the one convincing proof
of His religion's superhuman origin. By following
His words we shall see that this unity is not
simple but fourfold, and we shall trace the mutual
relation and subordination to the divine Headship
of its several kinds.

1. And first, "In[1] that day," says He, that is,
after His own resurrection, " ye shall know that I
am in My Father, and you in Me, and I in you,"
whereby He declares that, in the completion of
the dispensation, the union between Himself and
the faithful shall be such as to image out the
mutual indwelling of the Father and the Son.
Which again is further expressed, " I am the true
vine, and My Father is the husbandman. Every
branch in Me that beareth not fruit He will take
away : and every one that beareth fruit, He will
purge it, that it may bring forth more fruit. . . . I
am the vine ; you the branches : he that abideth
in Me, and I in him, the same beareth much fruit :
for without Me you can do nothing. If any one
abide not in Me, he shall be cast forth as a branch,
and shall wither, and they shall gather him up and
cast him into the fire, and he burneth. If you
abide in Me, and My words abide in you, you shall
ask whatever you will, and it shall be done unto

1 John xiv. 20.

you." [1] In these words He sets forth that union of mystical influx, by co-operation with which His disciples keep His words and abide in His love, and of which He is Himself the immediate principle.

2. But He does not stop at this interior and invisible union between His disciples and Himself: He speaks likewise of a new and special command, and of a special gift, by which their union with each other should be known. " A new command I give unto you, that you love one another : as I have loved you, that you also love one another. By this shall all men know that you are My disciples, if you have love one to another." [2] And again, " This is My command, that you love one another, as I have loved you. Greater love than this hath no man, that any one lay down his life for his friends. . . . These things I command you, that you love one another." [3] But the Holy Spirit, whom our Lord was about to send forth, is the efficient principle of the love here enjoined, by His substantial indwelling, as we are told, " The charity of God is poured forth in our hearts by the Holy Ghost who is given to us ". [4] From Him, therefore, bestowed by the Head of the Church, springs that unity of charity, which, being itself internal, is shown in outward signs, and constitutes that distinctive spirit of the Christian people, the spirit

---

[1] John xv. 1, 2, 5-7.
[2] John xiii. 34-36.
[3] John xv. 12.
[4] Rom. v. 5.

characterizing it, and analogous to the national spirit in civil organization.

3. But our Lord likewise speaks of a third unity, springing from the direction of one and the same Divine Spirit. "And I will ask the Father, and He shall give you another Paraclete, that He may abide with you for ever : the Spirit of truth, whom the world cannot receive, because it seeth Him not, nor knoweth Him : but you shall know Him, because He shall abide with you, and shall be in you." "The Paraclete, the Holy Ghost, whom the Father will send in My name, He will teach you all things, and bring all things to your mind whatsoever I shall have said to you."[1] "It is expedient to you that I go : for if I go not, the Paraclete will not come to you ; but if I go, I will send Him to you." "But when He, the Spirit of truth, is come, He will teach you all truth. For He shall not speak of Himself, but what things soever He shall hear, He shall speak ; and the things that are to come, He shall show you. He shall glorify Me, because He shall receive of Mine, and shall show it to you."[2] Of the nature of this unity we may judge by the gifts and offices assigned to that Spirit and Paraclete from whom it springs. Now He is repeatedly termed, "the Spirit of truth," and His office, to *suggest*, to *announce*, to *teach*, and *to lead into all truth*. This unity, therefore, is opposed to the division produced by ignorance and error, and so is the unity of faith, or Christian profession. Thus our Lord promises,

[1] John xiv. 16-18, 26.   [2] John xvi. 7, 13-15.

besides the unity of charity, that of faith, the efficient principle of which, as well as of the former, is contained in the communication of the Holy Spirit. But it is no less true in the super-natural order of divine gifts, than in the order of nature, that the first cause produces its effects by means of second causes. And here, as often as the Lord promises the Spirit of truth, He promises Him *to the Apostles*, and assures His perpetual abidance with them and the successors in their charge, thus, " That He may abide with you for ever": " He shall abide with you, and shall be in you " : " He shall teach you all things, and bring all things to your mind which I have said unto you": " Whom I will send unto you from the Father": " I will send Him unto you " : " He shall lead you into all truth": " He shall show the things that are to come ". And so the unity of faith may be expected from its *supreme* cause, the Holy Spirit the Paraclete, *through the medium* of the Apostles and their legitimate successors : the Holy Spirit is its *ultimate*, but they its *subordinate* principle : He is the *source*, but they the *channel*. Thus to trust to the invisible action of the Spirit, but to despise the office and direction of the teachers ordained by Christ, in the very virtue of that Spirit, is to reject His divine institution, and to risk a shipwreck of the promised gift of faith and truth.

For in exact accordance with our Lord's words here, St. Paul has set forth not only the institution, but the source, as well as the end and purpose, of

the whole visible hierarchy. It is instituted by our
Lord, as an act of His divine Headship ; its source
is in " one and the same Spirit dividing to every
one according as He will " ; its end and purpose is,
" the edifying the body of Christ, until we all meet
into the unity of faith ".[1]

Each of these points is important. Our Lord's
divine Headship over the Church, all-encom-
passing as it is, and the spring of all blessing and
unity, does not dispense with the establishment of
a visible hierarchy, but rather is specially shown
therein. And again, the Holy Spirit is the source
and superior principle of all spiritual gifts to all,
but yet He acts *through* this hierarchy. He is the
Spirit who maintains faith and truth, but it is by
the instruments of His own appointing.

Now these three points, the bestowal of all
spiritual gifts and offices by Christ in virtue of His
mystical Headship, the Holy Spirit being the one
superior principle of such gifts and offices, and His
manifold operation therein through the visible
hierarchy, are set forth most distinctly in two
passages of St. Paul, the twelfth chapter of the
First to the Corinthians, and the fourth chapter to
the Ephesians. " To every one of us is given
grace, according to the measure of the giving of
Christ. Wherefore He saith, Ascending on high
He led captivity captive ; He gave gifts to men.
Now that He ascended, what is it but because He
also descended first into the lower parts of the
earth ? He that descended is the same also that

[1] I Cor. xii. 11 ; Eph. iv. 13.

ascended above all the heavens, that He might fill all things. And He gave some apostles, and some prophets, and other some evangelists, and other some pastors and doctors, for the perfecting of the saints, unto the work of the ministry, unto the edifying of the body of Christ, until we all meet into the unity of faith and of the knowledge of the Son of God, unto a perfect man, unto the measure of the age of the fulness of Christ ; that henceforth we be no more children tossed to and fro, and carried about with every wind of doctrine by the wickedness of men, by cunning craftiness by which they lie in wait to deceive. But doing the truth in charity, we may in all things grow up in Him who is the Head, even Christ ; from whom the whole body, being compactly and fitly joined together, by what every joint supplieth, according to the operation in the measure of every part, maketh increase of the body, unto the edifying of itself in charity." "And the manifestation of the Spirit is given to every man unto profit. To one indeed by the Spirit is given the word of wisdom ; and to another the word of knowledge, according to the same Spirit ; to another, faith, in the same Spirit ; to another, the grace of healing, in one Spirit ; to another, the working of miracles ; to another, prophecy ; to another, the discerning of spirits ; to another, divers kinds of tongues ; to another, interpretation of speeches. But all these things one and the same Spirit worketh, dividing to every one according as He will. For as the body is one, and hath many members ; and all the

15

members of the body, whereas they are many, yet are one body, so also is Christ. For in one Spirit were we all baptized into one body, whether Jews or Gentiles, whether bond or free, and in one Spirit we have all been made to drink." [1]

Thus, then, we have been brought by the words both of our Lord and of St. Paul, through an inward invisible unity, that of mystical influx from the vine to its branches, and again, that of charity, and that of faith and truth, to an outward and visible unity, one of social organization, called forth by the great Head for the purpose of exhibiting, defending, maintaining, and conveying the former, since it is expressly said that He gave it "for the perfecting of the saints, unto the work of the ministry, unto the edifying of the body of Christ," and in order that "we may be no more children tossed to and fro, and carried about by every wind of doctrine". And the inward source and cause of this unity are indeed invisible, being the Holy Spirit of God, sent down by Christ, when He ascended up on high, to dwell permanently among men, but its effects are external and most visible, even the growth of a body "unto a perfect man, unto the measure of the age of the fulness of Christ," a body which has an orderly arrangement of all its parts, and a hierarchy of officers to continue till the end of all. And the function of this hierarchy is one never to be superseded, and which none but itself, the organ of the Holy Spirit, can perform, namely, to bring its members "to meet

[1] Eph. iv. 7-16; 1 Cor. xii. 7-13.

in the unity of the faith, and of the knowledge of the. Son of God". As our Lord says, in the promise, before His passion, "I will ask the Father, and He shall give you (the Apostles) another Paraclete, that He may abide with you for ever, the Spirit of Truth," so St. Paul of the accomplishment after His ascension, "He gave some apostles, and some prophets, and other some evangelists, and other some pastors and doctors," yet "all these things worketh one and the same Spirit". For as the divine Head took to Himself a body, bridging thereby the worlds of matter and of spirit, and as "in Him dwelt all the fulness of the Godhead *corporally*," so in His Church, in perfect analogy with the Archetype, the visible is the channel of the invisible, and the outward organization is instinct with inward life, and the hierarchy is the gift of the mystical Head, and the instrument of the one sanctifying Spirit. To think otherwise, to disregard the external framework, under a pretence of exalting the inward spirit, is to undo so far the work of Incarnation, and to renew the insanity of those early heretics who in one way or another would "dissolve" Christ; for there is no less "one Body," than there is "one Spirit".

But if His headship of mystical influx is *alone* and *immediately* sufficient, as is so often objected, for the maintenance of external unity, to what end is the creation of this visible hierarchy? For the objection that the invisible Headship of Christ renders a visible headship unnecessary, and indeed an infringement on His sole divine prerogative, whatever force it may have, tells not more against an œcumenical head of the Church, than against every order and officer of the hierarchy. These all, and with them the whole system of sacraments as well as symbols, become alike unnecessary and even injurious, if each member of the mystical body be knit to Christ *immediately* without any outward framework. And with what face especially can those maintain that the Bishop is the visible head of each diocese, and in being such does not contradict, but illustrate, the Headship of Christ, who yet deny that there is one in the whole Church put in the like place over Bishops, and see in such an appointment an infringement on the office of Christ? Such an argument is so profoundly illogical and inconsistent, that one has difficulty in believing it to be seriously held, or is hopeless of bringing conviction to those who cannot see an absurdity.

Let those, then, who confound together the supreme Headship of Christ over His Church, whereby He communicates to it life and grace, with the inferior and subordinate headship of external unity, see to what their objection tends. It stops at nothing short of destroying the whole visible hierarchy, and the sacramental grace of which it is the channel. Holy Scripture, on the contrary, tells us in these passages that the providence by which the Church is governed resembles that by which this outward universe is ruled, in the subordination of second causes to the supreme

cause. Christ repeats as Redeemer His work as
Creator, to give life and force to these second
causes, and while He works in the members of
His body both "to will and to do," bestows on
them the privilege of co-operating with Him.
Thus the dignity of supreme Head which belongs
to Christ, and is incommunicable, no more takes
away the ministry of the external head who is
charged with the office of effecting and maintaining
unity, than it impedes the ministry of "apostles,
prophets, evangelists, pastors, and doctors," to
whom Christ entrusted the Church, that by their
means it might be brought to sanctity and perfection.

4. And these words bring us to the fourth unity
mentioned by our Lord. For not until " He
ascended up on high" did " He give gifts to men ".
And this visible hierarchy, the sign and token of
His mystical Headship and fostering care, is by
Him quickened and informed with the Holy Spirit,
when He is Himself invisible at the right hand of
the majesty of God. This absence, too, is what
He foretold, saying, " And now I am not in the
world, and these are in the world, and I come to
Thee ; Holy Father, keep them in Thy name whom
Thou hast given Me ; that they may be one, as
We also are. While I was with them, I kept them
in Thy name. . . . And now I come to Thee."
These words of our Lord show that it was His will
that His believers should be no less one among
each other, by an outward and visible union, than
they were one by the internal bond of charity, the
guidance of one Spirit of Truth, and the influx of

the one Vine.   And so far we have seen that to
guard and maintain that unity under the guidance
of the Spirit of Truth, He called forth the visible
hierarchy, in all its degrees.   But what, then, was
the external root and efficient principle of this
visible hierarchy, when He was gone to the Father?
Did He not likewise provide for the loss occasioned
by His own absence, which He had foretold ?   The
argument of St. Paul proves that He did so provide,
as well as His own words.   For St. Paul declares
the Church to be "one Body".   Was it then a
body without a head, or a body with a head
invisible ?   Or did the Lord of all, having with
complete wisdom framed His mystical body in all
its parts and proportions, and having set *first*
Apostles, and then, in their various degree, doctors
and pastors, in one single, and that the main point,
reverse the analogy of all His doings ?   Did He
appoint every officer in His household, except the
one who should rule all ?   Did He construct the
entire arch, save only the keystone ?   Did He
make a Bishop to represent His person, and be the
centre of visible unity in every diocese, but none
to represent that person in the highest degree and
to be the centre of unity to the whole Church ?
Was it the end of His whole design " to gather
together in one the children of God, that were
dispersed," in order that there might be " One
Fold," and did He fail to add " One Shepherd" ?
Yet St. Paul declares that " there are many
members, but one body".   How can the distinct
and diverse members be reduced to the unity of a

body, but by the unity of the head, as the efficient principle ?   In accordance with which we may observe that never is the image of a body used in Scripture to represent the Church, but it is thereby shown to be visible ; and never is it compared with a body as a type, but that body is shown complete with its head.   Such are the well-known images of one House, Kingdom, City, Fold, and Temple, to which we have had so often to appeal.   Even the unity of things in themselves dissimilar is derived in Scripture from the unity of the Head.   Thus the man and the woman are said in marriage to be one, and that in a great mystery, representing Christ and the Church, but this because " the husband is the head of the wife ".   And Christ is said to be one with the faithful, because " the head of every man is Christ " : and God one with Christ, because " the head of Christ is God ".   If, then,[1] the Church is one body, it receives, according to the reasoning of Holy Scripture, that property from the unity of its head.

But such a one body, while yet militant upon earth, St. Paul declares it to be, setting forth at the same time the various orders of its hierarchy. Is it then a body complete, or incomplete ?   With a head or without one ?   For it is no reply to say that it has indeed a head, but one invisible.   That invisible headship did not obviate, as we have seen, the necessity of a visible hierarchy : why then does it obviate the like and even more striking necessity, that the hierarchy too must

---

[1] Passaglia, p. 254.

have its visible head? If it was, so to say, the very first act of our Lord's supreme headship over all to the Church—the very token that He had led captivity captive—to quicken the visible ministry which He had established by sending down the Holy Spirit to abide with it for ever, is the one place most necessary in that ministry to be the only one left vacant by Him? Is the one officer most fully representing Himself to be alone omitted? "The *perfecting* of the saints" (a metaphor taken, as we have seen, from the exact fitting together of the stones in a building), and "the edifying of the body of Christ," are described as the end to be reached by those to whom "the work of the ministry" is committed; but as this applies in a higher degree to the Bishop than to the priest, so it applies in the highest of all to the Bishop of bishops.

Again, God's method of teaching by symbols, which runs through the whole Scripture, and the institution of Sacraments, proves to us His will to lead us on from the visible to the invisible, and to make the former a channel]to the latter. For "we are all baptized into one body," and the outward act both images and conveys the inward privilege. And again in the highest conceivable instance, "because the bread is one, we being many are one body, who all partake of that one bread".[1] In like manner the outward unity of the Church must accurately represent, and answer to the inward, which, we know, is derived from the Person of Christ, who is its head. And so that

[1] 1 Cor. x. 17.

Person must be specially represented in the outward unity.

And this is one reason why no unity of a college, whether of Apostles, or of Bishops, will adequately express that visible headship of which our Lord's Person is the exemplar. For the root of all lies in a personal unity, that of the Godhead and Manhood, and therefore a merely collective or representative unity cannot express it. And if the Apostle wrote, "God hath set in the Church *first* Apostles," yet he also wrote that the grand result, "the perfecting of the saints, and the edifying of the body of Christ," was due to the ministry, not only of Apostles, but of prophets, evangelists, pastors, and doctors, each in their degree ; they all conspire to a joint action, which does not impede the existence of distinct orders in the hierarchy. And his expression that the Apostles are *first* in this hierarchy without defining their mutual relations to each other, does not exclude those other passages of Scripture which *do* define those relations, and which make Peter among the Apostles "the First," "the Ruler," "the Greater," the Judah among his brethren, the foundation of the whole building, and the one shepherd in the universal fold. And the more so because St. Paul uses three expressions of the Church, two of which are *relative*, but one *absolute*. He calls it "the body of Christ," and "Christ," which are relative ; but he also calls it "one body," which is absolute. Now, these expressions are not to be severed from each other, as if each

by itself would convey the whole idea of the
Church, which rather is to be drawn from them
altogether.   In answer to what the Church is, we
must not say that it is *either* "the body of Christ,"
or mystically called "Christ," *or* set before us as
" one body," for it is *all* of these at once, relatively
" Christ," and "the body of Christ," and
absolutely "one body".

As, then, the former expressions show that the
Church is one *in reference to Christ*, so the latter
shows that it is so *in itself*, and *simply*. For as
the Church is called " Christ," and " the body of
Christ," because it is one with Christ by mystical
union, drawing its supernatural life from Christ
its head, so it is called " one body," because in the
variety of members and parts, of which it consists,
no one is wanting to its being one body in itself,
and to its being seen to be such.   But it would
neither be so, nor seem to be so, if it were without
a visible head, the origin and principle of its
inherent visible unity.   And so where the Church
is called by St. Paul " one body," he declares that
it has a visible head.

Thus it is that the inherent notion of the
Church, as one visible body, and the whole dispensation by which visible things answer to
invisible, as their archetypes, demand one visible
head.   Now to this *inherent* necessity let us add
the force of *positive* teaching.   When our Lord in
almost His last words to His Church prays to His
Father, "while I was with them in the world, I
kept them in Thy name—but now I come to

Thee," what does He but suggest the appointment
of another visible head to take that place which
He was leaving? and further, what does He but
name one to that high dignity, when He calls him
"the Greater" and "the Ruler" among his
brethren, commits them to him to be confirmed by
him, and makes him the shepherd of the whole
flock? What else had He done but prepare them
for such a nomination, when He promised *one* that
he should be the foundation of His Church, and
the bearer of the keys? What else did Christians
from the beginning see in such an one, when they
called him the *head*, the *centre*, the *fountain*, the
root, the *principle*, of ecclesiastical unity?

Let us remark, once more, as a confirmation of
the above, that the archetype of visible unity in
the Church, which our Lord sets before us in His
prayer to the Father, is no other than that most
high and solemn of all things conceivable, the
mutual indwelling of the Father and the Son.
" Holy Father, keep them in Thy name whom Thou
hast given Me, that they may be one, as We also
are;" and again, for all successive generations of the
faithful, " that they all may be one, as Thou, Father,
art in Me, and I in Thee, that they also may be
one in Us, that the world may believe that Thou
hast sent Me ". Now, the relation established by
our Lord between Peter and the rest of the
Apostles, by appointing him the visible head of
the Church, and between Peter's successor and all
Bishops, does represent, so far as earthly things
may, and in a degree which nothing else on earth

reaches to, the mutual relation of the three divine Persons to each other. For as these are distinct, but inseparable, so, too, are the Apostles. As the fulness of the Godhead is *first* in the Father and *then* in the Son and in the Holy Spirit, so the fulness of power *first* promised and given to Peter, is *then* propagated to the other Apostles united with him. As in the Father the economy of the divine Persons is summed up under one head, and gathered into a monarchy, so in Peter is gathered up the fulness of ecclesiastical power, which, through union with him, is one in all, as the Church is one, and the Episcopate one. More-over, as it is the dignity of the Father to be the exemplar, principle, root, and fountain of unity in the Trinity, so is it the dignity of Peter to be the exemplar, principle, root, and fountain of visible unity in the kingdom of God, which is the Church. This is alluded to by Pope Symmachus, thirteen hundred and fifty years ago : " There is one single priesthood in the different prelates (of the Apostolic See), after the example of the Trinity, whose power is one and indivisible".[1] And long before him St. Cyprian : " The Lord says, ' I and the Father are one'. And again it is written of the Father and the Son and the Holy Spirit, ' And these three are one '. Is there a man who believes that this unity, coming from the divine solidity, cohering by heavenly sacraments, can possibly be broken in the Church, and torn asunder by the collision of adverse wills ? This unity he who

---

[1] Mansi, Concil. tom. 8, 208.

holds not, holds not the law of God, holds not the faith of the Father and the Son, holds not the truth unto salvation."[1]

Whereas, then, all unity in the Body of Christ, the Church, is derived ultimately from the person of its Head, the Word Incarnate, that unity is yet fourfold in its operation, and the efficient principle of one sort is not to be confounded with that of another. There is the *mystical* unity, which consists in the perpetual divine influx from the great invisible Head to His members; there is the *moral* or *spiritual* unity of charity, consisting in the presence of the Holy Spirit in the hearts of believers, and these two are internal, and in closest correspondence. There are two likewise external, which may be called the *civil* or *political* unity, consisting in the public profession of the same faith, the same truth, for what the *law* is to temporal states, the *faith* is to the great spiritual kingdom of Christ; and this unity is indeed inspired by the Holy Spirit, but is maintained by Him through the visible hierarchy; and lastly, correspondent to the unity of faith, there is the *visible* unity of external organization, the immediate or efficient principle of which lies in the visible headship over the Church attached by the Lord to St. Peter's chair. The latter two, while they correspond to each other, are indeed subordinate to the former, the unity of faith to that of charity, as the unity of the visible headship to that of the invisible; yet the very truth of the Body which

[1] St. Cyprian, de Unitate.

the Lord has assumed, and in which He reigns, and the whole analogy of His dealings with men, and the sacraments whereby He makes us " partakers of the divine nature," warn us that it is of the highest importance for us to see how external unity is the channel of internal, and the visible the road to the invisible. No words can be more emphatic to this effect than those with which the Apostle introduces the description of the visible hierarchy, and the divine headship which called it forth. " There is *one Body* and one Spirit, as you are called in one hope of your calling. One Lord, one faith, one baptism. One God and Father of all, who is above all, and through all, and in us all." From which he goes on to say, " Ascending up on high, He gave gifts to men—some apostles, and some prophets, and some evangelists, and some pastors, and teachers ". And lastly, " the Head over all things to the Church," is " the Saviour *of the Body* ".[1]

But if this be so, we can say nothing more highly to exalt St. Peter's office in the Church, for he is the great bond and stay of this outward unity, as even enemies[2] confess. As surely as

[1] Eph. iv. 4, 8, 11 ; i. 22 ; v. 23.

[2] That such was the belief of the most ancient Fathers, Ignatius, Irenæus, Tertullian, Cyprian, and others, see a most curious admission of the Lutheran Mosheim, in his dissertation, De Gallorum Appellationibus, etc., s. 13. And his way of extricating himself is at least as curious as the admission. His words are, " Cyprian and the rest cannot have known the corollaries which follow from their precepts about the Church. For no one is so dull as not to see that between a certain unity

in a real monarchy the person of the sovereign ties together every part of the political edifice, and is endued with majesty because he is at once the type of God, and concentrates in one the power and dignity of the whole community, so it is in that divine structure in which "the manifold wisdom of God" is disclosed to all creation. The point of strength is felt alike by friend and foe. On the Rock of Peter has fallen every storm which the enmity of the evil one has raised for eighteen hundred years; but yet the gates of hell have not prevailed against it. In the Rock of Peter, and the divine promise attached to it, every heart faithful to God and the Church trusts now, as it trusted from the beginning. Many temporal monarchs in their hour of pride have risen against St. Peter's See, but the greatest of them all [1] declared that no one had ever gained honour or victory in that conflict, and he lived to be the most signal instance of his own observation. "God is patient,

of the universal Church, terminating in the Roman pontiff, and such a community as we have described out of Irenæus and Cyprian, there is scarcely so much room as between hall and chamber, or between hand and fingers. If the *innocence* of the first ages stood in the way of their anticipating the snares which ignorantly and unintentionally they were laying against sacred liberty, those succeeding at least were more sharp-sighted, and it was not long in becoming clear to the pontiffs what force in establishing their own power and authority such tenets possessed." So the ancient Fathers were not intelligent enough to see that *the hand was joined to the fingers*. But the other alternative was still harder to Mosheim, that Lutheranism was fundamentally heretical and schismatical.

[1] Napoleon.

because He is eternal," and the Holy See pre-
vails in its weakness over power, and in its justice
over cupidity, because while temporal dominion
passes from hand to hand, and stays not with
any nation, following the gift of God which the
poet calls fortune,—

" Perchè una gente impera, e l' altra langue,
Seguendo lo giudizio di costei
Che è occulta, come in l' erba l' angue," —[1]

the visible kingdom of Christ, which is His
Church, lasts for ever and is built upon the rock
of Peter. The long line of descendants, from Con-
stantine and from Charlemagne, have in their turn
impugned and illustrated this glorious privilege
of the Papal See. What is there so stable in an
empire of commerce, or so solid in the nicely
balanced and delicate machinery of a constitu-
tional monarchy, as to exempt them from the
action of a universal law, or to ensure their victory
in the doomed contest with the Vicar of Christ?
Mightier things than they have done their worst,
have oppressed, triumphed, and become extinct,
and if it be allowed them in the crisis of their
trial to crucify Christ afresh, He will yet reign
from the cross, and "draw all men unto Him".

[1] Dante, Inferno.

CHAPTER VIII.

SUMMARY OF PROOF GIVEN FOR ST. PETER'S PRIMACY.

It would now seem to be made clear to all that the controversy on St. Peter's Primacy relates *generally* to the question of inequality in the Apostolic college, and *specially* to the question, whether Christ, the Founder of the Church, set any one of the Apostles, and whom of them in particular, over the rest. For as, on the one hand, there would have been no room for the superior dignity of the Primacy, had all the Apostles been completely equal, and undistinguished in honour and authority from each other; so on the other hand, it is the nature of the Primacy to be incapable of even being contemplated, save as fixed on some certain definite subject.

But to determine the two questions, whether the Apostles stood, or did not stand, on a complete equality, and whether one of them was superior to the rest in honour and dignity, it seemed requisite to examine chiefly four points.

First, the words and the acts of Christ respecting the Apostles.

Secondly, His expressions which seemed to mark the institution of a *singular* authority.

16

Thirdly, the mode of writing and speaking usually and constantly employed by the Evangelists and other inspired writers.

Lastly, the history of the Church, from its beginning, from which might be drawn conjectures, or even certain proofs, of the power which either all the Apostles had exercised equally, or one had held above the rest.

For should it become plain, from the agreement of these four sources, that a certain one of the Apostles, and that one Simon Peter, had been distinguished from the rest by the acts and words of Christ, and set over the Apostles; had been invariably described by the inspired writers, as the Head and supreme authority; and in the history of the rising Church, been portrayed in a way which could only befit the universal ruler, no difficulty would remain, and there would be arguments abundant to prove that Christ was the author both of the inequality among the Apostles, and of Peter's Primacy.

Now we seem to have proved *absolutely*, what we proposed *hypothetically*. For we have shown that Christ declared by His whole method of acting, and by solemn words and deeds, that He did not account Peter as one of the rest, but as their Leader, Chief, and Head.

We have shown it to have been the will of Christ to concentrate in Peter the distinctions which belong to Himself, as Supreme Ruler of the Church. For such must be deemed the properties of being the Foundation, the Bearer of the keys, the Holder of universal authority, the Supporter, and lastly, the Chief Shepherd. Of these there is no one which He did not promise to Peter singly, and confer on Peter singly : no one with which He did not associate Peter, and Peter only, in making him the foundation of His Church, bestowing on him the keys and universal power of binding and loosing, in setting him over his brethren to confirm them, and over His fold as universal Pastor.

We have shown that the Evangelists place almost the same distinction between the Apostles and Peter, as between Peter and Christ, while still among us. For as they set forth Peter as second after Christ, so do they subject the Apostles to Peter ; as the acts and words of Christ occupy the foreground in respect to those of Peter, so do his in respect to those of the Apostles ; as Christ, in their histories, is pre-eminent above Peter, so is Peter more conspicuous than the Apostles ; and as the Gospels cannot be read without seeing in them Christ as the prototype, so neither can they without seeing that Peter approaches the nearest to Christ.

We have shown that St. Paul spoke of St. Peter in no other way than the Evangelists, and that his pre-eminence is evident in St. Paul's Epistles, as well as in the Gospels.

Lastly, we have shown that Peter shines as the superior luminary in the history of the rising Church. The lustre of his deeds in the Acts recalls that of Christ in the Gospels. In the

Gospels Christ is named by far most frequently; in the Acts no one occurs so often as Peter. The discourses, the acts, the miracles of Christ occupy every page of the Gospels; and in that portion of the Acts which embraces the history of the whole Church, a very large part has reference to the discourses, the acts, and the miracles of Peter. In the Gospels, Christ leads, the Apostles follow; in the Acts, Peter takes the precedence, the Apostles attend him. In the Gospels, Christ teaches, and the Apostles, in silence, consent; in the Acts, Peter alone makes speeches, and explains the doctrine of salvation; the Apostles by their silence consent. In the Gospels, Christ provides for the Apostolic college, guards it from injury, defends it when attacked; in the Acts, Peter provides for filling up the place of Judas, determines the conditions of eligibility, enjoins the election, and defends the Apostles before people, rulers, and chief priests, in quality of their head.

Moreover, he alone is pre-eminent in exercising the triple power of *authoritative Teacher, Judge, and Legislator.* Of *authoritative Teacher,* not only towards Jews and Gentiles, whom he is the first to join to Christ, so that the same person who was the Church's rock and foundation also became its chief architect; but towards the Apostles likewise, who are taught by his ministry that the time was come for the blessing of redemption to be extended no less to Gentiles than to Jews, and that the burden of legal rites could not be laid on the Gentile converts without tempting God. Of *Judge*, because, while the Apostles are silent, he is the first to hear the causes of the faithful, to erect a tribunal to examine the accused, to issue sentence, and to support and confirm it by inflicting excommunication. Of *Head and Supreme Legislator*, both when he singly visits Christians in all parts, and provides for their needs, or when he uses the prerogative of first voting, and draws with authority the wording of the law to which the rest are to give a unanimous consent.

From this compendious enumeration we draw a multifold proof, both of inequality in the Apostolic college, and of Peter's superiority at once in rank and in real government.

I. For, *first*, a college cannot be considered equal, out of which Christ chose one, Simon Peter, whom, by His words and His actions, He showed to be set over all. Now, Christ's whole course of speaking and acting, of which the Gospels give us the picture, tends to exhibit Peter as chosen out from the rest, and set over them. Accordingly, neither is the college of the Apostles equal, nor can Peter be accounted as one of the rest.

II. Again, one who has received all in common with the rest, but much besides peculiar to himself, special and distinguishing, must seem to be taken out of the common number. Now, such must Peter have been among the Apostles, since Christ granted nothing to them which He denied to Peter, but did grant to Peter many most distinguishing gifts which He gave not to the rest.

III. And, further, it is apparent that the Foundation and the Superstructure, the Bearer of the keys, and those who inhabit the house or city whose keys he bears, the Confirmer, and those whom he is to confirm, the universal Pastor, and the sheep committed to his charge, cannot be comprehended under the same order and rank. Now the distinctions expressed by the terms Foundation, Bearer of the keys, Confirmer, and universal Pastor, are Peter's official insignia in reference to, and over, the Apostles themselves. His distinction from them, therefore, and the inequality of the Apostolic college, are plain.

Perhaps this may be put somewhat otherwise even more clearly. And so, IV. Let it first be considered, what is plain in itself, that a distinction carrying pre-eminence depends on distinction in perfection and gifts, and follows in a greater or less degree from the greater or less inequality of these, or in case of their parity exists not at all. Next, be what we hold both of reason and of faith remembered, that "every best gift and every perfect gift is from above, coming down from the Father of lights," that God is the fountain-head of all good, and that all gifts whatsoever flow over from Him to His creatures. From both points it follows that the amount of the creature's dignity and perfection lies in the participation of divine goods, and is greater or less in proportion to the participation and association with divine goods. So, then, the controversy on Peter's Primacy and the inequality of the Apostolic college, comes ultimately to this: *whether Christ, the God-man, associated Peter singly, above all, with Himself, in the possession of those properties on account of which He stands Himself related to the Church as its supreme Ruler.* For let it be once evident that Christ did so, and it will of necessity be evident also, not only that Peter was preferred to all, but wherein his leadership and headship consisted. And since we have made the inquiry, there is abundant evidence to prove that Christ really did associate Peter singly in five properties, which, belonging to Himself *primarily* and *chiefly*, contain the special cause for which He is the Prince and Supreme Head of the Church.

For, in truth, it is specially due to the properties and distinctions of *Foundation, Bearer of the keys, Establisher, Chief Shepherd*, and *Lord*, who has received all authority from the Father, that the Church has an entire dependence on Christ, is subject to Him, and that He enjoys over the Church the right and authority of Supreme Lord and Ruler. But which of these properties did He not choose to communicate to Peter, according to the degree in which they were communicable? He bestowed them all upon Peter, and upon Peter alone, so that Peter also is termed *the Foundation, the Bearer of the keys, the Confirmer, the universal Pastor*, and *the Chief*[1] *of the whole Church.* We see,

---

[1] ἡγούμενος, Luke xxii. 26, the very term still given in the East to the head of a religious community; and also, as has been said, that which marks our Lord in the great prophecy of Micah, recorded in Matt. ii. 6.

therefore, a remarkable proof of Peter being distinguished from the rest of the Apostles, and set over them, in his singular and special association with these gifts.

Again, V., to this tends that disposition of divine wisdom which provides that Peter holds in the Church, and among the Apostles, a rank of dignity greatly resembling that which Abraham among the Patriarchs, and Judah among his brethren, received from God. The former of these relations has been exhibited, and shown not to be arbitrarily conceived, but grounded on due proof. The latter will be presently farther touched upon. Now who shall deny Abraham that superiority whereby he was made the Father and Teacher of all the faithful, or strip Judah of the dignity in which he excelled his brethren, and was in many points preferred to them? As little may any one strip Peter of his authority as supreme teacher, and take from him those singular endowments which make him "the Greater one" among his brethren and Apostles.

Especially as, VI., this authority of Peter is clearly confirmed by the mode of writing usual to the Evangelists. For it is monstrous and preposterous to confound with the rest one whom the Evangelists constantly distinguish and prefer to all. For what more could they do to show their purpose to distinguish Peter, select him from the rest, and place him at all times before all the Apostles? We may venture to say that they omitted nothing to this end. And so it is absurd to doubt of Peter's prerogatives, or set him on the same footing with the rest.

For, indeed, VII., no one would endure it to be denied, from the usual more of writing of the Evangelists, that Christ was pre-eminent among the Apostles as their Supreme Head, and was removed from them in dignity by an infinite interval. Now, though the Evangelists do not give Peter all things, nor in the same degree, yet they do give him much, and in a degree not dissimilar, to distinguish him from the rest, showing him, as in a nearer relation to Christ, so proportionably exalted above the other Apostles.

And this proof, VIII., is the more persuasive because St. Paul follows the very same mode of speaking as the Evangelists. For in repeatedly mentioning St. Peter in his Epistles, he always gives him the place of honour, and joins him as near as may be with Christ. Who then can doubt Peter held a certain pre-eminent rank?

And the more, IX., because what is read in the Acts, and the view of primitive history therein contained, looks the same way, and seems set forth with the same purpose. For if you compare together the Acts and the Gospels, the mind at once suggests that the position of Prototype which Christ holds in the Gospels, belongs to Peter in the Acts, and that Peter seems distinguished above the rest of the Apostles in the Acts, as Christ is pre-eminent far above all in the Gospels. Now what is the result of so apparent a likeness? What is it fair to deduce from such a bearing in

the Evangelical and Apostolical history? Those
who are obedient to reasoning, and follow the
bright torch of the Scriptures, must confess with
us that in this parallelism of both histories, and
so of Christ and Peter, is contained a mark and
sign, proving that Peter follows next after Christ
in dignity and authority.

X. In authority, I repeat, and, therefore, in that
kind of superiority which very far surpasses the
limits of precedence and order. For what are the
grounds on which we see Peter's eminence in the
Acts, or a resemblance between the Acts when
speaking of Peter, and the Gospels when speaking
of Christ? Chiefly these, that Peter is set forth
as remarkable, singly, above all, for the use and
exercise of the triple power of Judge, Legislator,
and authoritative Teacher. Now, the superiority
herein asserted not merely distinguishes Peter
from the rest, but attaches to him a greater
authority over the rest.

XI. And, indeed, propose an hypothesis which
is necessary to solve a complex and undoubted
series of facts; such an hypothesis is thereby
made a certainty. At least these are the principles of philosophy, from which the laws of
reasoning will not allow us to depart. Now,
Peter's pre-eminence and supremacy are such an
hypothesis, without which you can render no
sufficient cause of the facts narrated in the first
twelve chapters of the Acts. Accordingly, this
supremacy of Peter may be considered as proved.

XII. Or to put the argument somewhat differently, thus: As the existence of causes is deduced, *a posteriori*, from effects, so it is perfectly established, *a priori*, whenever the series and sum of effects, of which the senses are cognizant, are foretold from it with certainty. We deduce the force of gravity necessarily from its effects, *a posteriori*, but we likewise determine it to exist, with a judgment no less invariable, *a priori*, when it is such that we do not merely guess at, but certainly anticipate, its sensible effects. Now, Peter's supremacy is not inaptly compared with this very force of gravity. For it is a characteristic of each to be, in its proper order of things, the source and principle in which effects are involved which afterwards become apparent, whether in this physical universe, or in the supernatural region of the Church.

Suppose, then, Peter to have held the dignity which we claim for him. What happens in the Acts which might not, nay, which should not, have been anticipated? Is it his being mentioned above all, his speaking in the name of all, his constantly taking the lead, and his eminence, as if he were the head? But it could not be otherwise if he alone received from Christ a higher dignity than all the rest. Is it his discharging the office of supreme Judge, Legislator, Teacher, and Doctor? Is not this just what was to be expected from the rank of Head and universal Pastor? The Primacy, then, the larger authority, and the unshared majesty of Peter, belong to that class of truths which are indubitably believed on the strength of deduction and rational anticipation.

Having noted, if not all, at least the greater
number of those arguments which we have alleged
hitherto in favour of our cause, we approach the question which was secondly to be cleared up, what,
namely, is *the force and nature of that Primacy*, which
the same arguments prove to belong to Peter. For I
know that all Protestants are possessed with the
notion that no other pre-eminence should be ascribed to Peter, on Scriptural authority, than one
limited to a certain precedency of honour and
order. That *precedency* should be granted Peter
they are not unwilling to admit, but *supremacy*,
they stoutly maintain, must not and cannot be
allowed him. As to which their opinion I consider
that it would be much the shorter way to strip
Peter utterly of every prerogative, than to attenuate the distinctions applied to him in Scripture to
a sort of shadowy precedency. I consider that
nothing is so foreign to truth and the Scripture,
as on their testimony to allow that Peter was
distinguished from the rest of the Apostles, but
to confine that superiority within the very narrow
bounds of honour and order.

For, *first*, whence do we most evidently and
chiefly draw the greater dignity which Peter clearly
possessed above the others? We draw it from
the endowments separately bestowed upon him
whereby he became the Foundation of the Church,
the Supreme Bearer of the keys, the Confirmer of
his brethren, and the universal Pastor. But are
these names, images, signs, expressing a naked
superiority of honour and order, or rather designat-

ing an authority of jurisdiction and power? I
cannot hesitate to assert either that these forms
are most fitted of all to express a singular authority,
or that none such exist in language. For, *secondly*,
their force is to ascribe to Peter the main sway,
and to mark him as set for the head and leader of
all. Who that hears them can, without pervert-
ing the natural force of words, or disregarding the
laws of interpretation, imagine anything merely
honorary, or figure to himself Peter with a mere
grant of precedency?

Especially as, *thirdly*, he is named in Scripture
not only *the First*, but, comparatively, the *Greater*,
and absolutely, the *Superior*.[1] Now these terms
do, of themselves, and far more if you consider
the context of the discourse in which they occur,
express a singular authority, and one without
rival. An authority, *fourthly*, kindred to that with
which Christ, while yet in His mortal life, presided
over the Apostolic college, and administered as
Supreme Head the company which He had formed.
For we can never sufficiently urge a point which,
being in itself most true, is of itself abundantly
sufficient completely to set at rest the present
controversy. It is this, that Peter's Primacy
proceeds from a singular association with those
distinctions, in virtue of which Christ is considered
the Head and Chief, and Supreme Ruler of the
Church. So that the more his Primacy is de-
pressed, the more Christ's prerogatives and dignity
are lowered; nor can he be confined to a pre-

---

[1] Πρῶτος, μείζων, ἡγούμενος. See ch. 2.

cedency of honour and order, without Christ's
superiority being shut within well-nigh the same
limits.

Besides, *fifthly*, are tokens wanting in Scripture
which disclose the nature of Peter's Primacy?
Are there not effects which unfold the force and
quality of the cause from which they spring?
Such tokens there are in abundance, and such
effects manifold. These are, the care with which
Peter guarded the Apostolic college; the authority
with which he visited Christians in every part;
the singular exercise of judicial power, by which
he established Church discipline, and provided for
its maintenance; his acts of authoritative teaching;
his drawing the form of laws which were to rule
the universal Church; and, in short, the wonderful
regard with which that Church followed Peter as
its Head, and the Steward of all the Lord's family.
What Primacy is it which these tokens set forth?
What cause which these effects demonstrate? Is
it one limited to a precedency of honour and order?
or one pre-eminent by an inherent jurisdiction
and authority? It is a point which needs no
further words. For if any there be whose minds
are not struck by a candid and sincere exposition
of facts, you will in vain attempt to persuade them
by arguments.

Unless, indeed, *sixthly*, they allow themselves
to be forced out of their prejudice by the Scriptures
exhibiting such a Primacy of Peter as compels all
others to profess one and the same faith with him,
and to maintain one and the same society. For

such an obligation could proceed neither from titles of honour, nor from precedency. It demanded a stronger cause—none other, in fact, but that supreme authority by which Peter is made head of all.

But we shall feel much more at home in the truth of this deduction, if we inquire a little more deeply into the reasons for selecting one among the rest, namely, Peter, and instituting the Primacy. For the purpose and end proposed in a work have the force of a *negative* rule by which we may judge with certainty what ought to be done, or could not be left undone. I know well that it does not follow, if anything has been instituted for a certain purpose, that it ought to be endowed *only* with those properties which appear necessary for the end to be gained; for it may be much more munificently established than the absolute need required. But at the same time I know that there would be a failure in prudence and wisdom in one who, desiring a certain work for a specific end, did not provide it with everything that could be deemed necessary. Thus the *knowledge of the intention and purpose* is equivalent, if not to a *positive* rule, determining all and singular the powers bestowed on any institution, at least to a *negative*, ascertaining what must be given to it, and what cannot be denied to it.

Now, is the purpose for which Christ instituted the Primacy, and honoured Peter with its dignity, unknown, or is it most truly ascertained? The end which moved Christ to make the college of

Apostles unequal, and to set Peter as head over
it, is it secret, or very conspicuous? There are
in all three *classes of reasons* which enable us to
form, not a mere guess, but an ascertained judgment, as to the purpose of Christ in instituting
the Primacy. There are *typical* reasons, drawn
from previous shadowings forth of it: there are
analogical, derived from relations of resemblance;
and there are *real*, inherent in the testimonies
themselves, and the Church's endowments. Let
us briefly exhibit these in order.

I. By, then, that signal agreement wherewith
the two dispensations, the old and the new, correspond to each other, the first in outline and
the last as filled up, this rudimental and that
complete, we are plainly instructed that it was
Christ's purpose for Peter, in the new dispensation, to bear the character whose lineaments had
been traced before in Abraham, and to be eminent
among the Apostles for the prerogative which
Abraham had possessed among the Patriarchs.
Now, Abraham's special prerogative and pre-
eminence was this, that no one could share either
promise, whether carnal or spiritual, which is
expressed in Scripture by "the Blessing," who
was not joined with Abraham by a double, that
is, a carnal and spiritual, a physical and moral,
bond.   For to him and to his seed were the
promises made, with the condition that only by
conjunction with him, and with his seed, they
could flow over to the rest. Since, then, in the
new dispensation, Peter was to sustain the char-

acter of Abraham in the old, and since the only-
begotten Son of the Father, having put on the
form of a servant, granted to Peter the prerogative
which, in prelude of His future order, He had
given to Abraham, it is plain that Simon was
chosen, honoured with the name of Cephas, and
preferred above all, in order that from him as
supreme minister of Christ, and by union with
him as visible head, all the members of the
Church's body might enjoy the blessings and
fruits of the Christian institution.

The deductions from this are easy to see. For
two things chiefly follow, specially declarative of
the nature of the Primacy, and showing its intent
to be the cause and efficient principle of that unity
by which the Church of Christ is one visible body.
First, there follows the *duty*, laid upon all the
faithful, of being joined with Peter, if they would
not fall from those promises with which Christ
has most bountifully enriched His mystical Body,
being no other than that which reverences Peter
as its visible head. Secondly, there follows Peter's
jurisdiction, in virtue of which he enjoins all to
form one communion and society with him, as
well as effects, defends, and maintains it. Now,
nothing can be stronger than this ordinance of
Christ, either to prove a Primacy of supreme
jurisdiction, or to unfold its purpose of effecting
and maintaining unity.

The same is the bearing of another type, no less
remarkable and no less adapted to explain the
whole matter. For, as Israel, " according to

the flesh," was the shadow of the "Israel of God," which was "according to promise":[1] and as the kingdom of Israel was a type and ensample of the kingdom of heaven, the approach of which Christ proclaimed in these words, "The time is fulfilled, and the kingdom of heaven is at hand": so the twelve sons of Israel, the heads of the Israelitish race, represented and imaged out those Twelve whom Christ chose, made princes in His Church, and endowed with supreme authority to build up that Church's structure, and enrich it day by day with new accessions of spiritual children. Of this type our Lord's words are the strongest guarantee: "Amen, I say unto you, that you who have followed Me in the regeneration, when the Son of Man shall sit on the throne of His Majesty, you also shall sit on twelve thrones, judging the twelve tribes of Israel". And, again, in the very discourse where He sets forth the future Superior, "I dispose to you, as My Father disposed to Me, a kingdom; that you may eat and drink at My table, in My kingdom; and may sit upon thrones, judging the twelve tribes of Israel".[2]

But now, though all the sons of Israel in the former typical kingdom were chiefs, and heads of tribes, yet one of them, that is Judah, had a special prerogative, which the Scriptures set forth, and which was called the *right of the first-born*. In virtue of this, on the one hand, Judah was

---

[1] 1 Cor. x. 18; Gal. vi. 16.
[2] Matt. xix. 28; Luke xxii. 29.

esteemed the lord of his brethren, whom they were to reverence as the parent of the whole family ; and on the other, it was only by union with him, and with the seed that was to spring from him, that the other chiefs could promise to themselves the divine blessing. And so the tribe of Judah had a great pre-eminence over the other eleven. It was its prerogative to take the lead :[1] it had received from God the promise of an authority[2] which was not to terminate before the old covenant should be transformed into the new : from it was the seed[2] to be expected, which should be the source of blessing to all nations, prefigured as they were by the twelve tribes ; the other tribes were bound[3] to union with it, and to the profession of its religion, on pain of falling into schism, and forfeiting the divine covenant. All this was expressed by Jacob in prophetic inspiration, when he addressed Judah as the head and root of his line : " Judah (praise) art thou, thy brethren shall praise thee : thy hand is on the neck of thine enemies : the sons of thy father shall bow down to thee ". It remains, then, to ask who was to represent Judah's person in the new kingdom, and on whom Christ bestowed the prerogative, the type and image of which had gone before in Judah. It is most plain that this was Simon Peter, for whom we have, therefore, to claim a double prerogative, the one of being the source and origin, from which no one may be

[1] See Num. ii. 3-9 ; x. 14 ; Judges i. 1-3 ; xx. 18.
[2] Gen. xlix. 10 ; and see John iv. 22.   [3] 3 Kings xii.

separated without severance from the kingdom and promises of Christ: the other of being the first-born, as betokening excellence, by which he was pre-eminent in the possession of special rights among his brethren, the Apostles.

The former prerogative was expressed by the Fathers of Aquileia, when, in the words of St. Ambrose, they stated their belief in St. Peter's chair: " For thence, as from a fountain-head, the rights of venerable communion flow unto all ".[1] The latter is confirmed and illustrated by the solemn expressions so often recurring in Christian records, wherein Peter is called " the Bishop of Bishops,"[2] " the Pastor of Pastors,"[3] " first pre-late of the Apostles,"[4] " Patriarch of the whole world,"[5] " universal bishop,"[6] " father of fathers,"[7] " having the dignity of pastoral headship,"[7] " the most divine of all heads, arch-pastor of the Church ".[7]

II. To these reasons, which, as we think, may be called *typical*, succeed the *analogical*, which prove with equal evidence the purpose of the Primacy as instituted, and its inherent powers. If we ask what are these reasons from analogy, and to what they point, one only answer can be given commended by any show of truth, that the

---

[1] St. Ambrose, Ep. 11.   [2] Arnobius Junior in Ps. 138.
[3] Eucherius of Lyons, Hom. in Vig. St. Petri.
[4] Proclus, Patriarch of Constantinople, on the Transfiguration.
[5] The Archimandrites of Syria to Pope Hormisdas, Mansi, 8, 428.
[6] St. Bernard, de Cons. lib. 2, c. 8.
[7] S. Theodore Studites to Pope Leo III., lib. I. Ep. 33.

Primacy was instituted in order that the Church of Christ might seem to be moulded after the analogy of one human body, one house, one kingdom, one city, and one fold. But whence the need that so very remarkable and clear an analogy should be obtained by the institution of the Primacy? Doubtless because the Primacy was created as a principle, by whose virtue and efficiency what was various and manifold should be gathered up into unity, because it was to be a head in which all the diverse members of the ecclesiastical body should be joined, the centre of the Church's circle.

Therefore the reasons drawn from analogy show that the unity of the Church is to be considered the special end for which the Primacy was instituted, and the Primacy itself a principle abundantly provided with all those means by which so admirable a blessing as unity may be first produced and then maintained.

And this is confirmed by another analogy, well worthy of close attention. This consists in the double and reciprocal relation in which the universal Church stands to particular Churches, and the institution of the Primacy to the institution of Bishops, who, by Christ's appointment, govern those particular Churches : an agreement which ought to have especial force with those who believe in the divine institution of Bishops. For as the whole society of true believers, and the particular congregations of which it is made up, are called in Holy Scripture and the Christian records by one and the same name of the Church, so is there the very closest analogy between the bond which connects the universal Church, and that which connects its several parts.

Exactly, then, as it is asserted with great truth of all these particular Churches that they are one house, one city, and one fold, so must this be repeated of the whole Church, since it is set forth in Scripture by no other images, and has no less right to claim the property of unity. Hence St. Chrysostom's golden saying, "If it is the Church of God, it is united and one, not at Corinth only, but in the whole world. For *the Church* is a name not of division, but of union and harmony;"[1] and St. Gregory calls it, "The tunic without seam, woven from the top throughout".[2]

Now, the same reason which existed for instituting particular Bishops to govern and preserve in unity particular flocks, moved Christ to institute a universal Primate, and to set him over the whole fold. If in the former case the best description of a particular Church is that of St. Cyprian, "A people united to its Priest, and a flock adhering to its Pastor";[3] in the latter the *form of unity*, which Christ established in the universal Primate, no less imposes on all, both taught and teachers, the necessity of saying with St. Jerome, "I, following none as the first save Christ, am joined in communion with your blessed-

---

[1] In 1 Cor. Hom. I. n. 1.
[2] St. Greg. Naz., Orat. 12, alluding to John xix. 23.
[3] St. Cyprian, Ep. 79.

ness, that is, with the chair of Peter. Upon that
rock the Church is built, I know. Whoever outside of this house eateth the lamb, is profane. If any
one was not in the ark of Noah, he shall perish. I
know not Vitalis; I reject Meletius; I am ignorant
of Paulinus. Whoever gathers not with thee, scat-
ters: that is, he who is not of Christ is of Antichrist."[1]

III. A great accession of evidence will accrue
to what we have said, if we attentively consider
the reasons deduced from the texts containing the
institution of the Primacy, and those proceeding
from the inherent properties of the Church. To
speak of the texts first :—

1. Either they carry no meaning with them, or
they prove at least this, that Christ, in instituting
the Primacy, intended,[2] while exhibiting the whole
Church under the usual image of a house and
building, to give it a *foundation*, the bond at once
of its strength and unity ; and, again, while communicating to one the special gift of unwavering
faith, to make him the channel for establishing
and *confirming* [3] all the faithful ; to render [4] the
fold which He had gathered out of all nations one
by the unity of a supreme visible *pastor*, and to
constitute [5] in the Lord's family, amid so manifold
a distinction of officers, one of such eminence as
to be *the Ruler* and *the Greater* among all.

But can we, or ought we, to conclude from this
as to the purpose of the Primacy, and as to its
constituent force and principle ? Assuredly these

---

[1] St. Jerome, Ep. 57.   [2] Matt. xvi. 18.   [3] Luke xxii. 31, 32.
		[4] John xxi. 15.			[5] Luke xxii. 26.

texts prove directly and categorically that the Primacy was set up as *the efficient principle* whereby to mould the Church's visible unity, and was endowed with all that authority, without which unity could neither have been produced nor maintained in existence.

2. And in this judgment we shall be confirmed if we investigate the properties of which the Church cannot be deprived, without taking a form and an appearance different from that which it received from Christ. The first which occurs is that *identity* by which the Church must always be like itself, and cannot be substantially different at its beginning and in its growth; one thing when it had Christ for its visible head, and another when His words had come to pass, "A little while, and now you shall not see Me, because I go to the Father". Now, at its first commencement in the time of our Lord's mortal life, the Church presented the form of a society governed by the supreme power of one, and deriving its visible unity from one supreme visible head. That it might not subsequently lose this identity, and put on another form, our Lord chose a Primate to be the principle of visible unity, and to have the power of a head over the whole body.

And indeed this was necessary to maintain the double character and test of *unity* [1] and *Catholicity*,[2]

---

[1] Unity. John x. 16; xvii. 20-23; 1 Cor. xii. 12-31; Ephes. ii. 14-22; iv. 5; 1 Cor. i. 10.

[2] Catholicity. Luke xxiv. 47; Mark xvi. 20; Acts i. 8; ix. 15; Rom. ix. 18; Colos. i. 8-23.

by which the Church is distinguished in Holy
Scripture and in the records of Christian antiquity.
As to *unity*, not only are the expressions in the
creeds, and the more ample explanation of them in
the Fathers,[1] most clear and emphatic, but likewise what is said in the Holy Scriptures of the
end for which the Church was founded by Christ.
For the grace[2] of God our Saviour hath appeared
to all men, instructing those who had[3] changed
the truth of God into a lie, and liked not to have
God in their knowledge, that denying[4] all these
things they might become an acceptable people,
and enlightened[5] by Christ, and sanctified in the
truth, might by the profession of one faith be one[6]
body and one spirit, in the same manner[7] in which
the Father and the Son are one, and might be
divided[8] by no sects and dissensions, which are
manifestly the works of the flesh, not of God, who
is not the God[9] of dissension but of peace. For
therefore Christ,[10] the only-begotten of the Father,
gave His blood for it, to present it to Himself a

---

[1] For all the Fathers hold the doctrine thus expressed by St.
Hilary of Poitiers on Ps. 121, n. 5. "The Church is one body,
not mixed up by a confusion of bodies, nor by each of these being
united in an indiscriminate heap and shapeless bundle ; but we
are all one by the unity of faith, by the society of charity, by
concord of works and will, by the one gift of the sacrament in
all." No notion of the Church's unity in England, it may be
remarked, outside of Catholicism, goes beyond " the indiscriminate
heap and shapeless bundle ".

[2] Tit. ii. 11.   [3] Rom. i. 25.   [4] Tit. ii. 14, with 1 Pet. ii. 25.

[5] John xvii. 17.   [6] Eph. iv. 4.   [7] John xvii. 21.

[8] Gal. v. 20, 19.   [9] 1 Cor. xiv. 33.   [10] Eph. v. 27.

glorious Church, not having spot, or wrinkle, or
any such thing, which would break peace and
disturb the agreement of faith ; but that it should
be holy and without blemish,[1] immovable through
that rock on which it rests, and against which not
even the gates of hell shall prevail ; wisely ordered
as the house of God,[2] in which[3] all hear his voice,
who is set over as the ruler,[4] and has received his
brethren to be confirmed,[5] and the care[6] of the
whole flock ; endued[7] with virtue from on high,
and strengthened by the Spirit of truth[8] who proceeds from the Father; possessing the power of
authoritative[9] teaching, which if any hear[10] not,
nor obey, they are to be accounted as heathens
and publicans, by a judgment which binds both in
heaven and on earth. Are there any who do not
see that in this description, which sets forth the
Church's pre-ordained end, its proper character
and very lineaments, the Primacy itself is included,
and exhibited as the principal cause which effects
the unity of the whole body ?   I hardly think that
any such can be, so apparent is the bond which
ties these several parts together.

Yet perhaps this may be more vividly brought
out if we shortly mention the common opinions
among Protestants on the Church's unity.   For,

[1] Matt. xvi. 18.

[2] 1 Tim. iii. 15.

[3] Matt. xviii. 17.

[4] Luke xxii. 26.

[5] Luke xxii. 31, 32.

[6] John xxi. 15.

[7] Acts i. 4-8.

[8] John xv. 26.

[9] Matt. xxviii. 20.

[10] Matt. xviii. 18.

omitting those who hold an invisible[1] Church, and so expunge visible unity from its attributes, all the other opinions may be reduced to three.

A. Anglicans, whose belief has been set forth, besides Pearson on the Creed, with more than usual care by Dodwell (in his Treatise on the Bishop as the Principle of Unity, and St. Peter's Primacy among the Apostles as the Exemplar of Unity), begin by noting that the question of visible unity cannot be determined in the same way as it respects the universal Church, or each particular Church. But why? Because, they say, it was indeed the will of Christ that each particular Church should have a double unity, inward and outward, but it was not His will that the whole Church, the sum of these particular Churches, should have the same mark and test. Because, it was His will that both unities should characterize the particular Churches, to use a school phrase, *separately* and *distributively*, but not the whole body, and the sum of these taken *collectively*. Whence they conclude that Bishops were chosen and made, by the command of Christ, to preside over particular Churches, and be in them the source and principle of external unity, but that a Primate was not chosen to whom the whole Church should be subject, and on whom its external unity should depend.

---

[1] The first Reformers fell into this grievous error because they had no other way to defend their schism. They may be passed over at present, as in most even of the Protestant confessions visibility is reckoned among the notes of the Church.

At this argument one is lost in astonishment, how it could have suggested itself to learned men, and gained their assent. For what had they to prove, or how could they assure themselves, or others, as to either of these two points, that external unity was necessary to particular Churches but not to the whole Church, or that the institution of Bishops presiding over particular Churches came from Christ, but not that of the Primate, whose charge was to rule, administer, and maintain in unity the whole Church? Had they texts wherein to trust? But as often as the Bible speaks of the Church's unity, it means that Church which is called "the kingdom of God," "the kingdom of Christ," and "the kingdom of heaven," which is termed "the inheritance of the Gentiles," and embraces with a mother's bosom and a mother's love the whole race of man from one end of the earth to the other. Had they creeds to cite? But in these unity is attributed to that Church only, which is so termed absolutely, and very often has the epithet of Catholic.

Moreover, is the word Church, in its unrestricted application, of doubtful meaning? On the contrary, it is specially defined as well in the Holy Scriptures,[1] where it expresses of itself the whole society of believers, as in the. Fathers, such as Irenæus,[2] Tertullian,[3] Clement[4] of Alex-

---

[1] 1 Cor. vi. 4; x. 32; xi. 22; xii. 28; Ephes. i. 22; iii. 10-21; v. 23, 24, 25, 27, 29, 32; Colos. i. 18-24; 1 Tim. iii. 15.
[2] Irenæus, lib. 1, c. 3, lib. 3, c. 4.   [3] Tertullian, de Præsc. c. 4.
[4] Clement, Stromat. lib. 7, 17.

andria, Origen,[1], Hilary,[2] Jerome,[3] and all the rest
without exception, who, in using it, express the
whole Christian people joined in one sole communion. It is defined also by Councils, as in
the Canons of Laodicea,[4] Carthage,[5] and Constantinople,[6] where the Church means the whole
assembly of orthodox believers, as distinct from
heretics and schismatics. It is defined in the
most ancient explanation of the creeds, the unanimous meaning of which Tertullian seems to
have rendered in saying: " And, therefore, so
many and so great Churches are that first one
from the Apostles, whence all come. So all are
first, and all Apostolical, while all set forth one
unity, while they have interchange of peace, the
appellation of brotherhood and the common rights
of friendship, privileges regulated by no other
principle than the tradition of the same sacrament."[7] Lastly, the very heretics[8] defined this
term, who, in order to make themselves understood,
could use the word Church in no other sense
than to express the universal assembly of the
faithful.

After this it is not at all necessary to ask
Anglicans afresh if they have ancient Fathers
whose authority they can quote. What these

---

[1] Origen in Cantic. Hom. 3.   [2] Hilary, de Trin. lib. 7, c. 12.
[3] Jerome, adv. Lucifer.   [4] Concil. Laodic. Can. 9, 10.
[5] Concil. Carthag. 4, Can. 71.   [6] Concil. Constant. 2, act 3.
[7] De Præsc. c. 20.

[8] See in the sixth act of the second Nicene Council the quotations from the iconoclast synod of Constantinople.

thought and believed about the Church's unity is fully shown by those whom we have quoted, and by the words of Irenæus, "The Church, though dispersed throughout the whole world, yet, as if it were contained in the same house, carefully preserves the rule of faith, and holds it as if she had one soul and one heart, nay, and teaches it with one consent, as if she spoke with one voice. For although different tongues occupy the world, yet, the force of tradition is one and the same, nor do the Churches of Germany, Spain, Gaul, the East, Egypt, Libya, and the middle of the world embrace any other faith. But as there is one and the same sun shining over the whole world, so the preaching of the truth shines everywhere, and enlightens all men who desire its knowledge."[1]

What, then, was the motive of Anglicans in maintaining the unity of particular Churches, and the institution of Bishops cohering with it, to be necessary, while they denied the necessity of unity in the Church universal, or of a Primate's institution, to effect universal unity? What induced them to assert incompatibilities, and defend them as a matter of life and death? The evidence of the Scriptures, and the unquestionable belief of all Christian antiquity, extorted from them the acknowledgment that unity was a mark of the Church, and the ascription to Christ of the institution of Bishops as necessary for the forming and maintaining unity. *But the fixed purpose of defending their schism, and their determination to reject the*

[1] Adv. Hæreses, lib. 1, c. 3.

Primacy, urged them to deny that unity in the whole Church was ordered and provided for by Christ. The result of these affirmatives and negatives was a doctrinal[1] monster of incomparable ugliness, an outrage on the light both of nature and of revelation, as incapable of defence as abhorrent from reason and from grace.

B. The second Protestant opinion has been set forth at length by Vitringa,[2] and supported with all his ingenuity. It is that of those who distinguish a twofold unity of the Church, one interior, spiritual, proceeding from union with one and the same invisible Head, Jesus Christ, and completed and perfected by the inhabitation of the Holy Spirit, and the bestowal of heavenly gifts; the other exterior, visible, depending on profession of the same faith, participation of the same sacraments, obedience to the same superiors. Having made this distinction, they proceed to argue for the purpose of proving that while the former unity is universal and absolutely necessary, the latter is neither universal nor necessary, save hypothetically (of which hypothesis Vitringa nowhere explains the nature), and so is capable both of extension and restriction. In a word, they attach simple

---

[1] Even the Puritan Cartwright observed, " If it be necessary to the unity of the Church that an Archbishop should preside over other Bishops, why not on the same principle should one Archbishop preside over the whole Church of God?" Defence of Whitgift.

[2] Sacred Observations, lib. 5, c. 7, on the hypothetical external communion of Christians.

and absolute necessity and universality to the
spiritual and invisible unity, but by no means to
the external and visible.

But for this what are their authorities? Can
they allege the most ancient Fathers in unbroken
succession from the Apostles? Nay, they candidly
confess that the Fathers thought external and
visible unity simply and absolutely necessary,
and not those only of the fourth and fifth century,
but those of the second and third. Witness Vitringa, [1] who says, "If we consult on this point the
doctors of the ancient Christian Church, they
seem on all hands to have embraced the view that
the communion of believers in holy rites, in the
supper of the Lord, and in reciprocal offices of
brotherly love, was maintained absolutely, not
hypothetically. They supposed, and seem to
have persuaded themselves, that all who were
joined to the Christian Church by the due rite
of baptism after previous preparation, were really
regenerated by the grace of the Holy Spirit, and
so that the Christian Church was an assembly of
men, who in far greater part, saving hypocrites
of whom a few might exist in secret, participated
in the renewing and sanctifying grace of the Holy
Spirit. Accordingly, to be joined to the Church
was much the same as being joined to the heavenly
city; to have one's name on the Church's books,
much the same as to have it in God's book of life.
On the other hand, to be severed from Church

---

[1] See also the testimony of Mosheim, quoted above, p. 216,
note.

communion, or, to use Tertullian's words, 'to be deprived of the sacrament of the Body and Blood of the Lord, and to be debarred from all brotherly communion,' was to risk salvation, and incur the danger of eternal death. That is, they supposed that no one was saved out of the external communion of the Church, which they confounded with the mystical and spiritual communion of the Saints. And again, kindred points to these and resting on the same principle, that Bishops represent the office and person of Jesus Christ Himself in the Christian Church; that those who separated themselves from them when rightly and duly elected, separated themselves at the same time from the communion of Christ Himself; that those who were absolved by the bishops after penance publicly performed according to the canons of ecclesiastical discipline, restored to their rank, and honoured with the kiss of peace, were absolved in the heavenly court by God Himself, and Christ the Judge. Lastly, which was the most *audacious*[1] of all such hypotheses, that it was all over with the salvation of all who separated themselves in schism from the external communion of the Church and its rites, although hitherto they had neither been tainted with heresy,

---

[1] Thus the universal belief of the Fathers from the beginning is charged with *audacity*. It is difficult not to be struck with the utter antagonism of feeling which separates Protestants from the whole body of the Fathers. The statements here ascribed, and truly, by Vitringa to them, would be viewed in modern Englis society as the very insanity of bigotry.

nor involved in crimes destructive of the Christian [1] profession. It would be easy for me to support at length each one of these particulars by the sentiments and the discipline of the doctors of the primitive Church, were they unknown to the more instructed, or did my purpose allow it. I now only appeal to Cyprian's letter to Magnus, in the whole of which he supposes and urges the very hypotheses which I have been enumerating; and amongst the rest, speaking of Novatian's schism, he writes thus distinctly: 'But if there is one Church which is beloved by Christ, and alone is cleansed in His laver, how can he who is not in the Church,' (that is, in communion with that particular external assembly which makes a part of the external Catholic Church) 'be loved by Christ, or washed and cleansed in His laver? Wherefore as the Church alone possesses the water of life, and the power of baptizing and washing a man, let him who asserts that any one can be baptized and sanctified with Novatian, first show and teach that Novatian is in the Church, or *presides over the Church*.[2] For the

---

[1] Because to rend Christ's mystical body, and to subvert that unity for which He had prayed the Father, was regarded by them as a crime of the deepest dye. In modern England it would be consecrated by the glorious principle of "civil and religious liberty". •

[2] The unrestricted expression, "to preside over the Church," used by Cyprian of Novatian, who claimed to be Peter's successor, contains a clear indication that the fold entrusted to Peter was as wide as the Church itself. It is the same Church in the two clauses, but in the former it *must* be understood universally.

Church is one, which, being one, cannot be at once within and without. For if it is with Novatian, it was not with Cornelius. But if it was with Cornelius, who succeeded the Bishop Fabian in regular order, and whom the Lord hath glorified with martyrdom over and above the rank of his high priesthood, Novatian is not in the Church.'[1] It is the precise thing which we have been stating."

But where did Vitringa and the supporters of his doctrine get courage to contradict the whole line of Fathers and their unbroken tradition? You would surely expect from them decisive arguments, and expressions from Holy Writ distinctly laying down no other than a *hypothetical* necessity of visible and external unity. But you may search in vain all over the Gospels, the Epistles, and the Acts, for any such. Not only is there no mention in them of such a distinction as that invisible unity is absolutely necessary, while external and visible unity is but hypothetically so; but this latter is plainly enjoined and set forth as the note which the mystical body of Christ, the true Church, cannot be without; and its violation is reckoned among those works of the flesh which exclude from the kingdom of God.

How, besides, can that be deemed necessary only under hypothesis, without holding and faithfully maintaining which you cut yourself off from the very fountain of blessing, and transgress and subvert the order appointed by God for attaining

[1] Ep. 69.

salvation ? Such an assertion would be senseless.
Yet in most of the Protestant professions,—the
Helvetic, art. xiv., the Gallican, art. xvi., the
Scotch, art. xxvii., the Belgian, art. xxviii., the
Saxon, art. xii., the Bohemian, art. viii., and that
of the Remonstrants, art. xxii.,—it is laid down
as an indisputable principle, "That the heirs of
eternal life are only to be found in the assembly of
those called ". What then do those who violate
outward and visible unity, and withdraw from the
outward and visible body of the Church ? They
stop up the very way which Providence has opened
for their obtaining " the inheritance of sons ".

For indeed Christ is the Saviour, but of His
mystical body, which is the Church,[1] which therefore He purchased with His own blood, joined to
Himself by that closest bond of being His spouse,
enriched with promises,[2] provided with all manner
of graces, and most nobly dowered with truth,
charity, and the Holy Spirit,[3] to give her at last
salvation, and "the weight of eternal glory".[4]
But have these things reference to a visible or an
invisible Church ? To a Church one and coherent,
or rent and torn by factions ? It is the Church
which Christ founded, which He made to be " the
light of the world,"[5] bound together by manifold[6]

---

[1] Ephes. v. 23-25.   [2] Ephes. iv. 15-17.
[3] John xiv. 16-26; xv. 26; xvi. 7.   [4] 2 Cor. iv. 17.   [5] Matt. v. 14.
[6] Compare Luke xii. 8, 9, with Matt. x. 32; Mark viii. 38;
Rom. x. 10; and again, Mark xvi. 15, with Matt. xxviii. 19; Acts
ii. 41; viii. 36; xix. 5; 1 Cor. xii. 13; and Matt. xxvi. 28, with
Luke xxii. 19; 1 Cor. x. 17; xi. 21; and Ephes. iv. 11, with Acts
xx. 28; Tit. i. 5.

external links, ordered to be one with the unity
of a house, a family, a city, a kingdom ; with that
unity wherewith the Father and the Son are one ;
in which He placed [1] pastor and doctors to bind
and to loose, and to watch over the agreement of
all the parts ; which He founded upon Peter,
committed in chief to Peter to rule and to feed.
Such, then, as fall off from one single visible
Church are of the condition of those whom the
Apostles of the Lord foretold, that "in the
last time there should come mockers, walking
according to their own desires in ungodliness :
these are they who separate themselves, sensual
men, having not the Spirit" : [2] these tear themselves from their Saviour, lose the fruit purchased
by His blood, and fall from the inheritance which
the Head obtained for His body and His members.

Therefore the necessity of union with the one
single visible Church is as great as the necessity
of union with Christ the Head, as the necessity of
the remission of sins, "for outside of it they are
not remitted : for this Church has specially received the Holy Spirit in earnest, without whom
no sins are remitted :" [3] as the necessity of
charity, "for it is this very charity which those
who are cut off from the communion of the Catholic
Church do not possess," [4] whence "whatsoever

---

[1] Compare Ephes. iv. 11-16, with 1 Cor. xii. 13-31 ; and Matt.
xviii. 18, with John xx. 21 ; Acts xv. 41 ; xvi. 4 ; 2 Cor. x. 6 ; 1 Tim.
v. 20 ; Tit. i. 13 ; ii. 15.   [2] Jude 18 ; 2 Pet. iii. 2, 3.

[3] Augustin. in Enchirid. c. 63.

[4] Aug. in Tract. de Symb. c. 11.

thing heretics and schismatics receive, the charity
which covers a multitude of sins is the gift of
Catholic unity and peace ":[1] as great, in fine, as
the necessity not to involve oneself "in a horrible
crime and sacrilege,"[2] "in the greatest of evils,"[3]
one "by which Christ's passion is rendered of no
effect, and His body is rent,"[4] by which[5] the sin
is committed of which Christ said, "It shall not
be forgiven, neither in this world nor in the world
to come ": by which one is estranged "from the
sole Catholic Church, which retains the true worship, in which is the fountain of truth, the home
of faith, the temple of God, into which if any one
enter not, or from which if any one go out, he loses
the hope of life and eternal salvation. Let no one
flatter himself in the spirit of obstinate contention, for life is at issue, and salvation, which without care and caution will be forfeited."[6] Can any
necessity be greater, or less conditional than this?
Or what can be more plain than this statement of
the simple and absolute necessity of visible unity
and outward communion?

Where, then, are we to find the cause which
induced so many learned and able Protestants
first to imagine this distinction between the necessity of internal and external communion and
unity, and then to deceive themselves and others

[1] Aug. de Baptismo, cont. Donat. lib. 3, c. 16.
[2] Aug. Cont. Litt. Petiliani, lib. 1, c. 21-22; lib. 22, c. 13-23;
lib. 3, c. 52.   [3] Optat. lib. 1.
[4] Ambros. de Obitu Satyri Fratris, lib. 1, n. 47.
[5] Idem de Pœnit. lib. 2, 4.
[6] Lactant. Div, Instit. lib. 3, c. 30.

with such a mockery ? The real cause was, as I believe, that having denied the institution of the Primacy, and the authority lodged in it for the purpose of forming and maintaining unity, they were without a criterion or proof in virtue of which, among so many Christian societies divided from and condemning each other, they could safely choose the one with which they were to be joined in communion, and the outward unity of duty and obedience. For they would readily conclude that the unity so often commended in Scripture, and so earnestly enjoined, could not be external, since God, who does not command impossibilities, had instituted no visible sign to mark that company of Christians, which alone among all the rest was the continuation and development of the Church founded by Christ, and built up by the Apostles.

C. From the same source must the third Protestant doctrine on unity be derived. Jurien[1] filled up the sketch of this, which Casaubon,[2] Claude,[3] and Mestrezat[4] had drawn, and it became so popular as not only to infect a large number of Protestants, but to exert a withering influence on certain unstable members of the Catholic body. It teaches that we must believe not only in an internal and spiritual, but in a visible and external unity, for the Scriptures plainly urge its necessity, and Christian tradition fully describes it, so that there is not a truth

[1] Le vrai Système de l'Église.   [2] Answer to Cardinal Perron.
[3] Défense de la Réforme, p. 200.   [4] Traité de l'Église, p. 286.

more patent or established on greater authority; but this unity is restricted within narrow bounds, and confined to the articles called fundamental, though as to how many these are no one defender of the system is agreed with another. For it is sufficient for Christians not to differ in the profession of such articles for them to be deemed members of one and the same Church. Whence they infer that one and the same true Church is made up out of almost all Christian societies, the Roman, the Greek, the Nestorian, the Eutychian, the Waldensian, the Lutheran, the Anglican, and the Calvinist; for their differences, important as they are, offer no hindrance to the unity which Christ enjoined, the Apostles preached, the creeds express, and universal tradition demands.

As Bossuet,[1] the brothers Walemburg,[2] Nicole,[3] and even some Protestants have most fully dealt with this portentous opinion, there is no need to urge much against it here. I prefer repeating the question, What *occasion* the Protestants had to get up so unheard-of a paradox, and a system so absurd? It was twofold: one theoretical, and the other practical.

The theoretical was this. The crime of heresy, depicted in Scripture and Christian antiquity with colours so dark, had gradually lost its foulness and its magnitude in the minds of Protes-

[1] Bossuet, writings against Jurien.

[2] The brothers Walemburg, Treatise on Necessary and Fundamental Articles.　　　　[3] Nicole, de l'Unité de l'Église.

tants, who had, at length, come to the pass of reckoning religious, as well as civil, liberty, among the unquestionable rights of man. As if, all other human acts being subject to a law, those alone which proceed from the intellect are exempt : as if the difference between right and wrong, which embraces the whole range of man's life, did not relate to its noblest part, in the acts of the intellect and the reason : as if God had laid down a law of justice, charity, fortitude, and prudence, but entirely omitted a *law*[1] *of faith :* as if the will submitted to a law of *good*, but the mind owned no law of *truth :* or as if God cared for the boughs and leaves, but took no thought of the root.[2] But what could Protestants do ? Having allowed to all full licence of thought, and overthrown the authority which ruled the mind, they were forced, while they kept the *name* of heresy, to give up the *thing* meant by it, and the effects springing from that thing : they were forced to attenuate to the utmost the crime of heresy, and to reduce to the smallest possible number articles necessary to be believed by all; they were forced to extend beyond all measure the Church's limits, while they contracted beyond all measure the range of necessary unity.

---

[1] See the recognition of this law, Mark xvi. 16; Matt. xxvii. 18-20; Luke xii. 8, 9; Rom. x. 10.

[2] Such the Fathers call Faith, terming it, "the beginning and foundation," "the greatest mother of virtues," "the principle of salvation," "the prelude of immortality," "the clear eye of divine knowledge," "the fountain of all wisdom". See Suicer, art. πίστις.

Besides the theoretical, there was a practical occasion in those schisms which, not merely in later or in mediæval times, but in the first ages also, rent the Christian society. Jurien and Pfaff appeal to these, pretentiously enumerating those which arose under Popes Victor, Cornelius, Stephen, Urban VI., and Clement VII., and those named from Donatus, Meletius, and Acacius. Then they ask if the true Church of Christ can be thought to consist in one single society perfectly at union with itself. They allege many conjectures against this, but dwell on the argument that *in defect of a visible external test*, such an assertion could not be maintained without *imposing upon all a most intolerable burden of searching out where is the true doctrine and the legitimate ministerial succession :* for it is not until these are found, that, at length, that one single society will be recognized, with which, as the only true Church, unity of communion is to be kept.

Now, I profess that I do not see how this argument can be met, if the institution of the Primacy, and its proper function to form and maintain unity, be rejected. For, without this, by what visible token among so many Christian societies, divided by intestine dissension, and condemning each other, can you distinguish the one which has the character of the true Church, and the right to exact communion with itself? There is none to be found ; and so, either all hopes of finding the true Church must be relinquished, *or* an inquiry must be undertaken into purity of doctrine and legitimate ministerial succession, on the termination of which the only true Church will at last be found. But as this latter course is to by far the greater number of men impossible, dangerous[1] to all without exception, and most foreign to the Christian temper, the only conclusion remaining is, that the selection of a Primacy with the power of effecting unity impressed upon it *is most intimately involved and bound up in the visibility and unity of the true Church.*

And quite as closely is it bound up with that other test of the Church, its Catholicism. We are not to believe Voss and King,[2] in their assertion that this test began to be applied first in the fourth century, for the purpose of distinguishing the genuine company of the orthodox, and the true body of Christ, from heretics and schismatics. For we find the Church distinguished by the epithet of Catholic, not merely in the records of the fourth[3] and fifth[4] century, but in those of

---

[1] After having gone through the search for ten long years, I may be allowed to express how great its danger, and how great too the blessedness of those who are not exposed to it. It is worth the experience of half a life to receive the truth, without personal inquiry, from a competent authority. Protestantism begins its existence by casting away one of the greatest blessings which man can have.

[2] De Symbolo, Diss. 1, 39, and Hist. Symb. Apostol. cap. 6, 16.

[3] Pacian, Ep. 1, n. 4. Cyril of Jerusalem, Catech. 18, n. 23. Eusebius on Isai. xxxii. 18. Chrysostom on Colos. hom. 1, n. 2 ; on 1 Cor. hom. 32, n. 1. Jerome on Matt. xxiv. 26.

[4] Augustine on Ps. 41, n. 7 ; Epist. 49, n. 3-52, n. 1, and elsewhere,

the third,[1] and the second,[2] at the beginning of
which St. Ignatius wrote, " Follow all of you
the Bishop, as Jesus Christ the Father; and the
body of Presbyters, as Apostles. But reverence
deacons, as the command of Christ. Without
the Bishop let nothing of what concerns the
Church be done by any one. Let that be deemed
a proper Eucharist which is under the Bishop,
or with his sanction. Where the Bishop is,
there also let the multitude be; as, where Christ
Jesus is, *there is the Catholic Church.*"[3] As, therefore,
that cannot be the Church of Christ, which is
not Catholic, we ought to investigate the meaning
which is given to this word by the consent of all
orthodox believers.

Now, two points are signified in it, one of which
is its *material*, the other its *formal*, or *essential*, part.
Its *material* part is, that the geographical extension of the true Church be such that its mass be
morally[4] universal, *absolutely* great, and eminently
visible, but *comparatively* with all heretical and
schismatical sects, larger and more numerous.
Of this *material* meaning attached to the epithet
Catholic, we find abundant witnesses in all[5] the

[1] Council of Antioch, quoted by Euseb. Hist. lib. 7, c. 30.
Origen on Romans, lib. 8, n. 1; Cyprian, Epist. 52; Acts of St.
Fructuosus, n. 3, and of St. Pionius, n. 9.

[2] Irenæus, lib. 3, c. 17, and Epistle on Martyrdom of St.
Polycarp, n. 19.   [3] Epist. to Smyrneans, n. 8.

[4] Augustine, Ep. 52, n. 1, Serm. 238, n. 3.

[5] As Optatus, lib. 2, Aug. de Unitate Ecc. c. 2, etc.; cont.
Cresconium, l. 2, c. 63. Contr. Petilian, 1. 2, c. 12-55, 58-73; on
Ps. 21, 47, 147, and on 1 Ep. John Tract. 1, 2.

orthodox writers who defended the cause of the Church against the Donatists, and again, against the Luciferians[1] and Novatians; and likewise, in those who have explained the creeds,[2] and, as occasion offered, have touched on the force of the term Catholic.[3] But the same first-cited witnesses tell us that universal diffusion is not sufficient, and that we require another element to infuse a soul into this universally extended body, and to bring it to unity.

For two properties are continually recurring in Christian records, one of which may be called *negative*, the other *affirmative*. The force of the former is *to expel from the circle of the one true Catholic Church all sects of heretics and schismatics :* of the latter, that this Church *consist in one single communion and society, whose members cohere together by hierarchical subordination.*

But is it true that both these points are so plainly and constantly inculcated? To remove all doubt we will quote the authors who most distinctly assert the one and the other. As to the first, there are Clement of Alexandria,[4] Tertullian,[5] Alexander of Alexandria,[6] Celestine,[7] Leander,[8]

---

[1] Pacian, Ep. 3, Jerome cont. Luciferianos.

[2] Cyril of Jerusalem, Cat. 18.

[3] Irenæus, lib. 1, c. 10; lib. 4, c. 19. Tertullian adv. Judæos, c. 7. Bernard in Cantica, serm. 65.

[4] Clement, Stromat. l. 7, § 15-17.

[5] Tertullian de Præsc. c. 30.

[6] Alexander, apud Theodoret, H. E. lib. 1, c. 4.

[7] Cœlestinus, Homil. in laud. eccles.

[8] Leander, Cont. Origenistas in Actis Synodi V.

the Emperor Justinian;[1] then again the Councils
of Nice,[2] Sardica,[3] and the third of Carthage;[4]
nay, the heretics[5] themselves; and all these agree
in asserting that *there is one only ancient Catholic
Church*, outside of which the Divine patience
endures and bears with heresies, which are as
thorns. Thus in language ecclesiastical and
Christian nothing can be considered as more
certainly proved than that the epithet of Catholic
is *distinctive*, and shows the communion which
rejects from its bosom all heresies and all schisms.
It was with great reason, therefore, that Pacian[6]
wrote what Cyril of Jerusalem[7] and Augustine
very frequently repeated, "Our people is divided
from the heretical name by this appellation, that
it is called Catholic ".[8]

Moreover, this unity, which we have said may
be called *negative*, is necessary indeed to the
understanding of the Church as Catholic, but is
by no means sufficient to complete the idea of
Catholicity. To it therefore must be added the
affirmative unity, by which Catholicism is not
only divided from heretics and schismatics, but
becomes in itself a coherent body with members
and articulations. That which we so often read

---

[1] Justinianus, Epist. ad Mennam Constantinopolitanum.

[2] Council of Nice, in the Creed, and Canon 8.

[3] Sardica, in letter to all Bishops, quoted by Athanasius, Apol. 2.

[4] 22nd Canon of Codex Africanus.

[5] The Nestorian profession of faith, in fifth act of Council
of Ephesus.

[6] Pacian, Ep. 1.   [7] Cyril, Catech. 18.

[8] Aug. de Vera Relig. c. 6, de Utilit. Credendi, c. 7.

in the monuments of antiquity, about the necessity[1] of communion among the members of
the Church and the tokens[2] and means of that
communion, has reference to the assertion and
maintenance of this unity, which is the soul of
Catholicity, and without which it cannot even be
conceived. There are very distinct and innumerable testimonies about it in the ancient
Fathers,[3] declaring its *necessity*, and setting forth
its *mode* of composition and coherence.

For to set forth the *mode* of this is the plain drift
of what Irenæus[4] writes in confutation of heretics
by the tradition of the Apostolical Churches:
" For since it would be very long in the compass
of our present work to enumerate the successions
of all the Churches, taking that Church which
is the greatest, the most ancient, and well known
to all, founded and established at Rome by the
two most glorious Apostles Peter and Paul, by
indicating that tradition which it has from the
Apostles, and the faith which it announces to
men, which has reached even to us by the succession of Bishops, we confound all those, who,
in whatsoever manner, either through self-pleasing,

---

[1] Pacian, Ep. 3, " The Church is a full and solid body, diffused
already through the whole world. As a city, I say, whose parts
are in unity. Not as you Novatians, an insolent particle, or a
gathered wen, separated from the rest of the body."

[2] Such as are γράμματα κοινωνικά, Euseb. H. E. lib. 7, c. 30;
ἐπιστολαὶ κοινωνικαί, Basil. Ep. 190, or κανωνικαί, Ep. 224, letters
of peace commendatory, ecclesiastical, etc.

[3] See especially Chrys. Hom. 30 on 1 Cor.

[4] Irenæus, lib. 3, c. 3.

or vainglory, or blindness and evil intention, gather[1] otherwise than they ought. *For* to this Church on account of its superior principate, it is necessary that every Church should come together,[2] that is, the faithful who are everywhere; for in this Church the tradition which is from the Apostles has been ever preserved by those who are everywhere. . . . By this ordination and succession, the tradition and preaching of the truth, which is from the Apostles in the Church, has reached down to us. And this proof is most complete, that it is one and the same vivifying faith, which has been preserved and handed down in truth in the Church from the Apostles to the present day."

The Churches, therefore, which are everywhere diffused, derive that strength and harmony of parts, out of which the whole body of the Catholic Church is made up, from the fact of their agreeing in the unity of faith and preaching with that Church of Peter, which is the greatest, the chief, and the more powerful. It follows that the Primacy of Peter, and the authority inherent in

[1] Compare Jerome's often-quoted passage, Ep. 15, to Pope Damasus, "Whoso gathereth not with thee, scattereth; that is, whoso is not of Christ is of Antichrist".

[2] For the meaning of "come together," see further on, c. 40. "God hath placed in the Church Apostles, Prophets, Doctors, and all the rest of the operation of the Spirit, of which all those are not partakers who do not *run together to the Church*, but defraud themselves of life by an evil intention and a very bad conduct. For where the Church is, there is the Spirit; and where is the Spirit of God, there is the Church and all grace."

it to effect unity, is that principle which Christ selected, that the Church which He had set up might be Catholic, and bear the note of Catholicity on its brow.

And Cyprian would set forth the same *mode* of communion, when he speaks of the *coherence of Bishops*, by which both *the Catholic episcopate is* made *one, and the Church one and Catholic*. For as the *several communities draw the unity of the body from the unity of the prelates* to whom they are subject ; so all prelates, and the communities subject to them, constitute *one Catholic episcopate and one Catholic Church*, because they cohere with the *principal* Church, *the root and matrix*, which is the Church of Peter, *upon whom* the Lord founded the whole building, and whom He instituted *to be the fountain and source of Catholic unity*.[1]

These words are a clue to understand Tertullian's[2] meaning, when, already become a Montanist, he called the Catholic Church, whose discipline he was attacking, *the Church near to Peter*—" concerning your opinion, I now inquire whence you claim this right to the Church. If because the Lord

[1] See St. Cyprian's letters, 69, 55, 45, 70, 73, 40. Consider the force of the words, " Peter, upon whom the Church had been built by the ' Lord, speaking one for all, and *answering with the voice of the Church*, says, Lord, to whom shall we go ?'" Ep. 55, on which Fenelon (de sum. Pontif. auct. c. 12) remarks, " What wonder, then, if Pope Hormisdas and other ancient Fathers say, ' the Roman, that is, the Catholic Church,' since Peter was wont to answer *with the voice of the Church ?* What wonder if the body of the Church speaks by the mouth of its head ? "

[2] De Pudicitia, c. 21.

said to Peter, ' Upon this rock I will build My Church,' ' to thee will I give the keys of the kingdom of heaven,' or ' whatsoever thou shalt bind or loose on earth, shall be bound or loosed in heaven,' you, therefore, pretend that the power of binding and loosing is derived to you, that is, to all the Church near to Peter; how do you overthrow and change the manifest intention of the Lord in conferring this on Peter *personally*,[1] ' Upon thee I will build My Church,' and ' I will give to thee the keys,' not to the Church, and , whatsoever thou bindest or loosest,' not what they bind or loose ? " Now, he used this mode of speaking because it was customary with Catholics, who are wont to exhibit *nearness with Peter* as the characteristic of the Church, and the necessary condition for sharing that power, whose plenitude and native source Christ had lodged in Peter.

This certain and undoubting judgment of Catholics Tertullian himself, before his error, had clearly expressed in his book, *De Scorpiace*, c. x., where he says, " For if you yet think the heaven

---

[1] This Montanist corruption (into which Ambrose on Ps. 38, n. 37, and Pacian in his three letters to Sempronius, state that the Novatians also fell) induced some Fathers, and especially Augustine (Enarrat. on Ps. 108, n. 1, Tract. 118 on John, n. 4, and last Tract. n. 7), to teach that the keys were bestowed on Peter so far forth as he represented the person of the Church in right of his Primacy. By which mode of speaking they meant this one thing, that the power of the keys, as being necessary to the Church, and instituted for her good, began indeed in Peter, and was communicated to him in a peculiar manner, but by no means dropt, or could possibly drop, with him.

shut, remember that the Lord here (Matt. xvi. 19)
left its keys to Peter, and *through him to the Church*".
Nearness, then, with Peter, and *consanguinity of
doctrine*[1] thence proceeding, are no less necessary
to the Church, that it may be the Catholic Church
which Christ founded and built upon Peter, than
that it be partaker in those gifts which, again, He
Himself granted only to unity, as it is effected in
Peter and by Peter.

Now, not only the most ancient Fathers, as
Irenæus, Tertullian, and Cyprian, but the whole
body of them, assign the origin of this to Peter.
This they make the vivifying principle of agreement, society and unity, without which the Church
can neither be intrinsically Catholic, nor the
mind conceive it as such. It is so stated by
Pacian,[2] Ambrose,[3] the Fathers[4] of Aquileia,
Optatus,[5] Gregory Nazianzen,[6] Jerome,[7] Augustine,[8] Gelasius,[9] Hormisdas,[10] Agatho,[11] Maximus

[1] Tertull. de Præsc. c. 32.
[2] Pacian. ad Sempronium, Epist. 3, § 11.
[3] Ambrose, de Pœnit. lib. 1, c. 7, n. 33.
[4] Synodical Epistle, among the letters of Ambrose.
[5] Optatus, de Schism. Donat. lib. 2, c. 2, and lib. 7, c. 3.
[6] Gregory, de Vita sua, tom. 2, p. 9.
[7] Jerome, adv. Jovin. lib. 1, n. 14.
[8] Augustine, in Ps. Cont. partem Donati, cont. Epist. Fundam.
c. 4, de Utilitate Credendi, c. 17, and Epist. 43.
[9] Gelasius, Epist. 14.
[10] Hormisdas, Mansi, tom. 8, 451, in the conditions on which he
readmitted the Patriarch of Constantinople and the Eastern
Bishops to communion.
[11] Agatho, in a letter to the sixth council, read and accepted at
its fourth sitting.

Martyr,[1] and to shorten the list, by Leo the Great.[2]
It is in setting forth the unity of the Catholic
episcopate that he writes what ought never to be
forgotten by Christian minds : " For the compact-
ness of our unity cannot remain firm, unless the
bond of charity weld us into an inseparable whole,.
because, as we have many members in one body,
and all members have not the same office, so we,
being many, are one body in Christ, and every one
members one of another.   For it is the connection
of the whole body which makes one soundness and
one beauty ; and this connection, as it requires
unanimity in the whole body, so especially demands concord among Bishops.   For though these
have a like dignity, yet have ·they not an equal
jurisdiction ; since even among the most blessed
Apostles, as there was a likeness of honour, so
was there a certain distinction of power, and the
election of all being equal, pre-eminence over the
rest was given to one, from which mould, or type,.
the distinction also between Bishops has arisen,
and it was provided by a great ordering, that all
should not claim to themselves all things, but
that in every province there should be one whose
sentence should be considered the first among
his brethren ; and others, again, seated in the
greater cities, should undertake a larger care,
through whom the direction of the universal
Church should converge to the one See of Peter,.
and nothing anywhere disagree from its head."

[1] Maximus, Bibl. Patr. tom. 2, p. 76.
[2] Leo, Epist. 10, c. 1.

And, if I do not deceive myself, the direct drift of all this is to answer the question, whether the doctrine of Peter's Primacy, and its virtue as the constituent of unity and Catholicity, is contained in the most solemn standard of faith, the creed. For although there are unimpeachable testimonies to prove that the creeds were not published and explained to Catechumens, in order to convey to them a full and complete Christian instruction ; and though it be proved further to have been the purpose of the Church's ancient teachers to omit many points in the creeds which were to be set before the initiated at a more suitable season afterwards, it may nevertheless be said that the most commonly received articles of the creeds may be regarded as so many most faithful germs, from which the remaining doctrines would spontaneously spring. And so, to keep within our present point, what is more plain than that the sum of doctrine, concerning Peter's Primacy, contained in the Bible, illustrated by the Fathers, and defined by Councils, is involved in that article of the creed in which we profess that the Church is one and Catholic ? No doubt there nowhere occurs in the creeds, *expressed in so many words*, mention of Peter, or of the Primacy bestowed on him, or of hierarchical subordination ; yet it is most distinctly stated that the Church is one and Catholic. What meaning, then, were the faithful to give to those epithets ? What were they to intend in the words, I believe one Catholic Church ? What but the meaning of the words themselves which they received from the Church's teachers together with the creeds? But they could not form the conception of one Church and that Catholic, without thinking likewise of one Catholic *principle* of the Church; nor could they assign the dignity of that one Catholic principle to any other but Peter, whom alone they had invariably been taught to have been set over all. For what St. Bernard [1] wrote in mediæval times, " For this purpose the solicitude of all Churches rests on that one Apostolic See, that all may be united under it and in it, and it may be careful in behalf of all to preserve the unity of the Spirit in the bond of peace," must be considered nothing but a repetition of the faith which resounded through the whole world, from the very beginning of the Christian religion.

Unless, therefore, any can be found who prefer asserting *either* that true believers *never* understood what they believed, in professing the Church to be one and Catholic, *or* that they understood this *otherwise* than it had been universally and constantly explained by the Church's teachers, it must be admitted that faith in Peter's Primacy, and in the power bestowed upon it for the purpose of making the visible kingdom of Christ one and Catholic, is coeval with that profession of the creeds which sets forth the Church as one and as Catholic.[2]

---

[1] Ep. 358, to Pope Celestine.
[2] The above chapter is translated from Passaglia, pp. 298-336.

CHAPTER IX.

THE NATURE, MULTIPLICITY, AND FORCE OF PROOF FOR ST. PETER'S PRIMACY.

[1] As the natural end of all proof is to give assurance, every kind of it must be considered a mean to persuade and determine the mind. Not but that there are different kinds, and that in great variety. If we refer these to their respective topics, some are *internal* and *artificial*, others *external* and *inartificial ;* some belong to the philosopher, others to the theologian, the former having their source in nature, the latter in revelation ; another sort, again, rests on *witnesses*, and another on *documents*. But if we consider their persuasive force, they may be conveniently ranged under the two classes of *probable*, and *certain* or *demonstrative*.

But if it be asked what sort of proof we have hitherto used, and drawn out to the best of our ability, we must distinguish between the *principal* and prevailing proof, and this in form is inartificial, theological, and drawn from the inspired documents ; and the proofs *occasionally inserted* and confirmatory of the principal : these, it will be evident, are sometimes artificial and internal, such

---

[1] The following chapter is translated from Passaglia, pp. 339-360.

as those drawn from analogy, and the harmonious
coherence of doctrines, from the unity and Catholicity of the Church, and the institution of Bishops
to rule particular flocks; and sometimes derived
from witnesses, for such we may deem the ancient
Fathers, whose importance and force, as testimonies, no prudent mind will reject. To embrace, then, the full extent of our proof, it ranges
over all forms and modes, is artificial and inartificial, and rests not only on documents, but on
witnesses. Now, two things follow from this
mixed and manifold character of our proof, of too
great importance to be passed over in silence.

The first of these is, the standard and criterion
of resistance which our proof presents to opponents. For consisting, as it does, of so many
elements, confirmed, as it is, by the absolute
harmony of so many various parts, that only can
be a satisfactory answer, which meets at once
every particular proof, and the whole sum of it.
For it would be to small purpose to give another
sense, with some speciousness, to one or two
points, if the great mass of matter and argument
remained untouched. The only valid answer
would be *to reject and deny the Primacy of supreme
authority, presenting at the same time a sufficient
cause for all those results of which the proof consists.*
For so long as the institution of the Primacy is
necessary to supply a sufficient cause for these
results, so long the force of our proof remains
untouched, and the institution of the Primacy
unquestionable. We can therefore demand of our

opponents this alternative, either to acquiesce in our proof, or, rejecting the Primacy, to find, and when they have found to establish, an hypothesis equal to the explanation of all that is contained in our arguments artificial and inartificial, in our documents and our witnesses.

The second point is one which all will admit. The proof we have given is such that *unless* it be deceptive, the institution of the Primacy is demonstrated to be not only *true*, but also *revealed*, not only *tenable*, but matter of *faith*. For although we have interwoven testimonies and artificial arguments, this was to confirm what was already demonstrated, and to shed fresh light on what was already clear; but the *proper* source from which we have drawn our proofs, was the documents of the Holy Scriptures themselves. Now what is thence drawn is revealed,[1] and enters into the number of things which, being revealed, are matter of *faith*.

These two points are clear, but a third may be somewhat less so. Many will ask, what *is* the force of the proof, its power to persuade, and whether it carry complete certitude or be defective? Now, to this we shall reply, that the proof which we have presented is not only probable, but altogether decisive. It wants nothing to produce the fullest assurance. This is a subject which I have judged fit for special and separate investi-

---

[1] This is not said as *limiting* revelation to such points, but to exhibit the scope of the present work, which uses testimony merely as a human, though very important, support of the cause.

gation, as due both to myself, my readers, and the cause which I am defending. For it is not a happiness of our nature to catch the whole and the pure truth at a single glance. This requires repeated acts of the mind; we have to make the effort again and again, and only terminate our examination when we have submitted our supposed discovery to reiterated reflection. Thus it is that truth comes out in full light, imposition is detected, the line drawn between doubt and certainty, and every point located in its due place. This inquiry, then, into the proof itself I consider due not only to myself and my readers, but to a cause, which requires the utmost attention as being of the highest importance, and the source of the deepest dissensions; for it is not too much to say that the origin of all those divisions which we see and lament in the Christian name may be referred to the reception or the denial of this doctrine concerning the Primacy.

Now we shall best reach the subject by first considering the inherent force of the proof *in itself*, and *absolutely*, and then *comparatively* with those arguments to which the most distinguished Protestant sects ascribe a full and complete demonstrative power.

I. First, then, as to the force of proof *absolutely*. We must reflect that two conditions complete a proof derived from documents : *first*, the authenticity of the document ; *secondly*, either the immediate and unquestionable evidence of the testimonies quoted from it, or their meaning being rendered certain by argument.   If these two conspire, nothing is wanting to produce assurance.   Now, as to the documents whence our proof is derived, no Christian doubts their authenticity; and as to the testimonies drawn from them, part[1] belong to a class of such evidence as to admit of no doubt; and part,[2] being equally clear and marked in themselves, have had to be defended from false interpretations.   Accordingly, our proof is peremptory in both particulars.

Moreover, our proof was not restricted to one or two passages of Holy Scripture, but extended over a great series, all tending to support and consolidate the argument.   We have set forth, not a naked institution of the Primacy, but multifold foreshadowings and promises of it, its daily operation and notoriety.   From its first anticipation we went on to its progressively clearer expression, its promise, its institution, its exercise, and the everywhere diffused knowledge of it in the primitive Church.   So far, then, as I see, nothing more can, with reason, be asked, to remove all doubts as to Peter's prerogative of Primacy; for, when the bestowal of certain privileges can be proved by documents, all question

---

[1] The texts relating to the Primacy, the Evangelists' mode of writing, that of St. Luke in the first twelve chapters of the Acts, and that of St. Paul.

[2] The Apostles' contest about "the greater," the distinction between the founder, and the visible head of the Church, and for false interpretations, the Primacy of mere precedency, the perversion of John xxi. 15-20, the assertion of Apostolic equality, and Gal. i. 18-20.

as to their existence is terminated. But here we find in documents, not their bestowal merely, but antecedents and consequences, a beginning, a progress, and a manifold explanation, which stands to the Primacy as signs to the thing signified.

Accordingly, the demonstration which we have given of the Primacy, considered *in itself*, and *absolutely*, needs nothing to challenge assent.

For, suppose it disputed whether Cæsar surpassed the other Roman Senators in honour and power. Could it be proved by undoubted records, that he so conducted himself as gradually to smooth his path to the supreme power; that he next gained from the senate and Roman people the title of Emperor and Prince ; 'that he exercised these powers at home and abroad, and received universal testimony to the dignity he had acquired ; in such case the judgment would be unanimous that he was Emperor, and head of the Roman Senators. Now, substitute Peter for Cæsar, the Apostles for the Senators ; Christ, the Evangelists, Luke and Paul, for the senate and people ; and you will see all the proofs enumerated for Cæsar, to square exactly with Peter. For we learn from Scripture *the steps* by which he rose to the Primacy, *the time* when he received it, *how* he exercised it, and the lucid testimonies to it which he received from Christ, the Evangelists, the Apostolic Church, and Paul. Accordingly, his Primacy and supreme authority among the Apostles rests on a proof which gives complete assurance, and challenges assent. It is a consequence deduced, not from a single, but from manifold inference; not merely drawn from results, but foreseen in its causes; declared not merely in the words of institution, but in the very acts of its exercise; supported not only by sundry texts, but by a cloud of conspiring witnesses; proved by an interpretation, not obscure, and far-fetched, but clear and obvious. A thing of such a nature it is folly to deny and temerity to doubt.

But, further, reflect on the other arguments which come in collaterally to support that from the Holy Scriptures. Then it will be found that our proof consists in the harmonious concurrence of these four sources: 1. *The authentic Scriptural documents* distinctly setting forth the promises, the bestowal, the exercise, and the everywhere diffused knowledge of the Primacy; 2. *Witnesses* the most ancient, well-nigh coeval with the Apostles, of great number, renowned for their holiness, or their martyrdom, excellent in learning, far removed from each other in situation, faithful maintainers of the Apostolic teaching, who, with one mouth, acknowledge the Primacy; 3. *The analogy of doctrines*, for the Church, which we profess to be one, and Catholic, can neither exist, nor even be conceived as such, without the Primacy; 4. *The facts of Christian history*, which are so entwined with the institution of the Primacy, that they cannot be even contemplated without it. For there are no less than fourteen distinct classes of facts in Christian history, all of which bear witness to the Primacy, and which cannot be studied

without coming across that power. Such are,
1. *The history of heresies*, where, in ancient times
alone, consider the acts and statutes of Pope
Dionysius in the causes of Paul of Samosata, and
Dionysius of Alexandria ; of Popes Sylvester and
Julius, in the cause of Arius; of Pope Damasus,
in that of Apollinarius; of Popes Innocent and
Zosimus, in that of Pelagius; of Pope Celestine,
in that of Nestorius; and of Pope Leo, in that of
Eutyches; so that Ferrandus [1] of Carthage wrote
in the sixth century, " If you desire to hear aught
of truth, ask in the first place the prelate of the
Apostolic See, whose sound doctrine is known by
the judgment of truth, and grounded on the weight
of authority ". 2. *The history of schisms* which
have arisen in the Church, when we consider the
unquestionable facts about Novatian, Fortunatus
and Felicissimus, the Donatists, and Acacius of
Constantinople, so that Bede, in our own country,
wrote in the seventh century, commenting on
Matt. xvi. 10, " All believers in the world understand, that whosoever in any way separate themselves from the unity of the faith, or from the
society of Peter, such can neither be absolved from
the bonds of their sins, nor enter the threshold of
the heavenly kingdom ". 3. *The history of the
liturgy*, as the contests about the paschal time,
and what Eusebius, in the fifth book of his

---

[1] " Interroga igitur, si quid veritatis cupis audire, principaliter
sedis Apostolicæ antistitem, cujus sana doctrina constat judicio
veritatis, et fulcitur munimine auctoritatis."—Ferrandus in Epist.
ad Severum.

history, c. 22-25, says about Pope Victor. 4. *The history* of the *summoning*, the *holding*, and the *confirming general councils*, wherein the Acts of Synods, the letters of the supreme Pontiffs, and the writings of the Fathers, show the entire truth of what is stated by the ancient Greek historians, Socrates and Sozomen,[1] that an ecclesiastical Canon had always been in force, "that the Churches should not pass Canons contrary to the decision of the Bishop of Rome," which Pope Pelagius[2] in the sixth century thus expressed, "the right of calling councils is entrusted by a special power to the Apostolic See, nor do we read that a general council has been valid, which was not assembled or supported by its authority. This is attested by the authority of canons, corroborated by ecclesiastical history, and confirmed by the holy Fathers." And Ferrandus says, "Universal councils, more especially those to which the authority of the Roman Church has been given, hold the place of second authority after the canonical books ".[3] 5. *The history of ecclesiastical laws*, for the regulation of discipline, a summary of which, enacted by the successors of Peter from Victor I. to Gregory II., may be found in Zaccaria's Antifebronius, tom. ii. p. 425, and his Antifebronius Vindicatus, Diss. vi. c. 1. 6. *The history of judgments*, specially the most remarkable in the Church, of which, if we are

---

[1] Socrates, Hist. l. 2, c. 8-17. Sozomen, Hist. l. 3, c. 10.
[2] In Fragm. Epist. apud Baluzium, Miscell. lib. 5, p. 467.
[3] Ferrandus in Litteris ad Pelagium.

to believe history, we can only repeat what Pope Gelasius wrote at the end of the fifth century, to the Bishops of Dardania, "We must not omit that the Apostolic See has frequently, to use our Roman phrase, *more majorum*, even without any council preceding, had the power to absolve those whom a council had justly condemned, or to condemn, without any council, those who required condemnation": and as he wrote to the Greek Emperor, Anastasius, "that the authority of the Apostolic See has in all Christian ages been set over the Church universal, is established by the series of the canons of the Fathers, and by manifold tradition".[1]   7. *The history of references* which were wont to be made to the chair of Peter, in the greater causes of faith and in those respecting Catholic unity.   Thus, Avitus, Bishop of Vienne, A.D. 500, said, "It is a rule of synodical laws, that, in matters relating to the state of the Church, if any doubt arises, we, as obedient members, recur to the Priest of the Roman Church, who is the greatest, as to our head".[2] To the same effect is the letter of Pope Innocent I., to St. Victrice, of Rouen, at the beginning of the fifth century, and again, the African Fathers to Pope Theodore; or again, St. Bernard, writing to Pope Innocent II., against the errors of Abelard, "All dangers and scandals emerging in the kingdom of God, specially those which concern faith, must be referred to your Apostolate: for I esteem it fitting that the injuries done to faith should be

---

[1] Mansi, tom. 8, 54, 34.   [2] Avitus, Epist. 36.

repaired there in particular, where faith cannot fail. That is the prerogative of this See." 8. *The history of appeals*, of which a vast number of remarkable instances exist. Take, as the key, the words of Pope Gelasius once more : " It is the canons themselves which have ordered the appeals of the whole Church to be carried to the examination of this See. But from it they have allowed of no appeal in any case ; and, therefore, they enjoin that it should judge of the whole Church, but go itself before the judgment of none : nor do they allow of appeal from its sentence, but rather require obedience to its decrees." [1] And Pope Agatho, in the Roman Council, pronouncing on the appeal of our own St. Wilfrid of York, the contemporary of Bede, A.D. 688, declares that " Wilfrid the Bishop, beloved of God, knowing himself unjustly deposed from his bishopric, did not *contumaciously resist by means of the secular power*, but with humility of mind sought the canonical aid of our founder, blessed Peter, prince of the Apostles, and declared in his supplication that he would accept what by our mouth, blessed Peter, our founder, whose office we discharge, should determine ".[2] 9. *The history of the ecclesiastical hierarchy* [3] and of the *rights possessed by certain episcopal Sees over others*, of which we may take an instance in the grants of Pope Gregory the Great, and his successors, to the See of Canterbury,

---

[1] Gelasius, Epist. 4, ad Faustum. Mansi, 8, 17.

[2] Mansi, tom. 11, 184.

[3] See Peter Ballerini, de Potestate Ecclesiastica, cap. 1, § 1-6.

which alone made it a Primacy. For the Bishops
of Canterbury had no power whatever over the
other Bishops of this country, save what they
derived from St. Peter's See. And the documents
and original letters conferring these powers still
exist, giving the fullest proof that Pope Pius only
did in 1850, what Pope Gregory did in 596.   10.
*The history of the universal propagation of the
Christian religion.*[1]   11. *The history of those tokens
and pledges,*[2] such as letters of communion, whereby Catholic unity was exhibited and maintained.
12. *The history of Christian archæology,*[3] inscriptions,
paintings, and other monuments of this kind.   13.
The history of the Emperors, as, for instance, what
Ammianus Marcellinus[4] says of. Constantius; the
letter of the Emperor Marcian to Pope Leo, entreating him to confirm the Council of Chalcedon ;
that of Galla Placidia, the 130th novel of Justinian,
and the remarkable constitution of Valentinian III.,
A.D. 445. "Since the merit of St. Peter, who
is the chief of the episcopal coronet, and the
dignity of the Roman city, moreover, the authority of a sacred synod " (that of Sardica, A.D.
347) " have confirmed the Primacy of the Apostolic
See, let presumption not endeavour to attempt
anything unlawful, contrary to the authority of
that See : for, then, at length, the peace of the

---

[1] See Mamachi, Origines et Antiquitates Christianæ, tom. 2.
[2] See Muzzarelli, de Auctoritate Rom. Pontificis in Conciliis
Generalibus, c. v. § 9.
[3] See Mamachi, as above, tom. v. part 1, c. 2.
[4] Ammn. Marcellinus, lib. 15, c. 7.

Church will everywhere be preserved, if the whole (universitas) acknowledge its ruler." And, 14, lastly, *the history of codes*, in which is contained the legislation of Christian kingdoms, wherein we may refer to the capitulars of the Franks, and the laws of the Lombards.

Now, from these concordant proofs thus slightly sketched, it follows that the institution of the Primacy belongs to that class of facts which is most certain, and which is absolutely demonstrated. For would it be possible to find a concurrence of proofs so various in case it had never been instituted? Is it possible to imagine so many various results of a cause which never existed?—so many various tokens of reality in a fiction? What are the chances for letters thrown at random forming themselves into an eloquent speech? Or a beautiful portrait coming out from a mere assemblage of colours? Or a whole discourse in an unknown tongue being elegantly rendered by a guess? If these be sheer absurdities, although a few letters have sometimes tumbled at random into a word, or a single clause been deciphered though in ignorance of the alphabet, then we may be sure that the Primacy, attested by so vast a variety of convergent results, can no more be untrue, than effects can exist without a cause, splendour without light, or vocal harmony without sound. Accordingly an institution established by such a union of proof, carries prisoner the assent. It may indeed be disregarded by a resolution of the *will*, but can neither be passed by, nor refuted, by a judgment of the *reason.*

And [1] having on the one hand this vast amount of *positive* proof, from sources so various, in its behalf, so that without it the whole Christian history of eighteen centuries, in all its manifold blendings with secular history, becomes unintelligible, a tangle which it is impossible to arrange; when we come on the other hand to consider what its opponents allege of *positive* on their own side, we find nothing. They content themselves with objections to this or that detached point, with historical difficulties, and obscurations of the full proof. such, for instance, as the conduct of St. Cyprian in one controversy, the occasional resistance of a metropolitan, the secular instinct of an imperial government stirring up Eastern Bishops to revolt, and fostering an Erastian spirit in the Church, the ambition of thoroughly bad men, such as Acacius or Photius, and the like. But what we may fairly ask of opponents, and what we never find the most distant approach to in them is, if, as they say, St. Peter's Primacy be not legitimate, and instituted by Christ for the government of the Church, what *counter system* have they, which they can prove by ancient documents, and whereby they can solve the manifold facts of history ? In all their arguments against the Primacy they are so absolutely *negative,* that the grand result, if they were successful, would be

[1] The following paragraph, down to " within and without," I have introduced here.   It is not in F. Passaglia.

to reduce the Church to a heap of ruins, to show
that she, who is entrusted with the authoritative
teaching of the world, has no internal coherence
either of government or doctrine, in fact, no mes-
sage from God to deliver, and no power to enforce
it when delivered. In the arguments of Greeks
and Anglicans, Lutherans and Calvinists, and all
the Protestant sects, the gates of hell have long
ago prevailed against the Church, and the devil
has built up at his ease a city of confusion on the
rock which Christ chose for her foundation. If we
listen to them, never has victory been more complete than that of the evil one over the Son of God:
the promised unity he has scattered to the winds :
the doctrine of truth he has utterly corrupted : the
charity wherewith Christians loved one another he
has turned into gall and wormwood. That is, the
opponents of St. Peter's Primacy are one and all
simply *destructives ;* they inspire despair, and are
the pioneers of infidelity, but are utterly powerless
to build up. Ask the Anglican what is the source
of spiritual jurisdiction, and the bond of the episcopate which he affects to defend ? *He makes no
reply.* All he can say is, it is *not* St. Peter. Ask
the Greek, if Bishops and Patriarch disagree, and
come to opposite judgments on the faith, or to
schisms in communion, which party make the
Church ? *He has no solution to offer,* save that it is
not the party which sides with St. Peter's successor.
Ask the pure Protestant, who maintains the sole
authority of the written Word, if you disagree
about the meaning of Scripture in points which

you admit to touch salvation, who is to determine what is the true meaning of the Word of God? *He has nothing to reply*, save that he is sure it is *not* the Pope. Contrast, then, on the one side, a complete coherent system, fully delineated and set forth in the Bible, attested by the Fathers, corroborated by analogy, and harmonizing the history of eighteen hundred years in its infinitely numerous relations, with, on the other side, a mere heap of objections and denials, with shreds of truths held without cohesion, with analogy violated, history thrown into hopeless confusion, and, to crown the whole, Holy Scripture incessantly appealed to, yet its plainest declarations recklessly disregarded, and its most consoling promises utterly evacuated. Choose, upon this, between *within* and *without*.

II. But such being the argument for the Primacy *of itself* and *absolutely*, look at it now in a *comparative* point of view with other doctrines. Let us ask Anglicans, Lutherans, and Calvinists, respectively, to compare it in order with the proofs with which they, each in behalf of his own sect, defend either the authority of Bishops, and their distinction from Presbyters, as instituted by Christ, or the real presence of the Lord's body in the Eucharist, or the divine nature of Christ, and His consubstantiality with the Father. Can they state, upon a comparison of these, that there are *more* testimonies of Holy Scripture in behalf of these latter doctrines than for the Primacy of Peter? As for the articles of the real presence, and the superiority of Bishops, this cannot be asserted with any show of truth, since in behalf of both there are undoubtedly fewer. Certainly there are a great number for the divinity of Christ, yet not much less are those which the same Scriptures contain in support of Peter's Primacy. So that if the force of proof is to be judged of by the *number of texts*, that in behalf of the Primacy will either be preferred to the rest, or at least yield to none.

But I anticipate the answer that it is not the number of texts which will decide the question, but their perspicuity and evidence, which constitute their force. To meet which objection I shall merely set these several parties against each other. What, then, do Lutherans think of the perspicuity of those texts by which Anglicans maintain the superiority of Bishops over Presbyters ? They are unanimous in thinking them not merely most obscure, but absolutely foreign to the purpose for which they are cited. Just the same is the Calvinist opinion of the Lutheran proofs for the real presence, and the Socinian view of the texts alleged by Calvinists in behalf of Christ's divinity. Both obstinately refuse to admit that their opponents urge anything decisive. It would be easy to quote instances of this, if it was not notorious. It is, then, no unfair inference that Protestants have no particular reason to boast triumphantly of the perspicuity and evidence of the texts on which they severally rely.

But who, they retort, cannot see that the cause of the Primacy, which we defend, is far inferior ? For our exposition is opposed not by one or two parties, but by them all in a mass, Anglicans, Lutherans, Calvinists, and *all who are not Catholics*. The addition is significant, *all who are not Catholics*, for indeed all these, and these alone, are our opponents. Yet their very name creates the gravest prejudice against them, and shows them to be unworthy of attention. As St. Augustine said, " The Catholic Church is one, to which different heresies give various names, they themselves each possessing their own name, which they dare not refuse. Whence judges unaffected by partiality can form an opinion to whom the name of Catholic, which all aim at, ought to be given." [1] If, then, the name of Catholic is a note of truth, the negation of that name is a test of error and heresy. But no one will imagine that heretics, that is, the enemies of Christ and the Apostles, have a right to be followed in what concerns the doctrine of Christ, and the Apostolic institutions. Thus, what Tertullian said is to the point, " Though we had to search still and for ever, yet *where* are we to search ? Is it among heretics, where all is foreign and opposed to our own truth, whom we are not allowed to approach ? [2] What servant expects food from a stranger, not to say an enemy of his lord ? What soldier takes donative or pay from confederate, not to say from hostile kings, except he be an open deserter and rebel ? Even the woman in the Gospel searched for her piece of silver within her own house. Even he

[1] Aug. de Utilitate Credendi, c. 7, n. 19.
[2] Tit. iii. 10.

who knocked, struck the door of a friend.[1] Even
the widow solicited a judge, who was hard indeed,
but not her enemy. No one can be built up by the
person who destroys him : no one be enlightened
by one who shuts him up in darkness. Let us
search then in our own, and from our own, and
about our own, and only that which can be
questioned without harm to the rule of faith."[2]

But if we look closer into the matter, we shall
find that even in the interpretation of our texts
Protestants are not so agreed with each other as
uniformly to oppose us. Some of the greatest
names amongst them, such as Cameron, Grotius,
Hammond, Leclerc, Dodwell, Michaelis, Rosen-
müller, and Kuinoel, differ from the rest and agree
with us in interpreting, "upon this rock I will
build My Church," words of great importance in
the controversy about the Primacy. So that we
were not wrong in stating that Protestants do not
entirely agree among each other in their interpretation, nor disagree with ours.

But grant that they were one and all opposed to
it, it would not prove much. For, *first*, it could
hardly happen otherwise, since the old Protestant
cause is so contained in this matter of the Primacy,
that, were they to confess themselves wrong in it,
they would pronounce themselves guilty of the
most groundless schism. Therefore it is a matter
of life and death with them to resist us. *Secondly*,
as they dissent from us, so do they desert that

---

[1] Luke xv. 9 ; xi. 5 ; xviii. 2.
[2] Tertullian, de Præsc. c. 21.

doctrine which the whole Christian body solemnly professed and defined before the sixteenth century in Ecumenical Councils, that of Florence held in 1439, the second of Lyons in 1274, and the fourth Lateran in 1215. We, then, follow antiquity, and they take up novelty. And so it follows that while we have Protestants against us, we have the earlier Christians for us, whilst Protestants are opposed not only to the present race of Catholics, but to those whose children these are, and whose doctrines they have preserved. For as to the ancient interpretation of these texts take the following proof, contained in a letter of Pope Agatho to the Greek Emperor Heraclius, read and approved in the sixth General Council, A.D. 680 : " The true confession of Peter was revealed by the Father from heaven, for which Peter was pronounced to be blessed by the Lord of all, who likewise by a triple commendation was entrusted with the feeding of the spiritual sheep of the Church by the Redeemer of all Himself ; in virtue of whose assistance this His Apostolical Church hath never turned aside from the path of truth to any error whatsoever ; whose authority, as of the Prince of all the Apostles, the whole Catholic Church at all times and the universal councils faithfully embracing, have in all respects followed, and all the venerable Fathers have entertained its Apostolic doctrine ; through which there have shone the most approved lights of the Church ; which, while, the holy orthodox Fathers have venerated and followed, *heretics have pursued with false accusations, and calumnies inspired*

*by hatred. This is the living tradition of Christ's
Apostles, which His Church everywhere holds."* [1] We
might imagine that Sir Thomas More had these
words before his eyes when he answered Luther,
" Not only all that learned and holy men have
collected to the point moves me to give willing
obedience to that See, but especially what we have
so often witnessed, that not only there never was
an enemy to the Christian faith who did not at
the same time declare war against that See, but
also that there never has been one who professed
himself an enemy of that See without shortly after
declaring himself signally a capital foe and traitor
of Christ and our religion. Another thing, too,
has great weight with me, that if, in this matter,
the faults of individuals are laid to the charge of
their office, all authority will collapse, and the
people will be without ruler, law, or order. And
if this ever happens, as it seems likely to happen
in parts of Germany, at length they will learn to
their cost how much more it is to the interest of
society to have even bad rulers rather than none." [2]

Protestants, then, have many more opponents
than we ; to which we may add, *thirdly*, that we
assert and maintain a doctrine which for several
ages had no opponent worth mentioning, and
which received a general belief and assent. Protestants, on the contrary, no sooner brought their
doctrine to light than they roused the whole
Catholic Church against them ; that very Church,

[1] Mansi, Concilia, tom. 11, 239.
[2] Responsio ad Lutheram, c. x.

fourthly, from which they had rebelled, in which they had been washed in the laver of regeneration, whose motherly care had enrolled them as Christians, from which they had received the Bible and all other Christian blessings, which, before that fatal schism, alone presented the appearance of the true Church, and was invested with attributes which inspired belief and fostered obedience. For such were antiquity, the hierarchy, unity, the agreement of its members, universality ; such, again, the splendour of sanctity and learning ; zeal in the guardianship of primeval tradition, hatred of profane novelties ; and, lastly, the renown of those heavenly gifts, which cannot fail the true Church of Christ, and were ascribed to no other body.

But, *fifthly*, it would be very apposite to compare the Catholic Church with herself, and contrast her state and condition in the nineteenth century with that same state and condition in the fourth, the fifth, and the sixth. Now who, in the fourth century, professed the consubstantiality of the Trinity ? Well-nigh Catholics alone, while innumerable sects of heretics opposed this doctrine. War to the knife was waged against it by Praxeans, Noetians, Sabellians, Paulianists, Arians, and their worst portion, the Anomœans, Macedonians, and those who then made their appearance, Tritheists. Again, in the fifth and the sixth centuries, who were they who retained the true faith in Christ the God-Man, and His dispensation in taking flesh ? Once more the true faith was hardly found outside the Catholics, while the followers of Theodore of Mopsuestia, and Diodorus of Tarsus, Nestorius and the Nestorians, Eutyches, and the Eutychean sects at daggers drawn with each other, and in fine, the Monothelites and their sects, who hated one another and the Catholics with equal bitterness, clubbed all their forces together to oppose it. Now, do any Protestants venture to infer that in the fourth and following centuries the cause of the Catholic Church was less certain, on account of this mob of hostile sects? I should consider such an insinuation an insult to them. They must accordingly allow my parallel inference, that it is fair to pass the same judgment on the cause of the Primacy now for some centuries defended by the Catholics against the Protestants.

Lastly, to address specially Lutherans and Anglicans. They are well aware that almost all sects are not more opposed to the supremacy of Peter than to the superiority of Bishops, and the verity of the Lord's body in the Eucharist. But are they therefore deterred by the number of their enemies, or do they distrust the goodness of their cause, or doubt the perspicuity of those documents on which they rely for the victory? They can afford to disdain the tricks of their opponents, as well as repulse their attacks. They must, accordingly, agree with us that the assertions or denials of contesting parties, ought not to be, and cannot be, the test of a cause's goodness, and of documentary evidence.

But, then, by what standard are we to go ? I reply, by those criteria which are not subject to just exception, and which must be approved by all who seek the truth, and obey the dictate of reason. Now, four such criteria in chief I think may be assigned, the two former of which are *immediate* and *internal*, the third *internal*, but somewhat more remote ; the fourth, *external*, but of great weight, and not to be overlooked. To speak of the former first : one of these is *verbal*, and belongs to the words and phrases of which the text consists ; the other *real*, and regards the meaning of the sentence. Indeed, no other sources of obscurity or of clearness can be imagined than either the *words* which express the *matter*, or the *matter* intended by the *words*. If both words and matter are plain, and perspicuous, the discourse will be clear, and the language distinct ; but if either the matter exceed the power of reason, or the words do not run clear, or both these conspire, the evidence of the meaning will be more or less impaired.

1. Now, to begin with *words*, I shall not be severe, but allow to Anglicans, Lutherans, and Calvinists, that the texts alleged by each of them in behalf of his own cause consist of words which are either immediately perspicuous, or become mediately clear upon definite principles. But in turn I should ask them repeatedly to consider whether such a perspicuity can be denied to the words of which the texts cited for the Primacy of Peter consist. These words are in general and vulgar use, continually repeated in the Bible, but

so connected together that their certain meaning
is either immediately evident, or fixed with very
little trouble. But are not most of them metaphorical, such as *rock, building, keys, binding,
loosing, lambs, sheep, feeding?* Undoubtedly some
are such, yet not that words used in their *proper*
sense are wanting, as when Peter is called *the first,
the greater,* the *superior;* also when he is charged
to confirm his brethren; and what we collect from
the Acts of the Apostles, the Epistles of St. Paul,
and the Evangelists' mode of writing. Not,
secondly, that it is not evident, from the connection of the discourse, what fixed and established
meaning must be given to those metaphorical
expressions. Not, thirdly, that the meaning of
those formulas is not shown by the exercise of the
powers conferred in them. Not, fourthly, that
there is any inability, if you remove the metaphor,
to express in *proper* words what the metaphor
shadows out. Not, fifthly, as if the literal and
immediate sense were therefore wanting; for it is
very plain that the metaphorical[1] sense likewise
is literal and immediate. And sixthly, not that
metaphorical can be considered equivalent to
obscure, for obscurity is most opposed to the very

---

[1] Sense, says Jahn, is the connection or mutual relation of
notions intended by the author in his words, or, according to
others, which is the same thing, the conception of the mind
which the author has expressed in words, and wishes to raise in
his readers. This sense, whether it springs from the proper or
whether from the improper and metaphorical meaning of words,
or from allegorical language, is immediate, grammatical, and
literal.

genius of metaphor, and such a canon would
destroy the perspicuity of human language. For
there is no language, ancient or modern, rude or
polished, semitic, chamitic, or japhetic, whose
metaphorical is not much more copious than its
proper vocabulary.

Metaphor, then, and obscurity are very far
removed from each other, and there is nothing to
prevent a metaphorical expression bearing the
plainest sense. For such the sense will be, whenever what is called the *foundation* of the metaphor
is clear, and the series of the discourse indicates
the point of likeness, and usage of speech unfolds *the
force* of the metaphor. Now, all these conditions,
which ensure perspicuity in the metaphor, are
found in interpreting the metaphors which contain
the singular prerogatives of Peter. For as it is
perfectly plain whence the metaphors of *foundation, building, keys, binding, loosing, sheep, lambs,
shepherd*, are drawn, so the context defines the
point of similitude, and usage of speech does not
allow ignorance of the force of such metaphors.
And thus the texts on Peter's Primacy have a
verbal perspicuity which will bear a favourable
comparison with those texts on which Anglicans,
Lutherans, and Calvinists rely. For indeed all
the difficulties, in the invention of which Protestants have shown their ingenuity, are introduced, put upon the words, not drawn from them.
So, on the contrary, the haters of the Primacy
evidently wince at their clearness.

2. *Verbal* perspicuity is followed by *real*, or that

which concerns the *subject-matter*. And this, I assert, is far inferior, far more slender, in the above-named Protestant controversies, than in this of the Catholics. Indeed, both the controversies, on the real presence and on the divinity of Christ, have a super-intelligible object, so far exceeding the natural power of reason, as to admit of the mind's conceiving it by analogy, but not by a *distinct* and *proper* knowledge. For this is the nature of mysteries, whence it follows in them that neither single words have distinct notions, nor a whole proposition distinct sense. Whereas in the controversy about the Primacy, there is nothing which is not commensurate with reason, and which has not the advantage of proper and distinct notions. For, of revealed truths, some being *rational*, some *beyond* reason, and some *above* reason, the proper character of those which are called *beyond* reason is, that, *if* revealed, they are cognizable by reason. Now, to such an order of truths the institution of the Primacy belongs. Thus its *real* evidence, that, namely, which concerns its *subject-matter*, is much superior to that which the others admit of. But should we grant as much to the controversy in which Anglicans defend the superiority of Bishops over Presbyters? Grant this, yet still it remains that in this species of *real* evidence the cause of the Primacy is far superior to that of the real presence, or that of the divinity of Christ. But, in truth, the Anglican doctrine on Bishops may be considered from two points of view, either as severed from the Catholic

dogma on Peter's Primacy, or as in connection
and coherence with it.   From the latter point of
view I should admit it to be so agreeable to
reason, that this power calls for it, and rests in it,
when once illuminated by faith, so as to know,
that is, the purpose of Christ that each particular
Church should present the aspect of a united
family.   But sever this superiority of Bishops
over Presbyters from the dogma of the Primacy,
and inveigh as keenly against Peter's supremacy
as you defend their presidency, which is what
Anglicans do, and then I could only conclude that
this doctrine is plainly contrary to reason instead
of agreeing with it.

For whence do Anglicans deduce its agreement
with reason?   Hammond, Pearson, Beveridge,
Bingham, and their other great theologians, tell us
that it follows very plainly, because we know that
Christ carefully provided for the unity of particular
Churches, which, they say, it seems impossible to
obtain without the superior power of Bishops.   It
is a good inference ; but did Christ show less care
for the unity of the whole Church than for that of
particular Churches ?   Who can seriously maintain this ?   For what is the unity recommended
by Christ and so earnestly urged by the Apostles,
save that of the whole Church ?   And when we
acknowledge in the Creed *one* Church, do we
mean a particular or the universal Church ?   We
mean that which we also acknowledge to be
Catholic, and therefore the unity is that of the
Catholic Church.   And therefore it was Christ's

intention, and His certain will, that not only particular Churches, but the universal body of the Church, should possess the test and the dower of unity. And this Anglican notion, which denies of the universal Church what it affirms of particular Churches, may suit very well an island, holding itself aloof from the rest of the world, but it is quite incompatible with the radical idea of the kingdom of Christ.

Moreover, if it was necessary for the production and maintenance of unity in particular Churches to set Bishops over them, with authority superior to that of Presbyters; if reason demands that it being Christ's will for particular Churches to live in unity, He should likewise have instituted the power which distinguishes Bishops from Presbyters; can we suppose either that it was not necessary for the production and maintenance of unity in the Catholic Church, to commit its government to a universal superior, or that reason does not *equally* require, that Christ, who enjoined the Catholic Church to maintain unity, should have instituted the universal Pastor? Nay, as the necessity is not equal on the two sides, but so much stronger on the side of unity in the *Catholic* Church, as it is more difficult to hold together in one an innumerable than a limited number, men scattered over the globe than men within a narrow region, nations differing in genius, habits, and laws, than those who resemble each other in these; so reason, which for particular Churches requires their respective Bishops, *much more* requires the institution of a *universal* superior, lest the end should appear to have been devised without the means, and the divine work of Christ be deficient in wisdom. What, then, are Anglicans about in dividing these two doctrines, and contending for the institution of Bishops, while they obstinately deny the institution of the Primacy? They strip of its authority the very truth which they defend, and by severing doctrines which derive their consistency from their cohesion, put weapons in the hands of Presbyterians to assault and even overthrow the very dogma from which they take their name of Episcopalians. Accordingly the evidence derived from the *subject-matter* is much clearer in those texts which are alleged for Peter's Primacy, than in those by which the superiority of Bishops over Presbyters, the real presence, and the divine Person of Christ, are proved.

Now the force of demonstration derived from documents corresponds to the sum of *verbal* and *real* evidence in the texts, being greater or less as this is stronger or weaker. In other words, the force of demonstration belongs to that class of evidence which mathematicians call *direct*. But both these sorts of evidence exist in the same, or even in a fuller degree, in those texts which concern the Primacy, and set forth its divine institution. Accordingly the force of demonstration for the Primacy is equal or superior to that belonging to the arguments which prove the superiority of Bishops, the real presence, and Christ's divine

Person. Yet these arguments have such force, that the articles which they prove cannot, in the opinion of the Anglicans, Lutherans, and Calvinists, be questioned without incurring the deepest guilt of heresy. We have, then, the same or even a stronger reason to affirm that the Primacy of Peter, resting on the same, or even a stronger evidence, as *revealed*, cannot be denied without heresy.

And this is a corollary which I would entreat Anglicans, Lutherans, and Calvinists, carefully to consider, and then say whether they are consistent; for then I feel assured they would become discontented with themselves, by reflecting that, in the choice of the articles which they hold, they are not following the clearness of revelation, but party spirit and factious prejudices. What satisfactory answer can they ever return to the Catholic who asks why they, who on equal or less evidence defend the superiority of Bishops, deny the Primacy which rests on similar or greater proof? Or why they attack the Primacy, while they defend the real presence, or the divinity of Christ, which are supported by no more evident arguments? And how will they satisfy their own conscience, should this thought ever cross them, "Why do I at one time obey, at another time resist, the same evidence of revelation?" That same faith with which they severally believe the divine appointment of Bishops, the real presence, and the consubstantiality of Christ, compels them, if they would maintain consistency, and not repel conviction, to confess the Primacy of Peter.

And this argument might be carried much farther, if they would reflect how great is the brilliancy of evidence in behalf of the Primacy, compared with sundry other capital Christian doctrines, some or all of which they hold without question : such are the consubstantiality of the Trinity, the unity of Christ's Person, the propagation of original sin, the eternity of punishment, regeneration in baptism, and gratuitous justification. They will find, on reflection, that they hold these doctrines not because they are proved by stronger scriptural evidence than the Primacy, for quite the reverse is the truth, nor because they are encompassed with less obscurity in their own character, for the subject-matter of the Primacy is clear and distinct in comparison with them all, but because the doctrines do not oppose the particular tradition which they have received, and so their minds are not set against them. Let them once come to compare the whole evidence for the Primacy, scriptural, traditional, analogical, and historical, which last alone comprehends the fourteen heads above enumerated, with the same evidence in behalf of any or all of those, and they cannot but admit its great superiority.

3. But we must proceed to the *third* criterion, which increases not a little the evidence from revelation for the Primacy. For Catholics and Protestants are agreed in considering *analogy* as one of the best helps in interpretation, and in assigning to it the force of a real parallelism, a proceeding which rests on the necessity of the

Scripture presenting one whole and harmonious body of doctrine in its several parts. And in order not to deprive this help of its efficacy, both parties give two conditions for its exercise : the first, *that no sense be put upon passages of Scripture contrary to analogy ;* the second, *that no violence be used to the language of Scripture to confirm it with analogy, which would be imposing on Holy Writ the sense wanted from it.* These two faults carefully avoided, analogy is of great service, and throws much light upon interpretation.

But, now, is there such a sum of doctrine, so remarkable, and so diffused through all the books of the New Testament, that the texts expressing the gifts and prerogatives of Peter, can be tried by the touchstone of this analogy ? Such, indeed, there is, very remarkable, and threefold in character. The first point is found in the texts [1] which regard the divine institution of Bishops : the other two in those which show the unity [2] and the Catholicity [3] of the Church. For what can stand in closer connection with these articles of doctrine, than the appointment of a supreme ruler to discharge over the universal Church the office which every Bishop exercises over his own particular Church, and his own portion of the flock ? What,

---

[1] Acts xiv. 22 ; xx. 28 ; 1 Tim. v. 19-22 ; 2 Tim. iv. 2-5 ; Tit. i. 5 ; 1 Pet. v. 2, 3.

[2] Matt. xvi. 18 ; xviii. 18 ; John x. 16 ; Eph. v. 25 ; 1 Cor. xii. ; John xvii. 20-26.

[3] Luke xxiv. 47 ; Acts i. 8 ; ix. 15 ; Coloss. i. 8 ; 1 Cor. i. 23 ; ix. 20 ; Rom. x. 18.

again, can be more opposed to them, than the
supposition that provision was made, by the
institution of Bishops, for *the parts*, but none, by
the institution of a supreme pastor, for *the whole
body*, which is to be one and Catholic ?   Therefore,
that exposition of the texts concerning Peter,
which exhibits him as ruler of the Church universal, and as made to be the visible cause of that
same Catholic unity, so admirably agrees with
analogy, that it must be considered unquestionable,
unless texts contradictory to it can be produced.
But so far is it from the case that texts *considered
in themselves* contradict it, that, on the contrary,
they *immediately* express it *of themselves*, and can be
distorted from it only by violating all the laws of
interpretation.   Accordingly, that view of the
texts about Peter, which establishes his Primacy,
is wonderfully confirmed by analogy, and by its
harmony with what the Scriptures tell us of the
Church, as instituted by Christ.

4. And nothing will be wanting to give full
assurance to this confirmation, if we add the *fourth
or external* criterion, that derived from consent of
witnesses.   I am not going to urge here the divine
force and infallible authority of Christian tradition :
I shall merely allege what no person of discretion
can deny or question.   The first point is, that in
the actual controversy the testimony of the most
ancient witnesses cannot be disregarded ; and the
second, that it carries the very strongest prejudice
in favour of whichever interpretation it supports.

Now, here we have to do, first, with the interpretation of a series of dogmatic texts ; and, secondly, with a point of doctrine, which, being of the utmost moment, could not be unknown to any one.   But are these matters on which ancient witnesses, such as the Christian Fathers, and ecclesiastical writers, can be safely passed by unheard ?   If it were a matter of geography, chronology, or archæology, one might allow it, though with regret : but this is out of the question, in a matter of dogmatic texts, and those relating to a most important doctrine.   For notorious is the zeal with which the ancient Fathers laboured to preserve and interpret the dogmatic texts of Scripture.   We know their care to prevent the introduction of new and false interpretations, and new and false doctrines thence arising.   And we know that, together with the Scriptures, they received from the Apostolic teaching the kindred power of interpreting them.   For, as Origen re-marked, " Since there are many who think that they believe what is of Christ, and some of them believe what is different from those before them, yet, since the preaching of the Church is preserved, as handed down by the order of succession from the Apostles, and to the present day abiding in the Church, that verity alone is to be believed which in nothing is discordant from the ecclesiastical and Apostolical tradition ".[1]

Moreover, can it seem safe to enter upon a track most divergent from that which the Apostles marked out, and the Christian people constantly

---

[1] Origen, preface περὶ ἀρχῶν, n. 2.

followed ? St. Paul[1] taught us to listen to witnesses, and Christendom, whether assembled in council, or everywhere diffused, was content to depend on them. Most clear is what is said on this point about the Fathers at Nicæa[2] and Ephesus,[3] and no less so the words of Leontius of Byzantium,[4] John Cassian,[5] Theodoret,[6] Augustine,[7] Jerome,[8] Epiphanius,[9] Basil,[10] Origen,[11] Tertullian,[12] Clement of Alexandria,[13] and the oldest of all, Irenæus,[14] who says, " The true knowledge is the doctrine of the Apostles, and the ancient state of the Church in the whole world, and the character of the body of Christ, according to the succession of Bishops, by which they handed down the Church, which is in every place, which hath reached even to us, being guarded without fiction, *with a most full interpretation of the Scriptures*, admitting neither addition nor subtraction, and the reading without falsification, and legitimate and diligent exposition according to

[1] 2 Tim. ii. 2.

[2] See Athanas. de decretis Nic. Synodi, and also Hist. tripartit. lib. 2, 2, 3.

[3] See Vincent of Lerins, Commonit. c. 32, 33.

[4] Leontius, contr. Nestorium, lib. 1.

[5] Cassian, de Incarn. lib. 1.

[6] Theodoret, in the three dialogues.

[7] Augustine, cont. Cresconium, 1, c. 32, 33.

[8] Jerome, Ep. 126, and Dialog. adv. Luciferianos.

[9] Epiphanius, Hæres. 61, 75, 78.

[10] Basil, cont. Eunomium, lib. 1 ; de Spiritu S. c. 29.

[11] Origen in Matt. Tract. 29.

[12] Tertullian, throughout the book De Prescriptionibus.

[13] Clement, Stromatum, lib. 7.

[14] Irenæus, lib. 4, c. 63 and 45.

the Scriptures, without danger, and without blasphemy, and the chief gift of charity, which is more precious than knowledge, more glorious than prophecy, more eminent than all graces ". For, as he says elsewhere, "We ought to learn the truth, where the gifts of the Lord are placed; among whom is that succession of the Church, which is from the Apostles, sound and irreproachable conversation, and discourse unadulterated and incorrupt. For these maintain that faith of ours in one God, who made all things: these increase that love towards the Son of God, who has made for our sake so great dispositions : *these explain to us the Scriptures without peril.*"

And, besides, where is the Protestant who does not praise the Hebrew illustrations of Lightfoot, Schoettgen, and Meuschen? or who does not at least make much of the commentaries of Aben Ezra, Kimchi, Jarchi, and others, in the interpretation of the Hebrew Scriptures? They all see the advantage of approaching such sources of information, and using them for their own purpose. But are we to refuse to the Fathers and ancient doctors of the Church the deference which we allow to Rabbins and Talmudists? This is at least a reason for hearing the testimony of the Fathers.

And if it be concordant, constant, and universal, it most powerfully recommends that scriptural interpretation which agrees with it. In this, all Catholics without exception, and the most judicious and learned Protestants, are agreed. In

good truth, it would be incredible that an interpretation could be false, which was adopted
unanimously by the Fathers of every age and
country.   And it ought to be as incredible to find
any one so conceited, as not to be greatly moved
by the witness and consent of Christian antiquity.

One point of inquiry remains, whether the
Fathers have given their opinion, and that
unanimously, on Peter and the texts which relate
to him.   But their words inserted in the foregoing pages entirely terminate this controversy,
and show that they were all of the mind expressed
by Gregory the Great, in these words, which, it is
well to remember, were directed to the supreme civil
authority of those days, for he tells the emperor—

"To all who know the Gospel, it is manifest
that the charge of the whole Church was entrusted
by the voice of the Lord to the holy Apostle
Peter, Prince of all the Apostles.   For to him it
is said, 'Peter, lovest thou Me?   Feed My sheep.'
To him is said, 'Behold, Satan hath desired to
sift you as wheat, but I have prayed for thee,
Peter, that thy faith fail not ; and do thou, one
day, in turn, confirm thy brethren'.   To him is
said, 'Thou art Peter, and upon this rock I will
build My Church,' and the gates of hell shall not
prevail against it.   And I will give to thee the
keys of the kingdom of heaven.   And whatsoever
thou shalt bind upon earth, it shall be bound also
in heaven ; and whatsoever thou shalt loose on
earth, it shall be loosed also in heaven."[1]

[1] St. Greg. Ep. lib. 5, 20.

www.ingramcontent.com/pod-product-compliance
Lightning Source LLC
Chambersburg PA
CBHW021801110726
47902CB00006B/1607